Travel Page

Every publication from Rippple Books has this special page to document where the book travels, who has it and when.

True Blue Tucker

Campbell Jefferys

Rippple
Books

First published in 2011 by
Rippple Books

Editor: Jeff Kavanagh
Cover design: Claudia Bode
Layout: Susanne Hock

The title of this book, *True Blue Tucker*, was conceived by the author.
If any media, companies or businesses have used this title or phrase,
it's purely coincidental.

Rippple Books
Postfach 304263
20325 Hamburg
Germany
www.rippplebooks.com

A CIP catalogue record for this book is available from
the British Library.

ISBN: 978-3-9814585-0-3

From the television program *Australia's Own Heroes.*

The opening sequence shows paintings and photographs from the mid-19th century up to the First World War, with pictures of famous people and events to create a clear timeline, from stoic early settlers, to the miners of the Eureka Stockade, to the steel hat wearing Ned Kelly, to grainy images of the landing at Gallipoli. The background music is quaint and folksy, the light notes of flutes and oboes alluding to pastoral promise and then the cellos and drums signalling war. The pictures change to modern images of Sydney and Melbourne: gridlocked streets, crowded beaches, packed cafés, young people in business clothes speaking on mobile phones and rushing to work; many of the people are overweight. The sequence ends with beautiful scenes of the outback landscape and the smiling, contented faces of the people who live there.

Mike Lewis: Portraying the character and essence of the Australian bush once played an essential part in the development of our cultural and social identity. Our values rose from stories of heroic bushrangers, selfless Anzacs and the ballads of Banjo Paterson and Henry Lawson. As the country developed and became more urbanised, attention naturally turned to the cityscape and to celebrating the exceptional way of life Australians enjoy. The bush as a literary and cultural element was in many ways forgotten. But the recent rise of an outstanding young poet has changed that. With poems like *City Fella*, *Dad's Bush Burial* and *Ballad of the Ripper*, this West Australian balladeer has sparked a revival in bush culture, causing many of us to long for the simple bush life of hard work, mateship and fair go that this country was founded on.

Poet: Our land's who we are, ya know. These days, a city can pretty much be a city anywhere, but our landscape's unique. There's no place like the bush.

Lewis: Your poetry not only captures the land but also the character and values of the people, true Australian values.

Poet: Growing up in the bush is a completely different experience to growing up in the city.

Lewis: Let's start with your childhood. You grew up in the farming area south-east of Perth. What was it like?

Poet: I was lucky. I was born into a world that hasn't been ruined

1

by technology and fair-weather friends. Much of it's farmland, but there's still this overwhelming sense that the land's untamed, will always remain untameable, and that nature's more powerful than you and deserves your respect. Living and trying to survive in the bush is a constant battle and you won't make it unless you have the support of those around you. That's why the mateship's so strong, why everyone's prepared to help each other, and why you can go to sleep at night knowing nearly everyone in your community is there for you. The people are real and so's their loyalty, and there's honesty that city people know nothing about.

Lewis: But it's urban Australians, and suburban Australians, who have so readily embraced your poetry. Surely that's because they relate in some way to the world you describe.

Poet: They probably see what's been missing from their own life. It's always been like that, ya know. The people in Sydney and Melbourne looking to the bush and admiring the people there and how they are. They want to be them, want all the things they're missing. Bushman, swagman, *Waltzing Matilda*. All that. In the cities, they talk about mateship, learned it from their fathers, but it's not like it is in the country. There, it really means something, and mate's not just some word that gets thrown around. For people who live in the city but grew up in the country, I can understand they might relate to it, because it reminds them of what they once had. You know, the world they lost.

Lewis: So, a child growing up in the country has it better than a child in the city?

Poet: Well, everyone has their own opinion of what better means, but our values are essentially country values, even if they get watered down in the cities. If a child grows up with those values in their truest sense, then I'd say they have it better. They may not go to university or make a million dollars, but they'll be better people, that's for sure. Honest, fair, real and true blue.

~~~

Walkabout

He pulled the sleeve of his woollen jumper over his hand and tried to rub away the grubby mist on the window. He didn't have to pull very hard. The sleeves went way over his wrists, and the whole thing was so loose and big he got lost inside it.

"Grow into it," gran had said last Christmas.

The window stayed dirty. He rubbed harder, the wool squeaking against the glass. Did they hear that? Even if they did, they wouldn't see him. Not down here. He was safe in the darkness, crouched under his desk, hidden. His bedroom window was low, almost at the level of the floorboards, and he had to look up to see them both. Through the scratched glass, he watched her walk across the veranda. Her curly hair bounced as she kept turning her head to look towards the road. Her floral dress turned with her, fanning out and billowing like a garbage bag kite grabbing the wind.

His dad hated the dress. "Better off as curtains, I reckon," he often joked.

The dress was bright in the fading light, and the red sun streaming through the gum trees illuminated its colourful design. It reminded him of the theatre she had taken him to in Mandurah, last year when his dad was out shearing. They had sat in the darkness, in the front row. Then the lights had come on, round spots in reds and yellows and greens, lighting up the dusty wooden floor she had called the stage. Now, from his vantage point, with his eyes peering above the window ledge, the veranda looked just like that stage, the thick wooden boards splintered and the cracks filled with dust.

He rubbed at the glass again, trying so hard that he made a hole in his sleeve; more, the wool came loose, and he rolled the sleeve up to hide the hole. He hated these jumpers but his dad made him wear them. He felt so small in them. His gran seemed to have lofty ideas about his growing ability; the pencil scratches on her doorway charted his limited progress and hanging from the gum tree behind the house wasn't making any difference. His dad was so big and tall. Would he ever be even close to that?

His breath steamed the window over. He didn't want to be scared, but whenever they were on the veranda like this, he felt sick in his

3

stomach and his palms became slippery and cold. The same had happened that night at Tim's house when Cody had told them scary stories about the empty shearing shed on old Gary Johnstone's farm, about how Gary had killed his family in the shed and then hung himself, or, and then Cody's eyes had narrowed, "Or did he?" And Cody had laughed. "Ya not scared, are ya, Daz?" And he had tried so hard not to look afraid and weak, but those stories scared him, enough to make him secretly sleep with the light on. If he didn't, the shadows would form shapes in the darkness, slowly separating into arms, legs and a face, morphing somehow into the murderous outline of Gary Johnstone, coming towards him.

But his parents shouting on the veranda inspired more fear than any story Cody told. The sounds of his dad's boots slamming the boards would wake him, as they did tonight. He couldn't hear exactly what his parents said, and never opened the window in fear they would catch him, but would watch through the glass, secure in the darkness. Nearly every fight ended with his dad jumping into the ute and driving into the night. But he always woke up for breakfast the next morning to find them in the kitchen as usual, their positions and actions the same as all the preceding days.

This time, it seemed different. He didn't know why but there was something strange about the way his mum kept looking out into the darkness, towards the road. Her feet were bare, her soles a deep shade of sandstone and just as cracked, and her shins and calves the colour and texture of dusty chocolate. She stood at the edge of the veranda, searching the darkness. She shook her head slightly, her curls tangling, and when she turned to face his dad, her brownish-red lips were pulled down in a frown. All the other kids at school had teased Justin for having a black mum, but nobody had ever teased him. At bedtime, she sometimes told him fantastic stories about warriors and spirits, of tribes who defended their lands against the invading white men. Dreaming, she called them. It was in his veins, she said, but so was the blood of the invaders. He was both, like her, and her face would become flat and lifeless when she said that.

The floorboards thumped as his dad paced up and down. His boots were open, the laces loose, dangling like long yellow worms. As they dragged across the wood, they gathered dust and splinters, and even tempted a huntsman out from a crack between the wood.

4

The spider grabbed the worm with its front legs and was along for the ride. It hung on for a few seconds and then let go. It stayed in the middle of the veranda, until the boot came down hard on its back, leaving a sticky brown and cream mess behind.

His dad was shouting, but all he could hear was a muffled drone. Then he remembered; the science lesson from last week. He grabbed the greasy glass from his bedside table and put it to the window. With his ear at the base, the voices became clear and this minor miracle made him grin in the darkness. The kids at school had made fun of him because he hadn't known the glass trick. Was it really something every eight year-old would know? Or had they just pretended to know? The nicknames Demented Darius and Daz the Spaz tormented him until another kid became the collective target. Then, he had joined in with the teasing.

"Where ya gonna go?" he heard his dad say. With the glass at his ear, he could only see his dad from the corners of his eyes.

"The city. I passed the exams. I'm goin. My brothers'll take care of me."

"They'll sell ya for a carton of piss."

"They're a better lot than your mates round here."

His dad shook his head. With an index finger the size of a sausage, he rubbed his nose, picked it a little. "They prefer my company to an empty can a petrol, that's for sure." He cleared his throat and jerked his thumb towards the front door behind him. "Carn, back in the house. You'll make a joke of yaself in the city."

"I'm goin. I'm gonna get funding."

"That fella again, eh?"

"That was a mistake. It just happened. I'm sorry."

"Too late."

"The funding's from the government."

"Bloody politicians. Whitlam gave you lot a bit of bloody wasteland and now ya reckon ya can take over the world." Then his tone softened slightly. Darius sometimes heard that murmured tone drifting through the house at night, often not long after the ute scrunching the gravel outside had woken him. "Come on, enuff of this bullshit. The uni's no place for ya. I know it. You'll get laughed outta there."

His dad was a man of few words, always said so, and what he

5

said now sounded like a lot because he took a long time saying it, stretching the words out. But his mum ignored him. She walked down the three veranda steps, no longer on the stage, but part of audience. She looked towards the main road. Darius put the glass aside and followed her stare. A set of headlights cut yellow swathes through the gum trees. The lights slowed and then were facing the house, drawing closer and jumping as the car took the bumps. The silky black outline of a kangaroo fled from the side of the road and leapt over the first fence. The big white station wagon pulled in front and stopped. The windows were filled with numerous shadowed heads, some big, some small, but all looking directly at his dad on the veranda.

Darius put the glass back to his ear.

"Called the whole clan, eh? You mob always stick together."

Darius looked at the car as three men got out. They fanned their hands at the dust. Two of them leaned casually against the car, their skinny dark arms folded. The third took a few steps towards the veranda, limping strangely.

"Uncle Will," he whispered, fogging up the window. He remembered the trip to Perth last year, when his mother had explained that Uncle Will had been a football star but had suffered a bad injury. But later that day, Uncle Will had told him "a jealous white fella done it on purpose."

"All right, Jack?"

His dad stayed rooted to the spot at the top of the steps, his huge body filling the entrance. "Yeah."

"The bags are round back," his mum said.

The two men leaning against the car went around to the back of the house, moving out of view. He heard their noises through the open back windows, heard something break and one of the men swear. Uncle Will stayed by the car, his hands in his pockets. The engine of the car was still running and Darius could just hear music coming from the radio. He marvelled again at the miracle of the glass, even took it from his ear, briefly, to check if it wasn't actually some kind of magic glass.

"Packed already, eh?" his dad said, the words coming out all chewed up from his big mouth. "Been plannin this walkabout for a while. I thought you lot just got up one day and left. No plannin or nuthin. I guess it's cause ya just a quarter."

6

"You don't have a clue, Jack. Never did and never will. I'll get Darius away from you. I've already applied."

His dad laughed loudly, that same nasty, mocking laugh Darius hated, especially when it was directed at him.

"Good luck with that. They gave ya land that no one wants but they'll never let ya take me kid away."

"Maybe the Great Protector'll come'n'take him," Uncle Will said.

"That's over," his mum said to her brother. Or was Uncle Will her half-brother? Darius couldn't remember. He had met a lot of brothers and cousins on that last trip to Perth.

"Only just." Uncle Will looked at the ground and kicked a rock towards the fence. He nearly lost his balance.

"Was right. Ya proved ya carn take care a yaselves. Ya take the government's money, piss it all away and then kill yaselves in our prisons."

Darius watched his mum slowly walk up the three steps onto the veranda, walking back onto the stage. She stumbled on the first step; the old milk crate wedged deeply into the ground at an angle. For as long as Darius could remember, his dad had talked about replacing the crate, but he often boasted that he liked its authenticity and heritage. "Me great granddad was the milkman round here," he would say slouching against one of the thick veranda posts, in between complaining about the mosquitoes and the weather. "Got round with a horse'n'cart and was one a the first in the area to drive a truck. Top bloke, he was, tough as nails. Good shearer, too." There were plenty of tough-as-nails top blokes in the family, and even the distant convict connection was spoken of with pride, as the reckless, lawless side of the family; the unfortunate Irishman who stole bread to feed his starving family, so the story went. Darius was determined to be just as tough, just as top a bloke.

"How dare you say that," his mum shouted. Her words made his dad shift in his boots, as if digging his feet into the sand. "Those fellas get beaten to death, everyone knows that. The government covers it up."

"For 200 years, they cover everythin up," Uncle Will said. He opened the back door of the car for the two other men to put the bags inside. "That somethin to celebrate."

"This one's made for you, eh?" one of the men said, and all three of them laughed.

"We're better than you," his mum said, standing on the top step just below his father, "were always better, will always be better. And you hate us for it. And don't give me any of that colonial civilisation bullshit. Raping women and stealing children is hardly the stuff of civilised people."

"And sittin under trees sniffin petrol is?"

"You put them there."

"You belong with em." And he reached out his burly shearer's arms, those monstrous hands of his, and shoved her from the veranda. She tumbled to the ground, her dress and the dust falling around her. She tried to find a way out of the tangled mess and coughed the grainy dirt her dress threw into the air. Uncle Will took a few short steps forward. The shadowy sneer on his dark face scared Darius.

"Now get the hell off my property."

She got slowly to her feet and then stood there barefoot, her legs apart, her dress covered in dirt and dust. There was dried grass in her curly hair that glittered like spider webs. Darius was startled by the aggressiveness of her stance, the shining heat of her eyes, the way her hands hung loosely at her sides, the fingers spread; like a cat about to attack. She looked at him then, searching his bedroom window, seeming to stare right at him, but not quite. He raised his head a little higher so she might see him. She smiled, her white teeth lighting up in the darkness, her body relaxing, softening.

"We'll be back for Darius. When I've got the papers, and I'll bring the police if I have to."

His dad laughed. "No chance in hell. Go fuck ya city fella."

There were sounds of car doors slamming. Darius watched the big white station wagon drive into the night. He saw a few heads hanging out from the open back window and their chirpy voices carried down the road, onto the veranda and magically into the glass and into his ear. They were the voices he remembered from the trip to Perth, when they had played that war game with all the kids in the neighbourhood. What fun that had been.

Alone on the veranda, his dad picked up an old steel bucket and hurled it through the air. Darius watched it, the silver metal glimmering as it caught the light, and then heard the soft clang as it hit the dirt. Bladders emerged from the darkness and jumped onto the veranda.

"Ya too late, ya bloody mongrel." His dad took a swinging kick at the dog who retreated just in time.

"Digger?"

The dog barked.

"Not you, ya stupid dog." His dad was now moving heavily through the house. "Digger?"

Darius dropped the glass and scrambled back to bed. He wrestled with the sheets and blankets, briefly unable to find an entry, before just getting under as the door swung open. The light streamed in from the hallway.

His dad's bulk was shadowed in the doorway, his pumpkin-sized head just a few centimetres from the top. "Up ya get."

Darius made a show of pretending to wake up, blinking his eyes and raising himself slowly; he even did some melodramatic stretching and yawning. But his dad reached a long arm into the room and roughly threw back the blankets.

"I know ya awake. Ya got some of that devious black blood in ya. I'll beat it outta ya if I haveta." He thumped down the hall. "At least she won't be feedin ya shit about bloody walkabouts and dreamin no more. Ah, fuck it."

The front fly-screen door slammed loudly.

When Darius came out of the house, his dad was already behind the wheel. He revved the engine. Bladders was in the tray, dripping tongue hanging out and tail wagging madly, anticipating the journey.

"Getta move on. Ya slow as a wet weekend."

Darius climbed in and the tires tore into the dirt before he got the door closed.

"Where we goin?"

His father didn't look at him, but also didn't look left or right as he pulled onto the main road. "Town."

The gravel road was potholed and indented with tire marks. A few of the bordering gum trees had small white crosses in front of them and these swished past in greyish blurs, briefly catching the ute's one working headlight. Walking to school, he sometimes saw people laying fresh flowers at those crosses and scattering white powder to keep the ants away.

But at night, the road was deserted.

His dad swerved around the potholes and drove in the middle

9

where the gravel was firmer. With one of the car's front lights out, it was doubly hard to see the road. But Darius was well aware, because he was often told so, that his dad could drive this road without lights.

Darius shrunk in the seat, hating the smell of the ute, the putrid pong of chemical sheep dip. The same smell hung around his dad too. It kept the flies off him, he claimed, even on the hottest, stinkiest summer day. He was proud of the smell, the same way he happily dug out tiny gristles of wool from under his fingernails and showed them to Darius, even when it wasn't shearing season.

"Where's mum?"

A car came from the other direction, its lights shining brightly.

"Bloody hell." The ute swerved on the gravel, sliding over the road. It took a while before the car was under control again.

"Stupid bloody city bastards. Not a fuckin clue."

They drove in silence. Occasionally, a pellet would ping against the steel frame of the ute, like a gunshot.

"She wasn't welcome no more," his dad said at last, his eyes on the road, his big hands draped over the steering wheel, almost hugging it. His face had an expression Darius hadn't seen before; it looked like he was sad. Darius thought that he felt something too. His dad was a mystery, someone who seemed to inhabit a different world to himself, a world of popular giants, of top blokes and mates, the world that was out of his reach.

"She comin back?"

His dad blew the air through his nose. A booger, or maybe a piece of old wool, flew out. "Hope not."

"But..."

"Me own fault, Digger. She's the worst kinda poison." He sighed and turned back to the road. "Shoulda listened to me mum. She warned me not to shack up with her."

Darius looked over the dashboard at the dark road, the chunky gravel lit by the single headlight which was shining from his side of the car. She was gone, he thought, but that didn't seem possible because she had always been there. And they had left all the lights on in the house. She must be coming back, he decided.

The scattered bulbs of the town shone through the trees. Darius could see the pub because the streetlight next to it shone the brightest. His dad parked the ute and got out. Darius had to hustle to catch up. His dad made his usual boisterous entry, greeted loudly by all present. Darius knew some of the other kids there and they struck up a variety of games to pass the time.

His dad drank with the other shearers and farmers. When Darius came inside for a drink, he saw them playing darts in the corner, and his dad's shouted laughter rang through the pub; the laughter seemed to make everyone gravitate towards him. Buoyed by the attention his dad got, Darius enjoyed himself, as king of the kids.

As the night grew late, the other kids were retrieved one by one by their mums and dragged home to bed amid much whining. Some of the kids threw tantrums and cried. Darius watched and listened to the arguments as their dads campaigned for "just one more hour", even though it was a school night. But the mums would have nothing of it. How the other kids envied him, but when there were no more kids to play with and it was too cold outside, he found himself sitting bored in the pub, listening to the slurred conversation of the remaining men.

"Did the right thing, Ripper."

"Carn trust any of em."

"I liked her, but with some people ya just never know."

"She was always up to something."

His dad frowned and gritted his teeth, the muscles on the side of his face flexing. The sleeves of his flannel shirt were rolled up to his elbows and his right hand gripped his glass tightly, the ligaments flexing long and straight like over-sized rubber bands.

"Can we go home now, dad?"

He felt the eyes of the men. Their close circle widened slightly so they all could look. Their big heads and lumpy shoulders towered above him. They looked like they were playing some kind of copying game, because each stood in the same way: beer glass in the right hand, left hand deep in the trouser pocket, shoulders slouching, mouth formed in a thin smile, eyes crinkled with lines. There wore the same clothes too.

"The little fella's beat, Ripper."

"Hasn't got my stamina," his dad said. "Least not yet."

The men laughed and took their left hands out of their pockets to slap each other on the back. As one, they drained their glasses.

"One more beer, Digger."

11

Darius felt a big hand ruffling his hair. His dad only ever did such things at the pub, and they always struck him as surprising, strange and undeserved.

Outside, he climbed into the cab of the ute. He wound down the window, despite the cold. There was a mouldy blanket on the floor which he could have used, but that stank of sheep dip too. So he curled up on the seat and fell to sleep shivering.

~~~

The snaking, random movements of the car woke him. He opened his eyes to see his dad's big drooping face, his chin nearly touching his chest. His eyes, almost squinted shut, were staring at the road like he was seeing it for the first time. His shoulders were hunched forward and his hands gripped the steering wheel so loosely it looked like they might slip and he would fall face first onto it. As Darius sat up, he saw the flash of a roo in full flight. It jumped clear across the road, just in front of the car. His father swerved, too late, but also too slowly, and managed to keep control of the car.

"Just you'n'me now, Digger." His dad's moist mouth forced itself into a vague smile. The wheels ripped into the gravel, sending the pellets pinging into the steel frame. "No worries, mate," he said, rubbing his eyes with his woolly knuckles.

Lewis: You became a shearer, but went to the north-west to work in the mines. What made you go up there?

Poet: It was me dad's idea, to get some other skills and more work experience. But I think he wanted me to see my own state. Tough country up north. You gotta be made of strong stuff just to stand upright in the wind. I think he wanted me to know that, to survive that test. He did the same thing when he was younger. He travelled all over WA.

Lewis: Your poems about the north reflect a certain despondency, a solitude and emptiness. "Far beneath the dusty plains, the country's shiny riches lie, where men of miscellaneous names, as one for corporate profits die." Was it a shock to discover that some of the miners were unhappy enough to take their own lives?

Poet: No, no, sorry, Mike. You've missed the point. I don't mean they literally die, and they certainly don't kill themselves. I mean that the time working in the mines is for many of them the high point of their lives. On your first day, you're forced to trust complete strangers with your life. That builds an incredible mateship between them. They have to depend on each other. The problem is that every other experience with people on any level pales in comparison. They die for profits because they leave their souls in the mines, and the companies get all the rewards. That's why you find fellas up there who have been miners their whole lives, even after they'd promised their wives they'd quit and even when they were no longer physically up to it.

Lewis: Because of the mateship.

Poet: You think you know what I mean, but you don't. Sorry, mate, but you need to go up north and spend six months or a year working there. These guys depend on each other. In those towns, there's nothing. They're not even towns. You've only got your mates, and if you don't have any mates and you're not willing to put your life in their hands or take their lives in yours, then you won't survive. Simple as that. But if you embrace it, then you'll experience mateship in its truest form, and it'll kill you because you'll never have mates like that again. And any time you have a mate who does the dirty on you, you think back to the mines and how it was there and you see everything you've lost.

Lewis: Now I understand what you mean.

Poet: Maybe. They talk about mates in the cities, but they don't know the first thing about it.

~~~

Up North

The company four-wheel drive burned through the dust-blown haze, churning up a cloud of dirt and sand the same colour as the late afternoon sky.

"I like the dead roos," Humphrey said.

"Why's that?"

"It's a good reminder of the way of things."

Darius looked at Humphrey from the sides of his eyes, readying himself for another strangely delivered yet amusing rant. He sometimes got lost in the jumble of meanings, but it was simply refreshing to hear someone talk about stuff he had only ever thought about, all those taboo topics he had never been brave enough to tackle, still wasn't. And there was the unique sensation of being spoken to directly, not in that roundabout, convoluted way the others always did. Darius would never say as much to someone, but Humphrey just didn't talk like an ordinary Australian.

"How?"

"You can be bounding along with a few of your friends, you know, not a care in the world. The sun's shining and the earth's hot against your paws making you jump even higher and..."

"You should be a poet," Darius said.

"And you should know never to interrupt a miner waxing lyrical." Humphrey wagged an oil-stained and dried-out index finger. The finger was dirty but the nail was clean and perfectly rounded. "It's such a rare event. Interrupt him and he'll slink back into his grubby, smelly, secretly homosexual closet."

"We're not all...poets."

Humphrey laughed, then coughed, then cleared his throat, seemingly trying to extract a sarcastic snort that was stuck there. "I'd say the H-closet's more crowded than the poet's corner. Maybe. The whore wagons aren't enough for our mates. Those grunts and groans in the night aren't the beery farts and manly snoring we wish they were."

"I never hear it."

"Relax, Darius. That's just mateship. A man finding a mate in the darkness. Or maybe they are just snoring and grunting in their sleep. Anyway, our country was built on it. Think of all those convicts bunking together. If there's one woman for a thousand men, it's pretty clear what will happen. And I don't mean a bunch of half-caste kids running around. Although, that was also the result. No, no. Our fair land had a lot of man-on-man action right from the start. And probably a lot more man-on-animal than was documented. Hah. In those 'joyful strains then let us sing.'"

Darius gripped the steering wheel, hating the image. Humphrey's laughter made it worse, but he often behaved like that, found things funny others didn't, and left unexpected comments hanging in the air, like flies buzzing around a pile of shit everyone pretended wasn't there. Darius decided to ignore the shit this time as well, and focused instead on the dusty track in front of him. It meandered far into the distance, flat and desolate, without any sense of purpose or destination. It was just there. It seemed the car wasn't moving at all, and the dust trailing behind was churned up by the wind.

He hated it up here, but didn't tell anyone that. The land was so unchanging and uninviting: the ochre sand that was good for nothing, that grew nothing; the grubby green shrubs that soaked up every drop of water just to grow one metre high; the land that offered only sweat and toil, dusty coughs, dried snot the colour and texture of mouldy orange peel, and a longing for water that can never be abated. He couldn't believe what some of the miners had said, that the local Aborigines had tried to secure Native Title on this land. Why would they possibly want it? Just to find a place to sit down where they could drink and shove their empty bottles neck-first into the dirt?

"See what happens when you interrupt?" Humphrey said at last.

"Sorry, mate."

Humphrey grimaced.

"So?" Darius wanted to get Humphrey talking again, to fill the air with words and relieve the boredom. "You were sayin, bout the way of things?"

Humphrey sighed, disinterested. "Yeah, bounding along, happy as a cashed up miner," he said, his voice gaining urgency as the words came, "then suddenly, out of nowhere, wham! This giant steel beast slams into you and leaves you as mangled bird food by the side of the road."

Darius laughed because just as Humphrey said this, they passed the picked clean skeleton of a dead kangaroo. It wasn't like down south where the roos caused accidents. Up here, the vehicles were built to withstand such encounters, with emus and stray sheep too, and with any manner of feral animal on the loose.

"They're a menace."

Humphrey turned to him. "Where's your sympathy? That's the point I'm trying to make. You can be doing your thing and then your life's ended by the idiocy and invasion of someone else. And then, fuck me, and then the sentiment's completely misplaced."

"Well, they're just animals." Darius remembered the crosses planted on the road connecting his house to town, the crosses that had slowly multiplied over the years. Roos were always blamed and no one ever mentioned that the victims were driving home from the one establishment still open so late at night.

"So are we, Darius. You've seen the monsters we work with. Enough hair on their backs that you could take a handful and lift them up by it."

"Yeah, you got a point there."

"I think we've both been up here too long."

"Too right."

They had known each other a short time and superficially at that. When Humphrey had arrived, he had been assigned the bed next to Darius. Humphrey was there to make money, like everyone else. There was plenty to be made if you had a strong back, a solid work ethic and could hold your liquor. Darius had gone north for the same reason as the others, though each miner could tell a different story of motivation, and tell it with conviction even if it were a lie; to make money and kill time. That was it. They were all killing time, getting away from something or trying to make enough money to get back. And despite the high wages, everyone seemed broke and paydays were marked on calendars in red pen, or blood. They all came for six months to fill their pockets with quick cash but became so adapted to the life, so settled, accepted and secure, they were scared to leave. The rhythm of their lives was struck on a drum that counted out the money earned and spent, and each day became the same as the last to the point where the cycle couldn't be broken. Darius was stuck in it as well. He wanted to leave but didn't know how to. There was always the next pay cheque coming.

They lived in a desperate town, a mess of houses built somewhere else and then thrown together here in the guise of frontier prosperity. It convinced no one, and was neither cared about nor cared for. The cheap white weatherboard shuddered and cracked when the wind blew hard off the desert, and threatened to get whisked away altogether when a cyclone tumbled in off the coast. Darius missed the soft rainy days and solid bricks of down south.

The pub was the central point, the dull sun this world revolved around, a place of worship so revered Humphrey often joked that it had almost church-like status. The miners showered for the nightly venture across the gravel avenue to "pray at the amber altar," as Humphrey said, and came back dirty and foul, arm in arm, another great night behind them, another day closer to pay. How the glasses clinked, and broke, and how loud was the laughter, like it was a competition. Darius had spent his childhood judging such competitions, his dad always the winner, and had grown up trying to copy and emulate him. In the mining town, everything was like it was back home: the men standing in tight circles; the expansive and jovial third-hand stories made riotous and believable by alcohol and etiquette; the blokey anecdotes squeezed through the gaps in their teeth; the faces that were square and rough, with deep enough lines for there to be traces of red dirt in them, and their necks were leathery and pink; the shirts stretched across their backs, with a vertical line of moisture slicing between the shoulder blades. They were safe here, secure in number, finding relief with six-month strangers who were copies of themselves. They happily pissed their wages away or threw them up. There were nightly fights with no backing down. The soft label would be socially damning enough to make those who got it slink away silently in the dull hours before dawn, never to be seen again. But Darius knew how effective the bush telegraph was and "soft" would surely travel the length of the state and find a way to torment the one who had received it.

This testosterone-fuelled theatre played against a backdrop of concrete and dust – on sacred land, apparently – with a soundtrack by Cold Chisel and Midnight Oil, though no one bothered to understand the lyrics. Everyone knew their part. People in positions of authority were potential villains and not to be trusted. The only thing different about this world from the one Darius had grown up with was the scenery. Still, he played his part, aptly if not at times reluctantly, and was sharp enough to see, from the moment he walked into the hut, that Humphrey wasn't like the others. Sure, Humphrey could do the act, but his delivery lacked the required conviction. The words were right but the shadowy hint of arrogance and mockery made the other men narrow their eyes at him. This was a drama, but Darius thought Humphrey was playing it as a satire.

Darius was wary at first. He knew what the other men said about Humphrey, knowingly bandying about words like fag and poof and calling him Humpy behind his back. Humphrey was different, they all sensed it, and they reacted to it with rehearsed and collective scepticism.

"I got ya," Darius said, breaking the silence. "Ya can't control what happens to ya. And everythin can end cause a someone else's mistake."

Humphrey nodded. "You get the analogy."

"The what?"

"Australia."

"Uh..."

"The roos are the peaceful inhabitants, the first Australians, and the trucks are the barbaric, invasive, industrial behemoths of colonialism."

"Yeah, right."

Humphrey looked over the cracked dashboard at the dusty road littered with kangaroos in various stages of decay. "They wrecked the place. 40,000 years. Fucked it." He sighed. "This isn't our land. What're we doing out here?"

"Makin money," Darius said, knowing roughly how much he had saved.

"Like the others, yeah? Well, just a few more weeks and that's it for me."

The familiar low white buildings of the makeshift settlement drifted in and out of the dusty haze, like a hellish mirage. Darius saw the town and wanted to keep on driving.

"Where ya goin?"

"Far away from here."

"What, to Sydney, or Melbun?" Darius had never been to those places and saying them did not make them seem less foreign.

"A bit further than that."

"You mean leave Stralia?"

"Don't give me all that this's-the-greatest-country bullshit. You know, all this nationalism with the Olympics coming up scares me. Aussie-Aussie-Aussie sounds too much like a fascist chant to me. I've had enough and I want out. I can't stand the people anymore."

"Come on, they're all right."

"Bullshit."

Darius shifted in his seat. "So, where ya gonna go then? Where're the people better?"

"Canada. Canadians are the most tolerant people in the world."

"That right? What'll ya do there?"

Humphrey seemed to take great enjoyment from just the possibility of a world outside of Australia. He put one dirty boot up onto the dashboard. "Dunno. Have a look. See what happens."

"What can ya do there that ya carn do here?"

"'There's more things in heaven and earth, Horatio, than are dreamt of in your philosophy.'"

"Yeah? Who said that?"

"Shakespeare."

"Never read his stuff."

"No. Not proper, is it?"

"Me old man thought school was bad for me. When I was fifteen, he took me out shearin'."

"A different kind of theatre, but about as scripted and predictable as anything old Bill wrote."

Darius pulled in front of the shabby hut he shared with Humphrey and half a dozen others. Immediately, the front door was thrown open and the men poured out, bored, thirsty, collectively distressed.

"Aaannnddd, action," Humphrey said.

The men shuffled around to the back of the vehicle and threw open the rear door.

"Took ya bloody time," one said.

Darius jumped out of the car. "Bridge was flooded." He stretched and tried to air the shirt that was stuck to him. The dusty easterly was refreshing only because it was a breeze of sorts, but it carried sand and smoke and grit that stuck to his sweat and made him feel even dirtier than before. Humphrey was out of the car too, his green shirt damp and darkened with sweat.

The cans opened with simultaneous, gaseous hisses. The men drank and "aaahed" in unison. The esky had been taken from the back and the men now stood around it in a small circle, worshipping it. Darius and Humphrey joined them, beers in hand. Darius was welcomed into the tight ring while Humphrey managed to squeeze into a gap left not quite wide enough, leaving him with one leg awkwardly on the outside.

They were a typical group, interchangeable with the men of the other huts. Words could be wasted describing each man in detail. Darius often forgot their names and just called them mate. They were basically cut from the same mould and had all trod similar paths in becoming men. Of course, some were tall and others short, some blond-haired and others brown, and some who spoke clearly and others who stuttered or mumbled. But their collective similarities, the way they seemed to so brazenly imitate each other, made them become almost a single functioning entity of Australian manhood. Darius didn't know what thoughts raged in their heads, as they didn't know his, or what personal pleasures they kept secret, or what dreams they held close to their hairy chests like a losing poker hand, trying to bluff their way to victory. What they really thought wasn't important, and Darius would never know anyway, would never be brave enough to ask. What was important was that their character was recognisable enough for them to gain acceptance without having to explain or reveal themselves. They all loved sport, held similar opinions about politics and foreigners, were well-versed in the outback gospel, and had no time or respect for people in positions of authority. And they all had a grandfather, or a great-grandfather, who had fought, and often died, at Gallipoli.

"Bridge was flooded, eh?"

"Yeah. Had to take a detour."

"The chinks sent down anotha bloody cyclone," Humphrey said.

"Lucky to make it before dark," Darius said. "Never seen the river so high."

He drank his beer, eyeing the men, wanting one of them to talk. The beer was already warm and it went down like velvet. But his tongue still had that dry, chalky feel that had been there since he had first driven into the town.

"Them roads are death at night."

"Only saw dead roos, Richo," Humphrey said, slapping the man on the back and trying to get more into the circle. But none of the men made room for him and Richo's shoulders tensed after the slap. Only after Humphrey had removed his hand did the man relax.

"Roos? Who gives a stuff about them? I'd be more worried about drunk bloody coons and lost boat people who'd slit ya throat for a bottle of distilled water."

"Or a beer," one said.

"Or a bottle of metho," another added, his nostrils broadening like he could smell it.

They all laughed. Humphrey attempted to join in. A big four-wheel drive stopped in front of the group. They all turned to the car, swatting the dust away from their faces and coughing at it. A head stuck out of the driver's side window.

"One of you Humphrey Boragart?" he shouted, reading the name from a scrap of paper fluttering from his fingertips. He laughed at the name. Darius was sure the man had already seen the name but found it funny now he was in front of the others. The other men jumped at the opportunity to laugh at Humphrey. They winked at each other too, but not at Darius.

Humphrey stepped out of the circle he was only half in and walked towards the car. "Yeah?"

"Ya look nothing like him. Ya mum got some sick sense of humour or somethin?"

"I guess she thought I was destined for a better life than this."

The driver's sunburned face went flat. "Call for ya at the office." He paused. "Wanna ride?"

"Ya gonna make more jokes about my name?"

"If that's ya attitude," the driver said, clearly relieved, "then stuff ya. You can bloody well walk."

He roared off, the tires churning the dirt road and leaving Humphrey in a cloud of dust. The men laughed harder than before. And when Humphrey started the long walk towards the office, striding not without a little dignity, Darius thought, the laughter became even louder. He joined in.

"Sorry we sent ya with him," Richo said after the men had recovered themselves. A few of them pretended to wipe their eyes, smiling and shaking their heads. Richo looked anything but sorry.

"He's all right. I reckon he's a bit sick of it up here."

"Shit, we all are."

"He just thinks he's special," the oldest of them said. "I heard he did a year at uni."

"That says it all, doesn't it?"

"Maybe he's doin research or somethin, sociology or some bullshit."

Nervous laughter.

"Probly just a poof."

"Yeah, likes bein round men."

Darius watched the men frown and nod, but none of them could speak. This loose, difficult end was left untied and made worse by the fact they'd heard rumours about what happened in some of the huts when the lights went out. The other huts.

Darius knew that, despite everything, Humphrey had a good work ethic, had carried the load while the others around him had tired, and the men had to respect that.

"I reckon no uni student would work as hard as he does," he said.

"I bet he slacks off," Richo said.

"Bit more clever bout it."

"Yeah, he's cunning, he is."

"Too clever to be up here."

The oldest man cleared his throat. He was more lined and withered than the others and he seemed to believe this lent him a kind of leadership rank within the group.

"I met a fella like him shearing down south. He thought he was better than the rest of us. This big local sent him straight. Jack his name was. Coor, he was a right goer. Sorted out that smart arse so he was never seen again."

Darius couldn't help but smile, even if it felt like a grimace. The story had evolved over the years, and he'd often heard it changed to fit the context. Sometimes the fella was from the city, sometimes he was a foreigner, other times an Aborigine. He wanted to let it go, was amazed he had lasted this long without needing his dad to secure his place.

"That was me dad."

"Who? The clever fella?"

"Nah, nah, Jack. Jack Tucker."

The men turned to him, their eyes shining and smiles creeping onto their faces, causing Darius to wonder how his life might have been different here if he had played this ace sooner.

"No shit?" said the elder, looking at Darius differently, almost as if noticing him for the first time. "I used to shear with the Ripper. Christ, he could put it away. A liver the size of Tassie. Still shearin?"

"Yeah. Got a few teams now. He's gettin on a bit but he still shears."

The elder smiled wistfully. "He broke all the records when I was there. Top bloke, Jack. A dyin breed."

"Why ya not shearin, Digger?"

"I remember you now," the elder said. "You was just a runny-nosed kid back then, Digger. But I see it now. You're a dead ringer for ya old man. I don't envy ya though. Hard act to follow, the Ripper."

"I wanted to try somethin new. Dad said it would be good for me to come up here. You know, see the state."

Liar, he thought, and he recalled his dad's big face red with anger, slamming the front door, and then turning the veranda lights out, so that he had to carry his bag down the stairs in the darkness. He tripped over the milk crate step and fell to the dirt. He lay there, hoping his dad might appear on the veranda, might forgive him and understand, just for once. But the front of the house remained dark. He had turned his back on shearing, rejected the one thing that defined his dad and so his dad had turned his back on him. Laying in the dirt, there was nothing left to do but leave.

So, he pointed his ute north, driving along lonely desert highways with the windows down and the radio blaring. The landscape changed from tall trees and farmlands to the dry desert plains of the mid-west. He forced himself to embrace this adventure, to turn it into something he had chosen to do, something his dad had encouraged him to do. He travelled the highways and pitched his tent in forgettable towns, struggling to fill his days, until he found himself driving to a place that wasn't even on the map because he heard there was work going there.

He missed the south but kept that to himself; tried not to even admit it to himself. He missed the way the crops grew higher than the men when there was enough rain.

Rain.

Sure, it rained up north, but with a force and intensity, like it was trying to wash you off the land. Puddles became lakes, dry-bed rivers flooded and the dirt roads turned into squishy clay that stranded trucks and cars. Then, you woke up the next day and it seemed as if it hadn't rained at all. But the rain down south, that was different. Another country entirely.

"I was a bit sick of the sheep, too," he added.

"I used to hate the smell." The elder sniffed at the air, sucking up the dust and grime. "Much better up here."

And he said it with just enough irony and honesty for the men to laugh. Making fun of yourself and your situation showed just how strong and resilient you were, and with humour and a willingness to give it a go, you could tolerate and survive anything.

"The Ripper would sort out Humpy," the elder said. He looked at Darius, his greying eyebrows raised, challenging and expectant.

"Someone should," one of them added, getting the drift.

"Here he comes."

The men were silent as they watched Humphrey saunter towards them. His heavy boots flicked small puffs of dust into the air. He even kicked at an old beer can.

"Inheritance come through?"

Humphrey shook his head. "Still one more brother to kill. But it'll have to wait. He's gettin married. Wants me to be best man."

Darius watched the men grin and exchange quietly satisfied squints and nods with each other.

"That mean ya leavin?"

Humphrey was suddenly boyish and sprightly. He pulled his square shoulders back as he realised, and showed it, that he would no longer have to put up with these men.

"No choice. Can't turn him down."

"Too right."

"Where's he live?"

"Esperance."

"Couldn't be further away if it was Sydney."

"Long drive ahead."

"Yeah," the elder said. "Better get started."

Humphrey looked down at the older man and then turned towards the fading sun. The sky was streaked with red and orange and purple.

"Reckon I'll start in the mornin," he said at last. "Wouldn't want to get robbed by some coon or a chink."

Darius watched each of the men suck in their stomachs and dig their boots into the dirt. Hands that weren't holding beers clenched into fists and then released.

"Worse things could happen," the elder said.

Humphrey was tall, over six feet, but skinny and bony. He put his hands on his hips to make himself look broader and more muscular. "Such as?"

"Car problems. Wouldn't wanna get stuck out there in the desert. You should leave that shitbox of yours here, or are ya not comin back?"

Humphrey took exception to the man's tone, as local decorum dictated he should, but he did so with apparent glee, struggling to keep the required straight face. "Ya havin a go at me, mate? Sayin I'm not welcome?"

The elder stepped out of the circle and stood half a metre from Humphrey. He was considerably shorter, barely coming up to Humphrey's shoulders, but he was stocky and experienced. His knuckles still bore the scabs of a recent fight, one he'd lost, but lost well.

Slowly and deliberately, he rolled up the sleeves of his shirt. "Reckon I am."

The other men reached for their wallets. Richo, who was the best at calculating and always profited from taking bets because the others were so bad at it, was made bookie again. He scribbled the bets down on the inside flap of his packet of cigarettes. Darius waited for all the men to bet against the old man and then bet a thousand dollars. Richo, going with the mood of a Humphrey victory, gave him good odds.

Humphrey made the required line in the dirt, but it was soon rubbed away as the two started to wrestle, the boots of both men throwing the dust into the air. The cheers and shouts of the small crowd dragged others from the huts and out from the shaded areas where they sat drinking and playing cards. Starved of entertainment, they rushed over and joined the tight circle. Richo took their fast, reckless bets. Darius, standing nearby in case Richo decided to run off with his money, was again surprised to hear everyone betting against the old man.

25

Neither could gain advantage from wrestling so they stood far from each other, rushing forward and swinging big punches that cut perfect arcs through the dust but never came close to connecting. Humphrey seemed inspired by the calling of his name, even if Darius heard it as "Humpy", and landed the first blows, putting the old man on the dirt to the cheers, and jeers, of the crowd. With the old man down, Humphrey should have jumped on him and gained a big advantage, as everyone expected, but he stood back and waited for the old man to get up. Darius thought of the money, and was glad Humphrey was fighting with honour. He'd never win that way.

Hearing the heckles of the crowd, coming from men he probably considered mates, the old man forced himself to his feet. He wiped his mouth with the back of his hand and spat a slimy globule of blood into the dirt.

"You hit like a girl," he said.

"Hit him, Humpy,"

"Carn, Dougie."

"Give that poof what he deserves."

Dougie edged forward, bent over, his arms extended and his fingers spread, an animal looking to strike. The two fighters staggered around in a small circle, coughing at the dust. With the right music, Darius thought, it might seem like they were dancing together, or performing some kind of tribal ritual.

Men from the office came running over to stop the fight, but seeing the two almost finished, stopped to watch, smoke cigarettes and give their opinion who they thought would win. It seemed they too were enjoying the break in the monotony.

Dougie landed a few soft jabs and as Humphrey shuffled backwards, the old man picked up a handful of dirt and threw it in Humphrey's face. Blinded, Dougie tripped him over, then fell on top of him, pinning him to the ground. Humphrey struggled as the punches rained down. It looked like he had given up and was simply taking the beating. He protected his face with his hands and arms until two office men forced their way into the circle and pulled Dougie off. The crowd let out a chorus of boos, but Dougie raised his fists in the air and everyone cheered. The two office men helped Humphrey to his feet and shouldered him towards the first aid station. The few men who had waged correctly crowded around Richo while the others patted Dougie on the back. Money changed hands rapidly; crumpled bills slithered to the ground and were stepped on before the wind could blow them away. A few men chased dropped bills and the others laughed at them. Darius pocketed his healthy clump of dirty notes and moved through the crowd to slap Dougie on the back.

"Just how the Ripper woulda done it," Dougie shouted. He took the beer handed to him and drank it down in one gulp to the cheers of the men.

Darius looked over the heads of the men towards the first aid station. Humphrey walked unassisted and alone towards the building. Darius was glad his friend hadn't backed down and had put up a good fight, and had lost.

In the heat of the moment, with adrenalin running high and some men keen to prove themselves and others just downright bored, small fights broke out and were quickly broken up by friends and workers from the office. The drinking continued, though, and they were soon all showered and in the pub.

The night passed quickly, and they were all thankful for that.

***

The high-pitched beep-beep of Humphrey's watch barely disturbed the chorus of snores that rose and fell in various octaves in the stuffy darkness. Darius propped himself up on one elbow and watched Humphrey move silently through the cramped hut, pulling his bags from under his bed and then going into the bathroom and pissing loudly.

Must've packed last night, Darius thought, before he came to the pub.

Sure, that was normal, that the two fighters had a drink together, but no one had expected Humphrey to show. His presence, greeted at first by surprised and suspicious stares, eventually seemed to win a certain kind of approval. Humphrey iced the cake by beating Dougie in a drinking contest, although the elder was already far beyond a sociable level of drunkenness and threw up on the floor immediately after, to everyone's delight. Dougie slapped Humphrey on the back, forgetting all that he'd said. Watching the two arm-in-arms and screaming out the words to Midnight Oil's *My Country*, Darius wondered if

27

Humphrey might have been better off getting into a fight earlier.

"You awake?" Humphrey whispered. He gestured with his head to go outside. Darius followed.

The dawn was chalky and dry. In the half light, Darius sucked at the gritty air, inhaling the dusty remnants of the one industry that gave politicians the chance, in air-conditioned offices on the other side of the country, to claim the economy was booming. But the air smelt and tasted of death, of intrusion, and the only thing Darius thought was booming was the sense of his own deterioration.

Carrying his dirty green backpack, Humphrey walked towards his old sedan.

"Listen," Darius began, his mouth dry, his voice rasping from the stale, over-breathed air of the hut, "I know a bit about cars, and I don't reckon you'll make it to Esperance in this thing."

"That so?"

"Mate, you'll be lucky to get to Hedland."

"It'll get me outta here, and that's a good start."

Darius looked past Humphrey towards the pub, to where the big dust-covered rigs were lined up. The truckers were probably already scoffing their breakfasts, eager to be on the road and out of this place.

"Jump in one of them. They're all goin south."

Humphrey caressed the roof of his car, tapped it with his fingers. "I think I'll stick with freedom."

Darius looked down at the dirt. He drew small circles with his boots. "Buy it off ya?"

"You've got a car. A big ute that blatantly points out your heterosexuality."

"Yeah, but I could fix er up, maybe sell her in Hedland. It'll give me somethin to do."

"Save ya pennies, Digger."

"What ya want for it?" Darius pulled out his wallet and counted out a mess of dirty, scrunched up bills. "It's your money anyway."

Humphrey raised his eyebrows. They already had a few white hairs and these glittered in the growing morning light. "You bet against me. What did my beating earn?"

"Three grand."

Humphrey whistled, so loudly that a dog came running towards him and then sat panting at his feet. He bent slightly and rubbed the dog's head. Another whistle came from over near the trucks, but the dog stayed.

Darius reached out the money. "Take it."

"What a capitalist you are. Trying to make a profit out of suffering."

Again, Darius looked down at the dirt. The dog whined and Humphrey patted it. With his free hand he dropped the key into Darius's palm and pocketed the money, not bothering to count it.

"That's the only key in my life. Take good care of it."

"I will."

They shook hands, with Humphrey lingering a little.

"I guess that's it then," Darius said when Humphrey let go of his hand. "Think you'll be back?"

Humphrey shook his head. "No chance. And you should get outta here too. The mines are as poisonous as all these so-called mates."

"Couple more months."

"Bluey," a man shouted. The dog's head turned, and both Humphrey and Darius looked towards the approaching man, his boots slamming into the dirt and sending small puffs into the air.

"Bloody dog," the truckie said to Humphrey, somewhat too loudly for the still morning. "Reckon he's blind and deaf."

"Ya headin south?" Darius asked, picking the dirt from under his nails.

"Yeah?"

"Got room for a passenger?"

The truckie watched Humphrey patting his dog, its tail wagging and stirring up the dirt. "Reckon he heard that." He gestured towards Humphrey's backpack. "That all ya stuff?"

"My chariot's now in the hands of this young profiteer."

"Yeah, right, well," the truckie said, already walking away, "get ya shit together. I'm startin right now. And no singin in the cab. I heard ya last night. Bloody awful."

Humphrey reached into his back pocket and handed Darius a scrap of paper. "My address in Esperance. My brother lives there too." He started to move towards the trucks, walking backwards and carrying the backpack awkwardly. "He always knows where I am. If you're in the area, drop by for a visit. He really is a top bloke."

Darius put the paper in his now empty wallet. "When's the wedding?"

Humphrey had turned and was walking away, but stopped and faced Darius. "There isn't one. My mum died."

"Yeah, right," Darius said. But when Humphrey didn't smile or laugh, he added, "I...I'm sorry."

"Yeah, me too. But I guess it's a good reminder of the way of things." He looked down at the dog and turned towards the trucks. "Come on, Bluey."

"Good luck, mate."

"You'll need it more than me. I don't believe in it anyway."

Through the dusty dawn haze, the desert wind already picking up and lifting dirt into the open tops of his boots, Darius watched Humphrey climb into the cab, the dog jumping in first. The rig shuddered as it dragged the three long trailers behind it. The wheels churned the dirt, throwing it into the air. The wind blew it towards Darius and he turned away, coughing.

Around him, the desolate town was slowly waking up. Men were pulling on soiled undershirts, washing out arid mouths, and sighing as it dawned on them, again, that they were here, in this place. More than a few of them staggered out of their huts to vomit into the dirt.

***

The car was all over the road, running well but too light to handle the strong easterly. Worse, the road trains nearly blew it clear off the road. When he saw one through the desert haze, coming towards him or shimmering in the rearview mirror, he would pull the car to the side of the road, roll the windows up and wait for the monstrous vehicle to pass.

The other men, driving the tank-like company utility, had left him far behind. He would catch up with them later at the pub, after they had done all their shopping and enjoyed their brothel visit. But he would probably be forced to drive them all back, being the most sober.

Working on Humphrey's car had made the last few months pass quickly. It had kept him out of the pub as well, for a reason the men accepted. They had crowded around the open bonnet when the working day was done.

"Fixin er up for one a me cousins," he had said.

"On ya, Digger."

"Yep. Always look after ya family and ya mates."

A few men, each claiming more knowledge of mechanics than the last, had offered advice. They stuck their big hands into the engine and then smeared grease on their beer cans. Darius had let them help and never said anything negative or contrary. None of them knew as much about cars as he did and he was sure to keep this hidden. One man, more electronically minded but reluctant to help, had got the radio-cassette player to work on a bet.

Now, with no cassettes to play and the land never looking so dull, Darius tried to relieve his boredom by listening to the radio. He could only get one station, with talk-back radio.

"A boat crammed with Asian refugees fell to pieces and sank," the announcer said. "They were rescued by a passing crayfish boat. They're now in a detention centre near Derby that our tax dollars pay for. How many more of these unwanted boat people are we going to let into our great country? We're open for calls and we've got Beryl from Carnarvan on the line."

"Yes, hi, Brian. Look, I'm not racist or anything, and I'm not a supporter of One Nation either, but something's got to be done about these boat people. They're just queue jumpers, wanting to live here because our way of life is so much better than theirs. And they make trouble in the detention camps just to get attention. Why should we help them if they set the camp on fire?"

"Thanks, Beryl. I think you've expressed a sentiment of many of our listeners. Gary from Roebourne, you're on the air."

"G'day, Brian. Always got ya on when I'm workin in me garden. You know, I think it's just terrible that these Asians wanna leave their own country, but if we take one boat load, then there'll be thousands more on the way. The government's got to do something. These people take and take and give nothing back in return. Why should they be our problem? Turn the boats around and push them out to sea, I say."

"Cheers, Gary. Statistics show that few of these people can apply for refugee status to begin with. They arrive without passports or identification which makes the process slower, and they can't speak English, yet they expect to be received with open arms. And all this happens while the jobless rate continues to rise. Kevin, you're on."

31

"Shut up, youse...G'day, Brian. I'm a policeman in Broome and we had some boat people in the lock up here a few weeks ago. Couldn't speak no English and then went on a hunger strike cause we couldn't help them. One of em even attacked Willsy, the prison guard. Send em all home, I say, and send a bill to their government. I don't want my tax dollars funding this no more. My grandfather fought and died for this country and it's time the government drew a line in the sand."

There came the sound of clapping and cheering in the background, from the police station in Broome or from the studio of the radio station, Darius couldn't tell.

"You're right, Kevin. These boat people are invaders, pure and simple, and we have the right to defend our borders. It's time the Howard government took a stronger stance on the refugee problem and Asian immigration."

And so it went, all the way to Port Hedland. There seemed to be no end of callers wanting to complain, and just when it sounded like Brian couldn't get more agitated, his voice rose another octave of anger. Darius listened so the time would pass, agreeing sometimes with the sentiment, but disagreeing with the harsh solutions suggested; he half expected to hear his dad call in.

It was a relief when the dreary outline of Hedland came into view. After the monotonous interior, it was like arriving at a highly disappointing oasis. It wasn't much bigger than the makeshift mining settlement. It should have been a coastal paradise, with ocean-front villas and five-star resorts. Driving towards it for the first time over a year ago, he had expected as much. He had been sure there would be moneyed tourists lounging beside hotel pools drinking cocktails from pineapples, the main street lined with luxury convertibles, and long-legged girls walking from their hotel rooms down to the beach in string bikinis and high heels. Instead, he had found a broad, windswept expanse of nothing, where ill-matching buildings sat side-by-side, where aged and weary locals glared at anyone they had never seen before, and where the main point of interest was a giant mound of salt.

At the first service station, he blasted salty water at the thick streaks of red and brown that fanned out from the wheels up to the roof. A few locals, standing in a tight group in front of the workshop, looked over their shoulders and watched him, having already taken note of the license plate. He knew Hedland to be a town of transients, a place where people were forever passing through. That was what Humphrey had said, that it should have been a melting pot of cultures and influences, closer to Indonesia than to Perth, but it was disgustingly provincial, where confirmed locals looked with disdain at every unfamiliar face and with downright suspicion at faces coloured anything other than white.

Or something like that. Humphrey had ranted about Hedland for a good half an hour when they'd driven here together.

The used car dealership was down the road from the petrol station. Darius pulled in and the salesman came out of his small office to meet him. He looked at Darius and spoke from the side of his mouth, looking back over his shoulder as if there was something more important somewhere else that deserved his attention, or something he didn't want to be left out of. He kicked the sedan's little tires with contempt, muttering about salt and rust, and grumbling about blacks who tried to sell him stolen cars. Darius let the man talk, assuming that this was part of the routine.

"How much ya want?" the man asked at last, grumpily chewing the words and then sniffing loudly. He looked bored, in an interested sort of way.

"Four grand."

"Ya dreamin. Maybe in Perth, if she'd make it that far. Probly not." He coughed loudly, feigning closure. "Look, mate, I'm a salesman, not a wrecker."

Darius turned to look down the street to see if there were any other dealerships and, when he saw none, looked at the man. He wasn't much to look at. A set of skinny legs poked out the bottom of a slightly stained pair of shorts; two poles barely holding up this one-man tent. The legs didn't look strong enough to carry the bulk of the man's torso. His belly was hanging far over his belt, so far it looked like he might need help closing his pants. He wore a white, short-sleeved business shirt that lent him an air of professionalism, but the sweat-stained, sticky yellow patches under the armpits gave him up for the slob he was, probably an unmarried one at that. His face, set rock solid and square on a thick, muscular neck, was locked in a different time: bushy moustache straggling over his top lip with a few crumbs of food stuck in the strands, thick sideburns too far down the side of his face, and thinning hair combed over so that when the wind blew from the right direction, the hair stood straight up. He had what Darius's dad called the "coastal squint", acquired from a lifetime of looking at the glimmering ocean and squinting against the salty sea breezes.

"Sell it for me then?"

The man sighed heavily. A trickle of sweat ran down the side of his face and was absorbed by a sideburn. "Take fifteen percent," he said, sniffing disinterestedly. "Got the right papers?"

Darius took the small file from the glovebox and the man ran his stumpy fingers through it, licking his thumb each time he turned a page and leaving an imprint. Darius saw that his nails were raw and bitten to the quick, making the fingers look even stubbier. With clear effort and causing more lines than intended, his face twisted into a smile.

"Humphrey Boragart." He chuckled, his torso bouncing. "For real?"

Darius nodded, missing his friend.

"I guess ya mum took one look at you and wasn't so impressed."

"He's a mate of mine. I fixed er up for him. He lost his license a few weeks ago."

The man's eyes narrowed. "That right? What's your name then?"

"Darius Tucker," he said, hoping it might lead to a connection.

But the man's eyes narrowed even further, comfortably squinting to very thin slits. "Yeah?"

"Everyone calls me Digger."

Slowly, the man began to grin, and he nodded a few times. "Lose a relly at Gallipoli?"

"Me great grandfather." Darius tried to muster an appropriate level of sorrow. "Me dad wanted to preserve the memory."

"He sounds like he's got his head on straight."

"He's a shearer." Darius was amazed there had been no connection. Didn't his father say he had worked up here when he was younger? Or was that just another lie?

"Still want four grand?" the man asked. He seemed to be loosening up, his arms no longer folded and resting on his belly, but hanging loose at his sides, ready to shake hands and do business.

"Yep."

"All right. But I sill reckon ya dreamin."

Darius handed the man the key. "The higher the price, the more you'll make."

"Won't motivate me. Boy, you do dream a lot. Sure you haven't got some black blood in ya?"

Darius shook his head. "Nah, mate."

"Ya stayin in town, Digger?" The man slid his meaty hands into his pockets, looking like he could spend the rest of the day chatting.

Darius handed the man a business card from the mining company. "Call the office and leave a message. I'll come back when she's sold."

They shook hands. The salesman's hand was sweaty and warm.

"If, not when. Look, you seem like a bright spark. What ya doin up here? The air's poison where ya workin, ya know."

Darius had heard those rumours, and a few workers had been shipped out of the town for guarded reasons. But nothing had been proven yet and the company constantly reassured them that the mine wasn't dangerous. And the last time someone had questioned the manager, they had all received a pay rise.

"Need the money. Like everyone else."

"Then don't wonder why the locals round here don't like youse too much. Temp workers bring a lot of negative influences with them. They come from the city and reckon they've got everything figured. They don't havva clue."

"I'm from down south," Darius said, eager to distance himself from the stigma of the city.

"Nice country. But I get lost among all them trees. It's better up here. There's no place to hide. You can see what's comin and what's behind. It's all out in the open."

Darius was suddenly homesick, missing those trees that gathered around like a support group, the most reliable circle of friends, offering shade from the sun and shelter from the rain. He had always liked losing himself in the small forest near his house, following the creeks and catching tadpoles that he took home but which never grew into frogs like he hoped. He remembered going there with his mum; she always knew how to find animals and insects.

Mum, he thought.

"Take my advice, Digger. Save ya wages and get outta here before ya lungs get poisoned forever."

Darius nodded, hating that people always tried to tell him what to do. "Good advice. Thanks."

"But don't expect this bird to walk outta here in a hurry. I'll put something in the local rag. The sheilas read it and this is definitely a sheila's car."

"Cheers, mate. Call us when she's sold."

"Will do, Digger."

He left the salesman standing next to the sedan, squinting west towards the water. The afternoon was getting on now, but the sun still burned brightly, making Darius wish he'd brought his sunglasses.

There was a waft of grilled sausage in the air and from behind tall backyard fences came the squeals of children playing. He walked Port Hedland's wide streets with his head down. He decided that once the car was sold, he would quit the mine and go home. Surely enough time had passed for his dad to welcome him back?

He found the mining company's white utility parked in front of the pub.

"Where the bloody hell have you been, Digger?" one of them demanded jovially. His drunkenness making him sway between hostility, humour and genuine concern.

"Sorry, fellas. That shitbox took a beatin on the way in." He spied their empty glasses. "My shout, eh?"

"Ah, we better get goin," the company man said. Darius recognised him as one of the office workers. "Be dark soon."

"Oh carn, Stevo," said one man. "What are ya, mate? It's not bloody company time, ya know."

"Yeah," seconded another. "There's time enough. Reckon Digger's dyin of thirst from all that whorin."

"One more round on me," Darius said, going to the bar. He pushed the five glasses together and carried them with both hands.

"Up ya bum," one of them said.

"Cheers, Digger."

They all drank. Darius took half his beer in one gulp. The others drank quickly as well. Darius noted that even though they had singled out the company man for his sensibility and had made fun of him for it, they all knew the dangers of driving at night.

"The road awaits," Darius said, putting down his empty glass.

They all got slowly to their feet. One man had to grip the table to balance himself. He laughed, and the others laughed with him. Darius shouldered him towards the door.

"I reckon Digger better drive," Stevo said as they walked to the car.

"Carn hold ya liquor, mate," one of them said.

"My old lady'd beat you in a boat race before breakfast."

More laughter.

"Here, gis the keys," one said. "I'm clean as a whistle. Look."

He cut a line in the dirt with his boot and then attempted to walk along it, but neither line nor his walking were straight and he tumbled to the ground amid the laughter of the others. Darius and Stevo bent down to help him up, but he pushed their hands away.

"Get in, you lot." Stevo handed Darius the keys. "We're losin light discussin it."

Still laughing and chiding each other, they settled into the car and the journey began. Darius felt the pressure of being responsible for this group; they were capable of doing anything.

"Turn the radio up."

"Change the station."

"Order a pizza over the CB. I'm starvin."

Laughter.

But the desert monotony and the straight highway soon dulled them, and they resigned themselves to the long drive. The sun had gone down and the sky was awash with thin, smoky yellow clouds. Port Hedland was far behind them now, the day's fun over.

The reality was sobering, for all of them. Darius hoped this would be the last time he would drive back to the mining town.

The men fell asleep, snoring and farting intermittently. The company man, in the front passenger seat, remained awake, forcing his eyes to stay open and rubbing them until they were red. Darius looked at him every time his head tipped forward and snapped back.

Up ahead, there was a car parked on the side of the road.

"Slow down, Digger," Stevo said.

Darius stopped alongside an old station wagon with half a dozen people leaning against it. Their black faces were stark against the orange of the dirt, even in the fading light.

Darius left the engine running and Stevo half wound down his window.

"All right?" Stevo asked.

"Gottafanbelt?"

Darius looked past Stevo and saw a lean black man, young, his trim body lank against the car. He was shirtless, his chest hairless, and the beginning of a scraggly, patchy beard gave his youth away. He stood patiently, almost bored, as if waiting for a bus and not caring whether it came or not. And he seemed to look not at Stevo or Darius but past them, at the desert behind. Darius turned, briefly, to look in that direction, fearing they might get blind-sided by a gang, that the whole broken-down-car was just a ruse to get people to stop.

Stevo made a show of looking in the glove box. He turned and asked the men in the back, but they shook their heads, after searching for a bit.

Through the open back window, Darius saw the curly head of a woman tending, rather disconsolately, to a small child. The child was crying so loudly, Darius wondered why he hadn't heard it earlier.

"Sorry, mate," Stevo said. "We don't have one."

"Pannyhose?"

Stevo shook his head.

Darius stared at the woman, the whites of her eyes glimmering. To his surprise, she smiled at him, a big toothy grin that seemed to stretch her face.

Stevo shrugged. "Sorry. You want us to call for a tow?"

"Nah. We's alright."

"Well, good luck." Stevo turned to Darius. "Come on, Digger."

Darius put the car in gear. He looked in the rearview mirror as the station wagon grew smaller. The same kind of car had taken his mum away, the windows filled with as many heads. He grimaced and swallowed.

"Stupid coons," grumbled one man from the back seat. "Askin for trouble. I hope the cops lock em up."

"What for?" Darius asked without thinking.

"You need a reason, Digger?"

Lewis: Many of your poems are about your father.

Poet: Yeah.

Lewis: He sounds like an incredible man who lived an amazing life.

Poet: A top bloke. You ask anyone who knew him. They'd all say that.

Lewis: Tell me about him. What was he like?

Poet: He's not really someone you can put into words. I could describe him, say what he did, ya know, but it would never do him justice.

Lewis: But he comes across very clearly in the metaphors of your poetry.

Poet: Yeah, well, perhaps that's the only way to understand him and really know him inside and out, in metaphor.

~~~

Down South

His head kept tipping forward, bouncing off his chest and snapping him awake. The black coffee he had gulped in the car salesman's office made no difference. The salesman, counting out the money, had happily offered up his thermos.

"I'd normally say you look like somethin the cat dragged in," he'd said, his beefy face a cheerful shade of red, the bills sticking to his fingers, "but you look more like somethin the cat threw up."

"Big night, last night."

He had wanted the open road, the silent, unquestioning surface of the highway. But the salesman had kept talking, kept making jokes and laughing loudly. He had even followed Darius to his car.

"What ya want for this one?"

"Nuthin. I'm keepin her."

"Headin home?"

"Yep."

It was mid-morning and good to be on the road, good to be driving south. The tarmac shimmered hazy blue, the heat distorting the approaching cars, when there were any. On the side of the road were fresh kills of kangaroos and even the lumpy remains of an emu, its skinny legs vertical, pointing to the sky.

The kilometres clicked over and slowly the land began to change. Or was it just the sun moving across the sky, breaking through the clouds and casting new light on this landscape that was only marginally different from the dusty mining town, from salt-streaked Port Hedland?

Whatever.

It was just good to be moving, distancing himself from the mining town, pushing it into his past, separating himself from the person he had been there.

He had staggered from the pub to his car, wanting to get the hell out, scared he might change his mind if he slept in the hut, that he might wake up stuck in the routine again. What a relief it had been to see the disappointing buildings shrink and disappear behind his own dust. But the boisterous send-off, the long night of drinking, so matey and intimate, left him longing for the comforting acceptance of the men. He had earned a place in the town, could have walked up to any tight circle and been accepted. Every esky would have opened for him now.

They had made speeches. Complete strangers had walked up to him, to tell him stories, impress him and make him laugh. The groups had circled around him, heckling and chaffing.

"You're a top bloke, Digger," they'd said, slapping him hard and squeezing his shoulder. There had been so much back slapping that it had made his shoulder blades raw. "Won't be the same without ya round here."

He had smiled painfully, touched, believing them. But driving away from the town, he knew he wouldn't be missed. Men drifted in and out of the town like inconsequential grains of dust, and he knew too well that the greatest of mates and most revered and indispensable of workers were soon replaced and forgotten. Of all those he had left during his time, only Humphrey seemed to linger in the conversations of the men.

His head dropped sleepily forward again and bounced off his chest. He wondered if he was actually sleeping, lying on that wafer-thin mattress back in the hut. The sluggish late-morning sky and hazy distorted highway had a dream-like quality. But the desert wind that gusted off the desolate landscape was too raw and hot, too full of souls and the poisons of progress to be imaginary. It blew in his open window and sliced through him.

He knew this wind.

On those terminal nights when the hut was stinking hot, the air humid and thick with second sweats, when he couldn't sleep. He had gone outside. In the blackness of the desert, away from the dim, pathetic lights of the town, he had lain down on the ground. The desert wind, as limp as it was in the dead of night, caressed him then. Without knowing why, he picked up handfuls of sand, watched it closely as it filtered through his fingers. The sand tingled, the tiny grains getting stuck in the contours and lines of his palm, the heat and history stringing the grains together, giving the sand an almost liquid quality. With his sleeping bag and blanket, he settled himself like an animal on the warm sand and stared up at the stars. The wind rustled the shrubs with a thousand comforting whispers and sleep would finally come.

But he was driving away from that as well. South.

Whim Creek.

Sherlock.

Roebourne.

Thousands of kilometres still, to get to where he wasn't sure he was even welcome.

At the turnoff to Karratha, he saw two people standing, arms extended. They looked like men, but when he was closer, he saw the inviting outline of their feminine curves. There was something foreign about their backpacks, and something strange about them being here, standing at the turnoff to Karratha, thumbs out; girls no less. One was large and tall, so his eyes fell on her skinnier, diminutive friend. She was actually regular height, he thought, but looked small compared to her friend. He stopped the car next to them and looked her up and down. He leaned his elbow casually on the open window and tried to smile in a friendly, disinterested way, but even he had to admit it had been a long year in the mines.

"Nice day for a walk," he said.

"Too hot for that," the smaller girl said with an accent. She stepped towards the car, but keeping a distance of sorts. The other girl stood behind her, her big hiking boots gripping the dirt. Darius tried to ignore her. But even as he looked at the smaller girl, he could feel the eyes of the taller one, and found himself peering past the smaller to look at her.

"Where ya headed?"

"Exmouth."

"Long way."

"We can give some money for petrol," the taller girl said.

Darius could look at her now, and the smaller girl seemed to step aside to broaden his view. She was long-limbed and athletic, and prettier than her friend, even though her face was hidden under a broad hat. He thought he might be attracted to her if she lost some weight, and shed the thousand issues she seemed to be carrying. The way she stood there, so large and so proud of it, her arms folded and cradling her breasts, it bothered him. She wore shorts, and when he looked at her legs, was surprised by their form, by their luscious hazelnut colour. They were thick and strong, but he had to admit, they had outstanding shape.

"Not necessary. It's just..." He looked at the taller girl again, admiring the way her boots dug into the dirt, the strong calves that rounded above the white socks stained orange by dirt. Legs that just kept on going. "It's just, just a long way, that's all."

"What can we say?" the smaller girl said, getting his attention. "We're ambitious."

He licked his dry lips and rubbed his eyes to be sure this was really happening. When he opened his eyes again and focused on the two girls, that last word was still ringing in his ears: ambitious. Did they earn their rides by spreading their legs? He thought about the smudged cheques in his pocket, those well-rounded zeros, and all the crisp bills in the little tin lunch box he kept hidden under the driver's seat.

"Could take ya to the turnoff."

The taller girl took a map from her back pocket and unfolded it. "Burkett Road?"

"Yeah."

He watched the girls exchange a brief look. The taller girl, her broader stature giving her a matronly, dominating air, chewed her red lips questioningly. But the smaller girl nodded her head and threw her backpack into the tray of the ute. It landed on top of the dusty canvas tent that was badly folded and took up more space than necessary. She climbed into the cab, shuffling her small frame across the squeaky vinyl next to Darius. Their hips touched. The other girl lifted her backpack somewhat reluctantly – though it appeared to Darius that she did many things that way – into the tray, wedging it between the two spare wheels and the box of parts and tools. She lowered herself into the cab, taking her time, and closed the door. She seemed even bigger crammed into the cab.

"Are we going to start?" she asked, winding down the window.

Darius pulled the car back onto the road.

"I'm Sabrina," the girl next to him said.

From the corners of his eyes, he saw her give her hair a shake. A few bits of grass fell out. He wanted to run his fingers through her blonde tresses, just touch them and maybe bring the tips to his nose. They were almost the colour of gold, and not the milky, chemically inspired yellow he was used to. He sniffed at the air, hoping to catch a whiff of feminine scent, some sweet, natural womanly smell his life had been so void of this past year. But all he got was old cigarette smoke, girly sweat – which was almost enough – and the rather insipid smell of seldom washed clothes, although that could have been coming from him. Still, they were girls, they were in his car and they were driving south. Anything could happen. He had never been to Exmouth, and as their long journey began, he contemplated the idea of taking them all the way there. He would rent a cabin at a caravan park and they could all jump into bed together; or he could just invite Sabrina in and pitch his tent for the other girl.

"That's Trudi," Sabrina added.

"Actually, my name is Waldtraut, but no one in this country can say it, or even remember it."

"I'm Darius. But everyone calls me Digger."

"How did you get that name?" Sabrina asked. "Do you work at a cemetery?"

Sabrina seemed keen and talkative, and he liked the sound of her accent. The adventurous look in her eyes and the comely shift of her shoulders made him want to launch into a romantic and dashing story of personal heroism, that the nickname resulted from him showing such raw courage that she would tell him to stop and let Trudi out and then blow him all the way to Exmouth.

"Me dad gave it to me. He didn't like me name so much."

"I like it," Sabrina said brightly. "It's cool and not like the other nicknames we've heard."

"We've met so many Thommos and Robbos and Jimmys," Trudi said. "They don't have much imagination here when it comes to names. Or nicknames. Everyone sounds the same."

Sabrina spoke to Trudi. To Darius, their language sounded harsh, yet strangely musical, and the foreign words made Sabrina even more attractive and exotic.

"What's that?"

"German," Sabrina said. "We're from..."

"Actually," Trudi interrupted, "it's Swabian, a dialect spoken near Stuttgart."

"No shit? I've never met a German before."

"Do we fit the stereotype?" Sabrina asked in what Darius hoped was a coy, seductive way. She turned towards him, awaiting his answer, and as she turned her limited cleavage bounced slightly; he saw she wasn't wearing a bra.

"He probably thinks we're Nazis," Trudi said.

That had been his first reference point, but he wouldn't let the girls know that. Rather, he decided to impress them with his tolerance and openness. But Sabrina being bra-less made it difficult to think straight; it made it difficult to drive straight.

"That was years ago," he said, his voice breaking on years. He cleared his throat and tried again. "Got nothing to do with you either. I reckon not even me dad remembers."

"Well," Trudi said, "everyone else here does, and they don't want to let us forget it. It's the same in the States."

"You always generalise," Sabrina said.

"Yes. That's true. Because people insist on being general." Trudi continued in their language and they argued briefly before Trudi looked out the window and Sabrina turned to Darius. He wanted to look down her shirt but kept his eyes on the road, fearing that she would catch him looking.

"Where are you going?" Sabrina asked.

"Home." And it sounded even to his ears like a place hardly worth visiting.

"Where's that?"

"Down south. You wouldn't know it."

He stared at the road ahead, his hands draped over the steering wheel, suddenly bored. The girls weren't going to rob him. Sabrina seemed all right, but he didn't like Trudi, and also didn't like the atmosphere between them. Given the choice, he would have been happy to pull over and let them out. There was their smell too. They smelled of highway, exhaustion and, if he got his smells right, horse manure. He wondered if they had worked on a farm near Karratha. The peculiar smell of Australian horse manure clung to them like a pathetic friend. He didn't smell it at first, but now, in the close confines of the cab, with the Exmouth threesome increasingly unlikely, it seemed he couldn't smell anything else.

"What's the place called? We might end up there."

"Reckon ya won't. No tourists. Just farms. Nothin to see, unless ya like sheep."

He didn't know why, but he wanted to keep it a secret. With country people, he said the name with pride, because he won their approval without having to earn it, and he could reel off the towns he had visited as a shearer as well. Eventually, he would hit on a common acquaintance. The shearing sheds were confined spaces, the world small and intimate, and it only took a few sentences between complete strangers for them to find someone or some place in common. Maybe that was it; he didn't want these girls to use him as their connection, to ingratiate themselves with locals.

"We've seen plenty of towns like that," Sabrina said, and her smile was thin with disappointment. "We came here thinking this place would be paradise, but look at it. I never thought so much of it would be so forgettable."

"Nothing but flies and sand," Trudi added, seeming to like the topic.

"I wonder what the first prisoners thought when they arrived."

"Ja. 'Look at this dump.'" Trudi laughed loudly, making Darius turn to her.

Sabrina laughed as well. Darius frowned at the road. He wanted to tell them that if they didn't like it, they could go back to their own country, and they could take their lousy opinions and their horse stink with them. It was just like his dad had always said; only immigrants and foreigners bad-mouthed Australia. This was far and away the best country in the world and anyone who thought otherwise didn't deserve to be here.

"Germans dream of living here," Trudi said. "But they have no idea of the reality of this place. And we're not as welcome as we might think we are."

Darius slammed on the brakes and pulled over to the side of the road. A cloud of dust floated past the car.

"Look, I'm not a bad bloke, but I'm not takin ya if ya gonna criticise my country."

Sabrina looked down at the floor of the car. Darius saw then what a mess it was, with chocolate wrappers stuck to crumpled beer cans, and even a grease-stained junk food bag from nearly a year ago.

"Sorry," Trudi said. She opened the door and her boots hit the ground with a thud.

"Sorry, too," Sabrina added, looking sufficiently apologetic. Darius wondered if that was only because she didn't want to be left out here.

"That's how we talk in Germany. Don't we, Sabrina? We complain. It normally sounds funny. Perhaps it's the kind of humour that doesn't translate."

"Well, I've never been to Germany so I don't know that. But ya carn criticise other people's countries. That's not fair. It's not done here."

Trudi turned in the seat to look at him. Her blue eyes were pale and clear, and the way her moist lips curled upwards at the sides made him think she was enjoying herself, that she got some strange pleasure from awkward confrontations.

"You're right." She smiled at him, quite petulantly, and in the position she was in, turning to look at him, he had a clear view down her shirt. She shook her head when his eyes drifted down to her chest and then jumped out of the car. She stretched slowly, like a fully grown wildcat, yawning loudly as she did so. Darius watched her, looking past Sabrina and tracing the contours of Trudi's form with his eyes. Her shapeliness was even starker when she stretched, when everything lifted. It pulled her shirt tighter around her, and a speck of tanned, surprising flat and taut stomach was revealed.

He found himself getting out of the car. He left the engine running and stood leaning on the open door pretending to look at the dreary landscape but squinting at Trudi. She turned to him.

"Well?" she asked, again with that cheekiness. It made Darius think she often asked questions she already knew the answer to, and only asked in order to give her own opinion.

"Well what?"

The broad hat cast her face in shadow. "Come on."

Darius looked down the highway in both directions, wondering what she meant. The afternoon heat made the road shimmer with haze. No cars in sight, from either direction. His sweaty toes made small, nervous fists inside his boots. One toe got caught in a hole, the nail tearing enough to make him stop.

"You'll never get a ride standin here."

Trudi smiled broadly at Darius. Her teeth were very white. "That's right."

"What's so funny?" He tried to stay friendly, but the brightness of the sun made his eyes hurt, made him squint at her again; made him try to find her face beneath the broad hat, to decipher what she thought about him.

She opened her mouth to speak, seemed ready to deliver a long speech, even took a deep breath, but then she just sighed. "Nothing."

Darius couldn't help thinking she wanted to say more, and for some reason, he didn't like it that she held back, that she perhaps thought he might not be able to handle it.

"Even if a car comes, it won't stop here," Sabrina said from inside the car, "and there's no trees too."

Trudi nodded her agreement, swatting at the flies. She looked out at the landscape, at the flat orange land that extended far to the horizon. Darius followed her gaze: no buildings, no trees, no life, nowhere to hide. Drop someone in the middle of it all and they wouldn't know which way to go. He couldn't leave them out here.

"Look, I'm sorry."

"For what?"

"Uh..."

"How old are you?"

"Twenty."

"You're a good person."

"That's what people tell me."

"Well, all right then." Trudi fell back into her seat. "Let's go, Digger."

Confused, but trying not to show it, Darius got back into the car. He shuffled it into gear and eased back onto the highway.

They drove in silence, except for a few comments from Sabrina to which no one responded. Darius could feel Trudi smiling, could hear her thinking, and the curiosity to know what was going on inside her head, what opinion she held of him, was almost enough to make him ask her directly. But he held his tongue, proud that he had stood up for his country, defended it against these negative foreigners, and also by the way he hadn't abandoned them. After all they'd said, he still gave them a fair go.

When they stopped for petrol, Trudi again offered to pay, but Darius waved her off. When he did, he saw that smirk again, that she knew he would refuse. He turned away from her and went inside to pay. When he came back out, he saw the two girls arguing, rather heatedly. He smiled, hoping they were fighting over him. They stopped when he handed them both a bottle of cold water.

"Look," he said, squinting first at the oil stained tarmac and then at the girls, "I'm sorry for what I said earlier. I'm a bit burned out. I've been working up in the mines, a year of twelve-hour days. But I never woulda left ya on the highway."

Trudi drank and wiped her mouth with the back of her hand. "No, never. Thanks for the water."

Back on the road, the kilometres ticked over and the girls were quiet. Eventually, Sabrina asked him what his plans were.

"Canada, I reckon."

"That sounds great." She turned to Trudi. "You were there as an exchange student."

Trudi nodded but said nothing. She stared at the road ahead, lost in thought.

"A mate a mine's there now. I'm gonna visit him. You know, see what happens."

It sounded good, like he was reckless and adventurous, but the sheer thought of leaving Australia, of being far away in a completely foreign land, scared him shitless. He didn't even have a passport. But he widened his eyes and spoke keenly of the future, working hard to convince the girls that such a trip was part of his normal life.

They talked a bit more about where they wanted to go, where Sabrina and Trudi had already been, but when Sabrina ran out of questions and Darius couldn't think of anything else to say, they fell into silence again. The Great Northern Highway drains even the most talkative people of words; but not Humphrey, Darius recalled. He wished then he had his friend's power of conversation. Lacking it, he tried now to present himself as a strong, silent type, but he was just as bored as the girls.

The blue bitumen started to seem rubbery, like it was absorbing the car, slowing it to a painful crawl. Each kilometre made a resounding click on the speedometer and the further the sun fell to the west, the hotter and brighter it became. The open windows let in only dust and flies, and not even the radio could relieve their boredom. It crackled and fizzled, picking up a station and then losing it, breaking halfway through a good song and making Darius switch it off in anger.

They drove the last two hours in silence. Sabrina fell asleep on Trudi's shoulder, like a child sleeping against her mother, but Trudi remained awake. She said nothing, and Darius wasn't going to try to get her talking, even if he had a few dozen questions lined up in his head. She had got into his car, a big powerful horse with a horse stink, but now she appeared to him as exceedingly feminine and voluptuous; he too wanted to rest his head against her shoulder and drift off to sleep.

49

At the turn off to Exmouth, the girls unstuck themselves from the vinyl seat. Darius got out as well, and stood trying not to look at them. Trudi seemed to be wondering how to say goodbye. She stretched, again cat-like, and Darius watched her round curves appear and then disappear. She had broad shoulders, almost as wide as his, and this gave her a masculine appearance from behind because her hips seemed narrow in proportion. She reached into the tray and lifted her dusty backpack out. She grabbed Sabrina's too, and looked like she could easily carry both.

Darius looked down the road, the bitumen darkening with the setting sun, turning into the colour of sea water. He thought that he could smell the ocean, and the stink of seaweed, but out here, it could have been the stink of anything; even the land smelt like it was decomposing.

He considered driving the girls up to Exmouth and staying there rather than attempting to get to Carnarvan in the dark. The road would be treacherous. But something made him think he would be disappointed in Exmouth, that Sabrina wasn't as free-wheeling as she acted while Trudi seemed only intent on making fun of him.

"I'll stay till ya get a ride," he said.

"Thanks," Sabrina said, sitting on her backpack.

They waited in silence. A few cars came, headlights beaming, but none of them slowed down to turn onto Burkett Road. Darius kicked at rocks on the ground, wanting to be back on the road. At one point, he suggested they all go to Carnarvan, but Sabrina shook her head.

"She wants to go diving," Trudi said.

Darius turned to her. "You don't?"

She took off her broad hat and gave her hair a shake. Darius was stunned to see she had long, wavy blonde hair that tumbled to her shoulders, soft and wild. It made Sabrina's hair look like trampled straw.

"Sure," she said, but Darius didn't believe her.

Sabrina was about to say something when a big truck slowed down and prepared to turn. Darius walked onto the road and stood in front of the headlights. Through the windscreen, he saw the driver peer down at him and then at the two girls. The truckie jumped down from the rig. Three trailers of sheep bleated and stank. The smell took Darius straight back to the shearing sheds; it was almost enough to make him get in his car and drive back to the mining town.

"G'day," the truckie said, his rough face moist with sweat. He wiped his forehead on his sleeve. "Top campin spot ya got here."

Darius sized him up. "Goin to Exmouth?"

"Thereabouts."

"Room for two more?"

The truckie looked at the girls again and grinned; he even licked his top lip. "No question."

Trudi and Sabrina picked up their backpacks and walked towards the truck. Darius took the driver aside.

"Listen, mate, no funny stuff, all right, or I'll have a few hundred miners onto ya."

"Oi, fair go. If that's ya attitude, then stuff ya."

"Come on, mate, no offence meant, but we both know this's no place for girls to be hitchin."

"Too right."

"So, take care a them, all right?"

"We can take care of ourselves," Trudi said.

The truckie gave them both a leering look and then turned back to Darius. "You look familiar," he said, his eyes narrowing.

"I'm from down south, a shearer," he said, and a connection was beyond certain. "Me dad's Jack Tucker."

"Fuck off. You're the son of the Ripper? No wonder ya such a hard cunt. Just like ya old man. Top bloke, Jack."

"Yep."

The truckie slapped Darius on the back. "They're safe with me. Wouldn't want the Ripper on me bad side."

"Onya."

Darius reached out his hand and the truckie took it firmly, greasily. He walked back towards the girls and the truckie climbed into the cab.

"Is it okay?" Sabrina asked.

Darius nodded. "He knows me dad."

"Jack Tucker," Trudi said.

Darius nodded again, smiling at the big girl who so confused and intrigued him, more so by being attractive in a way he should have found repulsive.

"Thanks for the ride," Sabrina said before she climbed into the cab. Darius wondered how long it would take before the truckie became aware she wasn't wearing a bra.

"Have a good trip."

Trudi lifted her long legs slowly up the steps and into the cab. At the open door, she turned and looked down at Darius, her body filling the doorway, all blonde hair and gleaming skin. Her eyes shone with mischief and experience. She gave him a seductive, lingering smile, almost inviting him to join her in the cab.

"It was really nice meeting you," she said.

And as the truck crawled forward, the sheep bleating nervously and the trailers creaking and rattling, her eyes were locked on him. She leaned out of the window to keep looking at him until the truck was around the first corner and out of sight.

***

So many nights he lay awake staring at the ceiling, hearing the grumbles and groans coming from each corner of the hut.

"Buggering each other," Humphrey had said, "like modern-day convicts."

No, Darius told himself, they moaned from the hard day. Still, a shadow sometimes moved in stealth. Or did it? It would make him turn away, towards the wall, but still lying on his back. To drown out the noise, he would envision his room back home. The rickety bed was too small, and he had grown up sleeping with his knees tucked under him, his body scrunched up and folded under the pile of homemade quilts; that booty from a decade of Christmases. He missed those quilts, the way in winter he would steam underneath them, the meat baking under the layers of pastry.

During those sleepless nights in the hut, when he found himself listening for sounds in the darkness, for confirmation he didn't want to hear, his vision of home turned into one of renovation. His longing extended the walls of his room, made the bed longer and the mattress thicker. He painted the walls in every room, raised the ceiling, moved the toilet inside, scrubbed every counter and floor, and fixed those bloody veranda steps. Ambitiously, he set to work renovating his dad: toned down his shouted insults, sobered him up, kept him out of the pub for months on end, managed to draw some affection from him.

His ideal put his renovated dad at the kitchen table, wading through paperwork with a thin smile on his face and drinking tea from his favourite red enamel mug, the paint of which had been scratched and chipped over time until there was almost no red left; shearing sheds throughout the south had a few tiny flecks of red embedded in their wooden floors. And when this utopic vision was almost complete, then she would drift into the scene, appearing from nothing to stand in the kitchen, barefoot, her face glowing by the light of the her homemade candles, reading a book while she cooked. With her arrival, exactly as he remembered her, though without the clarity he desired, sleep would come. In his dreams, her features became sharper: her hair was still dark and curly, her lips red and cracked, her legs long and chocolate brown. But then his dad would force his way in and ruin it, leaving Darius to wake up with a sour taste in his mouth that stayed with him the whole day. Sometimes, though, his dad would be the final touch to this conjured scene of tranquillity, and because it would be right then that Darius would say to himself that he never wanted to wake up again, he would do just that.

He drove south to the house of his youth, to the only home he had ever known. When people asked him about his origins and his background, he would see the house that tilted just slightly to the right, threatening with every stiff wind to crumble in a mess of brick, mud cement and sheet iron. For some reason, he always saw it from a distance, from the turn-off to the gravel road that led to town. It was his schoolboy perspective, he knew. It had seemed huge then, a farmer's palace.

Sure, it was an ugly house, but everyone knew this was where the Tuckers lived. Darius had never heard anyone say anything bad about it. The locals climbed over each other to help when repairs were needed. Because Jack Tucker was always there for them, no matter what. His dad saw potential when others saw hardship and was always prepared to give it a go even when the odds were against him. So, the locals treated the house and its occupants with respect. They drove up on Sunday mornings with problems they knew only Jack Tucker could solve, with questions they knew he could answer; his dad could have met them outside, but instead sat with them in the kitchen, made them a cuppa and offered biscuits baked by someone else's mum. The others would wait on the veranda. Darius would wait with them, ducking into the kitchen when his name was called and then going back to the veranda to say who was next. Waiting, he listened to the men talk about his dad and smiled proudly when they said he was a "top bloke" and "the best mate any fella could have." But as he grew older, he started to hate those Sundays, when he was his dad's go-between.

The gravel road was unchanged. The gum trees were tall and straight. The small white crosses had fresh flowers, faded photographs and those short, exaggerated eulogies written in haste. He drove past the Mackay farm, saw the barn where he lost his virginity to Taslyn Mackay when she was down from boarding school for summer holidays. She had come after him, claiming she had something to show him in the barn. In between all the stinking old farm machinery, she was suddenly naked and reached her hand into his pants. "I want some Tucker," she had whispered. Then she strapped a condom on him and was on top of him, already choking on an orgasm. He should have felt great, but all he could feel was the sensation that his dad was watching. It made him look around the barn, between the wheels of tractors and through the blades of ploughs. Taslyn had her eyes closed and was looking to the ceiling, her flat chest barely moving; her Hollywood groans almost made him tell her to shut up. His dad was in there somewhere, he was sure of it, looking with disapproval, expecting more. As indeed Taslyn had, because when it was over, she had her underwear back on before he had the condom off. And she had looked at him in the shadowy barn, scowling with disappointment, before pulling her dress on and running back to her house.

But he had boasted about his success, and this had led to a few more strange afternoon encounters in barns and to empty morning meet-ups in girls' bedrooms; yet always with the same sensation that his dad was in there with him, not just in the room, but inside the girl. They were almost all backdoor girls – like they'd agreed on it beforehand – too scared to go to the doctor to get the pill and desperate not to get pregnant.

The outline of his house cut through the gum trees. The shit-coloured walls and shiny, rusty roof made him swallow hard. He'd missed it. At the turn off, he stopped to look at it. It was smaller than he remembered, shrinking with age, and listing even more to the right. To the side of the house was his father's precious work shed, the door of which was the only one on the whole property with a lock. Behind the shed was the cramped, fermenting box of the outside toilet; his father had talked for years about moving it.

From the road, it all looked very shanty and unattractive, a house built in haste by a farmer struggling against the land and weather, unlucky every season, forever cursed because he had got the land for free. But it was home and Darius couldn't deny that he felt something, even if he had left the place in anger. Just the smell of the gum trees and the familiar lay of the land made him glad to have left the dusty north behind. Reminded of it, he coughed a dry rasping hack and spat a glob of greenish slime out the window. He would work all that gunk out of his system eventually and every phlegmy spit was satisfying.

He drove slowly towards his house. His dad's ute was parked under the tree in front, with the battered old farm ute next to the shed. The cream four-wheel drive was Murray Stevenson's.

"Still got the same old car."

He wondered again why Stevenson drove such a shitbox while sending every Stevenson child to private school in Perth and buying up property from failed farmers. He parked next to Stevenson's car. The bumpers were orange with rust, and the paint near the doors was bubbling and coming off in flakes.

He slammed his car door loudly, nervously, and walked towards the veranda, his boots dragging in the dirt. Nothing had changed. The windows were still caked with dirt, the milk crate was still the veranda's first step, and the only thing that shined was the big padlock on the shed door. He had one boot on the milk crate when the fly-screen was flung open.

"Digger?"

"G'day, dad."

The fly-screen whined shut. Darius climbed the steps onto the veranda. They took each other in, noting changes. Darius saw that his dad had aged, was broader than before. His receding hair was grey around the sides, but cut short so the grey could only be seen up close. He looked older with short hair, and the beard, recently grown and flecked with grey, added a few more years as well. The chest hairs poking out of his button-down shirt were silvery. Darius

55

couldn't believe all that ageing had taken place in twelve months; maybe he hadn't noticed it before. His dad's stomach bulged a little, but the forearms and shoulders were solid, and greying as he was, he still cast an intimidating figure. Darius gritted his teeth.

The fly-screen door opened a second time and Murray Stevenson came out.

"G'day, Digger. Where you been hiding?"

Darius shook Stevenson's hand. "Up north. A fella can get lost up there, that's for sure."

"Sent him to work in the mines," his dad said. "Shearin's too bloody technical these days. Any idiot can do it. Thought the mines might make a man outta him."

Stevenson nodded knowingly, looking like he too had worked in the mines. "Right in time for shearin. Bet ya happy to be back, aren't ya, Digger?"

"Yeah."

"Hard country up north," Stevenson said. "But lotsa money to be made."

"Christ, Muzza, is that all ya ever think about?"

"I'm no miner, but there's plenty of city fellas getting rich from the north."

"I prefer it down here, Murray. It was a tough experience, but it's good to be home."

"Onya, Digger."

"Just in time, too," his dad said.

"Your old man just scored a pretty healthy contract." Then Stevenson lowered his voice. "He thinks about money too, ya know."

"Bugger you, Muzza. You can stick ya contract up ya arse."

Stevenson laughed and slapped Darius's dad on the back. Stevenson even feigned a punch; great mates they were.

"We're gonna shear all his skinny sheep."

"That's bloody brilliant." Darius tried to sound enthusiastic, but a sweaty shearing shed was the last place he wanted to be. He liked the mateship, sure, the chatty tea breaks, the cold beers when the day was done, and those long drives out to the sheds when they all sat in the back of his dad's ute, joking and chaffing each other. But none of that detracted from the life inside the sheds, when the pressure was on and the time ran too quickly. He hated the dung, the rank smell and the coarse feel of the wool in his hands; and the bleated protests of the sheep sometimes sounded too much like the sound a child might make when having their tongue cut out. But worst of all was the pressure, that he was the only son of Jack Tucker and everyone expected him to rise to the same level. His dad often turned away from him when he finished so badly in the totals, wouldn't have anything positive to say. The other shearers were more supportive, saying with half smiles that it took his dad years to get good at it. But he also knew what some of the shearers said behind his back, that he was too tall and not strong enough, and, more harshly, that he didn't seem interested, that he thought himself too good for the sheds.

"Yeah, good news," his dad said. "This'll be your chance, Digger."

"Yeah, knock this old codger off his pedestal."

"I've still got a few more years left in me yet, Muzza."

Stevenson chuckled and shook his head. He took a few steps across the veranda, making to leave. "I'll let ya know when and where we'll start."

Darius shook the sheep farmer's big, crusty hand again. Stevenson was wealthy but he still had a worker's hands, cracked and scrubbed clean, but with stains embedded in the cracks that only the years would take away. More than one fingernail was black, with others chipped or broken, and Darius thought that every chip and stain could tell a story that would only succeed in taking him further away from the essence of the man's soul. His father had the same kind of hands, and when he looked at his own, though his skin was still relatively fresh, they were starting to look the same way.

"We missed ya last season, Digger," Stevenson said, but not looking Darius in the eye. "Good to have ya back."

Stevenson turned and walked down the steps to his car. He climbed in and drove away with a squirt of gravel and a double toot of the horn. Darius watched the car throw the dust into the air.

"I didn't think you'd last a month up there."

Darius sniffed and looked down at the wooden floorboards. "Money's good. I think about that too."

His dad nodded. "I got ya postcard. From Hedland."

"I was living inland."

"Hungry?"

"Bit."

"Let's go to the pub."

His dad went inside, leaving Darius standing awkwardly on the veranda. He thought about retrieving his bag of clothes and taking it into his room, but decided to wait until he was welcomed in. He could keep moving, down to Esperance, anywhere really. Money gave him options. Canada? he wondered, scared to pursue that dream.

Bladders came from behind the house and jumped onto the veranda. He circled Darius and barked loudly, once.

"He whined the first coupla days but then forgot about ya," his dad said, moving through the doorway.

Darius bent down to pat the dog and wondered if his dad's reaction had been the same.

They drove to the pub in silence, save for the crackle and snap of gravel. Darius had travelled this road so many times, that the dull familiarity of it made him feel like he had never left.

As they entered town, his dad asked, "So? How was it?"

"Yeah, all right."

He wanted to talk, to complain about the cramped hut, the dust, the long work days and the monotonous evenings; to complain about a thousand things. But he knew his dad wouldn't want to hear about it, that he would scold Darius for being too negative. Still, he had to say something, and it had to be positive.

"Made some good mates."

"Coor. Reckon they're hard as nails up there."

Darius couldn't resist the chance. "Few of em know you. From shearing."

"Yeah? Made a lotta good mates in the sheds. Mates for life."

Until there was more money to be made in the mines, Darius thought.

"Hard life, up north. A year's enough."

"I knew you'd come back for the season." His dad parked next to the pub. "Ask anyone, they'll tell ya."

Darius hadn't planned it that way, but he had to admit his timing was perfect. His dad's twisted story was coming true: toughened up by a tour in the mines, older, wiser and stronger, he was ready now to become the shearer his dad expected him to be, to morph into the Tucker heir the town demanded. He could even drag Taslyn Mackay back into the barn to gauge his own development; she wouldn't run away disappointed now. Hardened by experience and having been out on his own, battling, the locals would surely respect him more.

And that's exactly what happened in the pub. They crowded around him and toasted his return. After a couple of rounds, his dad took over, and Darius stepped back to allow the Ripper to emerge: everyone's mate, joking, teasing, laughing, advising, patronising. His dad set the place alight, set the tone, raised the volume, made everyone around him funnier and more interesting. He was the golden screws that bound the flat wooden planks of men together. Without him, it might have been just another pub in a country town where the men stood around sombrely holding their drinks and grasping at conversation.

It was a rousing welcome. Big things were talked up, punctuated and confirmed by clinking glasses and over-zealous backslapping. Of course he would shear again, become a key member, perhaps even a leader, of one of his dad's teams. Numbers flew from mouths, the kind of totals they would expect from him in what would be his break-out season. It made the shearers present seem even more excited for the coming season; they could watch him blossom, or perhaps savour his failure. Darius could see in their eyes and in the tightness of their shoulders how keen they were for the competition, how much they wanted the chance to better a Tucker, if not the one they actually wanted to beat.

Of course he would play in the footy team, resign his bony frame to the last line of defence. He took no enjoyment from the sport and had only succeeded at it because he played against boys much younger than himself, younger brothers and sons of players with jumpers down to their knees sent onto the field to make up the numbers. And then in the pub after the game, all the talk would be about how great a player his dad had been, and the men would crowd around, desperate to recount a story about the Ripper that had become more exaggerated with each telling.

Of course it was time he got married. The names of Stevenson girls were dropped without subtlety; a few were still in high school, but ready, as the men roundly claimed. Taslyn Mackay and her younger sister got a mention. The men spoke with winks and nudged each other, rating the girls like they were sheep in an auction pen. Beauty was important, they claimed, but loyalty meant more. At his age, or younger, most of them had married and started raising a family. Darius knew what nasty rumours might circulate if he waited too long, as they had done with Roy Stevenson, who had stayed single until he was almost thirty and then had moved to the city, never to be heard of again.

Of course he would take over his dad's shearing teams one day, keep the business in the family. His own sons would grow up on farms, barefoot and strong, maturing in sweaty shearing sheds as he had done, their lungs forever lined with minute, coarse slithers of wool. The circle would continue and no one would ever have the courage to break it.

It would all be so easy, he thought, as the men outlined his future, getting it so accurate that he could already see his grown sons shearing next to him, could already hear his own reproachful voice. He would assume his dad's mantle simply by playing the same character. He just had to say the right things, be the most loyal and honest of mates, and give everyone a fair go: be tough when required, be the centre of attention, and make everyone around him feel better about themselves. It sounded like a lot, but he knew it wouldn't be difficult. He just had to play along. The men around him would manufacture his legend, cut it from a similar mould as his dad's, out of necessity to fill the void. It would have a foundation of fallacy, built with half-truths and exaggeration, and the collective belief of the men around him would make it all true.

And of course he was a liar. Could he really stay in character for so long? Stand there and smile while all the lies raged around him? Could he spend the rest of his life shearing in this town, making babies with some teenaged Stevenson girl he didn't love who would balloon after the first pregnancy and then spend fifty years torturing him with passive aggression?

Of course he couldn't. He knew that, and as the drunks around him laid out his life before him, speaking in slurred hyperbole, he wanted to tell them all to shut up. He didn't want to shear, didn't want to stay here and didn't want to be the Darius he was before. He had only been back a few hours, but already he felt himself playing that character, as if nothing had happened in between. No, a year had passed. He'd driven the length of the state and survived without his dad. And he had met Humphrey.

He smiled then, still listening to the men, still agreeing to all the requests, demands and plans coming his way, because it would have been too difficult and damaging to disagree. How Humphrey would have hated this place, these men too. Grandsons of Anzacs and relics of bushmen, he would call them, idolising and clinging to an identity that was a construction. Or something like that. But looking at the scene now, Dairus thought Humphrey had a point. There was too much acting here, too much fake behaviour.

But of course he couldn't put these thoughts into words, at least not here. He kept his feelings to himself, laughed with the others, drank with them at the same speed, copied their actions and mimicked their behaviour. He didn't want their attention, didn't want to assume his dad's mantle, couldn't give a fuck about shearing totals. He didn't want to one day be giving advice to the sons of these men on a Sunday morning in the shanty house he would inherit.

And of course he said the opposite. Yes, he was raring to go, to get those shears buzzing and do his dad proud.

"Yeah, mate, carn wait for the season to start. Reckon I'm ready to settle down. There's no other place I'd rather be."

And on until, drunk and tired, he started to repeat himself, fearing he hadn't convinced any of them and that the truth might spill out.

Late in the evening, he sat alone at the bar, nursing his beer, watching the scene. The men still crowded around his dad. They were playing cards with drunken skill, gambling away hard earned money and laughing about it; sometimes laughing so hard their faces turned red and they were forced to swallow hard to keep themselves from throwing up. After midnight, they started to drift away, driving their utes home and weaving them all over the road, no doubt. Darius pictured them, still grinning and laughing as they barely missed a tree or a roo, and then bursting into their bedrooms to wake up their wives roughly, hard-ons like drawn pistols, only to fall asleep as soon as their goal had been achieved, be it sex or violence, or both.

That would be him if he stayed. His life for the next half century.

They were the last to leave, with Darius helping his dad into the car. The old man insisted on driving. Darius slouched in his seat, scared to look at the road as the car waddled towards the first pink cracks of dawn. He had survived many of these intoxicated drives and knew he could do no more than put his faith in his dad and hope for the best. He gripped the torn end of the seat belt and the buckle, as he had done all through childhood. He was himself too drunk to drive, more tired than he had ever been, but he would rather have been driving. He hated being in the car then, powerless as his dad ponderously worked the steering wheel and pedals. The old bastard was just guessing and getting lucky. He wanted to stop the car and get out, to pull the park brake as hard as he could and end this; not for his safety, but just to get back control. He'd had that for a year, but in just a few hours, his dad had wrenched it from him. He knew then he wouldn't shear, as much as he knew his dad wouldn't understand. He would go to Esperance, to Humphrey, and get away from everything; run before his dad threw him out again.

The car swerved across the gravel road. Rain had fallen, making the road softer so that the tires gripped the gravel better, giving his dad false confidence. The potholes were filled with shadowy, glassy water that looked like black ink from a distance.

His eyes were sticky and the slow, drifting motion of the car made him feel sick. His head tilted to the side, his cheek slapping against the passenger window. His eyes were stuck and he couldn't open them again.

~~~

The thump woke him. As his eyes slowly started to focus, he made out the bulky figure of his dad hunched over the wheel, jamming the car from reverse into drive while pumping the accelerator. The spinning and grinding sound was familiar. The back of the car slowly sank.

"Bloody hell," his dad said. "Only ever rains when ya don wan it to."

They walked home, his father moving quickly and Darius lagging several metres behind. The brisk dawn air was sobering and they were both under-dressed. It wasn't far, though, and the pale yellow lights of the veranda were soon stronger than the growing light of morning. He couldn't wait to climb into bed; he could already hear the springs twanging as he settled into his foetal sleeping position. He wouldn't even ask permission, and would just walk straight into his room and collapse.

At the house, he was first onto the veranda, had his hand reaching towards the fly-screen door, when his dad asked, "Where ya think you're goin?"

"I drove all the way from Carnarvan today. I'm goin ta bed."

"Like hell ya are."

Darius watched his dad move towards the shed. He unlocked the big steel padlock and retrieved two shovels from inside, then locked the shed again. They had to do this, Darius knew. If anyone saw the ute stuck, it would be all over town before lunchtime.

They set out side by side, shovels leaning on their shoulders, but his dad again set a fast pace, getting so far ahead he shouted a few times for Darius to catch up. A light rain was falling, giving the dawn a misty, dream-like quality, making them both sweep their hands in front of their faces to brush away the fog. Still drunk, Darius struggled to put one foot in front of the other, struggled to connect his mind with his motion. He wondered if he was already in bed, dreaming, and had conjured this wonderful image of his dad getting the car bogged. He knew what would happen next. They would get to the car, start digging, and then the whole town would drive past. They would all slow down, lower their windows and laugh. They would point and laugh at Jack Tucker, and no one would offer to help. Darius liked that part best of all; that all those mates might refuse to assist in such a crisis. His dad had never got bogged before, had never even driven off the road. It must be a dream.

The car seemed deeper than when they had left it, with the back bumper nestled on the dirt and the license plate buried. His dad set to work, shovelling strongly and quickly. Darius looked down the road, waiting for the convoy of cars.

"Oi. Get on with it."

And that was exactly the kind of thing his dad would say, Darius thought, driving his shovel into the dirt. The rain had turned the top layer of gravel into soft, spongy earth, making it easy to dig but heavy to lift. He shovelled with the kind of endeavour expected of him, unable to match his dad, but still doing a decent job. He kept sneaking looks at the road, though, narrowing his eyes at the fog, waiting for that moment when the headlights of every car in town would slice through. He was amazed that the suspense and expectation hadn't made him wake up. He heard his voice speaking and it had that strange sound it made in his dreams, like he was hearing it played from a recorded cassette tape.

"I'm not gonna shear this season."

His dad stopped shovelling and looked at him. "Bullshit." He slammed the shovel into the dirt. The tip hit the tire, almost puncturing it. "Ya came back for it."

"I wanna travel."

"What ya wanna do that for? Ya life's here. Stralia's the greatest country on earth. Ya bloody stupid to wanna leave."

Darius smiled, thinking that right then would have been a perfect moment for all the cars to come, to tarnish the legend forever.

"I wanna go to Canada."

"Wha for?"

Darius shrugged. "Dunno. See what's there."

"Anyone who leaves this country shouldn't be allowed back in. They let too many bloody chinks and wogs in as it is. They should get them and those who don't like it here outta my country."

It was so mean-spirited, so sober and stern, that Darius became distinctly aware that he wasn't scrunched up on his small bed breathing the old woolly air of his house. He had lost control, said too much, but there was no turning back now. His dad was not especially clever, was just a simple, hard-working honest man – wearing that simplicity like a comfortable old hat that everyone admired – but he seldom forgot things, even when drunk, and was well known for holding grudges with unchanging ferocity for decades; he also never forgot when someone did good by him.

"I'm goin. Anywhere's better than stayin here an shearin."

They had dug a hole deep enough to allow the car clear passage back onto the road. His dad ripped the shovel from his hands and threw both of them into the tray of the ute. They clanged against the metal, waking Bladders. The dog yawned.

"If that's how ya feel about it, ya might as well start now."

"Dad, wait."

But his dad was already in the ute and he managed to force the car out of the ditch. As the car roared down the road, throwing up a cloud of dust a shade darker grey than the fog, another car came from the other direction. Without thinking, Darius jumped into the ditch and stayed there until the car passed. Lying in the wet dirt, an apology formed in his head. He was kidding himself if he thought he could just fly to Canada and make things happen. He didn't think even Humphrey could manage that. Overworked, he could say after they had both slept it off, too many twelve hour days, and breathing all that air that's supposed to be poison. He just needed time, to get back into the rhythm of being home. Shearing would help, and what he had said on the road about not wanting to shear was just a bad attempt at a joke. It was the right thing: to grovel, to seek redemption, to lie and lie until all those lies become the truth.

At the house, the veranda lights were off, but it didn't matter because the morning light was stronger. It was a dull morning, soupy and moist, and the thin light cast the house in a dismal shade of grey. He walked up onto the veranda, thinking he could sneak into his room, sleep and sort everything out after lunch.

The fly-screen door made that familiar whine on opening and he reached for the front door. It was locked. He rattled the handle, thinking it was rusty or jammed. The handle turned but the door didn't move. He took a couple of stunned steps backwards. For as long as he could remember, the door had never been locked; he didn't even know it had a lock and that there was a key. He stared at the door, then backed away. He went down the veranda steps to stare at the whole house. No wonder his mum had never come back, he thought.

It hurt, that she hadn't come back for him. No sign, no word, nothing. Maybe, I'm like her. I want truth. I want more than this.

His dad was a world unto himself, and university and Perth and Canada and so many other things weren't part of that world. He forced people out, pushed them from verandas when they wanted more, threw them to the dirt and left them there. He locked doors to keep secrets inside, to keep the unwanted out. He drove away the people close to him, but got up in the middle of the night to help some farmer with a problem.

Darius had one foot on the milk crate. He stepped back to kick it, then bent down to rip it from the earth. But it was buried too deep and he wasn't strong enough to pull it out. Instead, he picked up a large rock and hurled onto the roof of the shed. It clanged on the sheet iron, denting it slightly, and thumped to the ground. He turned to the front door, half-expecting to see his dad's frame filling the doorway, perhaps even cradling the rifle he kept under the bed. But the door remained closed and no sound came from inside the house. Darius went to the shed, yanked at the big padlock a couple of times and then kicked the door. The shed was like his father's brain, he thought, unable to come up with a better comparison.

"Selfish bastard."

Still no sound came. There was nothing left to do but climb into his car and leave. He drove slowly along the road, kept his head low as he passed through town, and then pointed the car south-east towards Esperance.

***

The wind poured through the open windows, sobering and warm. By mid-morning, the sun was high, and any trace of the overnight rain and gloomy dawn were gone. Puddles had dried and it would have required an intimate knowledge of the trees to see that their leaves had turned a slightly darker shade of green. Those tall trees lined the road south, crowding around each other, their branches mingling and caressing like thousands of shaking hands.

The further he distanced himself from home, the more the road seemed to widen and the landscape expand. The sky was an exceedingly optimistic and hopeful shade of blue. The land seemed to breathe promise; he thought he could drive clear across the country, and wanted to.

He stopped for petrol just outside of Ravensthorpe.

"Fill it?"

He nodded at the old attendant whose lined face still looked wet from a morning shave. The man would look younger with a beard, he thought, stroking his own stubble and hoping it made him look older and more rugged, and it would protect his skin from the weather as well. But the attendant had no beard, perhaps never did, because his skin bore the brown and white marks of a lifetime spent under the sun.

The attendant squinted at the car's license plate, his eyes becoming narrow slits that made a fan of wrinkles at the sides. A meaty claw pumped the petrol. "You from over Wagin way?"

"Yep."

"Shearer or farmer?" The old man kept squinting, awaiting the answer on which most of his judgements would be passed.

Darius thought for a moment about saying miner, just to see the man's reaction. But even though he was tired of this manufactured hostility, these fledgling alliances that hinged on perceived commonality and acceptance, he stepped up and played his role.

"Shearer."

The squint disappeared and the man's face relaxed. His blue-grey eyes were glassy and shiny, as if he rubbed them every morning with Vaseline.

"Headin in the wrong direction, aren't ya?" He removed the pump and, without asking, popped the bonnet to check the oil. "Season's bout to start."

"Just takin a week off," Darius said, and then added, to prevent further questioning, "I gotta girl down in Esperance."

The old man whistled playfully. "Better get the most outta her before the sheep rule ya life again." He went into the workshop and came back with a large container of oil. With difficulty, he lifted it and filled the engine.

"She's a right goer. No worries there."

He would have liked to have said something funny, a dirty one-liner that would make the old man laugh and remember him, but couldn't think of anything better than what he said. He just wanted to get moving again and tried to hide his impatience as the old man tinkered with the engine.

"Ya hoses'll be religious soon. Very holey."

He laughed loudly, forcing Darius to laugh as well, to blend his dusty, contrived chuckles with the old man's boisterous cackles.

"We could do with you. Our servo couldn't crack a joke if it was burstin outta him."

The attendant slammed the bonnet shut. "Probly one of them unleaded fellas from the city."

"Probly. How much?"

He was sure to pay cash, though the old man proudly claimed that he took cards, and tried to pay a little extra for the oil and service. The old man waved him off. Darius knew better than to force the issue. He thought about sleeping a few hours in his car, but the scene's closure required that he drive out of the petrol station and continue down south to his Esperance girl.

He hoped Humphrey would be there. They needed to talk. Because he'd had reactions to things his friend had said that had only formed themselves into sentences long after Humphrey had left. Now, for the first time in his life, he would sit down with someone and talk, really talk, about all the things that had bothered and confused him. He would talk to Humphrey about his dad, and his mum; about everything.

Dad will make up a story, he thought. And he'll do it before word gets out, give them answers before they ask questions. He'll work hard to protect himself and the family name, tweak the story again, twist it once more to make himself safe; something about sending me off for more experience, to get more out of life than he had, to become a better man. Yeah, that sounds good. He'll make locking me out the ultimate sacrifice, and his mates will admire him even more.

"Fuck that."

As he drove deeper into WA's south-east corner, the road seemed to open its arms to him. It was unfamiliar landscape and the towns became more dispersed the further he drove. When he passed through those towns, locals would stare at him, their sunburned necks arching, heads turning to follow the car. A few people half-lifted their hands in greeting or gave an almost inperceptible nod.

In Esperance, he drove the grid of interlocking streets. The tarmac was wind-dried and a light, sandy blue. The few locals on the footpaths or watering their front lawns watched him pass with quiet wariness that forced him to keep on driving. He felt he couldn't stop and ask for directions. But after several laps of the town, he still hadn't found Humphrey's street. The locals answered his questions with smiles and laughs that bespoke friendliness. They made him do difficult u-turns, reeled off street names they were sure he knew as intimately as they did, and made references to shops and landmarks that he must know.

Still lost, and driving around in circles, he found the street by accident. It was a good-looking house, suburban in a country town kind of way. The high lawn and wild front garden made it stand out from the rest. All the other gardens in the street were well kept and orderly.

He parked on the street. Twice hungover, sleepless, dirty, and having driven nearly the length of WA in just over forty-eight hours, he knew he looked a sight. And smelled. When he took a whiff of himself, he could just make out the horsey smell the two German girls had brought into his car. He smiled, remembering Trudi.

He lingered in the car, hoping Humphrey might come rushing out to greet him. Not even after he got out and slammed the door loudly did the front door open. It was Saturday afternoon, cooler here on the coast, with a blustery breeze that would have made tennis or golf a ridiculous endeavour, though he was sure the courses and courts were full. He guessed, with the empty driveway, that no one was home, but he couldn't think of anywhere else to go and so walked up the drive, his boots slapping the concrete slabs then creaking the wood of the old veranda. There were three plastic chairs on the veranda, arranged in a small triangle; the people who had sat in them had faced each other rather than sitting in a line and looking towards the street. The nearby hibiscus bush had grown over the railing and had a flowery scent, but his own smell was stronger.

He knocked loudly on the door.

"Come in," said a man's voice, barely audible.

Darius hesitated before turning the handle. Strangely, the door opened outwards. He couldn't recall seeing a door open like that; fly-screen doors did but not front doors.

He stepped inside the house, peering down a long hallway, that had several shadowed doorways, towards a bright, sunny room that looked like the kitchen. At the end of the hallway, a head appeared from the side, the eyes squinting at the front door.

"Who're you?"

"Darius Tucker." He took a few steps into the hallway, his boots loudly clapping the wood. "Digger," he added. "I'm a mate of Humphrey."

In his nervousness, he spoke too loudly. From a nearby room came the sound of crying, softly at first but then louder as the baby found its voice. The head at the end of the hallway shook slightly from side to side and Darius heard the man sigh, making him feel it was his fault. He stepped backwards, into the strange doorway, guilty for having barged in unannounced, unexpected, at what was probably the wrong house. Humphrey had given him a false address.

The man came down the hallway, long-bodied and broad-shouldered. He moved with relaxed purpose, almost boredom, and stopped in front of Darius. He sniffed.

"The little devil's got the hearing of a dog. Not your fault. He wakes up even when I'm writing. He makes me type in whispers."

He ducked into a room, towards the crying baby, leaving Darius standing in the doorway, now about half sure he had the right house, but that was only because the man hadn't thrown him out. He thought about moving down the hall to the kitchen, and about turning and running. Either move might have been wrong, or right. The welcome had been strange, like the front garden, the door and the triangle of chairs on the veranda. No connection had been made, no attempt to establish him as less of a stranger. So he remained in the doorway, foreign, anxious, self-conscious, and smelling. He attempted to lean casually against the wall, as if he handled such disconcerting situations with ease, and even inspected his dirty fingernails to feign disinterest; under them were tiny grains of orange dirt from up north.

The crying stopped. The man reappeared, pulling the door behind him but leaving it just slightly ajar so that a slither of afternoon light sliced into the shadowed hallway. He motioned for Darius to follow him to the kitchen. Darius walked on his toes, so his boots wouldn't slam the wooden floorboards. Taller, his head hit the light hanging in the centre of the hallway.

"Careful. That's a family heirloom. It's worth half a million dollars."

"Sorry," he said, steadying it with his hands.

"So, you're Digger." He sat down at the large kitchen table. It was covered with scraps of paper.

Darius nodded. He glanced around the kitchen and then looked at the table, at the smudged printouts covered with markings and corrections in red; on one page, in the same red pen, someone had doodled a dog pissing against a tree. A white laptop floated in the middle of all the paper, the magnet connecting all those loose sheets together. The important keys were almost rubbed away, so it wasn't clear what key was for what letter.

"Heard a lot about you."

Darius shuffled in his boots, wanting to sit down, wanting to look directly at the man, to make a connection, but not wanting to come across as too eager or needy. In the sunlit kitchen, he finally got a good look him. He had shocking blonde hair, almost white, and this was made to seem even lighter because his face was heavily tanned, so dark it was almost reddish brown. But apart from the tan and the hair, he looked normal. Though, there was something in his blue eyes and in the cheeky curl of his mouth that spoke of complexity. Darius couldn't explain what it was exactly, but liked it because he had seen it before.

"All good I hope."

"Hobo said you might land on our doorstep, but he didn't say when." He kicked a chair out and Darius fell into it, slouching in a dishevelled and stinking heap.

"Thanks."

The man grinned playfully. "You look wrecked. Did you drive all the way today?"

"There was a bit of a welcome home party for me last night. Drank way too much."

The man raised his pale eyebrows, unimpressed.

"But I was worried I might miss Hobo," Darius said, liking the nickname and wanting to make their relationship seem more than just two guys who met in the mines.

"You have. He left last week." The man grabbed a red pen and started doodling on one of the pages, drawing over the printed words. "He had to get away. Mum's death really got to him."

"I'm sorry."

"For what? For my mum or for missing Humphrey."

"Uh, both."

"Well, he'll come back one day, but she won't." Then he smiled warmly, in a genuine way that made Darius smile back, and it made him discover muscles on his face he never knew he had. "I'm guessing Hobo didn't tell you my name. That's the way he is."

"Nah, he didn't."

The man shook his head. "I'm Lester, but unless you have something extremely profound to say, call me Les. Lucky for me, no one put my names together like they did with Humphrey's."

"Then you'd be Lesbo."

"Right."

They shook hands. Darius relaxed into the kitchen chair, embracing the surroundings as an accepted visitor and no longer some stinking stranger. He put his hands behind his head and stretched a little, but lowered them back down when he saw Les staring at the dark, damp circles of sweat under his armpits.

"He go to Canada?"

"Yep. Hobo's full of shit for the most part, but he sometimes goes through with what he says. He said only once that he would work in the mines, and one day he just left."

"Yeah, he left there in a hurry too."

"Always running. He thought he had a lot to get away from. What about you? Why were you up north? Humphrey said the mines are the ultimate great escape. You can disappear from society, and outlaws can work for double pay."

Darius stared at the floor, thoughtfully chewing his old lies, wondering which one he would spit out. Tell the truth, he ordered himself, wanting to change, not wanting to be like his dad.

"Just wanted to get away from me dad," he said.

Les laughed. "Better reason than Hobo's. He just wanted quick money. And there was also a small matter of a scholarship that he hadn't completed. He took all the money, did one year of uni and blew the rest travelling around Australia. Some of the letters they sent were really nasty. I guess Hobo's plan was to make quick cash and scamper to Canada."

In those few sentences Les had spoken, Darius thought he had learned more about Humphrey than in the eight months they had spent together. "Most of them are up there for the same reason."

"What d'you mean? Getting away from fathers or making money?"

"Uh, both."

Les laughed again. The baby's crying floated down the hallway and into the kitchen. Les rolled his eyes and stood up.

"Come on." In the hallway, he opened a door. "I'll be blunt, Darius. You need to visit this room first. Towels in the closet. Take any one you want. There are no favourites in this house."

"Okay, thanks."

The crying became more demanding.

"You'll have to take Hobo's room." He opened another door. "As you can see, he decorated it himself. If you can't stand the art work, crash on the couch. We wanted to make this the kid's room but I'm scared the walls will scar him for life. Hobo won't let me paint it."

Darius quickly took in the perfectly made bed, the battered stereo cassette player, the pile of tapes, the bedside table stacked with dog-eared books.

"I know. It's like looking inside his brain, isn't it?"

Darius nodded, chuckling.

"I'll be in the kitchen, eventually." Darius heard him shouting in the hallway. "I'm comin, you attention-starved little brat."

***

The kitchen was bathed in afternoon sunlight. There were long windows facing south that let in the sun once it had dropped below the line of the roof. But the windows faced the sea breeze too and were already banging in their frames. Outside, Darius could see tall trees with bent trunks and branches, their growth directed by the prevailing conditions. He breathed in the old kitchen smells, the kind of warm odours he had only ever smelt in other people's homes: dried-out bread, homemade cakes, fried eggs, over-ripe pears, an oven that dripped sweet lard and caramelised sugar. The pantry was well stocked, the door slightly ajar so he could confirm it, and the refrigerator hummed pleasurably.

"What do you do, Les?"

Les looked up from his laptop. The red pen was behind his ear; it looked like someone had slashed a long, deep cut into his blonde hair.

"I eat, sleep, breathe and try to be happy."

"Uh, I mean for work."

"That last part requires a lot of work. I guess Hobo didn't say much about the family, as always. Probably embarrassed. The family were some of the first settlers here, and are still pretty well-known, but not really in a positive way anymore."

"Really? First settlers?"

Darius didn't know what to make of it. Locals with a direct connection to the founding of a place were normally all too eager to claim birth rights, even if it was for useless rocky sand or withered plains of skinny brown grass. His dad could work into any conversation the fact that the Tuckers were the first shearers in the district, and say it in such a nonchalant way that no one could ever accuse him of bragging.

"Mum used to ruffle a lot of feathers round here. They all came to the funeral, and they cried a lot, but I reckon a lot of them were quietly glad to see her go."

73

"What'd she do?"

Les looked around the kitchen, perhaps seeing small grains of memories which he might be able to combine into a rich dough of recollection; something he could stick in the oven and perhaps consume and enjoy, some sweet reminder of the past that would remove the bitter taste of death and loss. Darius could never look around his own kitchen like that, or chance upon fond memories stored in cupboards and drawers. There was only dust and old hair, and rusted soup cans from previous decades.

"She was just different," Les said at last, "which is a good thing. She tried to do things other people disagreed with. She was bit too hippy and revolutionary for the folks round here. Raised two boys who had different fathers on her own." He laughed, sarcastically yet the hurt was clear. "Everyone thought our house was a brothel. Of course, Humphrey used to confirm a lot of those rumours. He liked to tease the locals."

"Are you older than Hobo?"

"Yeah. My dad was killed in Vietnam. Why the hell we were even in that war, I'll never know. Mum always said he should've just gone to prison instead of becoming a soldier." Les shook his head. "Died just after he got off the boat, so she said. The identity of Hobo's dad is a secret she's taken to the grave. When I was four, we went to New Zealand. Nine months after we came back, on Christmas Eve, out popped my brother. Funny, I can't remember the holiday, but I remember very clearly how the whole town talked about her. Some kids weren't allowed to play with me at kindergarten. Hobo had it harder. Of course, he made a lot of it worse for himself."

Darius frowned, picturing the locals talking in murmurs in the bakery, exchanging unpleasant remarks in the supermarket, shaking their heads in the pub, each with their own false theory about the Boragart family. At least, that's the way Darius remembered it happening to the Stapletons. They had lived outside the box and their kids were given a rough time at school. Rumour had it they smoked drugs, had wild orgies and worshipped the devil. He once saw Tony Stapleton, who seemed as normal as all the other kids, get beaten up by a gang of Stevenson boys. He recalled how the Stapleton name had been dropped with such disgusting familiarity, and the family's reputation trodden on with such force that it could never be mended;

the family soon moved away. Tony was apparently in jail for rape, and the continuous, greedy citing of this rumour had made it true for locals.

"Any idea where he went?" Darius asked. "In Canada?"

"Somewhere in the Rockies. He said he wanted the complete opposite to heat and dust. That's Hobo for you. Too much like mum to survive in this place. It's time I got out too. My wife's been at me to leave." He cleared his throat loudly. "She's from Melbourne," he added, as if that explained everything.

"Never been there."

"It's got the same problems as here, but it has a bit more culture and you see more than just white faces when you walk down the street. Melbourne makes Perth look like a village, a bubble town."

"Not a fan of Perth."

"Who is?"

"Think ya might move to Melbun?"

Les shrugged his shoulders. They were broad like Humphrey's but not as square. Looking at him now, Darius thought Les was more filled out than Humphrey, heavier and not as tall.

"There's not much left for us here. Loo's parents live in Melbourne and they could help out with Peer. I guess you don't have kids?"

"Nuh."

"Well, when you do, it makes it easier to have grandparents around, especially if father and mother want to keep a semblance of passion in their relationship. Shit, listen to me. I can see why Hobo likes you so much. You're a good listener and he loves to talk. You should be a therapist."

Darius smiled at the compliment, wondering what a therapist actually did. "Could you work in Melbun?"

"Maybe you've guessed from all this paper that I'm a reporter. I could say I'm a journalist but really I'm just a hack. I work for the local paper and I hope I'll be the last Boragart to do so."

Reminded of all the papers, Les started to clean them up, shuffling them together without care or order and folding the corners of the more stubborn sheets which refused to fall into line. His swift work revealed a table of dark, varnished jarrah of a red so molten and warm, Darius almost wanted to dive into it. He stared at the wood and yawned.

"But enough boring history," Les said, standing up.

"It's not boring. I've just had a long coupla days."

"Well, I've already said too much. Still, when we leave, I'm sure the Boragarts will be forgotten pretty quickly, first settlers or not. Or maybe the name will live on as the punchline of a thousand jokes."

Darius wondered if the same would happen eventually to the Tuckers. No chance. His dad would make sure of that.

Les clapped his bronze hands together, metaphorically snapping the big family history book shut. "What about goin outside? Loo'll be home in a minute and we can let Peer cry in the open air."

"Sounds good," Darius said, wanting to sleep. The table looked exceedingly inviting and he pictured himself stretched out on that broad expanse of jarrah, lying on the food stains of decades of family meals.

"Help yourself to anything," Les said, his voice echoing in the hallway.

Alone in the kitchen, Darius rubbed his eyes and looked around. He liked it here, felt comfortable and welcome. He took a large red apple and sank his teeth into it. It was the expensive, juicy kind his father never bought. What a delight it was now to have the sweet nectar squeeze between the gaps in his teeth; some of the flesh got stuck there, forcing him to dig at it with his tongue until it came loose.

The front door closed. Darius could see the shadowy, curvy outline of a smallish woman in the hallway. Her hair fell past her shoulders and bounced and swished when she moved. She dropped her bag on the floor with a clinking of empty glass bottles. When she saw Darius she stood perfectly still.

"Hello," she said, looking directly at him.

"G'day. I'm, uh, I'm Darius," he said through a mouthful of apple, perhaps an apple she herself had picked out, had touched and paid for. A slither of juice dribbled onto his chin and he wiped it away with the back of his hand. "Digger. A mate of Humphrey."

"Hi, Loo," Les said, his shadow joining hers in the hallway. He cradled the baby in his arms and the three of them became one dark outline. "Don't worry. He won't bite, but I might." He bent forward and bit his wife on the neck. Les led her towards the kitchen, holding the baby with one hand and his wife's hand with the other.

Darius straightened up to greet them, thankful he had already showered and that she hadn't been there when he had arrived.

But when she stood in the kitchen, he was speechless. Why hadn't Humphrey said something? He tried to smile, straining with the effort, and tried to chew the apple and swallow.

She wore a blue tracksuit and her long black hair was cut shorter at the front, the strands framing her face and curving around the sides of her almond-shaped eyes. Her smile was thin-lipped and friendly, but not without caution. Darius thought she seemed to be trying too hard to smile, just like he was, and it left him wondering whether she had to force herself to smile so often, that it always looked contrived. She wasn't tall but, he had to confess to himself, tall for her race. Most Asians, though he hadn't seen many, seemed to scurry along with thin bodies mounted on skinny short legs; like they were children who had stopped growing. That was his dad's joke, but it was the only reference point he had.

He wouldn't say any of this, but the way she looked at him, it seemed she already knew all of his thoughts and prejudices and smiled at him regardless.

"I'm Louise." She held out a hand the colour of the ginger biscuits his gran forced him to eat. "Call me Loo."

"Hi, Loo," Darius said formally, slowly, wondering if she would understand everything he said and whether he should speak even slower. He shook her hand and was surprised by her strength. The smooth, cool feel of her fingers tickled his palm, made the hairs on the back of his hand rise slightly. "Nice to meet you," he added, again slowly.

"I thought we'd go to the beach," Les said.

"Great." Loo smiled in an excited, girlish way that Darius found both curious and confusing; curious because it made her attractive to him and confusing for the same reason. He watched her bound athletically down the hallway. It looked like she had strong, lean legs.

Les held out the baby. "Here. Hold him while I put some stuff together."

It was only then that Darius noticed the baby. Les had fucked Loo, perhaps a thousand times, and here was the product to prove it. A part of him was jealous of Les for it, but he took little Peer, holding him like he was a large bottle of milk, gripping his sides with two hands, the baby's feet dangling and kicking the air. Then he took him closer and cradled him as he had done with hundreds of lambs. He looked into the tiny, sparkling blue eyes of the child and marvelled at his shiny black hair. Here was a little piece of the world, he thought, a bit of Asia, a bit of Australia, and, where was Humphrey from? That's right, a bit of Holland.

"He likes you. He's normally pretty sensitive with strangers. Just like his father."

Darius bounced Peer lightly in his arms and the child gurgled with delight. But when Loo burst into the kitchen, he nearly dropped him. Her blue summer dress clung tightly to her shapely form, the cotton thin enough for Darius to see the white bikini she wore underneath. A small pair of hazelnut coloured feet gripped white thongs and she rocked playfully on the balls of her feet, eager to be outside and down the beach. She came up close to him. The hem of her dress brushed his leg. He could smell her, a warm sweet scent that even Peer picked up, because the child turned his head to face her.

"Can you carry him?" she asked, her black eyes wide and moist.

"Light as a feather."

"Great. Then we don't have to take that bloody pram. It's impossible to push on the beach."

Darius followed them down the hallway. Les and Loo held hands.

Outside, the afternoon was warm and dry. The wind had dropped and dusk was slowly settling across the sky, splashing the scattered clouds with dusty yellows and traces of pink. It was a beautiful spring evening, with plenty of daylight left to enjoy the warmth. As they negotiated the plain, suburban streets, there came from more than one backyard the smoky fragrance of barbecue, voices and laughter carried with it. The few kids who played in their front yards stopped to stare as the three of them walked past. A couple of kids said hello.

Peer was asleep in his arms, and both Les and Loo turned to him to smile at this scene. From the passing cars, Darius saw there were not the standard waves and toots of horns locals gave each other, which could be heard when those cars were further down the street. Les and Loo didn't break stride or stop their conversation.

"Darius is passing through on his way to Canada," Les said. They had been talking about Melbourne and Loo had screamed with delight when Les said he wanted to move. She had even skipped a little and promised to cook up a big celebratory dinner; but first, she said, after they had earned it.

"A bit of a detour, isn't it?" Loo said, smiling at Darius.

"He's going to...what's the name of the place where Humphrey is?"

"Woodlow. I can't believe you forgot. We even went there together."

Les stopped to kiss his wife, then turned to Darius. "It's down the road from where we met."

The two of them shared a moment and then the trek to the beach continued. "Not far" had already turned into a twenty minute hike and Peer was starting to feel heavier with each step, but Darius didn't complain or even show that he was struggling.

"Hobo's got a job there," Les said. "He's gonna freeze to death on the local ski hill, checking tickets or something."

"Where is it?"

"About a day's drive from Vancouver. Isolated, but really beautiful."

"Like this beach," Loo said from the top of the path, "but minus the kangaroos."

They all looked down at the small cluster of kangaroos lounging in the late afternoon sun.

"And with just a little more culture and tolerance," she added softly.

"No beaches like this in Melbourne," Les said, draping an arm over her shoulders.

"No, but there's a bit more life. O brave knight, rescue me from this awful place."

Les laughed as Loo ran down the path towards the beach. She left a trail behind her – thongs, hat, sunglasses – then whipping off her dress and flinging that aside too. Darius watched her strangely coloured body glide through the water. She swam out past the breakers with long, firm strokes.

"Can you wait a bit?" Les asked.

Darius nodded and sat down on the sand. Les ran towards the water. His tanned body and blonde hair was much more suited to this scene, but it was Loo who seemed more at home in the water, a stronger swimmer and more confident in the surf.

Peer didn't stir. Darius was sure to keep the little guy's head covered by the small hat Les had tied to his head. He marvelled at the natural purity of the scene, that they shared the beach only with kangaroos and birds. The water looked cold and the surf rough, but he wanted to plunge into it, to swim out to where Loo was and frolic in the water like the two of them were doing.

To keep his jealousy at bay, he tried to imagine himself skiing down a Canadian mountain with Humphrey. It was so wild and adventurous; he wanted to start right now. He would ask Les how to get there, where to buy a ticket and how to get a passport. His legs felt jittery. The present, as enjoyable as it was, seemed nothing in comparison to the promising future.

Escape.

But the future was cradled in his arms; a bit of this, a bit of that, sleeping peacefully now but maybe headed for a hard life of sorts. He hoped that they would have a better time in Melbourne, hoped that the city really was as tolerant as they claimed. He didn't want little Peer getting teased or bullied at school, and he didn't want Loo to be seen as an unwanted foreigner. He had looked at her like that, but he wouldn't do that again. She was as Australian as he was. He wanted that to be true, to believe it, but he had spent his whole life listening to people complain about money-grubbing Asians, the multitude of foreigners who were overrunning the country, taking jobs from Australians, sticking to their groups and trying to sneak in the back way as refugees. He tried to imagine how hard it must have been for Les and Loo in Esperance; the Asian girl married to the son of the one woman the whole town gossiped about. But even he knew he wasn't worldly or experienced enough to understand just how tough it must have been.

Lewis: How poetic, to only know someone in metaphor. Do you think of the bush in the same way? That you can only describe and know the land in metaphor?

Poet: The land is a metaphor. The cities are cities.

Lewis: Yes, you're well known for you disregard for cities, namely Perth.

Poet: All those folks who live in cities, they need to spend some time in the bush. Ya know, they've been to Europe but not to the Kimberley. In cities, they, no one feels anything. They just live, pay bills, pass the days. For metaphor, you need emotion and passion and imagination. Perth's a gigantic, lifeless brick. But the area around Perth is amazing. Some great country there. It's a shame a lot of the locals never see it.

Lewis: But Perth is the fastest growing city in Australia. It has the kind of quality of life people dream of.

Poet: Yeah, it's a great lifestyle, but I'm not really sure it's a life.

Lewis: You're getting a few metaphors out of Perth.

Poet: There's not a lot of beauty in suburbs. When you've seen a bit more of the country, seen a cyclone flatten a town, or a mine collapse on a bunch of your mates, or a flood wash your whole crop away, you realise that having a beautiful beach on your doorstep and the best garden in the street doesn't amount to much of a life. But worse is how the locals think they're so superior, like they know everything better and have got life sorted. They really don't have a clue. There's a lot more to Australia than a house in the suburbs. A lot more. While racking up huge amounts of debt and chasing our Australian dreams, we've forgotten that. We've forgotten our country. Lost it. And that means we've lost ourselves.

~~~

The City

Squeezed between the two big bodies, he felt safe. The hot, dusty air that came through the vents made him thirsty, but he didn't complain. Above the cracked dashboard, the blue tarmac was a shade darker than the sky. Cars sometimes came from the other direction, gripping the road like enormous white erasers. His mum had bought him such an eraser, so big it was, for his third school year. He would transform it into a car when they were home, he decided, push some Lego wheels into the side.

The radio was on but not loud enough to be intrusive. When his parents spoke, those short, familiar sentences and the unexpected laughter amounted to the very sound of comfort, and just hearing it made him sink deeper in the seat. Next to him, his mum smelt raw and fresh, like roots just drawn from the ground, still covered with mossy, fertile earth and with stringy ends that almost dripped with moisture. Her smile was sunlight, beaming through a mouth ringed by cracked red lips that she kept licking to keep moist. She gave him small sweets from a bag stored in the glove box. He told himself to eat these slowly, to savour them, but gobbled them up as quickly as he could. She put them straight into his mouth, and when one of her dry, leathery fingers touched his lips, he shivered with pleasure.

His dad drove, one beefy, hairy forearm caressing the wheel, the other stretched out along the back of the bench seat, far enough that his fingers touched the curls of her hair. He was smiling more than usual, showing his teeth. Darius kept looking at the chipped left canine, the tooth his dad always showed with his crooked smile, but never spoke about.

"Ya too young fa that one, Digger," he would say, grinning secretly and making Darius wish he was older.

They drove along wide streets lined with factories and warehouses. There were large expanses of cleared land surrounded by fences, but nothing being built. Darius sat up to see the tall buildings and mansions his dad had promised, but saw only tiled roofs and plain brick houses sweltering under a sky the colour of stale cheese.

Still, the city held the wonder of the unknown, of everything big and new. It was a place people talked about and could boast they had visited. It was the setting for anecdotes, for small victories and humorous misadventures. And Darius knew, from his dad and the kids at school, that if things didn't go as planned, you could always blame the city people. For most of his friends, Perth remained a distant place they visited at Christmas or for special events. Some kids could brag that they had brothers or sisters at boarding schools in Perth, and that the same would happen to them. This elevated them in the school pecking order, for they had been chosen. Darius wondered if he too would be chosen. He didn't want to go, but was jealous of the kids who would.

They arrived at a grungy house crowded with cars. The front lawn was dead and brown. A large group of men lounged on the shadowed veranda. They all looked at the ute when it stopped in front of the house.

"Ya comin, dad?"

"Nah, Digger. Got some city business to take care of."

His mum got out. "Take your time." And then she took Darius by the hand and led him towards the veranda. His dad drove away and soon there was a dozen voices speaking to him, voices that spoke quickly, the words echoing in cavernous mouths crowded with teeth. They were all uncles or cousins, but he couldn't remember any of their names, except for Uncle Will who had once stayed a few days at their house. It was Uncle Will who led Darius around to the back of the house, to where a cluster of children were playing in a disorderly and aggressive fashion.

"Oi, you lot," Uncle Will shouted. "This's me nephya, Darius. He's one a them tough nuts from down south. Watch out for him, ha-ha."

When Uncle Will was gone, limping back into the house, the kids crowded around Darius. He looked from one dark face to another, hoping he might find a friendly or softer kid.

"Whatcha playin?"

"Wars," a taller kid said. "We was pickin teams."

The kids went through a complicated, drawn-out selection process, with Darius the last kid picked. They fashioned armour of sorts out of old cardboard beer cartons, with red for the Emu team and yellow for the Swan team, and the battle began. With hard, sun-dried eucalyptus nuts for bullets, they tried to hit the armour of the other team and capture prisoners. Hitting the armour was the goal, but they all aimed for the head. Whispers of tactics and strategy flew from mouths like gusts of wind. As the game went on, both teams started to branch out, going into neighbouring backyards and recruiting more kids along the way. As the afternoon grew late, it seemed every kid in the neighbourhood had pledged – or changed – allegiance to the Emu or Swan army. The adults lazing on the verandas snapped open their cans of beer and watched.

It was such fun. Darius wore his Swan armour with pride. He was an accurate thrower and had become a sniper of sorts, helping his army edge towards victory and winning friends along the way with his prowess. They already had a good number of Emu prisoners held in the backyard of Uncle Will's house, their headquarters.

But his brief, exultant military career ended when his dad returned just before sunset. He handed his battered and ripped armour to another comrade and more than a few hands patted him on the back.

In the car, squeezed again between the two big bodies, he sank into the seat, wishing they could stay. The argument steamed above his head, his mum campaigning to spend the night rather than risk driving the country roads in the dark. They shouted at each other. Darius saw through the window that everyone on the veranda was watching; there was even a group from the Swan army standing near the car, listening and staring. He hoped they were planning to rescue him.

But then the car pulled away from the curb with a jerk. His mum fell silent and he could feel his dad seething in that quiet, powerful way. His dad's whole body seemed to be able to emanate anger that everyone nearby felt and was intimidated by.

"That was fun," Darius said. "When we comin back?"

But he got no response. Both his parents were more interested in looking out the side windows than at each other, let alone at him. Tired, he lay down with his head on his mum's thigh, smiling as recalled the triumphs of the afternoon and the friends he had made.

~~~

He had been to Perth many times; twice a year with his dad to visit gran at the retirement home in Cottesloe. But it was that one trip to Midland that always came to mind when he thought of the city.

Not long after he got his license, his father sent him to Perth to run some errands and buy supplies at a cheaper price. He drove through Midland, looking for Uncle Will's house but, he had to admit, all the houses looked the same, especially the ones with Aboriginal residents, and he was too scared to stop and ask. He knew there was a time gap in between, but he always linked that trip to the city to his mum leaving. There were clues, he was sure of it, disjointed pieces he could have forced together, stuff he could have remembered if he thought hard enough, but his dad never gave him the chance, and now it was years ago.

She was gone. The end.

He drove the highway to Perth forlorn and eager. Conversations with Les had made him relaxed about journeying overseas and quiet moments with Loo when Les was tending to Peer had inspired him. There was a world out there, with different people and strange cultures, and he wanted to experience it. He wanted to meet exotic women who didn't follow the standard female behaviour like all the girls he had known. He wanted someone unpredictable, a girl who wouldn't be willing to settle for all the ordinary, expected things in life. Someone like Loo, but not necessarily exactly like her.

During the two weeks in Esperance, he became good friends with Les. They talked a lot about Australia and about travelling. Les had said that going abroad had made him see Australia differently, had made him accepting of the country's faults, because other countries had faults as well. For Les, it was all right that Australia wasn't perfect, and he was sure Darius would experience a similar realisation.

"You need comparison," Les had said, "and perspective. Don't worry. You'll get it. The fact that you want it already puts you ahead of everyone else. You'll probably come back more in love with Australia than ever. Because loving something means loving all the bad stuff too."

He was scared, sure, but he couldn't go home. He wanted to go to Canada. Les, Loo and Humphrey expected it of him. He hadn't known them long but felt he couldn't let them down. And he couldn't just start living in Perth.

"What a hole," he said to himself as he negotiated the streets of Fremantle and headed north towards Cottesloe.

Along the coast, the houses were wedged next to each other like acts of defiance against taste. The roads were as wide as highways, filled with cars and lined with petrol stations, fast food restaurants and hairdressing salons. Prime coastal real estate, he thought, but it looked little better than the industrial area of Midland. It could have been a stunning stretch of living space. Instead, it was a classic example of neighbours trying to better each other: no renovation was too far-fetched, no construction too inappropriate, no colour too garish, no addition too ill-conceived. The pristine lawns spoke of an abundance of water and landscape gardeners were probably grossly overpaid.

No, he could never live in Perth. He knew that. But he did stop at Cottesloe Beach for a swim and to stare out at the ocean that was so calm in mid-morning. He could have sat there all day, but he wanted to get the visit over with and so drove to the Eternal Sunset Home for the Elderly.

She wasn't surprised to see him, which made him believe she had spoken to his dad, even if she didn't say as much. Darius sat down and listened to her familiar lines. He drank the tepid, weak tea she served and nibbled a supermarket biscuit that was in a cake tin; to make it look like she baked them herself. The air of the small flat was musky and musty. He felt like a giant, because all the furniture had been designed for an old woman of shrunken stature. The ceiling was low and he had to be careful not to hit the hanging lights with his head. In the bathroom, the low toilet had safety handles and he once nearly pulled a hamstring straining to reach the taps in the sink. In the living room, the tan carpet was two inches thick, a plush safety mat. In one corner, Menzies was curled up within the carpet, almost buried in the strands and clawing at them subconsciously.

He wondered how long it would take her to ask him why he wasn't going to shear. He didn't know how to respond, and didn't want to contradict any stories his dad might have told. He decided to let her talk, which was easy because she needed little encouragement.

"I've written to the council but those idiots do nothing," she said, buttoning her big, lipsticked mouth together. "They're useless. The bloody teenagers hang around that mall like they own the place. Why, Ethel Johns had her handbag stolen and the police did nothing."

Darius sipped his tea and looked at his watch, wondering how long it would be appropriate to stay. He couldn't help feeling that she counted him amongst the group of out-of-control teenagers.

She looked at him over her tea cup. "They should send all you young boys into the army. That would sort you out. What you need is discipline and respect for your elders."

Darius forced a morsel of biscuit down his throat. So, that's what his dad had suggested: the army.

"They're all just bored, gran. There's nothing for them to do here."

"Rubbish. There's no better place in the world to be a child. You lot are spoiled these days. You've got the best weather and beaches and parks. School's a breeze. I never had any of that growing up. All I did was work. But all you lot do is sit inside playing with these computer thingies and watching TV."

She punctuated this by ramming a biscuit into her mouth. She lightly touched her pale blue hair, arranging it so it covered her very large and withered ears. Darius thought she looked much older than when he last saw her, and the wrinkled skin exposed at the base of her neck seemed to sag a millimetre for every year she had lived. She certainly looked older than the other women he saw padding around the grounds of the home. It was true, he decided, that living in the country aged women faster. The tough lifestyle, the closeting of expectations and dreams, the continuous battle with land and weather, and the overwhelmingly masculine ideals; it hardened their hands, put callouses on callouses, filled out their calves and wrecked their backs. They bore children and went out the next morning to feed the chickens. All those decades spent darning socks, frying bacon, sewing quilts, filling thermoses, taking hits, and living in silent compliance put extra, deeper lines on their faces, carved rings of bitterness into their necks. Darius had also seen it in the girls his own age, who had looked and talked like they were thirteen going on twenty-five, and then nineteen going on forty.

"Television," she continued sourly. "That's what's wrong with you people. You watch too much television. And all of it American rubbish."

Darius wondered why she wasn't more like the grandmothers on television, mellowing with age, always with a clever tip or piece of advice, and laying out homemade shortbread and not these crumbly, store-bought biscuits.

"I haven't watched it for yonks. We had no TV up north."

"Maybe you should've stayed up there. It was good for you."

His dad's words.

"Maybe. There's always the army, I guess. No TV there."

"Your grandfather was in the army, you know. Oh, he was so handsome in his uniform."

He hoped she wouldn't launch into more stories about his granddad, which she always seemed to find a way to do. Ironically, he wished his dad was here, because he would dominate the conversation, make it flow easily, with humour, so the time ran quickly. Now, as silence fell upon the room – his gran reminiscing and himself not wanting to say the wrong thing or give too much away – his dad's presence would have been ideal.

"How's your father?" She slurped her tea loudly and let a biscuit dissolve in her mouth. A few tan crumbs were stuck to her lipstick.

"Yeah, good." His dad wasn't big on telephoning – he was a face-to-face man – but his gran seemed to know the situation.

She took the teabags out of the pot and put them carefully to the side, perhaps to be dried out and used again. "Shearing will be starting soon."

"Yep."

"It's nice of you to visit before it starts." Then she lowered her voice. "I take it Jack was too busy to come."

"Yeah, lots to organise."

"Are you in Perth to do some shopping before it starts?"

"No. I'm, I'm skipping this season."

"What, dear?"

You liar, he thought. Dad told you everything.

"I'm going overseas. To Canada."

"It's about time you got married and settled down." She picked up her tea cup, hooking a large thumb under the handle and wrapping thick pink and purple fingers around the rim. Her rings glittered.

"Haven't met the right girl yet."

"You must be fending them off with a stick. Why, I bet all those Stevenson girls are fighting each other to snap up the one and only Tucker."

Darius looked down at the thick carpet. He had finished his tea, but his gran filled his cup again and then held the biscuits towards him. She shook the tin. He took one.

"You're only young once. You don't want to miss your chance. I don't want people talking."

"I just wanna see some of the world before I settle down. I'll only be gone a few months, maybe half a year. I'm comin back."

It sounded good, and it was only the slight raise of his gran's bushy grey eyebrows that made him think he hadn't been convincing enough. Still, what he had said would eventually reach his dad.

"Shearing's always been our bread and butter." She crossed one leg over the other and pulled up the hem of her white dress just enough for Darius to see the knee-high stockings which bulged her calves into chunky legs of ham. "It was always good enough for us."

How he hated that legacy, hated how everything was already decided and that he should feel special to be part of it, thankful and appreciative. Privileged. His life was already lived, all his sentences already spoken. Worse was that his gran made it sound like she was the matriarch of this clan of shearers, when she had married into it and delivered just one son.

"I'll be a shearer too," he said, sick of arguing, sick of explaining.

His gran nodded her round, puffed-up head. She was a thick-set woman, and although the skin sagged below her neck, the neck itself was gaunt and wiry, hinting perhaps to bygone days when her whole body had been svelte. But that stiff, skinny neck now made Darius wonder that if she nodded too aggressively, her head might snap off. Fortunately, he knew her to be a disagreeable woman who spent most of her time shaking her head, and that movement from side to side was safer – and much more practised – than up and down.

"Of course you will, dear."

They talked some more, until all the tea was drunk. His gran advised, commented and complained. She shook her head a lot, unable to comprehend all the stupidity and unfairness present in her world. She talked of foreign doctors who prescribed her medicine that did not work. She wouldn't say exactly what was wrong with her, but she most certainly was suffering.

Darius eventually kissed her goodbye, getting a smudge of face powder on his lips, and then bullied his car into Stirling Highway's peak hour traffic. The open windows let in a sea breeze that smelt more of car exhaust than salt.

The city bustled and seethed.

His reactions and abilities were by no means city quick, so horns sounded all around him and words were shouted in abuse in his direction, coming from lowered windows of vans, utes and trucks as they accelerated past him. All those tradesmen and couriers and gardeners heading home, none of them wanting to be slowed down or held up, none of them giving an inch. Inexperienced with the pace of the city, its self-important busyness, he got confused by the roads and highways, was intimidated by the endless streams of traffic, by the aggression and collective nastiness.

"Big ugly roads lined with big ugly buildings in a big ugly city," he said to himself.

He hoped Canada would look better than this. Humphrey had promised as much.

"You'll love it here," Humphrey had said when they'd spoken on the phone in Esperance. "The Canucks have got things sorted."

"Can't wait."

"I'd come and get you in Van, but you'll have more fun if you get here on your own. Hitchhike. There's only one highway and everyone'll pick you up. Things are totally different here."

"How'll I find ya?"

There had been a brief, crackling silence before Humphrey had said, "Let's make it interesting. There's a bar here called Joe's. Yeah, really, I eat there, hah. Go there the evening you arrive and we'll see if we can find each other."

"Right."

"I'm runnin out of coins. Give me Les again, will you?"

The last few days in Esperance had been fun. He got his ticket, waited for his passport and Les and Loo had made him feel like part of the household. But he was keen to get moving.

"Send us a postcard," Les had said. "And keep Hobo out of trouble."

Darius had nodded. Barely out of the city limits, eager for his big adventure, he already missed them. Nothing of the sort had been said, but when they were settled in Melbourne, he knew he could visit them and they would just pick up right where they had left off.

Now, crawling down Stirling Highway, he followed the street map towards the address Les had given him. He caused problems with the traffic, by trying to make ambitious turns with no drivers willing to let him in, and by stopping when the traffic lights were orange to buy time to look at the map. When he did this, tires squealed behind him, horns sounded and men shouted.

But he found the dealership and got a good price. Les had called ahead and the salesman treated him fairly. With the last material thing holding him to this place gone, he could fly to Canada with just a pocket jammed with traveller's cheques and a backpack full of clothes. It felt liberating to have so few possessions, and he laughed at all the locals in their suits, tied down by mortgages and full-time jobs, driving in their cars from one important appointment to another. How they crowded St George's Terrace and Hay Street, walking so quickly, with such necessity, throwing down lunches and drinking cappuccinos from cardboard cups, checking their watches and barking into mobile phones; doing all these things at once. They looked fit, healthy and handsome from a distance, but up close, a lot of them were lined and sun-dried. Darius thought they looked miserable, despite the smiles, jaunty steps and bright sunshine.

So he killed the last few days watching the locals who flooded downtown in the mornings and then hightailed it out in the evenings, leaving Hay Street mostly deserted by dark. The reality of Perth was suburbia, he decided. Each person's house was their sun and the rest of their world rotated around it.

But this was all just to stop him from feeling nervous, to keep him from giving up on Canada, cashing in his ticket and going back home to shear. He didn't want to face his dad, but what really kept him on course for Canada was not disappointing Humphrey and Les.

On the last evening, aching with loneliness, and boredom, he toured the bars of Northbridge, trying unsuccessfully to pick up girls. In the end, he let a tubby, middle-aged woman lead him to her apartment in East Perth. They had a good time, but she fell asleep in a heavy, damp mess on top of him. He squeezed out from under her and ducked out of the building. He had achieved a relief of sorts that made him think a little straighter; at the very least, he would be able to brag to Humphrey that he had left Perth with a bang.

The streets of East Perth were shadowed and dark, with every third streetlight out or glowing so dimly it cast no light at all. He walked quickly back towards his hotel and took a short cut through a park. He passed under the lone park light and saw shadows stretch out on the grass and leaning against the trunks of trees. The white shimmer of moist teeth caught his eye and made him stare as he passed. When he looked at them, the shadows began to stir, moving slowly and languidly at first, but then gliding fluidly in his direction, their bare feet slapping the grass. He started to run, stumbling over empty bottles, and headed for the nearest road. He heard voices behind him, the words coming rapidly and violently. Something – a bottle, a golf ball, a bullet – whizzed past his head. He got to the road, weaved between the cars and burst through the door of a bar.

"Orright?" the barman asked.

Darius sucked in stale cigarette smoke and wiped the sweat from his forehead.

"Beer," he said, trying to sound relaxed.

As the barman worked the tap, Darius looked out the front window to see if those chasing him had been brave enough to cross the street and enter the bar. They hadn't, but they lingered at the edge of the park, moving in and out of the darkness, before slinking one by one back into the shadows, liquid outlines of black against the dark velvet green of the park.

Lewis: You were twenty years old when you went to Canada. How did your time there change the way you saw Australia?

Poet: It gave me perspective.

Lewis: That's good, isn't it?

Poet. Yeah, but I also learned that you can experience a place, but not feel connected to it. I was in the Rockies, but it was nothing like being in the fields down south. I felt no connection to the Canadian land and that made me homesick. It made me appreciate the Australian bush even more.

Lewis: So you wanted to go straight home, because you felt no connection?

Poet: No. I toughed it out.

Lewis: Why?

Poet: You only appreciate what you have when you don't have it no more. I love Canada because it made me miss Australia. But I didn't go home. Sometimes it's good to suffer.

~~~

The Mountains

"It's right, isn't it?"

"Huh?"

"The snow. Christmas with snow."

Darius looked out over the porch and into the sparkling white night. The silky snow glistened under the streetlights, a million white stars that had descended to earth that afternoon. Adding to the colour were the flashing reds and bright yellows of the lights that hung from the roofs and verandas of every house. He could almost smell the fresh pine of each individual Christmas tree. The smell made his mouth sticky, as if he had licked the axe that had cut those trees down. He sipped his whiskey contentedly, rubbed his nose with his gloves and sighed, his steamy breath wafting into the night.

"Yes."

"You don't have to keep that up with me."

Darius wondered if it was that obvious. There were plenty of guys in Woodlow whose boisterous voices grew louder in competition. They spent their days on the ski hill and their nights at Joe's and would not stop talking about themselves and their exploits. Humphrey had been particularly outspoken about it. So Darius had morphed himself into a strong, silent type, a man of few but well-chosen words. The girls seemed to like that. His one word mumbles and sustained silences bored all the men but intrigued the women. They took it as a challenge to draw the shy Australian out of his shell. Darius was happy to oblige them as long as they didn't demand too much commitment, or get too clingy. Andy was starting to get that way, even though they'd only been together for a couple of weeks.

"Come on, Digger. You know what I'm talking about."

Darius grinned into his whiskey glass. "Finish ya rant."

"Three words, all for me? I feel so special. So, think about it. All the songs and imagery, right, all the movies and cards. It's all about 'dashing through the snow' and 'roasting chestnuts'. Why do the mates swallow it? Americanisation, that's what it is. Come on, everyone, let's sing *Jingle Bells* even though it's forty-five in the shade and none of us has ever seen snow."

Darius chuckled slowly. "Not homesick?"

"Makes me glad I left. It reminds me that back home everything is upside down and back to front."

Darius watched Humphrey light a cigarillo and puff on it. He claimed he liked the tobacco taste as opposed to the chemicals of cigarettes, but Darius knew Humphrey smoked those little cigars to be more exotic and worldly; Darius was still toying with the idea of smoking a pipe. Humphrey had taken to cigarillos not long after Darius had arrived. That was two months ago, when Darius had found Humphrey, not in Joe's as planned, but by accident the next morning at Mandrake's Café. Humphrey had looked up from his paper and said in his pompous British accent, like he had been waiting all this time, "Where the devil have you been, 007?" There was an empty room in the house Humphrey was sharing with Whits and Tony, two skiers from Winnipeg, and Darius moved straight in. He sent a postcard to his gran, explaining where he was and that he had found work in a local bar. He got no response but was sure the information had been passed on to his dad.

"You mean down under."

Humphrey puffed a few more times, pausing for effect. He tried, unsuccessfully, to blow a smoke ring. "No, upside down. Think about it. It's all wrong in Oz. We drive on the wrong side, trees lose bark and not leaves. Animals that live in holes lay eggs. The birds laugh and don't sing. Hot tea is drunk in the middle of summer. And, and, they talk about fair go and mateship, but an ocker would just as soon trade his mother for a new ute or tell on a mate if it lent him some advantage. Okay, they're not all like that and they will lend a mate a hand, but most of the time only when they'll get something for it, even if it's just a return favour. Respond please, and more than just three words."

"Could make it a very unique place. That's," he counted, "seven all for you."

"Unique? Now you're just talking about the people. All those mates trying so hard to be just like each other. Really, there's nothing more derivative than the Australian male. You saw them during the Olympics. It was embarrassing, and then getting Freeman to light the flame. Totally shameless."

"We're Aussie males too."

"Okay, we're not derivative. There are exceptions to the rule.

95

Maybe there's more than we think. But still, they could all be a bit more critical. I keep asking myself why they all try to live this stereotype."

"Not me. I'm just trying to be happy."

"Are you? My brother really worked his charms on you. He sold you the gospel of Les which is just a rehashed version of the Ecclesiastes."

"Ecc-what a?"

"Forget it. I bet you're happier here than you were at home."

"The snow's nice." Darius again marvelled at the winter evening in front of him.

Humphrey blew a big cloud of smoke and steam. "Me thinks that whiskey makes you talkative. Maybe I should ply you with it every night and not just on special occasions."

"Must be tough bein born on Christmas Eve."

"I wouldn't mind so much if I'd just been born somewhere else. Ever get the feeling you landed in the wrong location? And then, when you find the place that fits, you realise just how wrong it was?"

"Think ya shoulda been born here?"

Humphrey shook his head and flicked the ash from his cigarillo. "But it does make me believe in the stork after all, you know, the drunk one from the cartoons, always dropping the baby in the wrong place. That drunk stork dumped me in Esperance when he should've dropped me in Europe. I'm heading there after the winter, you know."

"Ya say that one more time, I'll rip ya bloody tongue out."

Humphrey laughed. "Then I'd just take yours. It never gets used anyway, except on young lovelies like your pal Andy."

"Fuck you, Hobo."

"You like her? I think she's nice."

"She's all right."

"You guys sound like you have a lot of fun together in the sack."

"Yeah."

"Oh, don't be so hung up. You can talk dirty with me." Humphrey looked down the street. "Here she comes now. Hannah too. Looks like we both better get back into character."

They watched the two girls trudge through the snow, walking on the road where the snow had been compressed by passing cars and pick-ups. Hannah was wearing her bright pink moonboots. She was running forward and then sliding on the street, sideways, like on a snowboard. Behind her, Andy was struggling to keep up in her sneakers. Hannah was first to push the creaky wooden gate open and clamber up to the porch. She stamped the snow from her boots and shook her jacket, spraying Darius and Humphrey with flakes of light Kootenay snow that was so dry, it could be brushed or blown away. Andy hopped up the stairs and sat down next to Darius. They kissed.

"Happy birthday, Humphrey Boragart," Hannah said, taking up quite a lot of space on the porch, with her boots and large, puffy jacket.

She was as tall as Humphrey, big-chested and long-limbed, and a very good snowboarder. Just out of her teens, she was able to maintain a sexy, athletic look; a lot of the guys in town flirted with her. In a few more years, Darius thought, she might start waddling towards her thirties, but in her flush of youth, she was like a mare primed for the track: big, strong, feisty and full of energy. Children and age would eventually get the better of her, and she already had a motherly air that made Darius certain she would breed a litter of equally sturdy kids, but for now, she was playful and fun, up for anything – so Humphrey had said with a wink – just slightly too tall and heavy to be thrown around and perhaps dangerous if she ever swung from a chandelier.

"Andrea and I followed the Northern Star to this barn of a house," she said in her warbling Texan accent. "And we come baring gifts to honour the chosen one."

"You can keep the other crap," Humphrey said. "Just give me the gold."

Hannah put her large hands on her hips and shook her head. "'He's not the messiah,'" she said, waving a gloved finger and making Humphrey wince at her accent, "'he's just a very naughty boy.'"

Humphrey pointed to the road. "Hollywood's that way, woman."

She laughed at her own cleverness and sat down on Humphrey's knees to kiss him. The wicker chair creaked in what sounded to Darius like agony.

"I hate it when you smoke that shit," she said, pulling back. "Y'all taste like an 80 year-old oil tycoon."

"And how would you know what that tastes like?"

"It's the kind of thing any red-blooded Texan girl knows. But the good news is Andy picked up some rocking weed in Nelson. So put those yucky cigarillos away, Humphrey Boragart, and smoke something organic instead."

"Nelson?" Darius asked Andy.

She nodded as she licked the paper and stuck the joint together. She ran the whole thing into her mouth, sucking it the way she liked to suck his fingers. It felt good having her close, to be reminded that she was pretty, even if her body was more tomboyish than he liked. He didn't feel anything that strong for her, but it was good to be together, to talk, fuck, ski and hang out.

She was from Toronto. They'd met at the ski hill, sharing a chair. He still didn't understand why, but she had seemed to like him straight away, whether he talked or not.

"Whitewater rocks," she said in that deep voice she had. She lit the joint and took a toke. "It's a few clicks from Nelson. They're up to their eyeballs in powder and there's no one on the hill. I'll take you there, if you want."

"Sure."

"Nelson's where Les and Loo met," Humphrey said. "I'm thinking of putting up a plaque on Baker Street to mark the significance of the event."

Hannah went misty eyed and gave Humphrey a long kiss, gripping his cheeks with her gloved hands so his face nearly disappeared; only his lips remained uncovered.

"How romantic. Would you do the same for me? For us?"

"For you, I'd build a statue."

Hannah melted into Humphrey's arms and they kissed. After taking a short puff, Darius tapped Humphrey's shoulder and passed the joint. Hannah and Humphrey both took short tokes and then went inside, leaving Darius alone with Andy. They smoked the rest of the joint, staring out into the night.

It was good weed.

Darius felt his brain start to melt. With the alcohol and now the joint, he felt comfortable and languid. Everything around him started to shimmer and bend a little. The snow glittered and rose, like it was going back up to the sky.

He rubbed his eyes.

"She's leaving, you know that?" Andy said at last. "Her dad's cut off her funds."

"Yeah? When?"

"After New Year. She's scared to tell Humphrey. She loves him," she added, speaking distantly and making Darius wonder if, like it was for him, that love was a far off land she knew nothing about and might never visit. "Do you think Humphrey would go with her if he knew?"

Darius shrugged, drowsy. "Dunno."

"What about you?" Andy shifted her chair closer to his and placed a gloved hand high up on his thigh. "When are you heading back home? Or are you planning to just move on after winter? Ontario's pretty nice in the spring."

It was the kind of questioning he feared. Even if Humphrey went to Texas with Hannah, he wouldn't let himself be dragged to Toronto to meet Andy's family and be her boyfriend. No. He wanted to go to Europe as well. All of Humphrey's talk had opened up that option.

"I'm just tryin to eat, sleep and be happy."

It was rubbish, he knew, and someone else's rubbish at that. Andy was sure to see through it, but she let it drop. Like other times, it was easier for them to get naked and fuck, and to forget about spring; just as it was easy to strap on skis, ride the chair and fly down the slopes than to talk about deeper feelings.

"It's cold."

He stood up. "I know a warm place."

In his room, they got quickly undressed. Through the wall, Hannah was shouting, grunting and panting, sounding more like she was working the heavy bag than banging Humphrey. Darius wondered if Humphrey's air mattress might explode and wake the whole neighbourhood. But she peaked before Darius and Andy had their limbs entwined, and soon her loud, masculine snoring drifted through the walls.

They shivered under the cold bedcovers and fumbled with each other. Andy giggled. Drunk and stoned, Darius had a bit of trouble to get it up, and really would have preferred to sleep. But even after just a couple of weeks, his body was trained to her touch, and they fell easily into a rhythm together, fucking quietly, as usual, as if Andy's parents were in the next room. When she finally orgasmed, she emitted the slightest of squeaks from the back of her throat. Through the closed window, Darius could hear a few guys walking back from

Joe's, already talking up the big air and wicked lifts they were going to get at the ski hill tomorrow. When he recognised the Australian accents, he wondered, briefly, where he was.

***

Woodlow had an Aussie clique, all snowboarders, all guys. They hung out at the Post and Bank bar, the Pab, where Darius worked. Rod and Gazza were the first to arrive, setting themselves up in the youth hostel a week before Christmas. The other Aussies from nearby towns got to know Rod and Gazza and came to Woodlow too. They all liked Darius, but not Humphrey, who did his best to avoid them. Normally, when the clique came into the Pab, Humphrey would leave. But the clique didn't always let him, especially if they had a reason to bait him.

Like tonight.

Hannah had left yesterday. She'd got a few more weeks of funds from her parents, but that had run out by late January. The goodbye hadn't gone well.

"Mate, I heard she let you have it," Rod said.

Sitting on a bar stool, Humphrey shrugged. "'Tis better to have loved and lost than not to have fucked anyone at all. How's your dorm room, fellas?"

"What'd ya say to her?" Rod asked.

"I told her the truth."

"Mate, that's the last thing ya say to a woman."

"Ya gotta tell them what they wanna hear," Gazza said. "Promise them the moon and the stars."

"And then make a run for it when they're not lookin'," Rod said, and he laughed very loudly. The clique joined in.

"It wasn't going to work," Humphrey said. "I didn't want to go to Texas. Shame. I liked her."

"Me too," Darius said from behind the bar.

"From what I heard," Rod said, "she'll only come back to murder you."

"Broken hearts mend fast in Texas. Apparently."

"You didn't break her heart."

Humphrey swivelled on the bar stool to face them. "Hey, fair go,

100

mates. I'm not as successful with the girls as you lot are. It's crap that Hannah left, and the way she did. Can we drop it and get on with our lives?"

"Good idea," Darius said. "Who wants a beer?"

Each member of the clique drained his glass and put it on the bar. Darius set to work.

"Where's your lass, Digger?" Gazza asked.

"Workin. Night reception at the Vantage Hotel."

"Now, Digger knows how to treat a girl," Rod said.

Humphrey nodded. "That's right. Darius, you should start a class. For all the dateless guys in Woodlow. Where could we find your first students?" Humphrey turned to the clique. "Do you guys know anyone at the hostel flying solo?"

"We're here for the snow," Rod said.

"Yeah, best boardin in the world," Gazza added.

Humphrey stood up. "Agreed. So, I'm going to bed so I can be at the hill early."

"That's a cold lonely bed, I bet."

"Is there a spare in your dorm, or do you all share the one bunk?"

Rod ran a hand through his closely cropped hair. "Glass houses, Humphrey," he said. The others in the clique murmured their agreement.

"What does that mean?"

"You know what it means."

"No, really. I don't."

"People in glass houses shouldn't throw stones."

"Okay, but how does that apply to what I said?"

"Here's you beers, fellas," Darius said, lining the glasses up on the bar.

Rod tried to smile, as if he felt sorry for Humphrey. "You bloody idiot."

Humphrey nodded. "Looks like it. When you just throw random idioms at me, with no context, I'm lost."

Darius attempted to change the subject. "Ya beers."

The clique reached forward and took their glasses.

"Cheers, Digger."

"Another beer, Hobo?"

"Nah, I'm off."

"Like cheese left in the sun," Gazza said, and the clique laughed.

"Hey, Digger," Rod said, "what ya doin tomorrow?"

"What's so special about tomorrow?" Humphrey asked.

"You just proved that you are a completely clueless idiot," Rod said. "It's the most important day of the year."

"Stralia Day," Gazza confirmed.

"Our day."

Humphrey took a few steps towards the door and stopped. "Not here it isn't."

"How ya gonna spend it?" Darius asked.

"We're havin a barbie and a few beers at the hostel," Gazza said. "We've gotta flag and everythin."

"Sounds great."

"You're invited, Digger," Rod said. "And bring that lovely girl of yours."

Humphrey laughed. "That'll make it a true celebration of invasion day. One girl and seven men."

"What's your fuckin problem, mate?" Rod demanded.

"No problem. It's just that, well, that was the ratio of men to women in our convict colony."

"Bullshit."

"Maybe you guys should do a bit more research about our country's early years. It's fascinating stuff. A bit like the Vikings, without the gods and heroes."

"What the fuck are you on about?"

"Nothing. Happy Australia Day." Humphrey headed towards the door and left the Pab.

"The greatest mother-fucking country on earth," Gazza shouted. "Aussie, Aussie, Aussie!"

And the clique chorused: "Oi, oi, oi!"

"What the fuck's his problem?" Rod asked, looking at Darius for an answer. "He's got his head so far up his own arse, it's come outta his neck so he looks normal."

The clique tried to laugh, but Darius saw they were struggling a little. It looked as if some of Humphrey's comments had rankled, though none of them would admit as much. Darius hadn't seen any of them with a girl and they often said they were here for the snow and only the snow.

"I'd like to knock his arrogant head right off," Rod said.

"Steady on, Rocket," Darius said. "That's my mate ya talkin about. We've been through a lot together."

"He pull ya outta a burnin house or somethin?"

"More than that. We worked up north. In the mines. We had some tough days."

"What's he mean by invasion?" Gazza asked.

Rod patted his friend on the back. "He's just bullshitting ya. You in tomorrow, Digger?"

Darius was surprised to see Rod was quite keen that he come. "Sorry, fellas. Gotta work. Boss's gone to Calgary."

"Calgary?" Rod said. "Is that a ski town as good as this one?"

"Reckon it's a bit bigger than here."

***

The lift stopped again. The chair swayed back and forth, creaking loudly. The ice-cold wind sliced right through him, through his down jacket, fleece and polyester undershirt. Minus twenty-five, Denise had said down at the base. She had smiled broadly, jumping in her snowboard boots, loving the cold, and had given Humphrey a big kiss when he lined up for the lift.

"When was your date?"

"With Denise? Two days ago. You were working." Humphrey pulled his jacket around him tighter and hunched his shoulders forward. His skis clattered together. "Don't be fooled by that kiss. No action. Dessert was way off the menu."

"How'd you meet her?"

"Shift meeting. She's new, started last week. There weren't enough chairs at the meeting and we sat on the floor together. Fuck it's cold."

"She seemed keen on you down at the base."

"Yeah? That was more like kiss hello. She was in Oz once, got family there. Hated it. Couldn't stand the people and how superficial they all are. Her words."

"You're made for each other."

"Nuh. I couldn't get a word in. She went on and on about our country and how crap it is. Actually, it was pretty funny, she's funny, but where does she get off talking like that?"

"Never stops you."

"Yeah, but I'm allowed to. I can criticise Australia but she can't. She doesn't know it well enough. You don't hear me badmouthing Canada."

"Not yet."

"I could make some informed comments, but only the Canucks can get stuck into their own country. They know it better."

"Sounds fair," Darius said, feeling very cold, but thankful that the lift started moving again. He was wearing two wool hats, as Humphrey had advised, but still he felt his bones were frozen. He could feel the cold steel of the chair right through his thick ski pants.

"To criticise something," Humphrey said, "you need to know all the angles, the history, the myths. Those ockers in your bar can't say anything critical about Oz because they don't know it well enough. They know Melbourne or Sydney, where they grew up, but they don't know their history. It's sad when you think about it. They revel in all that matey bushman bullshit and those heroic, ha, diggers."

"Ha-ha."

"Sorry. They're attached to an identity that was made up. Something put in to vill the void. Think about it. Today, we're supposed to be celebrating well over two centuries of Australia, our day, as they say. But it was an invasion, plain and simple, the end of cultures thousands of years old."

"You mean a culture."

"The Aborigines are not one group. The colonials called them that, put them all under one useful heading. Makes it easier to pass laws that way."

"Hobo, I'm really fucking cold. What are we doing up here? It's summer back home."

"Hot enough down under to drink yourself into a stupor. And today, everyone's drunk, celebrating. Celebrating what? Stealing Aboriginal children, the White Australia Policy, Aboriginal deaths in custody, 150 years of Asian racism? No, they're drinking to Ned Kelly and the Eureka Stockade. Fuck the Indigenous Australians."

"I failed history at school. Couldn't keep all those dates in my head."

"History is about why, not when."

The lift was almost at the top of the mountain. They had broken through the fog that clung to the tree line and conditions were clear at the peak. The bright sun made Darius feel warmer even though he knew it was much colder at the peak than at the base. The snow covered Kootenays were jagged and craggy, the rock exposed from the movements of small avalanches. He saw small specks of snowboarders hiking alongside one of the peaks, outside the ski area boundary, in search of untouched powder. He looked to see if Andy was one of them.

"Well, all what you said's news to me."

"You're not alone. That's probably why a lot of the mates get drunk today." Humphrey sighed loudly, sending out a cloud of steam. He prepared to get off the chair, the one part of skiing he found the most awkward and challenging, by shuffling forward to the edge of the seat. "Oh shit. Enough politics. I say we head down Sundance and then try our luck in the trees. If we get separated, you'll find Denise lecturing me down at the base."

"You're on."

"Maybe she'll kiss me hello again."

"Good luck with that."

They were terrible skiers. Darius had had a couple of lessons, but Humphrey had just strapped on his skis and started, barrelling down the hill with the kind of confidence and daring Darius couldn't match. They always got separated as Humphrey went as fast as he could, trying to make quick turns but often falling to the snow. Darius took his time, making slow turns and always picking a conservative line, scared of all the little bumps he couldn't quite see. He wondered how long it would take him to ski like the locals, who shimmied down the slopes with poetic ease, most of them stoned, and more than a few on telemark skis. Still, just making a few turns and gliding on the soft powder gave him enough of a rush to make him keep coming to the hill every day.

At the base, Humphrey was holding a place in line. Denise was next to him.

"You won't believe it, Darius."

"You fell?"

"Funny. No. Rod just tried to take me out."

"Sure it was him?" Darius had been keeping an eye on Rod and his clique; they were riding the lift a dozen or so chairs behind them and following their runs. Gazza had an Australian flag tied around his neck like a cape, making him easy to spot. Even now, standing in the lift line, he could hear them shouting and laughing, making everyone turn in their direction. They stood in a tight group and passed a silver flask between them.

Humphrey and Darius shuffled forward and fell onto the cold chair amid a clatter of skis and poles.

"Why, Darius. Why?"

"Why what?"

"Why do these guys travel? I've got this terrible feeling I'm gonna meet Rods everywhere I go. And worse, whenever I tell someone I'm Australian, they'll expect me to behave just like him."

"Ah, they're not bad blokes."

"Don't worry, Darius. I don't count you as one of them. You're friends with me and Les likes you too, and that must mean that you're not just taking what you're given. Otherwise, you'd be standing next to Rod and laughing at me."

The lift stopped. The chair creaked and swayed precariously. Darius grabbed onto the cold bar and shivered as the wind sliced through him.

***

They entered the Pab, a larger group than the night before. Darius assumed the clique had picked up other Australians at the hostel or met them at the ski hill; that flag had got everyone's attention. The Pab was already pretty full, with a few locals and tourists, but the atmosphere of quiet post-ski reverie quickly changed. The Aussies took up more space than was necessary, spoke and laughed loudly, and bumped the people standing nearby, making them spill their drinks. They sang a loud and lyrically confused version of *Waltzing Matilda*, and followed it with *Advance Australia Fair*. A few people clapped at the end, but mostly they started to move away, sitting at tables in the corners of the bar or moving to stools behind the pool tables. A few finished their drinks and left.

Humphrey was playing pool with Denise, Andy and some worker from the ski hill. When Rod saw Humphrey, he motioned the group towards the pool table. They walked so closely together, they almost seemed like one entity. Rod walked up to the table, but Humphrey kept his back to him.

"Makin the most of our day?" Rod asked.

Denise turned to him, her arms folded. "What day is it? And who says it yours?"

She leaned against the pool table, making some of the balls move; one even fell with a clunk into a pocket. Denise wasn't very pretty, Darius thought, but she was definitely shapely, especially from behind, and quite savagely alluring, a look heightened by her dark red hair and the rather whorish way she dressed. She was well-proportioned, but she still wore tight clothes that made bulges in the right areas, and wide-necked shirts that blatantly exposed red, pink or black bra straps. Tonight, she had on a white shirt, short enough so her pierced naval was on full display, and thin enough so her bra could be seen through. Darius thought she looked better at the ski hill, when she covered her body with her big jacket and fleece-lined pants. Indoors, she garnered so much attention with the way she dressed, Darius didn't know where else to look, and always found himself tracing the outline of her bra with his eyes.

"Most important day a the year," Rod said.

Denise looked him up and down and seemed less than impressed. She turned to Humphrey, her folded arms cradling her breasts. Darius thought she appeared to be lifting them a little, but the pool table was a good twenty metres from bar, making it hard to tell.

"Why's it important?" she asked Humphrey. "International moron's day?"

Humphrey turned around, looked at Rod, then looked past Rod towards Darius. "You could call it that, Denise," Humphrey said. "Today's the day we Aussies honour those men and women, well, mostly men, and plenty of them morons, who England no longer wanted, who had stolen one loaf of bread too many or buggered a sheep to death, or whatever. Today we honour those who were shipped to the other side of the world to start a colony, to invade an already long-inhabited land for King, God and Empire. Most certainly, that's worth celebrating."

"Don't listen to him," Rod said. "He's bullshitting ya."

"Yeah, Denise, don't listen to me. It's a proud day to be Australian."

"You guys don't have a lot to be proud of," Denise said.

"True. Maybe that's why we drink so much on Australia Day, to dull the pain and guilt. To forget."

Rod shook his head. "I've never in me life met anyone so un-Australian."

Humphrey pointed at Denise. "She's Canadian."

Rod stepped forward, looking like he might take a swing at Humphrey, but stopped when Denise burst out laughing.

"What's your problem?"

"It's just that," she said, trying to gain control of her voice, "it's just such a ludicrous thing to say. I couldn't call someone un-Canadian." She laughed again. "Okay, un-American I've heard before."

"We like copying the Yanks," Humphrey said.

"But un-Japanese, un-French," she went on, getting a smile from Humphrey and a laugh from a few other people in the bar.

"Un-Swedish," someone yelled out.

"Un-Mongolian."

"It means not being true to your country," Rod said. "We call people un-Australian when they go against our people and our values. But you, you just go round tellin lies."

"They're not lies." Humphrey absently rubbed blue chalk on the end of his cue. He turned his back to Rod and spoke to Andy. "Is it my shot?"

"Mate, ya just focus on the bad stuff. There's more to it than that."

"Yeah, there is. Damn, missed. Jake, you're up."

"Stralia's the most multicultural kuntree in the world," Gazza said.

Humphrey moved behind the pool table. "So, why do we hate boat people? Why does Pauline Hansen get elected?"

"We can't let everyone in," Rod said.

"You left out the second verse earlier." And then Humphrey sang, "'For those who've come across the seas, we've boundless plains to share, with courage let us all combine to Advance Australia Fair.'"

"That's not how it goes."

"You're right, Rod. I'm lying again." Humphrey turned to Denise. "Anthem. Second verse. They don't sing it anymore because apparently it's not appropriate, but I sang that verse when I was at school and these guys probably did too. What about you, Darius?"

Behind the bar, Darius recalled how when he was nine, his dad had bet him a dollar he couldn't memorise the anthem. "Yep. I can't sing as good as you Hobo, but 'Beneath our radiant Southern Cross, we'll toil with hearts and hands', and so on. We used to sing *God Save the Queen* too."

"Really?" Denise exclaimed.

Humphrey nodded. "Unfortunately not the Sex Pistols' version."

"They just sang it in the country," Gazza said. "I'm from Sydney. I never sang it."

"Yeah, we're a pretty backward lot in the country. Everyone's related. Me and Digger are probably far distant cousins."

"You're no country fella," Rod said.

"Believe whatever you want. Denise, it's your shot. And pot something, woman, before we lose."

Denise took the pool cue and then dropped it on the table. "I'm out. You roosters can puff your chests at each other all you want. Drop your pants and see who's got the biggest dick, I don't care. I'm going to Joe's. You guys coming?"

"Yeah," Gazza said. "We're in."

"I'm not talking to you, you pathetic, useless gorilla."

"We'll go wherever we want."

"If you want my opinion," Denise said, "you should go straight home. Steal something, so you can all be shipped back to where you belong."

Humphrey laughed so hard he had to grip the side of the pool table. Darius, sensing trouble, moved around the bar and towards the group.

Rod stepped right up to Denise so he was only inches from her face. "What do you cost?"

Darius moved in between them and pushed Rod backwards. "That's no way to talk to a girl."

"Steady on, Digger. It was just a joke."

"Yeah, well, I'm not laughing. And I've had enough of this shit for one night. Someone's gonna haveta leave."

"I'm already gone," Denise said, and she headed for the door.

"Sorry, Digger," Humphrey said, following her. "But it looks like you're stuck with these mates. Make sure they drink themselves into a stupor worthy of our great country's anniversary."

Rod stepped towards Humphrey but Darius got in the way and again he pushed Rod back.

"Don't make me call the cops."

Some of the clique grabbed Rod and tried to pull him back. He struggled a little, to show how much he wanted to fight.

"Fuck off," Rod said to Humphrey.

"I think I will."

Darius went with them to the door.

Outside, Humphrey asked, "Ya gonna be all right?"

"I reckon they won't last long. Most of them can barely stand up as it is. A couple more beers and they'll be done."

"Come to Joe's if you finish early. I hear they serve delightful cucumber sandwiches."

Darius laughed. "Have fun."

Back inside, he saw the group were looking at each other, wondering how to save face.

"Onya, Digger," Rod said, "for throwing em out."

"Troublemakers, eh? My shout."

He moved behind the bar, glad to put a big wedge of Canadian oak between him and the group; just a bit of symbolic separatism. He got the stereo going with some Midnight Oil and lined up the beers on the bar. They all drank for something to do and sang along to *Dead Heart* and *Beds are Burning*. The conversation became buoyant again and the old anecdotes were churned out as more beers were drunk. They talked about Humphrey and Denise, and their comments become nastier with each round; Gazza boasted that Denise gave him a hand job in toilets at the ski lodge last week. Rod joked that it actually was Humphrey, and they all laughed.

But they were already far gone and it wasn't long before a couple of them were running outside to vomit in the snow. Rod argued over the cost of their drinks, with Darius conceding in the end and taking what Rod wanted to pay. It was a relief to see them outside and to lock the door. He wondered what damage those drunk Aussies could do, even though it was after midnight and no longer Australia Day. He feared they would go to Joe's and look for trouble. Alone, they were harmless; he even quite liked Gazza and Rod. But as part of the group, their clique powered by alcohol, they had the potential to do anything.

He made himself a cup of tea and started cleaning the bar.

An hour later, walking home through the snow, he thought about going to Joe's, but it was past closing time. It was snowing too, which meant that most people had gone home to sleep so they could be the first on the hill tomorrow. The streets were deserted and no cars had cut tire marks through the fallen snow. It was peaceful then, to walk the few blocks up to the house.

The snow gave the little ski town that magical, festive quality that winter deserves. White powder clung to the Victorian buildings and covered big sedans with thick silvery blankets, making them look like giant lamingtons. He walked slowly, leaving neat tracks in the snow. He was in Canada, on the other side of the world, with snow falling into his hair. He was living, working and surviving in a completely foreign place, and what Les had said about travelling making you more confident, independent and developed was then the greatest truism he had ever heard. He smiled, wishing his dad could see him now, could know what he had achieved.

"You were wrong."

And he knew he would go with Humphrey to Europe and continue proving how wrong his dad was. He wanted to get moving again, to get to another new place and face new challenges.

Inside the dark, silent house, he made a cup of hot milk and took it upstairs. He grinned at Humphrey's closed door, guessing that his friend's wit and charm had earned a ticket into Denise's tight pants, if he could get them off. He stopped at the door to listen, for confirmation, but it was pretty late and they were probably both asleep.

***

The morning was dark and grey. It was completely uninviting if not for the huge amounts of snow piled on the footpaths, houses and cars. Darius smiled as he looked out the window. Humphrey's closed door didn't get a second glance; his friend had more than once declared his partiality for morning sex.

At the hitch-hiking point, Darius joined the long line of eager skiers and snowboarders but watched the road to see if Humphrey would come trudging up the hill. He didn't, and it wasn't long before Darius was at the head of line and then on his way to the base. Waiting in line for the rickety double chair, he saw Andy come flying towards him. He let her in and they fell together into the chair.

111

"How's it going?" she asked. Her hat was covered with enough ice to make Darius think she had fallen several times, or clipped the branches of trees.

"Orright."

"The snow's amazing. Me and Jake found this wild run where the tree wells were ten feet deep. I fell in one and I thought I was gonna die. Lucky, Jake had a shovel and he dug me out."

"Who's Jake again?"

"Digger, I nearly died."

"I'm glad ya didn't."

"Jake was at the bar last night. He's from Toronto, too."

"Ya know each other?"

"It's big city. But, yeah, we have some people in common. He's a nice guy. You'd like him."

Darius looked away, disagreeing. He watched the skiers below, spraying mounds of powder with each turn. "Seen Hobo?"

Andy shook her head. "No sign of Denise either. It's crap that they're missing out on this. They could fuck any time."

"What happened last night?"

Andy adjusted the straps of her gloves. "We waited for you, even after Humphrey and Denise left. We thought you might close early and come to Joe's."

"Who's we?"

"Me and Jake."

He shifted uncomfortably in the chair and licked his dry lips. "Denise go home with Hobo then?"

"Yeah. Well, they left together, but I can't say if they went home together. Humphrey was, like, putting the moves on her, you know, but Denise, nice girl that she is, has got this whole virginal attitude that's, like, the complete opposite to the way she dresses and acts. When you get the chance, warn him. That girl's got issues."

Darius wondered if Andy was talking about herself; that she was more trouble than she was worth. Was she already trying to disentangle their bond and make it easier for them both? What happened between her and Jake last night? Did they fuck?

"I'll tell him that."

The lift got close to the peak. They readied themselves to get off.

"Wanna do a few runs together?" Andy asked.

"Lead the way."

They spent the whole day together. When Jake called to Andy late in the day to go for another hike with him, she turned him down and took another flat run with Darius. A few times, they stopped to talk about their relationship, but neither had the courage to go deeper. It was pathetic really, and Darius half wished she would go away, take that hike with Jake out of bounds. He didn't want to go through the process of breaking up with her, or have her admit that she slept with Jake. He thought the whole thing would be made easier by him leaving.

They separated in town. Darius went home to shower and get ready for work. At the house, Tony and Whits were lounging on the porch, heavily rugged up with beers clutched in gloved hands; a six pack was wedged in the snow at the bottom of the stairs. They looked like they had been on the porch for a while and Darius was reminded that they often left the hill early, claiming that they took off before it was "skied out" or the snow "turned to mush".

He clambered onto the porch with all that gear he hated so much. It would be a relief at the end of winter to sell it all. "G'day, guys. What a great day, eh?"

"Yep," Whits said. Darius only knew his last name, which was Whitaker. Everyone knew him as Whits, and because the two were always seen together, whenever Tony was alone, more than one person would quip that Tony didn't have his Whits about him.

"Before it got skied into slop," Tony added.

Darius looked down at the six pack, wishing he could have a beer but knowing with these two he could never just take. They labelled all their food and even their toothpaste and toilet paper. And he had to go to work anyway.

"Seen Humphrey?"

"Nope," Tony said, sitting on the wicker chair like a big greedy dog.

"Guess he missed a good one."

That was the cue for Tony and Whits to relate the incredible feats of daring and excellence they had achieved that day. Darius listened impatiently, already running late for work. He was heading inside when Tony grabbed his arm.

"Hey, have you seen that car parked in front of the hostel? You know, that white boat your Aussie buddies drive?"

"Nuh."

"I ain't saying another word then," Tony said. "Go look for yourself."

"It's wild," Whits added. He took a drink and it looked like he was sucking his beer rather than drinking it.

Darius went inside and showered quickly. He walked down to the hostel with wet hair that quickly froze in long clumps. He had spent his first night in Woodlow at the hostel, in a musty basement dorm with seven skiers, after he hadn't found Humphrey in Joe's as planned.

It was a small hostel, recently renovated so it looked new and loved, but that was just the front. The dorms at the back and in the basement were cold, mouldy and run-down. On the street out the front, Rod and Gazza were hunched over their car, sponges in hand, the water steaming off the roof and bonnet. Written on the car in thick red pen were words like "racist", "homophobe", and "White Australia". Written in smaller letters were "top blokes", "best mates" and "fair go for all". On the boot was a large map of Australia, quite accurate, with the words "sacred land", "invaded", "raped" and "stolen" written as many times as would fit inside the map. Inside Tasmania was one word: "killed".

"G'day, Rod. Gazza."

Rod was rubbing the sponge hard, his face red with exertion. "Bugger off, Digger."

"Wasn't me."

"No. Your mate, though."

"You see him do it?"

"Who else would pull bullshit like this?"

"The paper photographed it and everythin," Gazza said. "Who's gonna pay to have my car repainted?"

Darius laughed a little while Rod and Gazza scrubbed fruitlessly in silence. Gazza was right, Darius thought; the car would have to be repainted.

"Maybe it's a bad idea to destroy the evidence."

"We can't drive around like this."

Gazza waved a sponge at Darius. "We're gonna get your mate. You tell him we're gonna fix him."

"He's just having a laugh. He'll pay to have it repainted. If it was him, that is."

"Your car?" asked a voice behind him.

"Not mine," Darius said, turning. "It's Jake, right?"

Jake nodded. They shook hands.

"What's this about?"

"Dunno."

"Ignore it," Rod said. "It's complete and utter bullshit."

"You comin to the Pab?" Darius asked Jake. "Everyone's meetin there."

"Yeah. Andy told me already."

"We'll be along soon," Rod said.

"All right," Darius said. "But no trouble."

"Then tell your mate to make himself scarce."

"Humphrey did this?" Jake asked.

"Dunno. I doubt it. He doesn't have the balls for that. Come on. Let's go to the Pab."

They made awkward conversation as they walked. Though he was hurt, Darius thought Jake wasn't such a bad guy, and maybe it would make everything easier with Andy; he could leave without needing to have a break up conversation. Plus, there would be no more questioning and searching for commitment.

At the Pab, Darius was happy to find the world much simpler. Andy and Denise were standing out the front waiting for the bar to open. They cheered when Darius produced his keys. Inside, Darius gave everyone a shot of Tequila and they threw these down with whoops of delight.

"Did anybody see Humphrey today?" Denise asked. She looked directly at Darius, but he just shrugged.

"No sign."

"Well, get this," she said. "He quit."

"What?"

"He was supposed to work today, but he didn't show up."

"Maybe he's sick," Andy said.

"You didn't see him today?"

"Not at the hill."

"Darius?"

"Sounds like you were the last to see him." Darius had a feeling Humphrey was gone. Without even saying goodbye; just graffitied Gazza's car and then ran for it. Coward, he thought.

"He walked me home and that was all," Denise said.

The group took this information, both said and unsaid, in silence.

"Say something, Darius," she demanded. "You two were so secretive together. You might be gay lovers for all we know."

Darius cleaned a few glasses before saying, "Could be he's gone."

Denise looked like she was just keeping herself in check. "What does that mean?"

Darius shrugged again. "He's done it before. Just up and left without tellin anybody. No goodbyes, no explanations. He just leaves. That's Humphrey for ya."

"I think it's pathetic," Denise said. "And weak. He's probably gone to Texas to see that tramp I heard about."

"Maybe you should've slept with him. Then he might've stayed. Just kiddin. Nah, nah, he's gone to Europe. I dunno where. He talked about it for months. Probably already had a ticket. Fuck knows."

"I'm glad he's gone. I never want to see him again. Give me another shot."

Darius poured out a second round of Tequila for everyone and they all threw them down, Denise whooping as she did so. But then she calmed herself again, even smiled. She saw some guys come in, all wearing the blue jackets of ski hill employees, and went over to them.

"What'll you do, Darius?" Andy asked.

He turned to her. She stood close to Jake, almost as if they were holding hands behind their backs. That's it, he thought. We're finished. Nothing would have to be said, no hearts broken and no long-winded explanations given. She felt something for Jake that she didn't feel for him. To his surprise, he was all right with it.

"Dunno. If Hobo's really gone, then I reckon I'll ski a few more weeks. Maybe hit some of the other hills. Like Whitewater. We never went to Nelson, Andy."

"No, we didn't."

"Or Europe. Who knows? Might go home. I'm pretty sick of the cold. It's summer down under, ya know."

"Scared of Europe?" Jake asked. "Lot of languages and cultures. You can speak another language, can't you?"

Darius hoped they wouldn't ask about his schooling and background because then he would have to come up with more lies and they would have to be consistent with the lies he had already told.

It would be easier, he thought, just to leave Woodlow and all these old lies behind.

"I'd like to," he said. "Maybe do a crash course when I'm there."

To show off, Jake, Andy and Denise had a quick conversation in French. Darius poured beers to show his was unimpressed. But they had something he wanted, a worldly skill he needed as part of his armoury. He also felt left out. It was then he realised that Humphrey had always been his link, the one who got invited to parties, and the one who conversations were always centred around. That link gone, and with his relationship with Andy over, he remained a precarious member of this group, by association only.

"I always wanted to go to Europe," Darius said when they finally stopped. "Maybe I'll go over."

"I recommend it," Jake said. "But you'll need cash and lots of it."

"I got some money saved. And I'd work if I had to."

"Being a bartender's a ticket to the world. My brother's one. He's worked everywhere, even done the Club Med thing, and worked on cruise ships."

"Like *The Love Boat*?" Andy asked.

"That campy show on the cruise ship? Yeah, like that."

Andy starting laughed, Jake too, and Denise came over to join in. Now they were all laughing, as if trying to convince each other they didn't need Humphrey or his humour; the winter fun could continue in his absence. In a week or two, Darius thought, they would all have forgotten Humphrey, and another jocular transient was sure to drift into town and fill the void. In the same way, they would forget him when he was gone and another guy tended the bar at the Pab.

It was a great night. Rod, Gazza and the clique showed up later and everything was all right. Rod even apologised for being rude to Darius. Outside it was dumping with snow again, which meant everyone would leave early. Andy left with Jake, sneaking out the door when they thought Darius wasn't looking. Denise lingered but soon left with a guy in a blue jacket; he had a bounce in his step, but Darius was sure he would get nowhere with her.

With the Pab empty and the streets deserted, Darius closed early and headed home. The house was dark and cavernous, with Tony and Whits fast asleep. He stopped in front of Humphrey's door, looked at it, then edged it open. He found the light switch, half-expecting to see the angular outline of his friend curled up on the bed.

But the bed was empty, as was the room, and all that remained was a stack of bedsheets folded in neat squares and placed at the end of the deflated air mattress. On the top of the sheets was a note.

Darius,

You found the note. That means you entered my room when the door was closed which I seem to recall was against house rules. Anyway, now that you're in here, you can return these sheets to the youth hostel. They lent them to me when I first arrived. Clever, huh?

You're probably wondering what happened and why I left. I guess you've seen the car. The pen is certainly mightier. Here's what happened. Last night, they waited for me around the corner from the house. Like always, they talk fair go and honour but will cheat you any chance they get, and fittingly on the day we celebrate all things Australian. A couple of them held me while Rod threw a few punches. But they were so drunk there wasn't much in it. They could barely stand up. I'm all right. A few scratches. I think it was more for show. My biggest fear at the time was that they'd gang-bang me. Thankfully, I was spared. Good thing Denise wasn't with me. She might not have been so lucky.

I waited for you to come home and then went out to beautify their car. I thought the map of Australia was a nice touch. Now I'm back, it's 4am, everything's packed and I'm about to walk out the door without saying a proper goodbye. I hate goodbyes anyway. Sometimes it's easier just to leave and let everyone deal with it. I'm sorry to do it like this, Darius, but I'm sure you can understand that I couldn't stay after marking their car. I hope they didn't go after you instead. No, they like you. And they don't want to bite the hand that serves them drinks.

I'm heading for Van, but I'm done with Canada. Too many Aussies here, too many guys I left home to get away from. When I land in Europe, I'll let you know where I am. Whenever you leave Woodlow, call Les first. You've got his new number. It'll be great to catch up again, but I'm not sure where I'll land. It'll probably depend on where I can get a job.

Let's meet up in Europe. You're a good friend, Darius. I'd hate to lose you because of this. We've got unfinished business and we both need a little culture. We grew up with none. You might not admit it to yourself, but I know you've got your share of complaints about our country, with the people too. I think you feel something is missing or confusing or just plain wrong, but can't say exactly what it is. That's why I like you, Darius. Keep questioning things and when you find a few answers, let me know, because I'm just as confused.

See you soon,
Humphrey

Darius folded the note and put it in his pocket. "My problems with Australia are all to do with my dad."

In his room, he counted the money he had saved. The assorted notes, cheques and bank statements were like comforting old friends, circling around him, including him. Then he lay back in bed, trying to decide what to do. It had only been a day and already it was less fun without Humphrey around. It was no fun to ski alone. Rod and Gazza had said they were moving on as well, and Andy was now with Jake.

"That went bad pretty quick."

Europe, he thought. Why not?

***

From Humphrey's shock departure, Darius's days in Woodlow became long, arduous and dull. He struggled to continue with the social groups he had. He knew a lot of people in town, but he now just played a brief part in their lives, serving them drinks at the Pab but not getting invited to parties. There was no one left, no one close, not even on a superficial level, which was how it seemed most of Woodlow's relationships were maintained. Rod and Gazza were gone. Rumour had it they were down in Rossiland and that the car was white again.

Humphrey sent an exuberant postcard from Oslo and a long letter from Munich, where he was now working at a youth hostel. Given a destination, Darius sold his ski gear and bought a flight to Munich. The thought of leaving Woodlow and starting again in a new place where nobody knew anything about him spurred him on those last weeks. He was sick of the cold, sick of the people, sick of being alone and unpopular, sick of the person he had become in this ski town.

And when it came time to leave, there wasn't even anybody left to say goodbye to. Tony and Whits were out backcountry skiing, perhaps conveniently forgetting his departure. The owner of the Pab was in Calgary again, and Andy and Jake had already gone home to Toronto together.

With just his backpack, he walked down to the highway bathed in spring sunshine, and started the long journey that would take him right to Humphrey's doorstep, again.

Lewis: Did Germany have the same effect? Did you also feel no connection to the land?

Poet: There's not really any land to connect with. There's forests and mountains, but not any kind of wilderness like in Australia or even Canada. Go ten k's in any direction and you hit a town. That's not a bad thing. It's just different. You can't get lost there, or feel insignificant.

Lewis: So, you felt homesick and wanted to go home again.

Poet: Yeah, but Munich's got an Aussie community. Sometimes, it felt like we were back home, especially when I was at work.

Lewis: What did you do?

Poet: I worked in an Aussie bar. It was great. The owner, this guy Freddie, was a real character. A top bloke, a German one at that. I didn't think that'd be possible. He really opened my eyes to the locals. I met a great bunch of people in Munich.

Lewis: Were you there for Oktoberfest?

Poet: For us, every night was Oktoberfest.

~~~

Storming Europe

The airport was huge. As he walked from terminal to terminal, he looked at every face hoping he might, just by pure chance, pick Humphrey out of the crowd. But Humphrey didn't know he was coming; that was part of the surprise. He followed the train symbol, walking with all the other bleary-eyed passengers towards the station and the main exit. He let the suited men walk past him, clutching their briefcases and yelling into their mobile phones, and smiled, glad not to be one of them.

At the station, he stared at the ticket machine, then at the coloured squiggles of the train map. After watching a few other people, and from asking for help, he got his ticket and got onto the right train, feeling a little like the world traveller he wanted so badly to be. It was exciting to have this new landscape, as unexciting as it looked through the train window. Canada was behind him now. He could start again from scratch. A new continent, a new Darius.

At the central station, Munich breathed and roared. The air was thick with damp breath, train fumes and the burning fat of grilled sausage. It made his mouth dry. He had never seen so many people crammed into one building, so many people rushing with such purpose and intent. He found himself standing in the middle of it, unable to move. Everyone knew where they were going. It looked like arrogance, the humourless Germans being as productive and servile as expected, but that was the stereotype. Forget that, he told himself.

The people brushed his shoulders as they rushed past, and more than one briefcase banged against his legs. No one apologised, and if they did, he didn't understand them. Their foreign words had the tone more of "Get out of the way" rather than "Sorry" or "Excuse me".

Outside, he went with the crowd, down a busy street, caught in this flow of people, wanting to look like he had purpose and knew where he was going. After five blocks, he went into the nearest café to drink a coffee and ask for directions.

So he found the hostel where Humphrey worked. It was disappointing to see what a shabby place it was, with the paint flaking from the building and the sign slightly askew. Inside, it was even worse, smelling of the combined body odour of a thousand passers-through;

like a warehouse full of old shoes and sports clothes. The ramshackle reception area spoke volumes about the state of the bathrooms and dormitories beyond. There was a disorderly rack of pamphlets and flyers, some taken out and put back in the wrong place, and others folded and ripped and jammed back in where they would fit. Maps, of Munich, Germany and Europe, which perhaps had once been tacked to the wall with good intentions, were faded and written all over, with highways traced in pencil and cities and places circled or crossed out. The corners were lifting from the wall because pins had been stolen and replaced by tape which had long ago lost its stickiness. Near the reception desk, there was a pile of thin, yellowing bed sheets, and in the corner was a crate over-full with empty beer bottles. He could smell the stale remains in the bottles, like they had been fermenting there for months.

He dropped his heavy backpack and pressed the bell. It chimed faintly through the building. He studied the map of Europe while he waited. Under the graffiti, he found Munich and located it in relation to the rest of the continent. For some reason, he had thought Europe was one country, but the map showed that wasn't the case, with each country having a different colour, the borders clear. Munich was pretty much right in the centre and he liked that. Italy was just down the road, Austria and Switzerland next door, Prague barely a few hours away.

"Bout time you got here."

He turned and saw Humphrey casually leaning against the doorway, his angular body a bit more filled out than he remembered. His hair was longer and wavier, and it made his shoulders seem less square while also softening his facial features. He smiled broadly, cracking a few lines on his face. Darius reached out his hand, but Humphrey came forward and embraced him. It felt awkward. Darius tried to relax, but his body was stiff. He was glad when Humphrey released him and he could put a more manly distance between them.

"Had a few delays," he said. And he recalled how he had sat around in Woodlow waiting for a letter or a postcard from Humphrey. "At the airports."

"Well, you made it, at last, and that's the important thing."

"Long bloody way."

"You should be happy about that. If it was easy, every idiot would do it, and then we'd have all these amateurs running around with no clue what they're doing."

"You all right?"

"Yep. Awesome. Brilliant. *Wunderbar.*"

Darius looked around the reception. "Yeah?"

"Munich's great, but not this place. This's just a means to an end. Come on. I'll give you the grand tour. Don't worry about your pack. It's safe."

Darius retrieved his traveller's cheques from the front pocket and followed Humphrey down the hallway.

"How's Woodlow?"

"Same. Things kinda died off towards the end of winter. A lot of people moved on."

"Sorry about that."

"Forget it. You coulda stayed. Rod and Gazza left not long after you."

"I really should've taken a photo of the car."

"It made the front page of the local rag."

Humphrey laughed. "Maybe I'll call them and get myself a copy. One for the ages."

They entered the communal kitchen. It was a bomb site of stained and chipped dishes and cups, unwashed plates, mismatched cutlery and almost empty packets of pasta. In the sink, Darius saw a pot filled with water; at the bottom was a good centimetre of burned rice.

"It's been worse," Humphrey said. "But now that you're here, you can help me out."

"Thanks."

Humphrey gave Darius a few jobs and together they set about cleaning up the mess. A few travellers drifted in and out, asking Humphrey for advice and tips, about how to get to the airport or where such and such a museum was. There were girls too, young Americans and assorted Europeans, travelling in twos and threes and wearing baggy jeans and coats. Darius tried not to stare. He looked forward to summer when girls would show their legs again. He liked legs, was not particular about length – if anything, he disliked overly long, bony legs, like supermodels have – and was more interested in shape and curve. He loved the way a woman's ankle could curve so smoothly into a calf, blend into a sumptuous knee and then widen through a broad thigh; like a golden path towards the promised land. He was rather disinterested in breasts, though he never told anyone as much, and liked the warm days when girls wore shorts and dresses. Andy had terrible legs, too skinny and bony; real chicken legs, they were. The other girls he had met in Woodlow had disappointed him too. Humphrey had joked that it was a winter cover-up. "Frump season," he'd called it, whatever that meant.

The girls shot through the kitchen quickly, skipping breakfast, with perhaps a full day's itinerary to plough through. The men lingered. Darius half-listened as they spoke with Humphrey. They slouched in world-weary and experienced, bored almost with being in another new city with another list of things to see and do. One man, seemingly reluctant to start the day, slowly drank three cups of tea in a row, each time stealing milk from a different carton in the communal fridge, all the time not saying a word.

"You can't believe the girls here," Humphrey said when they were alone. "From everywhere in the world. Wes, the boss, says we're not allowed to fraternise." He laughed. "His word. I love it. Fraternise. Like all the people here are the enemy, or we are. He's American and religious to boot. There's even separate boys and girls dorms." He emptied the recycling bins, tying the bags securely. Darius was surprised to see separate bins for different recyclable products. "But he's a good guy, once you get past the preaching. He doesn't like America, bless him, and has some pretty strong opinions about Oz too."

"How'd he end up here?"

"He was in the army, served here when the Yanks still wanted a foothold in Europe. He was against the Gulf War, resigned from the army, came here and opened this hostel. He still thinks the Arabs will band together and attack America. I reckon he wants it to happen."

"Yeah? I thought about joinin the army once."

"Before you went to the mines, right?"

"I guess goin up north was the right decision."

"Oh, the irony."

"Why'd you go?"

"Money. For the experience too, but mostly for the money. I wanted to hit the road. When I was younger, Les was always travelling and coming back with these amazing stories. It made Esperance

125

seem like such a small, meaningless little place. I spent my childhood begging mum to move." He sat down at the kitchen table and swept up crumbs and dust with his hands. "It was actually Les's idea, not to work in the mines, you know, but to get away from everything. Away from the locals who thought I was a bit off, away from all those social groups that tried so hard to exclude me. In high school, I was even voted off the cricket team, and I was the best player." He shook his head, smiling bitterly. "I didn't really fit in down there. I tried to, but people saw through me."

"How is it here? You like it?"

"Darius, I could live in this country. Not in Munich cause there's too many Australians. They've got their own little community. If I wanted to meet Aussies, I'd stay home, you know? The city's big enough to avoid them, but just knowing they're here annoys me. They say the place gets overrun with them during Oktoberfest."

"Yeah." Darius wondered what Oktoberfest was. With Humphrey already way ahead of him, knowing locals and speaking some of the language, he was starting to feel a bit out of his depth. Still, it was great to see Humphrey and to be in a new place. It dawned on him that he was really here, in Europe, in Germany, in Munich. Growing up, he'd never seen that in his future.

"There's an Aussie restaurant near Marienplatz. I'll take you there tonight. It's so tacky and contrived, it'll make you laugh. They even serve kangaroo steaks. Kangaroo!"

"Be nice to have some good old Aussie tucker."

"Kangaroo's hardly that. Besides, German food's much better, and the beer's incredible. Not like the watered-down piss we were reared on."

"I'm thirsty already."

"Well, slackers like you have to earn it. Keep it up and Wes might offer you a job."

Darius made a show of liking the idea but wanted nothing of it. He knew there would be a bar job for him somewhere in Munich. He would just need to spend a few days doing the rounds, as he had done in Woodlow. But he wouldn't have to lie about his experience this time.

"It's good to see you, Darius," Humphrey said.

"Yeah, you too."

126

"I'm still sorry for ditching you in Woodlow. All your drinks are on me tonight."

"Forget it."

"Look, I've got a lotta work to do. Go and check out the town. Let's hook up later at the Hole."

"The what?"

"The Waterhole Bar and Grill. But it really is a hole. Around seven?"

"Orright. Any tips on what to see?"

"You're a man of the world now. Go and decide for yourself."

He spent most of the day reading English newspapers in a café he chanced upon. He walked around a little bit, liked the historic centre, but struggled to put it all into a context he could understand. It was all too foreign and unfamiliar. In the end he arrived early at the Hole and was surprised to see Humphrey already there, sitting at a table with a middle-aged man in a Hawaiian shirt.

"*Gruess Gott*," Humphrey said. "Freddie, this is Darius, a good mate a mine and a top bloke all round." He turned to Darius and gave him a wink. "Freddie owns this marvellous establishment."

"G'day." Darius took a seat, but Freddie just smiled and turned to Humphrey.

"City fella, I reckon," Freddie said, his distinctly Australian accent undone by his German pronunciation. "Thinks he's clever, but I know he's taking money from the till."

"Well, we're all thieves at heart. You know, our ancestry. What you need is a solid country fella." Humphrey paused and drank from a long beer glass while Freddie waited for him to finish. "Someone with hard work and honesty ingrained in him. A fella whose self respect would be tarnished forever if someone said he wasn't true blue."

"Sounds good, but only city fellas on offer here. I'd hire locals, you know, but it's more authentic having Aussies at the bar."

"And cheaper, I bet."

"Germans complain too much, especially with all these *Ossis* running around." He cracked his mouth into smile. "I need Aussies, not *Ossis*."

Humphrey said to Darius, "They call people from East Germany *Ossis*."

Darius tried to laugh. Are there two Germanys? he wondered.

What he wanted was a beer, but if Humphrey was buying, he'd have to wait until the beer was ordered for him. Freddie and Humphrey continued talking. At first glance, Darius didn't much like Freddie but could see why Humphrey did. For here was a small, dark-haired German with a sun-studio tan who seemed to be trying to pass himself off as an Australian. It was exactly the kind of contradiction that Darius knew appealed to Humphrey. He could imagine Humphrey having spent many evenings here in the last few months, towing Freddie along, yet getting great enjoyment from the man's performance.

"They're overrunning us," Freddie went on. "*Ossis* everywhere. I wish the wall was still there."

"What? Your side won. You know that us Aussies don't like losing or losers. We'll do anything to win. That's why we cheat anyway we can."

"Must be all that convict blood in you, mate."

"No convicts in my family, Friedrich. Dutch settlers all the way." Humphrey drank again while Freddie laughed. "But if it's honest country blood you need, with the desperate convict roots you think all of us have, and perhaps a pinch of Aboriginal for flavour, then Darius here is your man, your mate."

Darius tried to smile modestly but felt uncomfortable when Freddie started staring at him, as if seeing him for the first time. He couldn't meet his eyes and instead looked around the restaurant, deciding if he could work here. He saw the made-in-China boomerangs on the walls, the generic, factory-produced Aboriginal paintings of goannas and emus, the enlarged but slightly out of focus photographs of the Harbour Bridge and the Opera House, photos Freddie had perhaps taken himself, the English-looking cricket bat, and the posters of a very eighties Boxing Kangaroo. Through the stereo came the faint sound of didgeridoo played to a disco beat.

"You work bar before?"

Darius nodded. It was all too easy. He could already see himself standing behind the bar, thickening his accent to impress the local girls. "In Canada. Ski town."

"Where are you from?"

"WA." He wondered if he might make a connection, even on the other side of the world, but doubted it. He didn't need it anyway. "Down near Wagin. You wouldn't know it."

"Your classic 200 people, four surname Australian farming town," Humphrey said, getting a thin smile from Freddie.

"Cut both those numbers in half and you'll be closer to the truth," Darius said, glad not to be living there, in some house with a Stevenson girl he'd married and impregnated.

"Can you make cocktails?"

"Few," he lied. "Most people drank beer and shots in Woodlow. Cocktails are for cruise ships."

"Yes. But we make a lot of them during happy hour."

"This's an Aussie bar," Humphrey said. "Every hour is happy hour."

"That's right." Freddie turned back to Darius. "Know what a *Radler* is? No helping, Humphrey."

"Nuh."

"You'll learn. We don't have light beer here. A *Radler* is beer and lemonade."

"Shandy."

"Never heard of it," Freddie replied.

Humphrey laughed. "Your Aussie vocabulary needs work, Friedrich."

"Bullshit. Crikey fair dinkum, mate."

"Yep. That's exactly how we talk. Even in business meetings. The pollies address parliament the same way."

"Got a permit?"

Darius shook his head. The glimmer in Freddie's eyes and the way he smiled made Darius think he got some kind of sick pleasure from asking questions Darius couldn't answer.

"Well, we can work around that. Speak any German?"

"Nuh." Again, the glimmer of satisfaction.

"Don't worry. Nobody orders in German anyway. They're here for the free English lesson as much as for the Aussie food and atmosphere."

"I'm here for the atmosphere," Humphrey said. "It reminds me so much of our pubs back home, especially those boomerangs on the wall. Every pub in Australia has them, you know. They're much preferred over dartboards."

Freddie beamed. "A lot of my customers say it reminds them of Australia, the ones who have been down under, that is."

"They're spot on."

"Want to earn his dinner and drinks?" Freddie asked, gesturing to Humphrey. "Get behind the bar and we'll see how you go."

"Now?"

Freddie's face brightened, his eyes shining. "Want the job or not?"

"That's how it is here, Digger," Humphrey said. "There's no messing about like there is back home, no standing around waiting for others to start or sitting back and hoping you get lucky. If they want you, they take you, and if they don't, they tell you straight." He leaned back in his chair and opened his arms. "I've embraced it, Digger. It's what I've been missing my whole life. At last, no more grey areas."

"Digger, is it?" Freddie asked, licking his lips over the nickname. He stood up and motioned for Darius to follow him. He was surprisingly short, and walked with quick, jumpy steps, bouncing a little. Behind the bar, he said, "Digger, this is Darren." From the tone of his voice, Darius guessed that this was the city fella whose honesty was in question. Darren nodded once, his stubbled face flat and disinterested. "He'll show you where everything is. If someone orders in German, say you're just off the boat. They'll love it that you're a real outback Aussie."

Freddie left him and went back to Humphrey's table. Darius tried to familiarise himself with the set up of this foreign bar.

"Most of the Aussie branded beers are in the fridge," Darren said. "If someone orders an Aussie beer without asking for a brand, give them Foster's." He pointed. "That's on tap. It's brewed here, so it's actually drinkable. Most people will ask for a *Weissbier*."

As he said this, a group came to the bar and ordered three of them. Darren showed how to pour one, putting the glass over the bottle, turning it upside down and then pulling the bottle out with the neck just below the surface. Darius spilt the first one all over the floor, much to the amusement of the customers.

"Keep the neck below the line if it starts to foam," Darren said. "Give it another go."

Darius tried it again and got it right. His small audience applauded when he held the glass up in triumph. Darren, Dazza now, slapped him on the back.

More people came to the bar and one order followed the next. The hours passed quickly. Nobody ordered a cocktail and the waitresses, all German, were pleasantly flirtatious if not a little too old and withered up close.

After midnight, the crowd started to thin out.

"Can you handle the cleaning, Digger?" Dazza asked.

"Yep." He turned around to pour a beer and from the corners of his eyes saw Dazza lift some notes out of the till and shove them quickly into his pocket. When Dazza disappeared into the back room, Darius called Freddie over.

"You look like you've been here all your life."

"Cheers, Freddie." Darius tilted his head towards the back room. "Look, I don't like tellin on fellas, but I'm honest, yeah?"

"Let's have it. If he's stealing, he's out and you're in."

Darius nodded. "He's liftin, big time."

"You see him?"

"Check the right pocket of his jeans, but don't say it was me that saw him."

Dazza came back and moved around the bar. "I'm off, Freddie," he said cheerfully, a small backpack slung over his shoulder. "Digger said he'd take care of the cleaning."

Dazza moved between the tables and Freddie followed him. Darius watched the owner lean close to Dazza, speaking quietly so no one could hear. Freddie reached his hand into Dazza's pocket. He pulled out the notes and held them up in the air between them. Dazza remonstrated innocently, but then pushed Freddie away. He raised his middle finger right in front of the owner's eyes and then slammed the door.

Humphrey was grinning as he walked up to the bar. "Oh, barkeep," he said in that ridiculous British accent he was able to do, "divvy up a *Radler* for me, will you, boy?"

Darius poured the drink and slid the glass across the bar. "Looks like I'm in."

"Of course you are. It was never in doubt. With that name of yours, it would be blasphemous for any Aussies or wannabe Aussies to reject you. Plus, you managed to step on another Aussie to get ahead."

Freddie appeared from behind Humphrey. "What a prick. I knew it when I hired him."

"Convicts never change," Humphrey said.

"Digger, I can offer you evening shifts from Wednesday to Saturday. Cash for the first month while I test you out. If you do well and want to stay, we can get you the right papers. We can make a case for you, because being Australian means you're specially skilled to work here." He turned to Humphrey. "Thanks, mate, for bringing him in."

"Do I get a commission? You know, a finder's fee?"

Freddie laughed loudly, slapped Humphrey on the shoulder and then walked away. He could still be heard laughing when he was in kitchen.

"Weird old coot," Darius said.

"Your boss now."

"Thanks for that. Easy."

"Now, we're square. For Woodlow. But be careful. He may talk like an Aussie but he's German to the core. Be honest, keep everything on the table and try to ignore his bizarre sense of humour. Just work hard, speak in that thick accent of yours and become another of the authentic attractions."

"You were joking earlier, about this place looking like an Aussie pub?"

"Freddie believed me. But I'm starting to doubt he's ever set foot in Oz. He knows too many lines from *Crocodile Dundee*. He probably learned everything from watching TV, which is pretty scary when you think about it. He probably thinks kangaroos are part of the police force and that the only way to see a doctor is to fly him in."

"Aussie pubs are nothing like this."

"I love it. Look at the Aboriginal artwork, the stuffed crocodile that's actually an alligator from Florida, all those stupid yellow animal road signs made in Taiwan. It's a living, breathing stereotype. Look at it, Darius. This is what the world thinks of us. When people meet Aussies or when they think about Oz, this is what comes to their minds. They expect this. I knew, even before I came in here, it would look like this."

"Maybe some if it's true."

"Some, yes. But I wonder how they would like it if they knew a few other truths. Two centuries of racism, a country with no culture, intellectuals the common man's enemy. There's an Australian restaurant I'd like to see."

132

"How many beers have you had?"

"Too many. But I'm still lucid. I want that Aussie pub, Darius. Tell the world how we really are. White Australia Policy, Stolen Generations, Truganini, Bennelong, mining sacred land, nuclear testing, refugee camps, convicts buggering animals and each other." He took a breath. "Gallipoli, Vietnam, Alan Bond, One Nation, Anzac myth, Gough Whitlam, and all this lucky country bullshit. No bloody boomerangs and didgeridoo muzak. No stereotypes. A restaurant that tells the truth."

"You're a blast when you're drunk. I forgot that. Go on. What's on the menu?"

"No bloody kangaroo steaks, that's for sure." Humphrey turned to the people who were listening nearby. "We make it into dog food, you know." He turned back to Darius. "No, we need real Aussie tucker. Tough chops and gritty mutton that has to be tenderised for a week before it can be eaten. You know, beating it with one of those spiky mallets first. Bacon swimming in lard, soggy frozen vegetables zapped in microwaves, bread full of air, coleslaws drowning in cheap mayonnaise. And don't forget all that glorious seafood forgotten at the bottom of the freezer that tastes like paper when it's finally defrosted and cooked, and the fish so full of bones you almost choke to death."

Darius laughed.

"You could make up names for it all, too. Like Convict Stew, which has the worst parts of all the leftover meat in the fridge. Or, or Ned Kelly Soup, a potato brew served in a steel bowl that has a few dents from bullets. Better than that, you could use all those names mums came up with for meals made from whatever was left. We had one called tub grub. Mum made it in this massive pot that looked like a bath tub. She even said she washed us in it when we were babies. 'Added to the spice,' she used to say. She just threw everything in it, cooked it for hours, and for some weird reason, it tasted great. We'd eat if for a week and it got better with every reheat."

"I reckon you're onto somethin'."

"Oh, God no. No one in the world would go to a restaurant like that. And there would be a national outcry in Oz. The government and all those patriotic mates would try to close it down or blow it up. Australia First, Sons of Anzacs, One Nation, they'll send people over to torch the place." He looked around the restaurant. "No, no. This is who we are. This is what the world thinks of us, and this is who we want to be."

"I guess we're stuck with fake boomerangs and kangaroo burgers," Darius said, going back to his cleaning.

"Probably for the best," Humphrey said. "I think you better give me a black coffee. German beer, Digger, it's powerful stuff."

***

A month passed. The spring was warm. Darius had never seen plants and trees burst to life like they did in Munich. One day there was nothing, and the next day the city was green.

Freddie made no mention of contracts or permits and Darius didn't ask. He was making more than enough working for cash; the Germans were great tippers. He needed most of it to cover his rent. The three room apartment he moved into with two other students was expensive, but it was the cheapest room he could find. He sent a postcard to his gran, giving his new address and telephone number. She had never responded to the card he sent from Woodlow and he doubted she would reply to this one, but word would trickle down. And while he hadn't left on the best of terms with his dad, he didn't want to cause him any worry. He wrote that he was happy in Munich, he was well and things were going great. It was superficial, but it was something.

Life quickly fell into a rhythm. Humphrey worked, and lived, at the hostel. He had talked his boss into working the evening shift so he and Darius could enjoy Munich in the mornings. More than once, over breakfast in one of the cafés that fanned out from Marienplatz, Humphrey mused that it was great to be in Europe and to have the time to appreciate it, without having to rush from city to city like it was a race, the way the backpackers staying in the hostel did. When they both had a day off, they took day trips: Dachau, Schloss Neuschwanstein, Salzburg, Innsbruck and Nuremberg. They also took the train down to Italy for a couple of days in Venice. On a working day, they would start with a long breakfast, read the British papers and watch the world go by. Spring had the city alive with blossoms and greenery, and the warm days brought girls out in shorts and skirts. Darius was greatly impressed by the array of fine legs.

Yes, it was a great life. Every day started with promise, if not with a trip to some amazing place nearby then with a relaxing, lazy breakfast. It seemed they had all the time in the world to eat their rolls and drink their coffee. After a month of this, Darius noted that he and Humphrey knew each other so well, they didn't need to speak any more. It was comfortable to sit together in silence and just look around. Of course, most days ended with hard work, but Humphrey normally came to the Hole after finishing at the hostel and this would make things more interesting. He always sat at the bar, trying to read the restaurant's copy of the *Sueddeutsche Zeitung*. Darius had to admit that Humphrey was getting quite good at German. It was always Humphrey who did the talking when buying train tickets or ordering in a café. Darius thought the language was just too complicated; it didn't even sound like there were gaps between the words.

It was on evening such as this, with Humphrey reading at the bar and Darius pouring drinks, that a girl walked in and headed straight for the bar. She spoke in German, what sounded like a question.

"*Sprechen Sie Englisch*?" Darius asked.

"Should've known you'd be an Aussie," she replied, smiling in a way that revealed her front teeth, which were wide and prominent, like a rabbit's.

She was an interesting looking girl, not beautiful, but striking and different. Her blonde hair darkened at the roots and her pale skin made the dusting of freckles across her nose stand out more. She had a large stud in her nose and a ring in her left eyebrow, while the long chain of earrings in her left ear glittered in the light. She was dressed all in black, but wore a bright pink scarf looped once around her neck.

"I'm from Australia, not East Germany."

"Don't believe him," Humphrey said from behind his paper. "I helped him escape back in '88. Folded him into a suitcase and smuggled him across the border. Taught him Strine too. Convincing accent, isn't it?"

"About as convincing as you trying to read that paper."

Humphrey lowered his broadsheet and looked at her. Darius watched as his friend made all those judgements he was apt to make, "trusting his instincts," he claimed. His eyes narrowed as he took in the bleached hair, the jewellery, the accessories, the effort she had put in.

"*Steuerunbedenktlichkeitsbescheinigung,*" Humphrey read. "Any idea what that means?"

She took a seat at the bar, one stool away from Humphrey, and shrugged. "Something with tax. A kind of declaration? I dunno. I'm a history student. I was supposed to meet some other students here." She turned to Darius and smiled, showing those rabbit teeth. "Has there been a rowdy bunch of Brits and Yanks in here? My name's Jane. Maybe there's a note for me."

"Fraid not."

"Probably at one of the Irish pubs," Humphrey said, again from behind the paper. "Going for genuine Irish spirit over contrived Aussie atmosphere."

"Probably. They don't have much imagination."

Humphrey lowered his paper and looked at her again, differently from before. His face was friendlier, not as harsh or judging.

"Oh, barkeep," he said to Darius, "give Miss Jane here the beverage of her choice."

"Now you're talking. I'll have a *Weissbier.* And no Mr Squiggle jokes."

Humphrey laughed. "I bet you get that a lot. Oooh, Miss Jane, Miss Jane."

"I was thinking more *Sweet Jane,*" Darius said, pouring the beer. "You know, Lou Reed."

Humphrey shook his head. "Christ almighty, you're just full of surprises."

"I listened to some of your tapes. When I stayed with Les."

"He's still trying to sell our house. My room, Darius. My beautiful murals."

Darius poured the beer and slid it across the bar. "God awful," he said to Jane. "Like a hundred drunks vomited on the wall."

She raised the glass and knocked the head off it. "It's nice to meet some fellow Aussies. Where you guys from?"

Humphrey had put his paper down, had even tidied it up a little, but as always, he let Darius answer this question.

"WA. Hobo's from Esperance and I'm from over Wagin way."

"I've never heard of those places. Near Perth?"

"Near enough," Humphrey said. Darius recognised the glint in his friend's eyes, again saw the thoughts being processed, the judgements passed. It was unfair that Humphrey did this, summed up people so quickly. Humphrey was the first to admit that he was cruel for doing it and often apologised afterwards, but Darius couldn't ignore that when it came to deciphering people's personalities and characters, his friend was seldom wrong.

"Big state," Jane said.

Humphrey propped an elbow on the bar and cupped the side of his face in his left hand. "May I guess where you're from?"

Jane sneered. To Darius, it seemed she was trying to act cheeky, but there was a menace in her sneer that made her look suspicious. Strangely, the sneer made him homesick.

"Think you're so clever?"

To her surprise, Humphrey grinned confidently. "I do. I am."

"If you're such a smart arse, I'll pay for your drinks if you get it right."

"Careful," Darius said, recalling how Humphrey had played the same game with Rod and how it had started all of their problems with each other. Humphrey had even pinpointed the Sydney suburb, Maroubra, where Rod had grown up. "He's good at this. He pulled this on some Aussies in Canada."

"Those idiots shoudn't tattoo their fucking postcode on their arms."

Jane took a drink. "I'll take my chances."

Darius leaned on the bar, awaiting Humphrey's delivery with a mix of excitement and fear. Humphrey would be harsh and Jane would surely take offence, but that would only increase his own chances with her.

Humphrey cleared his throat loudly. "Well, Miss Jane, let me say off the bat that I've been all over Oz, several times, and I spent extended periods in all of the major cities, so I know my stuff. Still wanna bet?"

Jane nodded. "You'll never get it."

"Okay, uh, well, as you don't know where Esperance is, that rules out WA, probably SA too, because Esperance isn't far from the border. A lot of Croweaters spend their holidays in the big E. It probably makes you a city girl who hasn't seen much of Australia. Country people make it a

137

habit of knowing places as obscure as their own, and they know other farming areas, like where Darius comes from. I know, it's ridiculous, but some sheep farmer in rural New South Wales knows where Wagin is. So, city girl. That makes it pretty easy. Just a toss up between Sydney and Melbourne. Brisbane could be an outside chance, and I might be wrong, but I'm getting a whiff of Canberra, a city girl tainted with provincialism. No. No. You've got that kind of false superiority from growing up in a big, important city and Canberra's not that. A sun tan is high fashion in Sydney which could rule it out, Brisbane too. You also strike me as being too smart to waste years and months at the beach. Melbourne's not exactly famous for beaches. Hmm, Melbourne. Maybe. Great city. I spent a couple of months there working at a fish and chip shop in Toorak. Something Fishy it's called, on Toorak Road. You know it? Don't answer. Your authentic alternative appearance looks like it's out of the Triple J handbook, and, forgive me if I'm wrong, but you look European, maybe south European, Greek, Italian or Slav roots. Your surname would give you away, but I don't need that. You're also here, in Germany, studying history, one of the least useful degrees, and that means your parents must be relatively open-minded and not focused only on McMansions, mortgages and Holdens. Sydney's a real estate melting pot, fucking location-location, but Melbourne's not all like that. Life has a lot more elements there. Yeah, the Victorian capital, maybe one of the footy suburbs. Collingwood, Carlton or Fitzroy. Somewhere in there. Lucky girl."

"Yeah?"

"Very lucky. Luckier than me, that's for sure. Melbourne's got more substance than any other place in Oz. I reckon it's the one city that actually goes beneath the surface. Take us, Janey. We never grew up seeing different kinds of people or hearing different languages. Darius here probably didn't even eat Chinese food until he went to Canada. But you grew up in Melbourne and that makes you a lot more cultured than us backward country hicks. It could also explain why I like you, a bit, already. I struggle with people from Sydney. Dunno why. They think they're so superior, like their city is so fucking great so they are too. No, it's cockroach town, with sewage beaches. The Bondi ashtray. Sorry. Maybe it's the Sandgroper in me. Can't stand the Sydney Swans."

Jane took a drink. Lost in her thoughts and slightly stunned, she burped softly. Darius smiled, thinking it rather sweet. He liked natural women who didn't try to put on all those feminine airs. If they were a little rough around the edges, a little weird, then all the better; hairy and unclean was taking it too far.

"Sweet Jane, I'll take your silence as the soundlessness of victory." Humphrey folded the sections of the newspaper together. He stood up. "I'll see you for breakfast tomorrow, Digger. Make sure she gets my bill."

Then he was off, strutting towards the door and giving Freddie a high-five on the way out.

Darius laughed. "He's insane. Sorry for that. He's a really top bloke when you get to know him." She was looking at him now and her pale face softened. "He likes Melbourne. He doesn't mean anything bad by it. No offence meant, really."

"It's a great city."

"You miss it?" he asked, but someone stepped up to the bar. "Don't go away."

While pouring the beer, he kept looking from the sides of his eyes to be sure she was still there. She saw him looking and smiled into her glass. It was a very attractive smile and it caused him to lose concentration. The beer flowed over the glass and onto his hands. She laughed. He did too, thinking it might bring them closer together. He served the beer and walked back to her end of the bar.

"First day?"

"Reckon it might look that way."

"How long've you been here?"

"A month. What about you?"

"Almost a year. I'm on exchange at uni."

Darius made a clucking sound with his tongue. "Must be hard cause of the language."

"I'm getting by, but I'm a bit sick of it here. The winter's so depressing."

Darius smiled thinly, trying to empathise with her homesickness, but he thought she sounded a bit too sour. She had chosen to come here and now could only say bad things about it. If she wasn't enjoying it, then why not go home?

"But you had a white Christmas," he said, remembering that magical evening sitting on the porch in Woodlow. "That's pretty special."

"Sure, but my family's on the other side of the planet. They wanted to come over, but the flights were too expensive."

139

Her expression, drifting between sadness and disappointment, made Darius wonder if she had come to Munich with high expectations only to have none of them fulfilled. He tried to think of something witty to say, something that would lift her spirits, the kind of thing Humphrey would say that would impress her, make her feel better and make her interested in him. But he could think of nothing and so said nothing. When a customer came to the bar, he was thankful to gain some reprieve.

"Back in a flash." But he took his time pouring the beer, even chatted a little with the customer, answering some questions about Australia and then giving the price in German.

"So, you've learned a couple of words," Jane said when Darius was back in front of her.

"Not enough for university."

"What did you study?"

"Not German, that's for sure."

"If you want, I could teach you some words and sentences. Stuff that'll help you get by."

"Sounds great. When?"

"How about breakfast tomorrow?"

"I'm in. Where?"

"Let's meet at Marienplatz. I know a good place around the corner, but it's too hard to explain how to get there."

"Great."

She stood up. "How much do I owe you for Bozo's drinks?"

Darius waved her off. "Forget it. I owe him money anyway."

"Thanks. See you tomorrow."

Darius tried to look at her legs as she walked for the door, but it was dark in the restaurant and the black pants she wore gave nothing away.

"You got rid of Hobo pretty fast," Freddie said, walking past the bar. "Was he cramping your style?"

Darius felt himself blushing. Then he remembered. Bozo.

"He'll understand," he said to himself.

***

"I don't know what you see in her," Humphrey said from behind his broadsheet.

"Maybe you should give her a chance. Hell, maybe you should give everyone a chance."

"You've been going out for two weeks and already you take her side. I guess she's been badmouthing me because of what I said."

"She keeps asking me why you don't give her a chance. She's not perfect, but no one is. Let it go."

"Come on, Darius. I'd expect you to know better than to shack up with some Aussie chick. Take a look around you. This country's bursting with independent girls who'd have Miss Jane for lunch, and as an appetiser."

"I don't see too many of them hangin round you."

"That's my choice. I'm not in the mood for females at the moment. Sometimes it's nice to be single. Those chicks in Canada wore me out. Anyway, I'd rather be single than caught by the short and curlies by a girl who wants to control me and change my opinions, and my hairstyle."

Darius ran a hand self-consciously through his blonde streaks. "It's not like that at all."

"It sure looks like it is."

"You want another beer or what?"

"Such service. When's Miss Jane due?"

"Can you stop calling her that? She hates it."

"That's part of the problem. No sense of humour. If she had the right attitude, we could have a massive laugh together. I've already got the jokes lined up. Am I the only one who thinks Mr Squiggle is one dirty scene from being porn? That pencil nose, looks like a giant dildo. There you go. Mr Squildo and Miss Jane."

Darius laughed, but stopped himself.

"See? You've got a sense of humour."

"She finds different things funny. Not like us, that much."

"She coming in tonight?"

"Are you gonna leave then? Why can't you just accept the way she is and try to like her?"

"I would accept her, if she actually was the way she really is and not pretending to be someone else."

"Everyone pretends, Hobo. You saw me in Woodlow." His honesty surprised him and it was a bitter reminder how he couldn't speak so freely with Jane.

Humphrey waggled a finger. "You weren't acting. I remember you weren't exactly talkative when we met either. Now we know each other better you talk a lot more. And keeping silent is a little different to dressing yourself up and decorating yourself in order to convince the world you are a certain way. I think Jane's alternative, independent presentation is all smoke and mirrors."

"Ya can't say someone's fake just cause they've got an earring or two."

"No, but I'm looking at the whole package. She might be dolled up like some brazen girl ready to take it from the whole footy team, but under all that makeup and all those accessories, she's just an insecure little Aussie girl looking for a man she can wrap around her finger."

"You are so wrong."

"Look, I'm sorry, Darius. Let me level with you. I don't give her a chance because I'm not here to meet Australians. I want us to mingle with the locals. Broaden our horizons a little, like we did in Canada."

"Yeah, that was good. But I like Jane."

"Sleep with her yet?"

Darius looked down at the bar.

"That's a no."

"Come on, Hobo, we can't talk about that here."

"That never stopped you in the Pab."

"That was different."

"You know, by not answering, you're answering."

Darius leaned across the bar. Right then, he hated his best friend, hated it that he was always right, always had to be right, and was so confident about it, he never even took any satisfaction from being right.

"She wants to get to know me better."

"You're definitely worth knowing. I've enjoyed getting to know you better. But I think Miss Jane is looking a bit further into the future than me. Maybe she's already mentally picturing how your kids will look and what kind of house you'll live in and what car's in the drive and at whose family you'll spend Christmas. Sorry, Darius, but it's not her fault. Our society conditions a lot of girls to be that way. Maybe it's changing. I hope so. But it was like that where I grew

142

up. And I'll tell you another thing. All those earrings will disappear once she's married and pregnant."

"Mate, let it go. Stop bein so negative."

Humphrey stood up. "I'll think I'll take that as my cue to exit, stage right. I'll take solitude over generic, unquestioning people any day. Hope you get your leg over. But I bet the farm you won't."

He turned and walked towards the door.

"Hobo, wait a minute," Darius shouted, but his friend was already outside. Darius could see him through the windows walking down the street with his head held high.

Freddie came behind the bar and stood next to Darius, standing close. "Everything all right?"

"Yeah." He went to the sink to clean some glasses, to look busy. It was what he had always wanted, to speak freely and say what he really felt, but look where it had got him. Humphrey always demanded truth and honesty, but couldn't handle it himself.

"He's just jealous," Freddie said.

"Of what?"

"Your girlfriend, mate."

"She's not really my girlfriend. We just hang out."

He wanted then to end the relationship, such as it was. Jane was moody, often seemed bored with him, and she was always late. Worst of all, he got nowhere with her, no matter how many drinks and dinners he bought, no matter how much praise he lavished on her. He had tried, in the chaste domain of her student room where the walls were so thin he could hear mouse clicks coming from adjacent rooms, to put his hand between her legs while they kissed. But she had pushed him away, delicately. He was sick of being towed along, of not having a clear idea where he stood and what she really felt.

"Well, Digger, you better make up your mind. Here she comes."

She came towards the bar with jumpy, excited steps as if just keeping herself from skipping like a child. She wore a knee length denim skirt covered in outlandish patches and, rather daringly, a black pullover with a Carlton jumper over the top. It was the first time he had seen her in a skirt. Before she propped herself on a stool, he spied her legs, seeing creamy shins and shapely calves flaunting themselves below the ragged hem.

"Have a win?" Freddie asked.

143

Jane put her small fists in the air, making people look at her. "The flag'll be ours this year."

Darius smiled thinly but kept his distance, still hunched over the sink.

"Don't I get a kiss?" she asked.

Darius hesitated, feeling Freddie's eyes, feeling like the whole world was watching him, judging. He even looked at the windows to see if Humphrey was watching from outside. He moved slowly along the bar, his hands still wet, and leaned across it to kiss his so-called girlfriend. To his surprise, she opened her mouth, something she rarely did, and he felt the warm stud in her tongue run along the roof of his mouth.

When he pulled back, Freddie said, drifting away, "You two look good together."

"I listened to it on the internet and dad called after the game. He was there. God, I miss the footy. We always go, you know, my dad and me, ever since I was a kid. I can't wait until we're all in Melbourne. You'll really like my dad."

"Sounds great."

She had once mentioned going to Melbourne together, dropping it into the conversation and then jumping quickly to something else, but now she talked like they had their flights booked. He wondered if tonight maybe the night he plays Mr Squildo to her Miss Jane, to use Humphrey's analogy. He laughed a little.

"There'll be plenty of games left for us to see," she went on, "and then there's the finals too."

He looked at her. She was sitting back from the bar a little, her legs crossed so that an attractive pair of knees, like two big scoops of vanilla ice cream, rose above the denim. He wanted to stroke them, to feel the shape of her knee caps, and then run his fingers up the insides of her thighs. She saw him looking a pulled the hem of her skirt down.

"We could go to the travel agent tomorrow and ask for flights." Yes, he really wanted to know what she looked like naked and if she would be as uninhibited as he believed. "There's a good one near my apartment."

"How late are they open?" she asked.

Darius was about to reply when Florian burst through the door and ran up to the bar.

"Hey, Flo. What's up?"

"Digger, you won't believe it. Your grandmother called. There was an accident."

"What?"

"Your father's in a coma."

Darius felt his mouth go dry. "No."

"I came so fast as I could. I tried to call here but someone was on the phone. You should get yourself a handy like I told you to."

His knees felt weak and the room began to spin, like all the blood was draining from his head. Someone came up to the bar and ordered a beer. He moved from behind the bar and found Freddie in the kitchen. He explained the situation and Freddie was sympathetic.

"Go," Freddie said. "We'll be here when you come back."

Then he was running through the restaurant, weaving between the tables and knocking empty chairs over.

"Where are you going?" Jane called out, stopping him with the door half open. The whole restaurant went silent.

She stood in front of the bar, her white shins gleaming, the Carlton jumper hugging her chest and narrowing at the waist. She was an attractive girl, but looking at her then, his life flashed before him.

Together in Melbourne, the university educated girl and the country boy. Hard to win the approval of her friends and parents, but Jane would be on his side, would sow seeds of mutual understanding. A big wedding, with distant relatives and long-forgotten friends, all from Jane's side. A mandatory two or three kids, early on, to keep up with her friends and to keep people from thinking their marriage a failure. A house in the suburbs, mortgage counter-signed by Jane's dad. Working like a dog because Jane wanted to stay home with the kids. Maybe borrowing money from his father-in-law to open a bar in Carlton. Football every weekend, with Carlton fans regulars at his bar. The football season ruling their lives, the quality of their marriage hinging on wins and losses, perhaps even getting broken down to percentage points, injuries and potential draft picks. The bar doing well. A bigger house. Jane wanting the kids to go to private schools. Not much money left for holidays. Not much time to spend together. Jane looking old fast, all the rings gone. Not fucking for months, maybe years. Jane never really satisfied with him, despite everything he provides. Jane always wanting more, maybe even fucking around.

His bar a good excuse to stay away from home, work late and come home when everyone is asleep. Keeping up appearances, a happy family at barbecues and football games. Arguing a lot as their kids become teenagers. Divorce. Staying in Melbourne for the kids, but then Jane marries a son of one of her dad's mates and he never gets to see the kids as much as he wants. Then they're grown up and gone anyway.

Time would pass until one day he would wake up and wonder what had happened to his life.

He looked at her, wanting to say something, to explain. "I'm sorry, Jane. I gotta go. He's my dad."

He pushed open the door and ran as fast as he could through the cold spring evening. Too cold for wearing a short skirt, he thought.

Lewis: But a tragedy interrupted your life in Germany.

Poet: Yeah.

Lewis: How did it feel to see your father, your hero and mentor, lying on a hospital bed?

Poet: Hard. I thought he was indestructible, you know, that he'd live forever. I couldn't imagine the world without him.

Lewis: The poem *Dad's Bush Burial* is a remarkable piece. "In a wool-lined casket, tailor-made, there lies the old bastard, face unmade. Ten feet under, in gold-dust dirt, laying crooked, asunder, in his same old shirt."

Poet: That doesn't really capture the hurt.

Lewis: It's still very touching.

Poet: That's the first poem I wrote.

Lewis: For the funeral?

Poet: I still can't believe he's gone.

Lewis: He's gone but he remains a great inspiration to you.

Poet: He was the greatest bloody bloke I ever knew.

~~~

In the Shed

The coffee machine was out of order. There was a machine in the children's ward that always worked, the skinny nurse explained. Her smile when relaying this information was sympathetic yet wan; a withered, anorexic attempt at motherly comfort. The nurses all knew his plight, all sympathised, and doled out condolences and grave, supportive smiles accordingly. This nurse, in a starched uniform that was flat and cornered without curves, slipped a skeletal claw into her front pocket and tried to smile warmly as she handed him a small chocolate egg.

"Thanks."

It dissolved into a sweet mess in his mouth as he walked down the crowded hall, his jetlagged eyes as sticky as the egg.

Easter holidays meant high season for Royal Perth. His dad wasn't the only accident victim transported in. The intensive care station didn't have an empty bed and even the hallways were full, making him slalom to get through the small gaps between beds, wheelchairs, gaggles of nurses and small clusters of distraught family members still wearing their holiday clothes, still smelling of sunscreen. These people drifted apart to let him through and then clung back together again. He heard crying, confusion, snippets of conversations that tried to put tragedy into words, long declarations of innocence and victimisation; always someone else was to blame. But listening closer, he also heard a disquieting satisfaction, a subtle glee, from a selected few who harboured secret joy at finally bidding this old bugger or that old broad farewell.

He was glad to be freed, momentarily, from all those stoic and sympathetic visitors who had driven up to deliver their mandatory phrases of optimism. They came with the best intentions, mates to the core, but they seldom stayed longer than the time it took to put flowers in a vase, find a place for the card – signed in all corners by members of the extended family, saving a few the trip – on the already full bedside table, and deliver their lines, looking down at their hands as if reading from palm cards. Their mission complete, their attendance duly recorded, they then claimed they had "business in Perth" and had to get going. He hated having to receive these visitors, to shake their hands and hear their condolences, to listen to them talk about his dad with such intimacy and potency when really they knew nothing about the man.

The visitors made no difference. His dad lay motionless on the bed, wired to a wall of machinery that sucked and pumped and beeped. His eyes were closed and his face expressionless, the first time Darius had ever seen his dad's face that way. The character drops only when he's in a coma, he thought. But the visitors came anyway, felt obliged to, surely well aware that his dad would do the same for them. The nurses made sure the room was never too crowded, so everyone had enough space to twist and turn and say their lines. Their grief seemed vaguely genuine even if the complimentary phrases were well-worn and generic. Handkerchiefs that wiped away single tears were perhaps not just moistened from the taps in the toilets, while the women dabbed at their tears with theatrical accuracy to keep their make-up from running.

Still, he was moved by these visitors, by their sentiment, real or not. His dad was dying. There was nothing the doctors could do, so they said, except wait and hope for the best. An Easter miracle, Darius thought, with his dad rising from the dead three days after the crash.

In the busy children's ward, he joined the small circle worshipping one of the hospital's few working coffee machines. The plastic coffee cup was barely firm enough for him to hold in his hands without crushing it. He had to hold it delicately, in the tips of his fingers, and his dainty sipping was far too feminine for his liking. But all the men around him, gritty middle-aged dads with tanned faces and big hands, were drinking their coffees the same way, so no one could single another out for sipping like a girl. Still, they avoided each others' eyes, unwilling to share their respective situations, but glad to be able to stand in this tight circle, united by tragedy and testosterone, by big hands clutching small plastic cups. They shared nods and made small talk. For something to look at, rather than at each other, they all stared at the television that hung from just below the ceiling. The evening news was on, the sound turned up loud. The first report was about the Easter road fatalities, the numbers called out with such fervency, and listened to so attentively, it reminded Darius of a lotto draw. The dead were tallied state by state and city by city with nearly every accident having happened in the country. There was footage of cars wrapped around trees and mangled white utes splattered with blood. The camera panned to the grieving families and stunned witnesses standing nearby. Then came the photos of the victims as the reporter delivered a heart wrenching story of "a life of such promise cut tragically short," of someone who "gave more to his family and community than he took."

Or something like that, because Darius wasn't really listening. He was wondering if his dad would be shocked to learn, if he woke up, that his crash hadn't made the news. He hadn't died, meaning a new number couldn't be shouted out. But what if he had? With microphones and cameras thrust in front of him, could Darius speak with such pride about Jack Tucker, say so sadly and dramatically that he had lost his best mate as well as his dad? Decorum dictated he would, and he knew, thrust into the spotlight, he would deliver the kind of convincing performance that would make his dad proud. And there would be some truth in it, because he already missed the old bugger, didn't want him to die, despite everything.

The group of men turned away from the television to look at the commotion coming down the hall. A bed was being quickly wheeled into the ward and on it was a young boy covered in blood stained bandages. Though small, the nurses were struggling to hold the boy down. His face was covered with scratches and his eyes were wide with fear and shock. The parents followed close behind but were stopped at the door while the bed passed through. The doctor had to almost tackle the boy's mother to keep her back.

"Lemme go," she shouted. "That's my Haydon in there."

Everyone watched, waiting for the doctor to reply and to see if the mother would become hysterical. She looked like she was going in that direction and she was already very red in the face. The doctor held her in a hard embrace, though she outweighed him by ten kilos at least, and then passed her to the short, squat man who Darius guessed was the father. But he seemed reluctant to take the woman in his arms. He did lean close, though, put a hand on her shoulder, not very intimately, and brushed away a few permed, bleached locks to whisper consoling words in her ear. Or perhaps to get their stories straight, Darius thought, watching the two policemen approach.

"Excuse me, Mr McLean," the officer with the clipboard said, pen at the ready. The whole room was listening and someone had even turned down the television, thinking live entertainment more diverting and real. "What kind of dog was it that attacked your son?"

McLean sniffed at the air. He let go of the mother's shoulder and she fell exhausted into a chair. A middle-aged busy-body came over to comfort her.

"A pit bull." McLean wiped his forehead with his sleeve as the officer made a note. Darius saw that McLean had a few drops of blood on his hands as well as some red scratches that had already clotted. "Completely placid," he added. "Never harmed a fly. Him and Haydon went everywhere together."

The officer made another note, moving the pen slowly, carving the words into stone. "Where's the dog now?"

"At me mum's."

The officers exchanged a glance.

"You'll put him down over my dead body," McLean said roughly.

The officer made another note, turning the page over. McLean took the chance to get himself a cup of coffee. He held it daintily, his hand shaking slightly.

"We need the address," the officer said. "We'll have to impound the dog."

McLean shook his head, as if he himself were to be impounded. "Like hell ya will."

"Just let them take the bloody dog, Shane," the woman shouted. "We'll get him back."

Darius dropped his empty plastic cup into the garbage and walked back down the crowded halls to intensive care. He thought about Bladders. As Murray had told it, Grant Stevenson had found the dog whimpering next to the wrecked ute. He had seen the car from the road, the ute upside down and wedged between two trees, the wheels still spinning, the red tail lights bright in the grey shadows of dawn. Frightened by Grant, Bladders had tried to run away, but couldn't get very far with one leg broken. Grant knew better than to move Darius's dad and called an ambulance on his CB. They cut him out and airlifted him to Royal Perth. Stuck in terminals on two continents, Darius had arrived two days after the accident, and had been forced to hear the story told second, third and even fourth hand.

And by day three, Easter Sunday, there had been no resurrection. From what he could gather from the visitors, the events leading up to the accident were sketchy. Drinking at the pub, yes, they had all said that, his dad in his usual high spirits. But the longer the evening goes on, the more the versions differ. Some said he left before midnight. Others said they saw him speaking with a woman: a school teacher from Wagin, Bill Lawford claimed. No, Trev Notts said, it was the widow of young Troy Mackie who died two years ago in that accident down near Boddington. But one thing they all agreed on, after Darius had asked them, was that his dad must've hit a roo, as it had been with the Troy Mackie and the two Barker brothers last Christmas.

Back in his dad's room, he wasn't surprised to see his gran sitting next to the bed, on time for her evening visit, which after just a few days had become part of her daily activities. She had even said to Darius that there were others from Eternal Sunset who were visiting loved ones at Royal Perth and they had coordinated themselves to share a taxi to the hospital and back twice a day.

"Hello, Darius," she said not getting up. She was made up as usual and her sickly perfume filled the room. It was so strong, Darius wondered whether it might pull his dad back from the land of the unconscious; surely this perfume could wake the dead. "Did that doctor say anything new, or at least anything comprehensible? Where is he anyway? I've already been waiting five minutes."

"Dunno."

"We really should get another doctor. I can't understand a word he says." She lowered her voice. "If they can't speak English, they shouldn't let those people in."

"They say he's the best. I understand him perfectly well."

"Hmpf. He doesn't even look old enough to drink. Probably just off the boat, with a forged degree and all."

"A nurse told me he went to UWA."

She shook her coiffed head. "I still don't trust him. They're planning to take us over. They couldn't beat us in the war so now they're trying to out-populate us. Your grandfather fought in the war, you know."

"He's as Aussie as you and me."

He wanted to argue more, to defend the doctor who had already proven himself apt and who was very much Australian, but he knew it was useless. He thought of Loo and frowned, understanding now a bit more about the problems and prejudices she faced every day of her life. How many Gladys Tuckers had snarled at her, wishing she would go back to that place they called Asia – like it was one country – and never even giving her a chance? Part of him wanted to see his gran lying on the bed connected to all those machines; then she would die and take all her prejudices and hatred with her.

"If my Jack dies," she said, "we'll know who to blame."

"He's not gonna die." Darius would have liked his dad to live just to prove to her that Doctor Xuan was a good doctor and deserved respect. But another part of him took more than a little satisfaction from seeing the old bastard so helpless and weak, put there by his own failings and mistakes and not by a roo or a big pothole. It was a terrible thought, he knew, but seeing his dad immovable, connected to so many machines and unable to cause him any damage or harm, strengthened him. This powerful, dominating man lying on this bed of cotton and wire, he couldn't abuse Darius from there, couldn't tower over him and make him feel second rate and useless, couldn't cut down his dreams or destroy his hopes.

His gran started to cry softly, almost sociably. "I hope you're right." She dabbed at her eyes carefully with a yellow handkerchief. "He's a tough man, my Jack. If anyone can survive a crash like that it's him. He'll walk again too."

And the way she looked at Darius, with the slight raise of her eyebrows and the questioning frown, he was convinced she didn't think he himself was so tough.

"Don't worry, gran. He'll pull through."

But just then, he wanted his dad to die, to prove to his gran and to all those false pilgrims who had journeyed up from the south that Jack Tucker wasn't nearly as tough as everyone thought. He was human, like all of them, with failings and imperfections, and from there, all the lies would unravel and the legend would be tarnished forever.

Darius turned as Doctor Xuan entered the room.

"You asked to see me, Mrs Tucker?"

She waved him off with a wrinkled, purple-veined hand, not even looking at him. "My grandson's told me everything there is to know. It's quite clear there's nothing you can do."

"Yes, well, there's something you can do. The outlook's not good, we know that, but you should talk to him. Let him know you're here, that you care about him and want him to wake up."

She didn't reply and kept looking at the bed-ridden figure, her back turned to the doctor.

"Thanks," Darius said. The doctor nodded politely and left the room.

"Don't listen to any of that eastern rubbish. My Jack just needs some time to get his strength back." She looked at her watch and stood up. "Well, must be off." She gave Darius a perfume-laced hug. "Call if he wakes up."

She bustled heavily from the room, but her flowery smell remained. Darius fell into the chair next to his dad's bed.

Talk to him, the doctor had said. Make him want to come back. Probably the best way, Darius thought, would be to provoke him, get his anger up.

"Gran's a racist."

He eyed his dad's face for a reaction, the slight shudder of an eyelid or a twitch at the corner of the mouth. Nothing.

"You are too. You were wrong about a lot of things, dad. Okay, you were right about some things. But why did you always care more about your mates in town than about me?"

He watched the frozen figure, wanting movement, wanting the bastard to wake up so he could confront him.

"I know you act with them. Fuck me if I don't do it to. I tried to stop that, you know, in Munich. Just tried to be myself, but I met this girl. Jane. Miss Jane. And I fell right back into my old role. Like putting on old shoes. Guess that's over now. Thanks for crashing and making me come back."

He sniffed.

"No crying allowed."

He swallowed hard. For distraction, to keep it together, he looked at the table covered with cards and gifts.

"They don't know it, but I do. Wait. Maybe they do know it, but just go along with it. You're a fake, dad. How could you keep it up for so long? I mean, I've tried it, but it's impossible to keep track of the lies. I was in Woodlow, dad, pretending to be this strong, silent type. Ya typical stoic Aussie. Hah. I went to bed every night exhausted. It was that hard to keep it going."

It felt good to talk, to talk freely in a way he had never talked with

154

his dad. He talked like this with Humphrey. He missed his friend, and Munich, the life they had there.

"I'm living in Germany at the moment, dad. It's great. You were totally wrong about the Germans. Really good people. Straight up, honest and fair. Not like us."

He sat back and folded his arms.

"Why didn't we ever talk like this? Anytime it got hard or personal, you left the room. You can't leave now, and you can't shout me down. Thanks for listening, dad. I hope I'm getting through to you. The doc says you don't have much of a chance, but hold on. You can't die. What am I gonna say when you're dead? Fuck me, dad, I don't know anything about you. I know stories, all those anecdotes. I know what other people say about you, but I know nothing about you. Who the fuck are you really?"

And there it was. The man on the bed was a stranger, a composite being, and that was why he didn't feel as much as he should. They were linked by blood, had spent their lives together, but nothing went below the surface.

Thirsty from talking, he left the room and took a drink from the water cooler. He checked his watch, surprised to see how long he had talked, how long he had sat there staring, thinking, trying to put the complicated pieces together. He let out a long breath. It was a relief to talk like that, and he rued the fact it had never been like that with his dad, that he could never say what he wanted or do what he wanted. And if his dad did wake up, then it would just be like it was before.

"In a coma, he's the perfect father."

He had a good chunk of change in his wallet; all those bus rides to and from the hospital. He walked over to the public phone and started pumping in the coins. There was a long delay before the phone started to ring.

"Munich Star Hostel."

"Humphrey, it's Darius."

"It's about bloody time you called."

"Sorry, mate."

"You need to get an email address."

"Can't use a computer."

"I'll teach you. Jesus, Darius. Freddie told me what happened. You all right?"

"Getting by."

155

"Where are you?"

"Perth."

"Ugh. Dullsville, Boretown. What's the verdict?"

"He's in a coma. The doc's pegged him at 70-30."

"Sounds like they've got a betting pool going."

"Maybe."

"What do you think? He gonna make it?"

"Dunno. Long odds. Even if he does wake up, he'll be in a wheelchair."

"Shit. I'm sorry, Darius."

"Me too."

"What happened?"

"His car ran off the road near our house. They say he hit a roo. Maybe he was drunk. Probably both. I can't tell ya how many times we drove that road home from the pub. I used to close my eyes and pray."

"Was it on the news? Being Easter and all."

"Nuh. There were other accidents that got the cameras. He's not even part of the road toll. But there's hundreds of cards."

"What're ya gonna do?"

"Stick around, I guess, until he wakes up. I dunno. We never really got on, but I don't want him to die. And I can't just leave him."

"He might sleep forever. That's a long wait. Munich misses you."

"Yeah? I miss Munich."

There was a pause. Darius knew what was coming. Humphrey deserved to know but Darius decided to wait until asked.

"What about Miss Jane? She keeps asking if I've heard from you. She even stopped calling me Bozo. What'll I tell her?"

Darius sighed. "Tell her, 'Go Eagles'. She'll know what that means."

"I didn't know you were a footy fan. I love it. Where plumbers and garbagemen become idols."

"I sure don't wanna spend the rest of my life goin to Carlton games."

"Don't worry. She'll find someone else soon enough. Probably a Victorian with the right allegiance, no imagination and no sense of adventure. Someone with a top of the line barbecue who mows a mean lawn."

Darius laughed loudly.

"Mate, a gotta go. A group of spring-breakers just walked in. I guess Florida's out and Munich's in for college kids. We're full of them at the moment."

"Nice talking."

"Touch base again. Whenever you get the chance."

"See ya, Hobo."

"Take care."

He hung up the phone. The unused coins jangled out and fell to the floor. He bent down to pick them up.

***

A week passed. The visitors slowed to a trickle, until it was just him and his gran. There had been no change in his dad's condition. The doctor said the longer he was out, the less likely he would pull through. There had already been a couple of hairy moments, where the hospital had called the youth hostel where Darius was staying in the middle of the night and he had come rushing to his dad's bedside.

Darius spent most of his time at the hospital. He sat in his dad's room and talked. He couldn't shut himself up. He went right back to his early memories, to when his mum was there and they were a family.

"Why didn't you marry her, dad? You got along with the Aboriginal shearers and stockmen all right. I mean, you spoke badly behind their backs, but you were always good to them in person. What happened with mum? What happened to her? She couldn't've just disappeared. I don't even know her name. Something with A, I think. We never talked about her. Not once. And you never married. You had women. Fuck, that was shocking, dad. The noises those women made. It was like you were slaughtering cattle in there. And you grunting like it was bloody hard work."

He laughed a little, then sniffed.

"I think it's awful that I don't know her. Yeah, she never came back, never called or wrote. Maybe she didn't wanna know me."

And on he talked. He took his dad through his ten years of schooling, described his tryst with Taslyn Mackay in the barn, and his other early experiences with girls; those quick fucks between farm machinery and animals, the anal sex all the girls insisted on having.

157

It was pretty embarrassing stuff, but it just felt great to talk about it all with his dad.

One night, he talked himself to sleep, having spoken thoroughly about his time up north. He told the story of the two German girls he picked up – he couldn't remember their names – and of his hopes for a threesome in Exmouth.

He woke up with a blanket over the top of him.

"Sorry, dad. I must've dozed off."

"Is okay, mate."

"Dad?"

"Digger?"

"Dad! Mornin."

"Where am I?"

"Hospital, in Perth."

His dad looked towards him, squinting. "Carn...carn move me legs."

"Don't worry about that. You made it."

"Huh?"

"You need the doctor?"

"Me legs, Digger."

Darius got up and ran out of the room. He told the nurse that his dad was awake. The nurse picked up a phone.

Back in the room, Darius said, "He's coming."

"Good. Good."

"You look like hell, dad. What happened?"

"Carn...remember. Drivin."

Darius could see his dad trying to move under the sheets, his upper body jerking a little, his teeth grimacing with frustration.

"A roo?"

His dad tried to look around the room, to see all the machines around him. His eyes fell on the table covered with cards and flowers in various stages of decay. "Right, a roo."

"You're lucky to be alive."

His dad looked at him, still squinting. "Yeah. Lucky."

The door opened. Doctor Xuan came in. "Good evening, Mr Tucker. Welcome back."

"Who the fuck're you?"

"I'm Doctor Xuan. I've been taking care of you."

"Doc?"

"Darius," the doctor said, leaning close, "I need a few minutes with your father, to check a few things."

Darius nodded and opened the door.

"Digger. Where ya goin?"

"He'll be back in a minute," the doctor said.

Darius closed the door and leaned against the wall. He could hear Doctor Xuan speaking but couldn't make out what he was saying. He could guess, though, and could imagine his father's reaction.

After a few minutes, the door opened and the doctor came out. His face was grave.

"He didn't take it very well, but no one does."

"What now?"

The doctor gestured towards the waiting area. "Let's sit down." He turned to the nurse. "Can you bring Mr Tucker some water, please?"

As they walked down the hall, Darius heard the door to his dad's room open and then close.

"Your father's going to need you," the doctor said as they sat down. "It will mean a lot of changes in both of your lives. And even though he's awake, there's still no guarantee he'll pull through."

Darius nodded, thinking about Munich and Humphrey. "Ya think he'll walk again?"

"I'm afraid not."

Darius looked at the floor, trying to picture his dad in a wheelchair. At least he'll have to get rid of that milk crate, he thought, and the other steps. The house will need a ramp.

The doctor continued to talk about the coming changes. Darius wasn't listening. He was thinking about how he would be forced to go back home to look after his dad, to become the old Darius again and take over the shearing business. But he wouldn't be able to do things his own way, because his dad would be there, wheeling into his life, pushing and needling and criticising, knowing everything better and getting everyone's sympathy while Darius struggled with so many responsibilities. He thought it would be a bit like marrying Jane, because he would wake up one day a middle-aged man and wonder where his life had gone.

"It was good that you talked to him," the doctor said.

"What? Oh, yeah."

"You were in there every night. You guys must be really close."

"Yep. Close. It was always just me and him."

"Go on. He needs you."

"Thanks, doctor."

Doctor Xuan smiled and nodded. Darius thought he was a pretty nice guy, but wondered how they might become friends. He walked back to his dad's room and sat back down.

His dad's face was grim. "Good to see ya, boy."

"You too."

"The quack said I... I was out for a couple weeks."

"Yeah."

"You just get here?"

"I've been here all along. I talked to ya the whole time."

"What about?"

"Everything."

"Ya sure? I didn't hear ya."

"I did."

"You were in...uh...Germany, right?"

"Munich."

"And? All villains?"

"The opposite. Great people."

"We never went to Germany."

Darius sat up. "What?"

"Ya...ya mum and me. We went to Europe. Once. You were two."

"That's funny, dad."

"We didn't have a camera. Ya don't remember? Too young, I guess. Alice, she wanted to travel."

"We never went anywhere," Darius said, the words coming with difficulty. "Not even when mum was around. Her name's Alice?"

"We had some hard years. Kiwis. Came over and worked for half the wages. Non-union, under the table. There were some fights back then."

"I remember that. I'd just started school."

"It brought the community together," his dad said. He took a long, laboured breath. "I got Muzza on our side. Told him to think about the future, not about money. He listened."

"We had a big party at our house."

"We did."

160

"Sheep on a spit. I remember mum standing there turning it."

"Yeah."

"Dad?"

"Yeah?"

"What happened to her?"

His dad sighed and closed his eyes. "Alice."

"Right. Alice."

"She was a fine woman. Everyone liked her."

"Tell me about her. Please."

His dad opened his eyes. "I'm sorry, Digger. I shouldna...she... nothing works out as planned."

"I wanna find her."

"Alice."

"Dad?"

He was asleep.

***

He came in a white sedan. Bladders stumbled down the stairs, jumped the gap, fell on landing, and then limped towards the car, stopping directly in front of it so the driver had to brake suddenly and swerve. The car missed the dog, just, and came to a dusty stop a sociable but not quite intrusive distance from the house, parking next to the old farm ute, which still had the funeral wreath on the bonnet.

Darius smiled at the dog's unexpected behaviour. He wondered if Bladders also felt liberated with the lord and master gone, even if he whined all night on the veranda.

The driver gathered up his papers and checked his hair in the mirror, seemingly unaware Darius was watching him. The sedan was gleaming on top so it reflected the sun but smudged around the rims and bumpers with yellow dust. Its blue license plate had the initials of the company and then 011. Darius pictured ten other reps driving around the state trying to buy up worthless old houses that stood on valuable property. They were quick, though, he thought. He had only made the call yesterday, after Murray had been so pushy at the funeral.

"You bein an international traveller an all," he had said, "you might wanna perhaps think about sellin." And then he had smiled in a friendly, dismissive way, moving closer to put an arm around Darius. "Of course, this's not the time or place to talk about such things. But think about it."

Darius knew he would sell. Murray knew it too. It seemed everyone had guessed his intentions and this made them doubly mournful.

The funeral.

It wasn't just the burial of Jack Tucker. There was also the passing of the Tucker mantle. It was his for the taking, had been pretty much laid out on a fake silver platter. The locals needed him, needed to be able to drop his name and claim acquaintance at opportune moments. And he knew he wouldn't need to be as famous or such a revered bloke as his dad; as long as he was around, shearing and keeping things going like before, the legacy would remain and a new legend would create itself. Easy. But he just couldn't do it.

The sales rep was reading through some papers. Stalling, Darius figured.

At the funeral, the locals had clustered around him, patting him on the back and asking questions he couldn't answer honestly. They rubbed their over-sized thumbs and index fingers into their eyes as if trying to plug a leaky faucet, to stick a finger in their own dyke. The tears were real, dripping singularly down cracked, sun-dried faces, sometimes getting lost in the deep furrows and lines. Their words came out broken and half-finished, from brittle voices choking back tears. More than one speaker had to swallow hard and start his sentence again. This behaviour made the eulogies and speeches drag on for longer than necessary. Darius struggled to keep his emotions in check; the outpouring from the town and surrounding community was staggering. He didn't know what to feel; there was as much relief as sadness. He felt liberated, yet alone. Then it was his turn to speak.

"I, I don't really have the words," he'd said. "None of us do. But, ah, I hope you don't think me foolish or nothin like that, but I wrote a poem. About me dad. I couldn't think of what else I could do. It's all, uh, all a bit too hard."

"Read it, Digger."

"Yeah, read it."

From a piece of paper shoved in the back pocket of the black pants bought especially for the funeral, he'd read, "It's called *Dad's Bush Burial*."

The whole town's here, dressed to mourn
A bloke held so dear, buried where born
A ute upside-down, wheels still spinnin
On a road outta town, much disbelievin
A roo lay twisted, in dirt and blood
But he's not the victim, he'll go with the flood
A roo for a man, a pitiful trade
Believe if you can, that God us all saves
My dad is dead, he's not comin back
With a feelin of dread, I've to pick up the slack
Big shoes for fillin, but everyone knows
He was one in a million, so the story goes
In a wool-lined casket, tailor-made
There lies the old bastard, face un-made
Ten feet under, in gold dust dirt
Laying crooked, asunder, in his same old shirt

The applause had been solemn and gratifying. They were greatly impressed. They came up to him after the funeral, wanting a copy of the poem, wishing they could express their sentiment in similar fashion. He said he would give a copy to Murray, who could then distribute it. Murray said he would give it to the local paper, to be run alongside Jack's obituary. Darius agreed to everything they asked, anything to make them all go away and for the funeral to be over. Jack Tucker, the Ripper, the faker, his father; he was gone. So he stood in the rickety church, which still had the decorations from Easter, shaking hands, inhaling the woolly dust and his gran's perfume, waiting for the ghastly event to be over. Yes, ghastly, because his dad was dead and he didn't really know how he felt about it. The poem was one part; selling the farm and taking off forever was the other part. No one could look him in the eye. They tried to, but couldn't hold it, didn't have the courage, because looking him in the eye just reminded them of what was gone. They looked at the floor, at their hands, or past him to their friends and family. Eye contact was too challenging and revealed too much. Not even the parade of Stevenson girls, each younger than the last – all of them in home-made black dresses cut just above the knee, their deep red lips parting as easily as their legs would – not even they, who would have so readily tacked

Tucker to their name, could look him in the eye. As they received his inattention, his lack of recognition of their beautiful willingness, they huddled together and talked behind cupped hands, looking sideways in his direction and giggling inappropriately. Only Murray Stevenson was stoically by his side the whole day, raising the topic of selling and then dropping it, again and again. Darius made no promises. He just wanted to get out of the town as soon as possible, far away from the house where all those disappointments and lies had seeped deeply into the wooden floor. Munich was waiting. Nothing was expected of him there and nobody could call his past into question; and nobody had ever heard of Jack Tucker.

The car door closed and the sales rep walked towards the house. He wore a white business shirt, short-sleeved, and it looked a little ridiculous with the tie, as if he had just clipped it on in the car. His black pants were creased from the long drive and the hems were scuffed with yellow dust, making Darius wonder if he had got out of the car to ask for directions. He was tall and stiff-limbed, yet he tried to move with the graceful ease of an athlete. He had an egg-shaped face that easily formed itself into a friendly smile, and a thin moustache and perfectly trimmed goatee. He took in the house, then stared briefly at the green tent pitched next to the shed.

"Darius Tucker?"

"You were quick."

The rep walked towards the veranda, but stopped at the stairs. He looked down at the wide gap between the ground and the second step, and seemed uncertain how to negotiate it. He looked up at Darius and smiled.

"You're missing a step."

The milk crate had been the first thing to go. He had dug it out with his own hands and then melted it on his campfire. He had cooked over it too, and it had felt good to eat from the fire of his heritage.

The rep took hold of what was left of the handrail and pulled himself up to the veranda. He wasn't fat, but had the kind of all-round heaviness that made him take up more space than necessary.

"Nick Bentley. We spoke on the phone."

They shook hands.

Nick walked across the veranda and knocked on the rail with a fist. "It was great to get your call. We're always on the lookout for good country properties. Though the circumstances in this case are not ideal."

"No, they're not. Ya wanna cuppa?"

Nick nodded.

Darius led the way into the house. As they moved through it, he felt Nick looking around, taking it all in. He wondered what the sales rep might be thinking. It was a mess, with all the same furnishings he had known his whole lifetime. But for the first time visitor, it probably held a kind of very frank sadness. On arriving two days ago, after the orderliness of Canada and Germany, he found the house miserable. What struck him was the loneliness, like the used porn magazines left in a sticky heap in the toilets of the mining hut. He'd realised then that maybe his dad had missed him, a lot more than he'd ever let on, and the house had gone to waste as a result. The dust gathered in healthy clumps in the corners, sewn together by old pubic hairs and spider webs. There was not a single sign of the place ever having had a woman's touch, or even a female visitor. It was a man's house, with rusted trophies on the fireplace mantle and portraits on the walls of pastoral scenes, yellowed at the edges and every frame dusty and slightly askew. The sofa clearly had a favoured side, and that arm was dented from having a heavy head sleeping against it. There was the comfort of the familiar, but Darius guessed Nick wasn't getting that.

"Nice place," the rep said at last.

Darius stood next to the stove, his arms folded, waiting for the kettle. "It's seen better days."

"Land's valuable. Why didn't he sell up and move into town?"

Darius chuckled. The kettle whistled and he poured the tea.

"He didn't wanna sell?"

"I keep thinkin he's gonna walk in and stop me from doin it." He laughed again, but stopped when Nick joined in. "He never would've sold. Because of the heritage."

"First settlers?"

"So I was told. Apparently, they tried to farm but had no success. My dad wouldn't tell it that way. I reckon they weren't very good farmers. Probably city people, from London, I think. Dad never said where. They came from England when they were giving the land away here. When the crops didn't take, they turned to sheep and to shearing. They leased the land to people who could farm it better. But that was years ago."

"I saw some houses on the way."

"The soil salinised. No crops planted in my lifetime. Maybe it's better now. You know, nature recovers, when you leave her alone."

Nick took the cup of tea Darius handed to him. "Thanks. Do you have any milk?"

"Nuh."

"Sugar?"

"Ah, yeah, but it's full of ants."

"Black's fine. So, those houses. They're on this property?"

"Yep."

"Anyone living there?"

"They've been empty for years." Darius sipped his tea, wishing he could have a cup of Munich coffee. "We used to play in them, until one kid got bitten by a redback. Cyril Stevenson. His dad, Grant Stevenson, drove like a maniac to get him to hospital."

"He survive?"

"Yeah, but he was always scared of spiders since then. He went to private school in Perth and stayed there. In Perth, not at the school."

"There are spiders in Perth too," the rep said, and Darius caught him sneaking looks into the dark corners and crevices of the kitchen, to all those places a redback might hide.

"Not as many. There's none in Europe."

"Are you living there at the moment?"

Darius sipped his tea. "In Munich. I'm going back when this place's sold. But don't think that means you'll get it cheaper. I already had it valued. I called you to see what you'd offer."

Nick smiled, trying to seem friendly but coming across as arrogant. "Well, sometimes it's not what a property's worth but what a buyer's prepared to pay."

"The house is worthless. Bulldoze it. My dad tried to fix everything himself. Your typical battler."

"Sounds like quite a bloke."

Darius looked at Nick, trying to guess what he might know, what he might have heard. "Yeah. Top bloke. A real ripper."

Nick drained his tea and cleared his throat loudly. "Can we, uh, have a look around?"

"Did you bring any riding gear? Your own saddle maybe?"

Nick shook his head. "I didn't think I'd be needing that."

"Just pullin your leg. I shot all the horses." He walked quickly through the house and the rep followed close behind. "I reckon your car's not up for the trip. We'll take me dad's old farm ute."

"Fine."

Darius jumped down the stairs, while the rep took the leap more gingerly, stumbling on landing.

In the car, Darius said, "Sorry bout the smell. Me dad used to use sheep dip for cologne."

"Kidding, right?"

Darius nodded. He started the car. The engine purred. The sound made him sniff; his dad was really good with engines.

"Something wrong?"

He swallowed. "Nah, mate. All good. Let's take a tour of the estate."

***

He dropped the thick contract on the table.

"Good kindling, but not reading."

He made himself another cup of tea. There was beer in the fridge, another half a slab leaning against it, but he refused to touch it, out of taste as much as principle. Alcohol had so ruled his house. Tea was better, he told himself, pouring the hot water into a stained and chipped enamel mug, and he wanted to face Stevenson sober.

He took his tea out onto the veranda. It was a warm afternoon, hot and sticky, typical of late April. It felt like rain was coming, but the sky was only dotted with clouds. A half dozen kangaroos lounged under the big tree in the front paddock, like humans at a picnic, yawning, munching and chatting.

He placed the mug on the railing and went back inside the house, first into his own room, which his dad had cleared out and turned into a study of sorts – with an ancient computer that was probably just a prop – and then into his dad's bedroom. The curtains were drawn. He stood in the doorway, the dusty darkness covering everything in multiple shadows. The bed had the same quilted cover, the same wasted, mouldy blankets, same home-made bedside tables that wobbled, same ugly pictures on the walls, now yellow with age and old breath, and under the bed, he saw, peering down, the same rifle. He pulled it out and picked it up. It was covered in dust and unloaded. Must be bullets in the shed, he thought.

That fucking shed.

"What're you hiding, dad?"

He searched through the drawers, tipping old, skid-marked underwear and withered woollen socks onto the floor. He cast badly-folded flannel shirts aside and threw the endless pairs of blue pants to the floor, rummaging through each of the pockets in turn.

No key.

Bladders limped into the room. The dog panted expectantly.

"You know, don't ya?" The dog barked in agreement. They stared at each other, the dog cocking his head sideways. "What's he got in there?"

He had a feeling he knew already; that secret kept from him.

"Alice. Fuck it."

Rifle in hand, he went to the back of the house. Bladders followed. Outside, the air seemed stickier than before, heavier. He grimaced when he got a whiff of the familiar stench of the toilet, which in his lifetime had never been moved. But his disgust turned into a smile when he saw the old axe wedged into the chopping block next to the pot belly water heater. It took some effort to get the axe out and the blade was shiny and sharp. He took the axe and the rifle around to the front of the house. He leaned the rifle against the veranda and reached up to the railing to get his tea. He took a sip and looked at the shed.

The axe felt lighter in his hand. That was good; it meant he was stronger. Cutting wood for the water heater would be easy now, not like it had been through his teens when lifting the big axe was hard and tiring; when his dad had sat on the back steps, drinking beer and laughing at him.

"Bastard."

He looked towards the road to see if anyone was coming. He put his tea cup back on the railing and lifted the axe. He walked towards the shed. The first chop echoed loudly and the roof rattled. After a couple of whacks, the dry beams splintered and fell in large pieces to the ground. Through the gap, he saw the shadowed outline of tools along one wall and a small work bench with jars of nails and screws.

There was a vice too, and assorted pieces of wood. It all looked very innocent. But he drove the axe in again, getting satisfaction from every snap and crack of wood. A few splinters pierced his hands, making the axe handle sticky with blood. Those splinters pushed deeper into his palms and fingers and he enjoyed the pain. He made a large enough gap to fit through and was about to shimmy inside when a large, billowing cloud of dust caught his eye. He heard the sound of an engine then and turned to see a car coming towards the house. The car scattered the herd of kangaroos. They bounced away, over the fence and towards the road.

"Perfect timing."

He leaned the axe against the shed and wiped his hands on his pants. The cream coloured car came to a dusty stop in front of the house, its wheels turned so he could see gravel pellets in the grooves of the tires.

The window lowered. Murray Stevenson's concerned face peered through, his smile supportive and sympathetic. He looked past Darius at the chopped up shed, then at the rifle leaning against the veranda.

"All right, Digger?"

Darius put his hands in his pockets. "Sort of. Yeah. Not really."

"What's with the rifle? You huntin?"

"Honestly? There was a herd of roos under the tree. I thought about shootin em all."

"Understandable. I'm really sorry, Digger."

"Thanks, Murray. I know."

Murray gestured towards the shed. "Lookin for somethin?"

"Carn find the key."

"Guess it's locked for a reason. Probly best to leave it."

"All his documents are in there. I'm tryin to sort everything out. Order from chaos, that kind of thing."

"Want some help?"

"Nah, she'll be right."

Murray opened the door and got out of the car. "Thought we might have a bit of a talk."

"What about?"

"You know Miranda, my daughter."

"Course."

"She wants to study in Germany. Got any advice for her?"

The passenger door opened and Miranda got out. Darius looked at the girl who had eyed him so eagerly at the funeral only to turn away and gossip with her sisters and cousins. It had hurt to see them talking behind cupped hands. They weren't bad girls – he'd fucked a few of them – but they could be a mean bunch when grouped together.

"Hey, Darius. I loved your poem."

"Yeah?"

"It was in the paper today. You see it?"

"Nuh."

Murray reached into his car. "Here. You can have my copy."

Darius took the paper. "Cheers. You interested in Germany, Mizzy?"

"What's it like?"

"Really nice. I met a girl there who was at uni. From Melbun. She was havin a great time. Bit homesick, but, you know, that's to be expected."

"We're a bit worried. She's just a girl."

"I'm 19, dad."

"There's plenty of Aussies there. I bet you could hook up with some. But best of all are the locals. Really nice people."

"What about Munich?"

"Great city. They've got an Aussie Rules team. Good bunch of blokes."

"Really?"

"Yeah. Amazing, eh? Munich's pretty big and expensive. You might need to sell a few flocks to see her right, Murray."

Murray laughed. "Be worth it."

"I'm heading back, when I've sold the place. I work at a bar called the Waterhole. An Aussie bar. Come by and I'll see if I can help you out. If you go to Munich, that is."

"Thanks, Digger."

"No worries."

Murray turned to his daughter. "Can you give us a moment, Mizzy?"

"Sure." Miranda got back into the car and shut the door.

"Let's go up on the veranda, Digger."

"All right. Watch the first step."

"Where's the crate?"

"Cremated."

On the veranda, Murray leaned against the railing and said, "I'm worried about you, Digger. Ya takin this hard."

"How else should I take it? He's me dad."

"I know, I know. We're all hurtin. So, stay here and take over. Keep it all goin."

Darius ran his hands through his hair. "I can't."

"Can't, or don't want to?"

"Both. No. Neither. I dunno. I can't stay here. Everything reminds me of him. I gotta get away. Close the book, you know, start again. With distance."

"I wanted to do the same thing when my dad died. But I had too many responsibilities. You've got none. Except the community."

"I'm sorry, Murray."

"Maybe it's for the best. You'll probly come back, one day. We'll all be here for you."

"Thanks."

"What about the property?"

"I wanna take care of gran. That's one of the reasons for sellin."

"You're a good bloke, Digger. You know I'm interested. I'm pretty sure if Jack ever sold, he'd want to keep it local."

Darius downed the last of his tea. It was cold. "A guy came today."

"Yeah?"

"From the city. Made me an offer."

"Whatever it is, I'll match it."

"It's high. I'll knock 10% off for ya."

Murray stuck out his hand. "Done."

Darius shook the farmer's hand. Murray must be loaded, he thought. Miranda will have her year in Germany fully funded. She won't have to pour drinks or serve them in some Aussie bar.

"Sorry about the blood."

"No key?"

"I'll do it old-fashioned way. I don't wanna leave ends untied."

"Atta boy."

"And now?" he asked.

Murray hopped down the steps. "We'll sort it all out in the next coupla days. Come over for dinner tomorrow night. I'll have the paperwork ready."

"You don't mess around."

"This place's got potential. Your dad, bless him, never really saw it. I'll call it Tucker's Run. In his honour."

"Thanks, Murray."

"You call if you need anything. Your poem was spot on. You've got some talent, Digger."

Darius nodded. The car pulled away and he waved. Miranda stuck her hand out the window and waved back.

"Tucker's Run? Fuck me."

He picked up the axe. After a few more whacks, the gap was plenty wide enough to get inside. A loose nail ripped his shirt and scratched his shoulder. He looked around, taking in the tools and wood, and became increasingly annoyed when he found only mundane, everyday things; the kind of stuff any man might have in his shed.

He began to laugh, softly and bitterly at first, and then with painful, hateful sobs that turned into crying shouts. He trashed the shed, throwing the jars and containers against the wall and smashing the work bench with the axe. The bench was fixed to the wall and he yanked and pulled at it until it came loose. It pulled half the wall with it and once it was free, a pile of envelopes spilled to the floor. They had been stored in the gap between the bench and the wall, covered by a thin piece of chipboard. A few redbacks crawled out and scurried into the shadows, getting lost amongst the mess.

He stared at the envelopes, yellow with age and all opened. Some were addressed to him, some to his dad.

"You complete bastard."

Lewis: Why did you sell the farm?

Poet: It wasn't a farm. We weren't farming anything.

Lewis: But Tucker's Run is a very prosperous farm.

Poet: Yeah, now. I sold it to a friend and he really made somethin of it.

Lewis: But why sell?

Poet: Everythin reminded, ya know. It was like he was still there, but wasn't. I couldn't stand it. I thought the only chance I had to keep from killing meself was to sell everything and try to move on.

Lewis: That farm was part of you, part of your family, your heritage.

Poet: Still is. I sold the place but I never forgot it. And there aren't many days when I don't feel like my dad's with me.

Lewis: You captured that in the poem *The Ghost*. It doesn't mention your father but now you say that, I can see it's him, the ghost drifting further out of your life, starting real and dissipating into nothing through the years. It's incredibly sad and touching.

Poet: That's one poem that's not about him.

~~~

Bloodline

They started early and picked up some croissants and coffee at the train station. They made the camp just as it opened, as Humphrey wanted.

"It's really shocking when it's desolate. When all the groups arrive, it's still shocking, but for all the wrong reasons."

"Why's that?"

"Because they treat the place like an amusement park, one more stop on their ten-countries-in-five-days itinerary."

Humphrey walked quickly across the vast field, towards the far end where there was a small cluster of buildings. He kept gesturing for Darius to follow, but Darius took his time, stopping to skim-read each board and look at the maps and photographs. Humphrey waited for him on the far side. Darius was happy to make him wait, glad to see his friend keeping to his time for a change; he was getting tired of doing everything to Humphrey's rhythm. So he walked slowly across the field, pausing to read, look and ponder. The vastness of this horror, it's brutal, inhuman orderliness, was made no less devastating by its fifty years of distance. It was history, but here he stood in the middle of the remnants, surrounded by proof that it all had happened. There was no hiding, no attempt to remove blame or to explain. Here it was in its shocking entirety, for all to see.

"What's this?"

"You get one guess." Humphrey led the way inside.

It was like a shower block, the walls tinged a chemical blue. There was a smell Darius couldn't describe, didn't want to. He also didn't want to picture how it had been in here, naked, thin and unwanted. So he turned away. Outside, he sat down on the grass, enjoying the sun on his face as he waited.

"Let's walk to town," Humphrey said. He looked in the direction of the first tour group that was heading towards the crematorium. "Here they come. Disneylanders, cameras at the ready."

It was a long walk and Darius kept silent. But when they entered the old town, he had cause to remark what an attractive place Dachau was. They sat at the outdoor cafe of Schloss Dachau, looking down at the valley below. Humphrey took a piece of apple cake with his coffee.

Darius sipped his tea. "Nice view."

"Isn't it?"

"You know, Hobo, sitting here, you'd never even know the camp was there."

"That's the whole point. Like the Aboriginal concentration camps in Australia."

"The what?"

"The camps where they put all the stolen kids. There was one not far from your home town. Carrolup, down near Katanning."

"Yeah? Didn't know that."

"Again, that's the whole point. It's a museum now."

"You went there?"

"I did a bit of tour, of the old camps. Carrolup, Gnowangerup, Roelands. I hit Moore River on the way to the mines. Shocking stuff. Christ, Darius, the things our forefathers did. Government policy no less."

Darius lowered his voice. "Like here."

"Yeah, but the difference is they face their history. We just try to sweep it under the rug. No black armband versions allowed. Positives only. Get Freeman to light the flame and everything's okay. Hmm. This's good cake. Home-made. You wanna piece?"

~~~

He recalled that day as he drove south. Like Dachau, this prison was removed from town, down narrow roads, hidden and unacknowledged. No doubt, very few Perth people knew it was there. The rotten posts and twisted fence wire along the road suggested this was once farming land, until the top soil had salinised from over-use and had blown away. Probably was Aboriginal land, too, he thought, watching the unattractive, dead fields rush past the window.

"Noongars," he said, wondering if he was one of them, wondering if he stopped the car and sat down in that lifeless dirt that it might speak to him. If he dug his hands into the sand and closed his eyes, would the spirits take him to that place she had called dreaming?

Probably not, he thought.

So he kept on driving. He just wanted to get away again, on the first plane to Europe once the money came through. Stevenson had it all organised.

He needed to call gran and tell her he'd sold the place. But there had been other calls to make. The Perth telephone book in his dad's study was a decade old. He found names and numbers and dialled them. He got disconnected lines, busy signals, and if anyone actually answered, they only did so after a dozen rings and then listened to his questions with silent suspicion. He had a name, Alice Pickering, and former addresses and phone numbers. But the people he got on the line just gave him newer old numbers, half-hearted follow-ups, vague leads and disjointed stories. "She far way," they said, but they wouldn't say where. The one concrete lead had brought him down this narrow, bumpy road. He drove with reluctant eagerness, wanting to know, but scared of the truth and what it all might mean.

There was a small rusted sign at the turn off, faded and pointing more to the sky than down the single lane road.

When the prison came into view, it seemed like it appeared from nothing, like a mirage of hopelessness. At the front gate, he was shown where to park and told which office to enter. There was only one, a building separate from the rest, like the crematorium at Dachau, but the guard ordered him towards it all the same. He filled out the forms and waited, thumbing through a two-week old newspaper that was smudged and oily, as if the reader had eaten fish and chips at the same time, or the meal had been wrapped in the newspaper.

Waited, staring at the floor, preparing his sentences and trying to predict responses. He was alone in the room but when the guard came in, he loudly called out "Tucker", and it sounded like he was calling a family to dinner.

Darius went into a smaller room, with a line of low wooden desks separated by a scratched pane of glass that didn't quite reach the ceiling. There were two other people, one large woman piled onto a children's chair and an old man whose faded suit was bundled around him, hanging on his bones like a big suit on a mannequin. These two people mumbled through the small holes in the glass. The guard pointed for Darius to take the empty chair between the two.

Waited some more, trying not listen as the old man's voice went into his right ear and the woman's into his left; a story of hardship on one side and betrayal on the other. He heard the word innocent several times, and it was the old man who kept drawing parallels with Ned Kelly. The prisoners were victims of rough justice, wrongdoings and cruel misunderstandings; the drugs planted on one side and the evidence faked on the other. It sounded good, sounded real.

But their voices drifted away when he walked in. He wore a dirty grey jumpsuit and limped worse than Darius remembered. He pulled the metal chair across the floor and sat down. The scruffy brown beard was interspersed with long strands of grey, lending him more years than he deserved and perhaps a wisdom he didn't possess. The bloodshot eyes were narrowed, suspicious and sad. He snarled with puffy lips, looking quizzically.

"Who the fuck're you?"

He didn't lean close, didn't whisper through the holes like the others, but shouted, sitting back in the chair, bored.

"It's me, Darius Tucker."

The eyes narrowed further until they were pink slits. He cocked his head to one side and rubbed his nose. Then he smiled, and the white purity and geometric straightness of his teeth made his face look even scruffier and uglier.

"Took ya bloody long enuff."

"I'm here now."

"Heard Jack carked it. Sorry."

"How d'you know?"

"Word gets round."

"Yeah."

"What ya want?"

Darius leaned forward and whispered into the glass. "I'm looking for me mum. For Alice."

He gave Darius a searching, questioning look. "Ya dunno?"

"What?"

"Ha-ha-ha. What a bastard. Ha-ha-ha. He kept it from ya, all this time."

"You don't know the half of it."

Uncle Will shot forward, his gnarled face close to the glass. Darius could smell his breath coming through the holes. "Reckon I know more than you, mate."

"Yeah?"

"Yeah."

"Well, you can start by tellin me where she is."

Uncle Will sat back. "Why should I?"

"Cause I wanna find her."

"Yeah, now, cause ya lost ya old man. Ha-ha."

"He kept the letters from me. I didn't know she tried to get custody."

"I warned her. She had no chance."

"She didn't give up."

"Yeah, gave it a go. Smart cookie. Reckon you are too cause ya here."

"Right, mate."

Uncle Will leaned back in the chair and thoughtfully scratched his beard. His fingers were long and thin, the nails bright pink. "What I get for tellin?"

"What're ya in for?"

"B'n'e, but I didn't do it." He leaned forward again, spraying the glass with bubbly drops of spit and pumping his bad breath through the holes. "I know who did, but I'm not sayin."

"Ya need a lawyer or somethin?"

"Nah, mate." A bushy brown eyebrow, also flecked with strands of grey, went quickly up and down, like it was a nervous tick. "Gotta bit a money?"

Darius looked down at the scarred and sticky wooden table, at all the initials that had been carved into the surface; a lot people once "woz ere".

"Maybe."

"Gis some. I owe a guy a bit. Carn pay him from here, ha-ha. Carn, mate. We's family."

Darius tried to forget all the nasty things his dad had said, to deal with Uncle Will here and now. Yet here he was with his uncle, who he hadn't seen for almost fifteen years, and already he was asking for money.

"Ya know where she is? I've gotta few leads. There are other people who know."

Uncle Will shook his head, as if this was impossible. "Big world, mate. She could be anywheres."

"Even here?"

"Nah, not her. Too clever for this shit. Carn, I knows it. Ya pay?"

"How much?"

"Five grand."

Darius whistled softly. "That's a lotta money."

"Carn, mate. I'll tell ya where Alice is. She'll pay ya back, guaranteed."

"Two minutes," the guard shouted. "For you too, Mrs Tallis."

"Bugger off," she replied.

Darius looked around. The old man had gone but the large woman to his left remained, parked on the chair and gripping the table as if getting up required too much effort.

Uncle Will was frowning expectantly, one eyebrow jittering.

"All right. Where is she and who do I pay?"

"Gotta pen?"

Darius wrote down the name of a bar in East Perth and a university in London. When he looked up, a guard had hauled his uncle to his feet and was leading him from the room.

"Whatcha gonna do?" He shrugged off the guard, who surprisingly let him walk back to the glass to get his answer.

"If she's really at the uni, I'll pay ya debt."

"Piss easy. Ya come back an visit?"

Darius stood up. "When the info's wrong."

His uncle laughed crazily. "Shoulda gave ya the wrong info then, ha-ha."

"Then I wouldn't pay ya debt."

The guard pulled Uncle Will back again, but he held his place. "Fucker. Reckon ya a bit of a bastard, like ya old man. Smart like her and a prick like him."

Darius watched Uncle Will get led from the room and then followed Mrs Tallis to the door.

"He's innocent, I tell ya," she said to the guard.

"Sure he is," the guard muttered. When she walked further down the hall, he said to Darius, "Like everyone in here is. I reckon he just does it to get away from her. She's way too much woman to handle."

***

They were staring, looking him up and down, judging. The big dusty backpack gave him away, but he hadn't thought they would all be so smartly dressed; he'd even seen a few guys wearing ties. The designer jeans, faded in all the right places, and scruffy shirt he thought would be the global uniform of university students made him stand out a mile.

He had gone a little overboard in Perth. His brand new credit card had got such a good swiping it started to feel soft in his fingers. It had felt good to blow some of the money needlessly. There was plenty of it to blow. He even flew business class to London.

"Now you be a good boy and put that in the bank," his gran had said after that long debate over who should get the money. Darius wanted all of it, but then she threatened, ever so delicately, to call a lawyer and fight for what was rightfully hers. So he agreed to split it, because even half of it was a lot, and his gran in turn promised to make him the main benefactor of her will.

"Yeah, the bank. I'll do that."

"Do your father proud." She had smiled thinly at the calculations she had made on her telephone notepad, the extravagant, confusing lines of long division. "I'm sure he'd roll over in his grave if he knew you sold, but," and again she'd looked at her narrow notepad, at the generous interest rates she'd allowed herself, "but maybe you did the right thing, to sell while it was still worth something. My Jack would never've sold, but he often said you weren't cut out for the sheds."

"If he'd ever bothered to get the land valued, maybe he might've sold it."

"Put it in the bank, dear. Don't go spending it on drugs or cars or whatever. Save it for when you marry and buy a house of your own. You are getting married soon, aren't you?"

"Come on, gran."

"It would be very good for you to do so. It would put all that nasty gossip to rest."

"What gossip?"

"Oh, never you mind. Just find yourself a nice girl and everything will take care of itself."

"I'm goin back to Europe."

"What on earth for? Stop wasting your time over there, especially with those Germans. Warmongers, all of them. And I don't like this Humphrey character. Sounds a bit fruity to me."

That had made Darius laugh; he couldn't wait to tell Humphrey exactly what she had said.

"I'm goin to London."

"Well, at least they're civilised. Have you got a job there?"

"I found me mum. I'm gonna visit her."

"You found Alice? She's probably living on the street. Her life could only have gone down after leaving my Jack."

"She didn't leave. He threw her out."

"Jack said she left. She cheated on him and left."

"Cheated?"

"Some fella from the city. At university, I think. Poor Jack was distraught. You don't remember?"

"No."

"You were too young. But my Jackie, he could carry a load and not bother anyone with it. So I don't know why you want to find her. She ruined it all."

"She's a uni professor in London."

"Hmpf. I'll believe that when I see it. Maybe she slept her way into that too. It's been a long time, Darius. I'd leave the past well alone if I were you."

But he couldn't leave it alone. That was why he stayed up all night to make those calls to London, why he bought himself a ticket on the next flight out, why he cleared Uncle Will's debt. Once again, he found himself in Perth taking care of business: selling a car, organising insurances and accounts, all the while just wanting to get the hell out. The city functioned for him like an enormous administration centre: a place where papers were shuffled from one side of the city to the other, where records were meticulously kept but took forever to find, where problems were bounced from person to person and from place to place, where ridiculous opening hours meant driving all the way back the next day. But also where dodgy hustlers in scungy back offices of bars lent money to people who would never even be able pay it back. While in Perth, going from place to place, standing in line and taking a number, he wondered how all these people could live here, in this giant city-office with its accommodation cubicles and clear hierarchy of wealth, position and status. The roads were long corridors that linked departments, the parks nice places where employees could eat lunch. Even the sky seemed fake, too eternally blue, and it made him wonder if the city really was inside a giant bubble.

The best thing to do was leave. It felt good to have a reason to do so, an objective to move towards.

"Just down there to the right," the Indian boy said, pointing, and speaking without the Indian accent Darius expected.

181

"Thanks."

He walked quickly towards the Humanities building, embarrassed, out of place and nervous.

Very nervous.

He told himself to be fair. To listen and not pre-judge. Let her explain, he told himself. Give her that chance.

He found the building, saw her name on the board, a room number. He lugged his backpack up the stairs, sweating, and then followed the numbers down the corridor until he stood in front of her office.

The knock on the door echoed loudly down the empty corridor. The door didn't open, but two doors down, another did. A grey-bearded man stuck his head out and squinted at Darius.

"I thought that was my door," he said in an American accent. Or maybe it was Canadian. Darius couldn't tell the difference.

"I'm looking for Professor Pickering." Even after saying the name on the phone, it still sounded foreign, and not in any way connected to him.

The man, probably a professor like Alice, came out of his office and walked a few steps down the corridor. His slippers squeaked on the linoleum floor, yet he exuded the kind of intelligence and worldliness that Darius so revered.

"I believe she's working from home today. Looks like you've come a long way to see her."

"From Australia."

"Are you a new student?"

"No, no. She's, uh, she's my mum."

"It's good of you to visit."

"Yeah, we haven't seen each other for a while."

"Then go with haste, pilgrim." The professor started shuffling back to his office.

"Uh," Darius said, making the professor stop and turn, "can you tell me where she lives?"

The professor had the address is his chunky Filofax. Outside, Darius walked to the car park and got into a weird looking taxi, which had a door that opened the opposite way. From the window of the taxi, London honked, dripped and intimidated. He couldn't imagine what it might be like to be out in it. He felt secure in the taxi, safe he would get to his destination.

When the taxi stopped at the address, he paid the driver and told him not to wait. It was a terraced house, narrow, with two storeys and a small, tidy garden in front. The limes on the tree in the garden were the size of grapes. He walked up to the door, dropped his heavy backpack and rang the bell. He heard the chime pass through the house, going up the stairs and probably slipping under closed doors. But no answer came. He bent forward to look through the front window, cupped his hands around his face to block out the light, but it was useless because the curtains were drawn. He could just see the bulky outline of a sofa, the blurred edges of a coffee table, the five levels of what looked to like a very large bookshelf.

"Can I help you?" said a voice behind him, making him jump.

He turned and was surprised to see a middle-aged Arab standing on the front path, just inside the low gate.

"Uh..."

He had a thick, dark moustache and closely cropped black hair that was receding and made his forehead more prominent; it was covered in lines because he had his bushy eyebrows raised, eyeing Darius curiously. The depth and multitude of the lines made Darius think the man raised his eyebrows a lot.

"Um..."

His eyes were dark and intent, yet opened widely and had a subtle softness that made Darius think the man might be friendly, when required, when it suited. He wore a blue tracksuit which steamed slightly and was damp around the chest and shoulders. His arms hung loosely at his sides, one hand holding a folded newspaper and the other a carton of milk. Darius thought there was something routine about the man, about his tracksuit and shopping, about his muddy running shoes that had small holes next to the little toes, about his smell.

"Um..."

"I don't mean to interrupt your meditation, but can I help you?"

"Uh, I think, I, uh, I've got the wrong house. Is this number 84?"

The man nodded.

"Well, I guess, I've got the wrong street then."

He fumbled with the straps of his backpack. His hands were shaking and he turned his back on the man so he wouldn't see. With

183

the backpack awkwardly across his shoulders, his arms hooking into the wrong straps, he started down the short path. The man blocked it. Darius tried to walk around him and brushed the lime tree with his pack. A few small, stony limes dropped to the grass with soft thuds.

"Sorry."

The man let him pass, but Darius still felt his eyes. He closed the small gate and started walking down the street.

"Darius?"

***

They sat at the small table in the kitchen. Hareem made a strong smelling tea that he served in small glasses with equally small saucers and spoons. He didn't offer milk, and Darius was afraid to ask. Instead, Hareem dropped a cube of sugar into both glasses. Then he waited, seemingly comfortable with the silence and with the whole kitchen smelling of his sweat. Darius looked around, searching for signs of his existence, for photographs or for his name written down somewhere. There was nothing.

"You made it," Hareem said at last. "I always said you would."

Darius nodded. He sipped his tea, trying not wince at the taste. "Yeah."

"I'll be honest. Alice doesn't talk about you a lot."

"Long time ago."

"How long?"

"I was eight."

Hareem drank his tea. He had very large, wide fingers yet the small glass seemed to nestle comfortably within them. Darius was having trouble lifting the glass, as it was almost too hot to touch. Hareem wiped his moustache each time he drank and small, salty flakes of dried sweat drifted down to the table, showing up blatantly on the red surface.

"I know she stopped writing, but she never gave up on you. She thought that because she got no response that, what was his name? John?"

"Jack."

"Yes, of course, that Jack had thrown the letters away."

"He hid them. He died a few weeks ago."

"I'm sorry."

"Yeah, well, it's a good reminder of the way of things. I found the letters while I was, ah, while I was sorting out his stuff. They were locked away."

"Harsh, but I guess he had his reasons. The way Alice told it, she really broke his heart. Made a big mistake. More than one."

"Yeah?"

Hareem sipped his tea. So did Darius. Outside, a car drove past.

"But now you're here. How did you find her? We only moved here a few years ago, just after we got married."

"You're married?" Darius had been wondering what place this Arab had in Alice's life. He had been taught not to trust them. They had a weird religion which made them hijack planes and blow themselves up. His dad had hated them, and had always cheered loudly when the Arabs, the perennial bad guys, were killed in the movies.

No, he told himself. I'm not him.

"I guess a lot of things are going to come as a shock," Hareem said.

"It's okay. It's nice to meet you. Do you work at the uni too?"

"No. We met in Edinburgh. She was lecturing there and I was doing research for a book." He smiled, seeming to enjoy the memory, his dark eyes twinkling. "She wasn't very interested in me at first, so I started attending her lectures. They were very interesting. You come from a country that has more than a few, hmm, let's call them complications."

"Does she lecture only about Australia?"

Hareem turned towards the front door when he heard it open. "Maybe you can ask her that yourself."

Darius stood up. He wanted to walk into the front room, to run, but he didn't think his legs were up to it. He spread his hands on the kitchen table for support. He heard noises in the front room: the tinkling of keys dropped on a wooden table, the solid thump of books, a coat being unzipped and taken off, a woman sighing, shoes clapping against the floorboards.

All those years, he thought, counting them in his head, dimly recalling the time when the kitchen was warm and full of cooking smells, the house clean and homely. Her walking him to school and him not wanting to go. But then all those empty years that followed:

the one-pot meals, the stacks of canned food, the dirty dishes his dad loaded in an old steel bathtub and then hosed down outside; he even bought a special nozzle to get a stronger stream of water. And those few women who drifted in and out of his life, the women who tried hard to be friends, who seldom stayed the night, and if they did, were gone before breakfast. And all those lonely nights when he and his father stared at the television, or those terminal evenings when the power was out and they listened to the radio, the cheap batteries running out quickly.

His dad had thrown her out. Or she had left, like gran had said. Either way she was gone, and she left him in that miserable house. It was her fault so many things had gone wrong for him, why he didn't fit in and had always struggled to maintain his place. If she had stayed, or at least tried to come back, everything would have been different. She could have filled the holes, made him stronger, prepared him for the world. She would have held him while he learned to swim and wouldn't have just thrown him in the water and walked away. But she never came back, and he was left trapped in a web of lies that had grown denser with every passing year, with every new lie that was spun into the web.

He should have hated her, could have blamed her for everything. But he decided not to. He would listen, would forgive, because even with the years in between, he wanted her in his life. She had run and so had he.

"Harry?"

Her voice. It's cracking, lilting tone caused a flood of memories, all of them so old, disjointed and vague it felt like they had happened to someone else, or was the echo of a dream from long ago.

"In the kitchen."

"Did you get the paper?"

"Of course."

The simple domesticity of the exchange made his heart ache.

"And you ran," she said, her voice closer now, echoing in the short hall that connected the front room to the kitchen. "I can smell you from here."

"Two out of two."

"It's normally one or the other. What's the occasion?"

Hareem smiled thinly at Darius. "I think it's a special day."

She entered the kitchen. She was shorter than he remembered, older too, and not nearly as lean and gangly. He recalled how one of her long, thin arms could wrap right around his stomach. Now, those same arms looked broad, short and stiff. Her fingers were still slender, though, and she held them to her mouth as she looked at him blankly, her eyes blinking continuously as if adjusting to the light. Her hair was shorter, touched with wiry streaks of grey, but still curly. Those few curls dangled over a wrinkled forehead. Her face had widened and fallen, so the skin of her cheeks hung over her jaw line, but that broad smile of hers pulled the skin back up, making her look like he remembered.

"My God."

"Hi."

She took a step forward. "Is it really you?"

"It's me."

"I'm so sorry. For everything."

"It's all right."

"It's not."

"It is."

"You look like your father. He was very handsome when he was your age. Excuse me, Harry."

She began to cry. She moved around the table, stumbling over the leg of a chair as she came towards him. Her arms reached around his back and she hugged him hard, her face crying against his chest.

"I can't believe it's you."

His dad had never allowed him to cry, and not even at the old bastard's funeral had he shed a tear. But now, breathing in the musty smell of his mum's hair and feeling the moisture of her tears soaking through his shirt, he let go.

The tears came easily.

"What happened?" she asked, pulling back and stroking the tears from his face. "I want to know everything."

"Not much to tell."

"Liar. I can see it in your eyes, just like Jack. He was so transparent. How is he anyway?"

"Yeah, he, uh, he's dead."

Her face went blank. Darius watched her closely; he saw that she had loved his dad, once.

187

"I can see that's no lie. What happened?"

"Car accident."

His mother chewed her bottom lip and nodded slightly. She understood, he could see, glad he wouldn't he have to do any explaining, any lying.

"When?"

"Last Easter."

She sat down at the table. "I'm sorry."

"It's okay," Darius said. "He was in a coma and fought on for a while, but then he fell asleep again and didn't wake up. The doctor said he gave up, mentally, you know."

"Were you hurt?"

"I wasn't in the car."

"Thank God for that."

"I was in Munich."

"Munich? Jack let you go overseas? I guess he changed over the years." She turned to Hareem. "He never wanted to go anywhere. We went to Europe, once. But he was such a fish out of water, he couldn't enjoy himself."

"He didn't let me go. I left."

She smiled at him and they shared a moment that made his stomach rumble with warmth.

"Good for you," she said. "Sometimes you have to make hard choices to get the things you want. To do what you want."

"Like you did?"

"I made mistakes. I still regret them, but I can't undo them. I tried, but..."

"He kept your letters from me."

"Yes, I guessed as much. The government was on his side. We went to court."

"What?" There was nothing of a court case in the letters he had read.

"He was such a stubborn bastard."

"Alice," Hareem said.

"He could be a darling, when he wanted to. A lot of what happened was my fault. He won, of course. Because we never married. And I didn't take it very well and called the judge a few names. He was, let's say, old school, and had no problem tacking on a restraining order.

188

So, you see, I could never go back to you, even though I wanted to."

"Does that still apply?"

"The order? We're in England, not Australia. We'll forget about it, all right?"

"Yep."

"So, the case was a shambles, ruined by yours truly, but there was one positive. I found out about my own mother. My lawyer did some research and found out she'd been stolen as a kid. Made my case more sympathetic, so he said. The old school judge didn't care in the slightest. He looked like he didn't know what we were on about, like we were making it all up. I was able to find her, and that was good. Very good."

"That's all news to me."

"I wrote about it, in the letters."

"I guess he threw those away. Bastard."

"Darius," Hareem said, "that's your father. I'm sure he did everything with the best of intentions. And I think it's not good to speak badly of the dead."

"What does that mean?" he asked.

"Harry's a theologian. What he means is that there are so many religions in the world, there must be something to it."

"Sort of like, pray to God, but tie your camel. And speaking of camels, I smell like one. If you need me, I'll be in the tub. I'll leave you to it."

Hareem left the kitchen.

His mum poured herself some tea, using Hareem's glass. She dropped a cube of sugar into it. Darius sat down.

"He's a good man."

Darius sipped his tea.

"Would you like to stay with us? I mean, if you have other plans, it's okay."

"That'd be nice." He thought about Munich, about Humphrey and Jane. She would still be there, at least for a few more weeks, and he didn't want to have to deal with her. "If it's okay," he added.

The brown lines cracked around her mouth and eyes, and her smile lifted the drooping skin of her cheeks. "Good. Now, I want to know everything."

"Me too."

"It's just amazing that you're here, that we're sitting opposite each other."

"It is."

"I'm really sorry. Nothing went as I wanted it to."

"Well, now we can fill in the gaps and catch up."

"Yes, we can. Let's work backwards. How did you find me?"

"After the funeral, I decided to sell the place. And to do that, I had to clean up. That's how I found the letters in the shed. Did he ever write back?

"A couple of times. I've got them. You can read them if you like."

Darius nodded. "I started calling around, and finally tracked down Uncle Will."

"Will? How is he? You know I sent him money for a knee operation, but he never wrote to me to tell me how it went, or even to say thank you."

"He's in jail."

"Again?"

"He told me you were here."

She cocked her head slightly. "Just like that?"

He nodded.

"That doesn't sound like Will. He's only my half brother, you know."

"He still limps." To his surprise, Alice cackled loudly.

"Well, that just says it all, doesn't it? And you were in Munich before that?"

"Yeah. It was great."

"You weren't homesick?"

"A bit. Not really. There was enough going on that I didn't think about it."

"Are you going back to Munich?"

"I think so. The property's sold. There's nothing for me back home anymore."

"Jack was a person, not a country."

Darius sipped his now cold tea. "I know."

"How do you feel about it?"

"I wrote a poem. For the funeral."

"Can I read it?"

"They put it in the local paper. I've got a copy with me."

He stood up and went into the living room. He took the newspaper out of the front pocket of his backpack. In the kitchen, she took it, unfolded it and read.

"You just made me homesick," she said, putting the paper down. "That's just how it is. And my son's grown up to be a poet."

"Not quite."

"Well, I think this's very good."

"Thanks."

***

He thought it would be difficult, but they came together easily. She was eager to take him into her life and he was receptive. The first story she told him was how she cheated on his dad, who didn't take it well. His mum had wanted to get together with Dennis, to take Darius as well, but it hadn't worked out like that. It was Dennis who had got the lawyer and pushed for the court case.

"In the end, it all fell apart," she said. "I lost you, I lost Jack, and eventually I lost Dennis."

"Sorry."

"But I found my mother, and I was free to pursue my life. It's awful, I know, but I never would've ended up here if I hadn't lost you. I would've been just another country housewife in some forgettable little town."

"Thanks for telling me. He always said he threw you out."

"I bet he called me everything under the sun."

"I don't really remember."

They spent several evenings like that, at the kitchen table, talking and catching up, just him and Alice. Hareem would sit with them for a while but then retire to the living room.

Darius started to like Hareem. He even went so far as to start running with him.

Every evening, they had dinner at the kitchen table, like a family. That table: how important it was for them. The red top was scratched and one leg was too short, making it wobble, but all manner of feelings, subjects and thoughts floated over its surface. Around it, any topic could be broached. In the cramped living room, sitting in sofas that were so close together three pairs of knees touched, they didn't have the same kind of success, and so always sat in the kitchen.

For Darius, home had always been a place of torment, a place he had never wanted to be, a place of hard work, restrictions and silence. It was a revelation to have a home life that was so pleasurable, intimate and inclusive.

He and Alice had to get know each other all over again. From the beginning. He found her to be pragmatic, passionate, humorous and sometimes cold. She was nothing like he remembered. Harry had told him, on their first run together, not to expect her to be the same person.

"You're not the same person she remembers either," he had said as they jogged through Regent's Park. "You're both different. That should actually make things easier. You can start from the start."

Darius felt a little out of his depth with Harry, with Alice too. They were both academics and sometimes used words he didn't understand; and they made references to books or quoted people that Darius had never heard of. Harry often quoted proverbs and the Bible.

But this inspired Darius, enough for him to start going with Alice to university to attend her Australian history lectures. He even copied the reading list from another student and forced himself through those weighty doctrines in the library. Often, he had to read paragraphs over and over to extract any meaning. Why did these stupid academics hide their theories in sentences that twisted and turned like tracks in the desert, leading nowhere? But he pressed on, because this was his history, and it had been kept from him his whole life. It was fascinating, revealing and shocking; he hadn't learnt any of this in history class at school.

The lectures were easier to follow than reading the books. He had his notepad, like the other students, and sat at the back of the theatre taking notes and trying to belong. Alice spoke heatedly and emotionally about Aboriginal tribes, lost languages, land rights, the Stolen Generations, and once or twice told mystic stories he was sure he had heard before.

The semester was almost over. For the students, there were papers to write and exams to sit. Only Darius seemed to walk unhurriedly, without stress. But no one looked at him like an impostor because he had a leather shoulder bag with the university's name on it and he dressed accordingly. He had a little tape recorder which he put on the table during the lectures. And he even went as far as to copy the posture and behaviour of the students, perfecting their peculiar kind of hurried slackness and passionate indifference. He entered lecture theatres like he was meant to be there, asked for books at the library as if they were put there for him and walked with academic purpose. He attended a couple of protests too, but when asked later by Harry what they were about, he mumbled his answers, focusing on where the protest was and who was there, rather than the topic. Harry laughed at this and explained that he used to go to protest rallies to meet girls as well.

To complete his performance, he set about writing the final essay assigned to the students of Alice's first year Introduction to Australian History course. Struggling to write like an academic, he went to Harry for help. They sat at the kitchen table, drinking tea from those small glasses that he now loved so much; he took it with two sugar cubes and promised himself one day he would have such a tea set. Harry read through the short essay, which Darius knew was far below the required word count.

"May I be honest?"

"Of course."

"It's not bad, but you're mixing things together. It confuses the reader, and it doesn't sound like you. That poem you wrote, that sounded like you."

"I can't write the essay as a poem."

"No, but this sounds like you've taken bits and pieces from other texts and stuck them together as your own ideas."

Darius snatched at his essay. To his surprise, Harry didn't let go; the papers ripped.

"Forget it." Darius dropped the torn paper on the table. He wanted to explain, wanted to shout that he had done his best to write just like the other students. He got up to leave the kitchen. Harry grabbed his arm as he tried to pass.

"A suggestion?"

"What's that?"

"You're blunt, just like your mother. It's a rare quality in the academic world. Too many professors waffle on and use so many words to say so little. Less really is more."

"So?"

"Take that tape recorder of yours and speak your essay. Talk like you talk. Ask questions and offer answers, both your own theories and those of others. If you don't agree with them, say so and try to explain why."

"Thanks, Harry."

In the study upstairs, which was doubling as his bedroom, Darius stared at the tape recorder, at the crumbled papers his notes were scribbled on, at all the books that filled the shelves around him. His dad would have laughed at him just for trying, for thinking he could pose as a student. His dad had been a smart man, everyone knew that, but he'd had no time for intellectuals.

Darius put his notes in order and picked up the recorder. When he pressed record, the doorbell rang. Downstairs, he heard Harry move through the house, open the door and greet the visitor.

"Yes?"

"G'day. I'm looking for a lost Australian, last seen in a tacky bar in old Munich town. Has he passed through here? I think he's on horseback."

Darius leapt out of his chair. He was at the top of the stairs when Humphrey added sheepishly, "That would be Darius Tucker. Have I got the wrong house?"

Darius jumped down the stairs. "Hobo."

"Hey, Digger."

"What the fuck're you doin here?"

"I'd had enough of the hostel." Humphrey came into the house and closed the door. The three men crowded the hallway. "I quit and decided it was time to visit Mother England. Ah," he sighed, "cruel Brittania."

Harry cleared his throat loudly.

"Humphrey, this is Harry. I wrote about him."

"Proverbman," Humphrey shouted, shaking Harry's hand enthusiastically. "Saving the world with a simple quote."

"Trying to. Come in, why don't you. Would you like some tea?"

"A coffee would be great."

"Let's go into the kitchen. Make yourself at home."

"Listen, Hobo. I'm sorry about Munich."

"Forgotten," Humphrey said, sweeping it all away with a wave of his hand. "Though you are not. Freddie's been asking about you. He said you could come back and work any time you want."

It felt good to be wanted somewhere, that he had left a space that couldn't be filled.

"He offered me a job, too. I'm starting in the kitchen when I get back."

"You know how to cook?"

"Sure. I worked in a few restaurants when I was in high school. In Esperance, a fish and chip shop counts as a first class eatery. I did that in Melbourne too. Kitchen work's a good travelling vocation."

Darius shook his head with amazement.

"Don't be impressed." Humphrey took a seat at the kitchen table and looked at the torn essay. He picked up a slither of paper and squinted at the handwriting. "So, what about you? Coming back to Munich?"

Darius picked up the loose paper and shoved it into his pocket. "Dunno. I'm thinkin about, uh, applyin for uni here."

"Digger goes to college. I don't believe it. Do they offer Applied Wool Removal here? Shearingology? Or did all that mining turn you on to Geology? Or did it just turn you on?"

"He has potential," Harry said. "He could study whatever he wants."

"And what would that be?" Humphrey sipped the coffee Harry put in front of him, grimaced, and then started spooning sugar into it.

"Australian history."

"Excellent, but that'll take decades. There's two centuries of lies to wade through, and nearly every book written on the topic is wrong."

"Alice, me mum, teaches it at the uni. You should come to one of her lectures. Some of the stuff's unbelievable. We were never told it at school."

"I know, I know. All the bad stuff doesn't get into your average Aussie high school history book. Maybe that's changed. Hope so."

"Take him to a lecture, Darius," Harry suggested. "Maybe you'll both learn something."

"Sounds marvy," Humphrey said in his British accent. "Tally ho. Off to uni we go."

"How long you stayin, Hobo?"

"Just a few days," he said, sipping his coffee and grimacing again. "When you wrote that you were here, I thought I'd better rescue you. You know, stop you from stealing a loaf of bread and getting transported back home. But you look pretty happy."

"I am." Darius traced all those steps that had got him here, proud of every decision he had made.

"Well, that means it's your job to show me ye olde London town, including a trip to that seat of learning your mother rules. You found her, Darius. How does it feel?"

"Great. Fantastic."

"She's an amazing woman," Harry said. "Maybe you should give him one of your notebooks, Darius, because she often explains herself better when speaking."

"Yeah, give me a notebook. I wanna pretend to be a student too. Do you have a beige cardigan I can wear? What are we protesting against?"

"Maybe against the conflict in the Middle East," Harry said.

"Is that where you hail from, Harry?"

"Yes. Iraq. I went to Oxford but decided not to go home after Hussein took power."

"He's still there, isn't he? Don't worry. The yanks will find a reason to have another crack at him."

"And trample over a few million innocent people in the process." Harry cleared his throat loudly and changed his tone. "If you want to make that lecture, you better get moving."

"I'm ready." Humphrey downed his coffee. The grains stuck to the corners of his mouth and he wiped them away with the back of his hand. "Do we go by bike, or do only the professors do that?"

"We'll take the bus."

"A red double-decker devil, I hope, but you'll have to pay. I haven't changed any money yet."

"How'd you get here then?"

"Hitched."

"From the airport?"

"Yep. I was in the mood for some adventure. But it was easy. Who knew the English would be so friendly, and to an Australian no less?"

Humphrey went upstairs to use the bathroom.

"He's an interesting one," Harry said.

"Yeah, everyone says that. He takes a bit of gettin used to, but he's a good bloke."

"He's got spirit."

"Yeah. I need to get my stuff together. We'll be back for dinner."

***

The bus sloshed through the London rain, the windscreen wipers making loud rubbing and squeaking sounds that could be heard from the back of the bus. Jackets and umbrellas steamed, misting the windows over and making passengers rub at the glass with their sleeves. Darius did the same, remembering how he had rubbed at the mist on his bedroom window and had watched his dad push Alice from the veranda. He leaned slightly to his left and felt her shoulder. She was there now. Dad was dead and couldn't send her away again. Everything in between could be forgotten.

"But it's more than just history," he heard her say. "And it doesn't matter who writes it or from what point of view."

"How can you say that?" Humphrey said. "History is written by elites who glorify themselves. It's always been that way. The Bible wasn't written by lepers. Knowledge is power, like Bacon said. And those in power would never make themselves look bad."

"So, it's about human nature. You're implying that those who don't have the power would do the same if given the power. If history is only about glorification, then you would do the same too."

"I'd tell the truth."

"Ah, but then it would depend on who believes your truth. What's the truth for you may not be the truth for others. And then, no one might believe you, especially if all the evidence is to the contrary."

"So how can you ever know if history is true or not?" Darius asked.

"That's the best question I've heard in a long time. In history, truth can be a false friend. Events occur, things happen, but the reasons for it and what drives the participants is open to interpretation. Most of the time, there can be no single truth. Nobody except Philip knows what Philip was thinking when they landed at Port Jackson."

"Exactly," Humphrey said. "So why isn't what you lectured about today taught in Australia?"

She frowned and chewed her bottom lip thoughtfully. She had

full lips, just as Darius remembered, cracked and dry, and she didn't attempt to cover them with lipstick or balm. Her bottom lip stuck out a little to the side, perhaps chewed too often.

"To a certain extent, it is," she said at last. "In fact, probably a lot more so than when you went to school. It's changing. More people want to know what happened, good and bad. The changes come with each generation. I'm not sure there'll ever be accountability, though how hard is it to say sorry. You can't really blame people for being ignorant. The media so readily shows images of drunk Aborigines doing nothing, so for most people, that's the only image they have, especially for those who live in cities. And if a crime's committed, they always make a point of saying 'a man of Aboriginal descent' did it, but they'll never say 'a man of English descent' or 'a white man'. It won't be easy removing those images, all that evidence."

Clearly unsatisfied, Humphrey offered his own answer. "They don't teach it because then everything will fall apart. Our identity is a myth."

"No, it isn't."

"It is. They mashed it together for Federation. A white male identity. Kipling, Boy Scouts, Britannia's disposable army, the Coming Man. All that."

"Yes, but it's not like that anymore. And even if it was constructed at the start, it's now very much part of Australia."

Humphrey sighed. "Yeah. I hate to say it, and I wish it wasn't like that, but yeah. You're right. What do we do about it?"

Darius rubbed at the misty window again. Outside, the road was a river, yet Londoners were marching straight through it, clutching their umbrellas with two hands, leaning into the wind, and walking into puddles without looking or caring.

"Educate," Alice said, "and fight. Mabo was very important, the *Bringing Them Home* report was too. Things will change."

"I can't see it happening in my lifetime."

"Then don't live there. If you don't like it, find a place that appeals to you more."

"I don't wanna live there."

"Don't worry, mate," the man in the seat in front of them said. He stood up and prepared to get off the bus, which was slowing for the next stop. "You won't be missed. They should throw people like you out and keep them out."

"What era are you from?" Humphrey asked. "You see, Alice? You see? This's who we are. This is what we're up against."

"You're the problem, mate," the man said. "Not me."

"Steady on."

"He's allowed to have an opinion," Alice said. "And so are you. Discussion's always good."

"Yeah, well I didn't like what you lot were talking about. Australia's the greatest country in the world, and Aussies are the greatest people."

"Says the Aussie living in London," Humphrey said. "Why are you here? If Oz is so great, go home."

The man stepped toward Humphrey but the bus stopped suddenly and the man was thrown off balance. His sunglasses fell from the perch on his head. Humphrey picked them up.

"Here."

"Thanks."

"Look, mate," Humphrey said, "Darius and me, we're students. Alice is our professor. We were just having discussion, that's all. Looking at all the sides of the story. I love Australia too. All of it."

The doors opened.

"Maybe you should think about more action than just talk." The man shook his head and got off the bus.

"Idiot," Humphrey said. "But he does have a point. Action. Action. Talk is nothing, doesn't change anything. We need action."

"London's full of Australians," Alice said.

"You mean it's full of idiots," Humphrey said.

"Maybe you can get a sorry rally going."

"No chance."

"You won't get them to protest with that kind of attitude. Humphrey, I think you're a really bright spark, and I know that you know that people like him are the products of their upbringing."

"Yeah, I get that."

"They do the best with what they have, like a lot of people. Australia's shot itself in the foot. For decades, many of the brightest people have left Australia for a life overseas. You think you're alone but there are plenty of others like you, people who want to change Australia for the better but who just give up and leave. So nothing ever changes."

Darius thought about how, after his time in the mines, he had arrived back home expecting everything to be different, but nothing had changed. Les had talked about the same sensation, of coming home after an absence of years and then feeling like he had never left; that during that time, only he had developed and changed.

"You've got a point," Humphrey said.

"I'm guilty of it too, and so are you. So's our young poet here. A lot of the people who could make a difference, leave."

"I'm not a poet," Darius said.

Humphrey turned to Darius. "Maybe we should open that restaurant we talked about. Get the truth out there. That'd be some serious action."

"What restaurant?" Alice asked.

"It was his idea," Darius said. "I had nothing to do with it."

"An Aussie restaurant that tells the true history of Australia." Humphrey seemed suddenly quite taken with the idea. "Real history. Not just a lot of stereotypical nonsense. We could open it in Munich. Hah. Freddie would blow a fuse."

"He owns the Aussie bar in Munich," Darius explained to Alice.

"And it's full of stereotypical nonsense," Humphrey said.

"And full of people," Darius added. "Who's gonna want to eat and drink in a place that's tellin them nothing but bad stuff?"

"That's a good point," Alice said.

"Can you imagine it, Darius? I can."

"Well, Humphrey, if you want to give the world your version of the truth and try to change Australia, from Germany mind you, then why not do it."

"I think I will."

Darius smiled. Humphrey could be as excited as he wanted right now, but Darius knew there was no way he would ever see it through. His friend was prone to fanciful ideas; he would get wired up about something, lay plans to get it started and then wake up the next day with other things on his mind.

"This's our stop," Darius said.

On the footpath, long trails of water streamed towards the drains, bubbling through the already overwhelmed grates. They tried to avoid the puddles but after only a few steps, Darius could feel the water coming through his socks.

Alice led the way, through the gate and the front door.

"How was it?" Harry asked when they all stood in the kitchen.

Alice tilted her head towards Humphrey. "I had a bit of a troublemaker today."

Harry stirred a large pot. "Oh, yes?"

"I may have asked a few questions," Humphrey said, "but only because the others were too scared to ask."

"Actually, it was good. Got some discussion going."

Humphrey dropped himself into one of the kitchen chairs. "I thought the audience involvement was great. Get the kids out of their books and talking in the open."

Darius sat down at the table as well. It was already set for dinner. He poured Alice a glass of wine. She smiled when she saw the label. Darius looked too; an Australian Cab Sav.

"You talk like a uni grad," she said, "but your behaviour today makes me think you never went."

"I started at UWA," Humphrey said, "but never finished."

"What happened?"

"I couldn't stand spending another half decade in an institution that was going to tell me how to think, live and breathe."

"What did you study?"

"Law."

At the stove, Harry chuckled softly.

"What's so funny?" Humphrey asked.

Harry turned from the stove to look directly at Humphrey. "You should go back and finish. I think you'd make a good lawyer. Still, that's one less to kill when the revolution comes."

"Lawyers are useless middlemen," Humphrey said.

"But well paid," Harry countered.

"'Poor and content is rich, and rich enough,'" Humphrey said.

"Shakespeare again?" Darius asked.

Alice said over her glass of wine, "Sounds like literature would've been more your forte."

"Or the theatre," Harry said.

Humphrey poured himself a glass of wine and took a long drink. "I was in a few school plays. Hmm, this's a nice drop. The Italians, they know how to make wine."

"You idiot," Darius said, laughing.

Alice laughed too. This made Darius laugh louder, because her laugh was contagious and he was just so bloody happy right then.

***

There were a few puddles on the footpath, but most of the rain from the night before had dried. It promised to be a beautiful day, one that actually resembled summer. The grass that was just coming out from the tree shadows glistened with moisture. As always, they ran to Harry's rhythm. He took short economical steps, barely lifting his feet from the ground and moving deceptively fast. Darius ploughed on, trying to keep up, but already planning how he would take Humphrey to the centre of London and show him the sights.

"I like Humphrey," Harry said between heavy breaths. "A real character."

"Yeah, he's amazing, eh? I can't believe all the stuff he knows."

"Think you'll go back to Munich? He said something about opening a restaurant."

"He gets a lot of crazy ideas." Darius was surprised his friend was still hanging on to that one.

They reached the edge of Regent's Park and Harry slowed to a walk.

"You know, if you do go to university, Alice and I, your mother and I, we could help you out, financially."

"Oh no, Harry. I could never let you do that. It's okay. I've got some money saved. From the property sale."

"He never remarried?"

Darius looked away from Harry and back towards the park, frowning as the memories filled his head: a dusty-hemmed dress left on the floor, or a frilly pair of underwear sometimes slung around the door handle of his dad's bedroom, like a code between room-mates. And he could still hear those cries in the night that sounded like his dad fighting chronic constipation and the woman straining vocally for the hand of God.

"There were women, but none of them stayed. Sounds like Alice was the only one he loved."

"You know we'd like you to stay. But if you decide to go, we'll always be here for you."

"Thanks, Harry. That means a lot."

"And if you do open this restaurant, we want to be invited to the opening night. From the sounds of things, Alice could be a big help."

It seemed Alice and Harry had already factored Humphrey's ridiculous idea into their lives. Soon, he and Humphrey would be compelled into action.

"I like Munich," he said, not committing.

"Yes, distance is useful, isn't it? You could study there."

"No, Harry, you don't understand. I can't speak a word of German."

"Well, you could learn, but it doesn't matter. You can also study in English."

Darius stopped. "Really?"

"Sure." Harry started jogging on the spot. "Come on. Let's get home before that friend of yours makes a play for my wife."

"He'd never do that."

As he started to run, he thought about Jane; how she had complained so long and loud about studying in German. Had she done all her courses in English? he wondered.

They stopped for the customary milk and paper and beat the footpaths until they were back home. Alice was sitting at the kitchen table, staring sombrely at the pile of unmarked essays in front of her.

"Mornin," Darius said cheerfully. He even went up to her, awkwardly but trying to look natural, and gave her a kiss on the cheek. He left the kitchen and started to go upstairs.

He was half way up when he heard Harry ask, "Where's our young revolutionary?"

"Still sleeping. I think all that discussion last night wore him out."

"Well, must be difficult staying in character for so long. They were more than a few cracks appearing towards the end, and not just in his make up."

Alice laughed loudly. "You don't miss a trick, Harry."

Lewis: If that poem's not about your father, then who is it about?

Poet: Not saying.

Lewis: Okay, um, well, after your father died, you went back to Munich. Why?

Poet: No one knew me there. It was like being able to start from scratch.

Lewis: And it made it easy for you to move on?

Poet: Somethin like that.

Lewis: Was it difficult being a foreigner in Germany?

Poet: Why would it be difficult?

Lewis: Because of the history.

Poet: It's the most tolerant and open country I've ever been in. The world thinks they're boring and humourless, but the Germans have got a lot of things sorted.

Lewis: History casts a long shadow.

Poet: As it does here. They know their history and they're better people for knowing it. We could learn a lot from them.

Lewis: With regards to our own history?

Poet: Yep.

~~~

Seeking Asylum

It wasn't foreign, but it was still exciting. He walked with confidence along the automatic walkways that strung the terminals together, weaving between the lazy people who just stood there, letting the machine do the work for them. At the ticket machine, he saw a few tourists struggling to figure it out, tracing the coloured squiggles on the train map with their fingers. He knew what to do and the thick silver coins fell solidly into the machine. He helped the two tourists at the machine next to him and pointed to where the train platform was. The ticket was printed swiftly, on stiff paper and without any smudges. He admired the ticket, missing Alice and Harry but not the rundown, over-used city in which they lived.

"Excuse me, zir," a man said from behind, "but ve muss zearch your baggages."

Darius turned around.

Humphrey poked Darius's shoulder accusingly. "Vot nasty dings have you Australians been schmuggling?"

"You got the wrong Aussie," Darius said, holding his hands up innocently.

Humphrey leaned closer. "Ve have vays of making you talk." Then he slapped Darius on the back. "And we'll start by getting you deeply intoxicated at the Hole."

"Hobo, it's not even lunchtime."

"You're right. It's too late already. You shearers have beer for breakfast. It's all these time zones. Too confusing." He started walking away. "Come on, I hate airports."

On the train, every seat was taken, mostly by bags and suitcases, so they stood near the doors. Darius thought Humphrey was standing a little too close. He tried to lean back, to give them a more manly distance, but Humphrey closed the gap.

"What took you so long? I've been waiting."

"I went with Alice and Harry on a bit of a holiday, after the semester ended."

"Where?"

"Up to Scotland. Edinburgh and Glasgow, even to Loch Ness. But we didn't see the monster."

"There is no monster," Humphrey said. "No Santa Claus. No Easter Bunny. No Simpson and certainly no fucking donkey. We've been fed bullshit our whole lives. We've gotta change this."

Darius looked away. In the weeks following Humphrey's departure for Munich, he had convinced himself that the restaurant was a bad idea. Alice, now the strongest voice of reason in his life, had warned him that presenting a negative view of Australia could cause trouble.

"Teaching history on the other side of the world is one thing," she had said, "but doing it to make a profit could be dangerous. There are plenty of organisations back home who might try to stop you."

And without Humphrey's incessant talk of the idea, right down to finding a location and hiring staff, Darius had focused on other things. He considered applying for university but feared rejection. Instead, he bought a ticket for Munich. He thought he was better off working at the Hole.

"Action, right?"

Humphrey nodded. "Affirmative."

"Don't tell me you're still thinkin about that restaurant?"

"It's already underway."

"You're joking."

"Oh, yeah, Digger. I don't fuck around. I've got an agent looking for a location. I've been on this since I got back. London inspired me." He poked Darius in the chest. "You inspired me. You're the guinea pig. The lab rat."

"Huh?"

"You're the reason the truth must be told. You can set the mates free. If you can be changed, they can too. Imagine it. A whole country purified."

Humphrey's eyes had their usual twinkle, but there was also intent there, a sparkle of ambition Darius had never noticed before. He had always thought of Humphrey as someone who had a lot of ideas but never saw them through. But he knew from the mines that Humphrey was a hard worker, when he wanted to be.

The train stopped at the next station and Darius, leaning against the doors, fell out as they opened. Humphrey laughed at him as he climbed back in.

"Hobo, let's think about this some more."

"Too late. The agent's already got a few places to show us."

"What d'you mean us? I'm not involved in this. It's your idea. And I'm not your bloody lab rat."

"I can't do this without you. Come on. We're mates."

"How are ya gonna finance it all?"

"Les transferred the money to my German account."

"What money?"

"He sold the house." Humphrey stood closer, as if he had all that money in his pockets and didn't want anyone on the train to hear. "Mum had life insurance too. We can do this. There's plenty of money, isn't there?"

Darius looked down at the floor. It was impeccably clean and again he missed Alice and Harry but not London, where the floors of trains were covered with dirt, grime and gum. And nobody complained about it, as if they had long ago accepted that their city was a giant rubbish can.

"Come on, Digger. You're father must've left you something. You said your family's been there for generations. What about the land? You sold it, right?"

Darius kept looking at the floor, hating it that he was so transparent and that Humphrey always guessed right.

"You did. Ha-ha. Get that money transferred over here and let's do this thing."

"I dunno, Hobo," Darius said, but it sounded pathetic even to him. He could already see himself signing whatever contract Humphrey might thrust in front of his face.

"And that, my friend, is the whole point. You don't know, at least you didn't until you met me. And you found your mum again. Darius, there's a good chunk of those twenty million people down under who dunno, and who don't wanna know, and a whole world that thinks we're crocodile wrestling drunks. And 'shrimps on the barbie'? We don't even have any bloody shrimps."

Darius looked out the window. Munich's suburbs rushed past. He had missed the city's orderliness, its symmetry and reliable functionality. He could see it even from here, not just in the shape and look of the city, but in the way people walked; how they rode their bicycles and drove their cars. He sighed, wanting to leave his mark on this place, to be known, to change things; but he also liked Munich because here he was no one, completely anonymous, without a past.

"This's our chance to make a difference," Humphrey went on. "We could bring Australia into the next century. We could snap all the mates out of their malaise. One of us will be elected the first president. And may God bury the Queen."

"President?"

"Okay, okay. Maybe president's too much. But come on. We gotta do this before someone else does."

"No one's gonna go to a restaurant like that."

"Yeah, they will. Uni students and all the smart Germans. They'll want more than the stuffed alligators at the Hole."

"I was thinking of working there again."

"You can, until we get organised. I'm working there too."

"It can't be that easy for two Aussies to start a business in Munich."

"I've got some people on it. It's all coming together. Easy as. You can't ignore that everything's fallen into place perfectly, with the money and all. It's like the gods are telling us to do this."

Darius ran his hands slowly through his hair. He felt the stiff gristle left by those blonde streaks Jane had convinced him to get. He thought of the money, the years spent squirming and writhing under his dad's calloused thumb, earning it in some sick way, suffering for his inheritance.

Fuck, he thought, missing the old bastard. He really is gone.

Humphrey's persuasive argument lent the restaurant a deeper purpose, and his confidence made it sound like it would succeed easily, but he often talked like that. Darius wanted more time to think about it, to get settled in Munich again, and not just to rush like this. But from the look on his friend's face, from his fidgety body language and impatient stance, he knew he wouldn't get it. Humphrey's mind was made up.

There came the intrusive sound of a mobile phone.

"Boragart...Yeah, we're almost there...Okay. *Bis bald.*"

Darius looked with disdain at the phone cupped in Humphrey's hand. "When did you get that thing? I thought you hated them."

"Yeah, well, everything I said was right, but you have to admit, they're pretty handy."

Darius wondered what other of his friend's strong opinions had swung 180 degrees.

"Look, Darius," Humphrey said, jamming the phone into his back pocket, "Wolfgang, the agent, is meeting us at the Hauptbahnhof. He's very gay, so don't show that it bothers you."

"I don't care if he's gay."

"Riiiight. He found me an apartment a few weeks ago, big enough for you too. He wants to show us a place in Maxvorstadt. He says it's a bargain."

"What about drinks at the Hole. I wanna tell Freddie I'm back and ready to work."

"We'll go there after. Get into celebrating mode."

"Can't hurt to have a look, I guess."

"Good, because you don't have a choice. Shit, Darius, we're gonna make history. No, we're gonna rewrite history, turn the whole thing on its head."

At the station, Humphrey weaved through the crowd, walking quickly, almost skipping. Darius laboured behind, struggling with his heavy backpack, but Humphrey was easy to follow because he was taller than everybody, and the wind rushing through the station made his hair stand up, adding a few more inches. The short break gave Darius the chance to arrange his thoughts. He wondered how much money Humphrey actually had, because he was prone to exaggerate. How would they split the profits? Would they share all the costs? Was it really so easy for two foreigners to open a restaurant in Germany? What about visas and red tape? Bank credit? Staff? Supplies? All the money they would lose if they failed?

"Thanks for waiting, Wolfie," Humphrey said, giving the agent's shoulder a light, friendly slap. "This is Darius, my partner. The guy I told you about."

They shook hands.

"G'day."

"My car's around the corner," Wolfgang said, leading them towards one of the exits. His baggy suit pants ruffled as he walked. "Double parked." He turned to Darius. "Good flight?"

"Yeah, all right."

"When you've done the haul from Australia," Humphrey said, "London to Munich's a cup of tea."

"Yes, they drink a lot of tea in England," Wolfgang said.

"No, he means it's easy," Darius said. "Cuppa tea. Like, no worries."

"Ah, I see." Outside, Wolfgang slid his sunglasses onto his face

209

and led them towards his car. "Then flying to Australia would not be a cup of tea. It's still my dream though. My aunt moved to Adelaide last year. She was a *Beamterin*. Worked for the city. What do you call them in English?"

"Civil servants," Humphrey said.

Wolfgang stopped. "Really? That makes them sound like waiters and waitresses." He turned to Darius again. "Excellent pension. She bought a house on the beach."

"She could have chosen about a thousand places better than Adelaide," Humphrey said. "I guess it was cheaper there."

"It was. She left at the right time too, before all this euro nonsense started. That currency's going to make prices higher than ever." He looked at Humphrey, lowering his glasses and showing his eyes. "You really should think of buying. When the euro comes, the value will double in five years."

"I'm a renter, Wolfie," Humphrey said.

"Then I suggest a longer contract with a fixed rent that can't be influenced by the euro, at least for the first few years."

"You're the man."

They climbed into the agent's silver BMW. The leather seats crunched and squeaked as they got comfortable. Humphrey sat up front while Darius shared the backseat with his pack. He tried not to think about what may have transpired on this backseat. Is leather always this sticky? he wondered.

"This is better than the one I showed you last week," Wolfgang said. The car drifted down the street, the engine only making a noise when Wolfgang accelerated hard, which he did often to squeeze through narrow gaps and beat orange lights. "Good location, also," he added airily, twisting his head to speak to Humphrey. "Seating for about sixty. Very intimate. The last tenants left everything. Furniture and all the stuff in the kitchen."

"What happened?"

"They were deported. Pakistanis."

"Perfect."

"And we'll be next," Darius said.

"I've got you covered," Wolfgang said. "My aunt, she was a, how do you say it?"

"Civil servant," Humphrey and Darius said together.

Wolfgang laughed. "You two make a great team. Yes, she was a civil servant and I've still got contacts in her department. You know what it's like. They're all linked. I'll take care of your permits. You'll just need to sign a few things and pay a bit of money. No drama."

Humphrey turned in his seat to nod eagerly at Darius. "We want to get going as soon as possible," he said to Wolfgang. "There's a ton of people already interested in the place."

"It will have to be good to compete with Friedrich's place," Wolfgang said. "I was there recently and it's very authentic."

Darius couldn't see Humphrey's face but he could feel him smiling. "Not nearly as authentic as ours will be."

"I will tell all my friends. I know a lot of people in Munich."

"Thanks, Wolfie."

"You know, there's also a German-Australian group that meets every month. Maybe they could do it at your place instead of the Waterhole? In the future."

"That's a great idea. I guarantee they'll have plenty to talk about."

Wolfgang steered his car into a loading bay, stopping in front of a graffiti-covered roller door. Humphrey jumped out like an exuberant child.

"It looks great," he shouted, already looking through the windows. "I can see it now. We can hang flags out the front. The Aussie flag, the Aboriginal flag, even the flag from the Eureka Stockade, the one made by a Canadian, ha-ha."

Wolfgang unlocked the front door. "It needs to be painted, but it sounds like you're planning to decorate, so you probably would paint it anyway."

Humphrey was the first inside. He was behind the bar, then turning taps on and off in the kitchen, then sitting in one of the many booths. His whooping even echoed from the women's bathroom.

"Breadwinners for men," he said, coming out, the toilet flush still sounding, "and housewives for women. Or maybe mates and non-mates. Certainly no blokes and sheilas."

"It's all right," Darius said, glad he hadn't suggested blokes and sheilas.

"I love it, Wolfie," Humphrey said. He looked around the room and smiled ambitiously. "Man, the things we can do with this place. It's all going to start here."

"So, you're interested?"

"I reckon we are, aren't we, Digger?"

Darius nodded slowly, but thinking it was all moving too fast. "Interested, yeah. But we've still got a lot to talk about."

"Don't mind him," Humphrey said. "That's just Aussie scepticism. The optimism will bubble to the surface once we get some alcohol into him."

"*Wunderbar.*" Wolfgang clapped his small hands together. "I've got the contract back at my office. You can have a read and tell me what you think."

"Is it in German?" Darius asked.

"Yes."

"I got it," Humphrey said. "*Ich lese durch der Vertrag.*"

"*Den Vertrag,*" Wolfgang said.

"Right."

Wolfgang led them out of the restaurant and soon they were all settled into the leathery, sticky comfort of the BMW. Wolfgang weaved through the traffic. Horns sounded.

"So I can tell my friends, what will the restaurant be called?"

"We don't have a name yet," Darius said.

Humphrey turned to smile at Darius. "Yes, we do." He turned back to the agent. "True Blue Tucker."

"Ooh, that's catchy."

"Isn't it?"

***

She settled herself on a stool at the bar. "Hey, Digger."

"G'day, Jane. Good to see ya."

"I heard you were back."

"Yeah. Coupla weeks now. Enjoying the summer?"

She nodded. She had added another ring to her left ear, and the lobe hung slightly lower than the right lobe as a result. She stared down at the bar, her black fingernails peeling away the layers of cardboard from a soggy beer mat. She rolled them into little balls and dropped them in the ashtray. Around her, the Hole bustled and echoed, and when she spoke again, he could barely hear her.

"How's your dad?"

"Not too good. He's dead."

"Oh, I'm really sorry," she said, vaguely sympathetic and sorrowful, clearly trying hard. "Really."

"Yeah, me too." And he was, but not sorry that his dad's accident had ended their relationship.

When she didn't say anything, they lapsed into silence. Darius let it hang, let it resonate. Jane looked at him. She opened her mouth to talk once or twice, but was swallowing again and again, the words stuck in her throat, trying to keep inside all the things she really wanted to say.

"I heard you and Bozo are gonna open a restaurant," she said at last.

"Rumours."

"That's not what I heard."

"You sure hear a lot."

"I listen." Then she looked up at him. "Not like some people."

"Well, I listen too, and I heard you got yourself another fella. One of the guys from the footy team."

"It's not that serious. We just hang out."

"Good fella?"

"He's a programmer. From Melbourne. He's working here until October."

"Cartlon supporter?"

She shook her head. "Unfortunately not. Collingwood, ugh."

"How's uni?"

"Finished."

"But you're still here."

"The summer's so nice in Munich. I decided to stay for it."

Darius washed a few glasses. "Too hot for me."

"Yeah, right. You're from WA."

"Guess I'm sick of the hot weather."

"You'd like Melbourne then."

He wanted to reply, to say something clever, but nothing came to mind, and really, he couldn't be bothered engaging Jane in more conversation. So he looked past her and watched a small man enter the restaurant. The way he searched the room and the keen way his eyes fell on Jane convinced Darius that here was the new boyfriend. He wondered, angrily recalling how she had only ever introduced him as "my boyfriend", if he would ever learn his name. The boyfriend took a bar stool next to her and kissed her on the cheek.

"Gis a beer," he said.

"Righto."

"Darius," Humphrey shouted, running out of the kitchen. "Turn on the TV. You won't believe it."

The television above the bar was normally used for football and rugby games. For big sporting events, like the AFL grand final, Freddie put up a screen and rented a projector. The bar television was a flat screen, but a cheap one. It made everything elongated and thinner, so fat men looked in proportion and normal-sized women seemed anorexic.

"Get a news channel," Humphrey said. "In English." Darius flicked through the channels. "Stop."

On the screen was a large freighter, rendered strange by the cheap television. A skinny helicopter was circling above it. Sometimes, a close up of the deck showed some dark-skinned people sitting and standing in a small space between the containers. A blue tarp provided some shade but most of the people lay in the sun, sprawled on the deck and bundled under blankets and sarongs of mismatched colours.

"We were watching in the kitchen," Humphrey said. "A boat of refugees was sinking near Christmas Island." He turned to the people at the bar. "That's part of Australia but miles from the mainland. Off the west coast. Anyway, this freighter rescued them and tried to bring them to Christmas Island. The Australian government has refused to let the ship dock. They'll probably send out the navy in a minute."

"Why don't they let them dock?" someone asked.

"Well, you probably don't know, because it's a pretty well-kept secret, outside of Australia, but us Aussies have a pretty bad relationship with illegal immigrants. Yellow peril, White Australia Policy and all that. We don't really want our lucky little country getting overrun by Asians. Never did. There's even a few political parties with that exact mandate, and the Liberals, well, they just word it better so it doesn't sound as offensive."

"Oi, steady on, mate," said the boyfriend. "Look, I don't support One Nation, and I'm not racist, but we can't just let everyone in. Then they'll all come."

Darius could look at him now, could judge him, could happily be reminded that he still hadn't served him a beer. The man had tanned skin and a blonde rinse styled scruffily so it looked like he had just got out of bed. Darius knew, because he had had the same style, that it took a long time to get it right. The corners of the man's mouth were turned upwards, as if everything in life was such a joke for him, and he would always be the first to smile and laugh.

"Thanks, mate," Humphrey said. "You've just proved my point. In fact, you proved a bunch of points I now don't have to make. But just to make it real clear for everyone else, if we don't let these people in, who do we let in? Huh?" He cupped a hand around his ear. "I can't hear you, mate."

"There's a limit to our generosity," the boyfriend said.

"Most of them aren't even refugees, Bozo," Jane said. "They pay thousands of dollars to people smugglers. Real refugees can't afford that."

"Thank you, Miss Jane. That's just what the pollies say to get your vote."

"It's true," the boyfriend said. "And it's not fair that they just come to our country uninvited when there are thousands of others who really are refugees. They should get in line and apply like everyone else. We'll help them out, but not these queue jumpers. They don't deserve a fair go."

"Well," Humphrey said, "we can't let everyone in, can we? But, if they apply and spend a few years, or ten, in a detention camp out in the desert, then they'll be welcome. Don't forget, 'we've boundless plains to share.'"

"Don't listen to him, Griff," Jane said. "He's always bashing Australia."

"No, no, Miss Jane. I just know more about it."

"Yeah, the negative stuff. And stop calling me Miss Jane."

Griff laughed. "Hey, like Mr Squiggle."

Darius laughed too. He thought Griff wasn't a bad sort.

Humphrey feigned being shot in the heart. "I'm hit, Digger. She got me with the silver bullet of negativity. I'll never recover. Low blow, Jane. All I'm doing is being critical, looking at all the angles. Aaah, but that's not allowed, is it? Can't be critical of Australia, can we? And why, Digger?"

Darius shrugged. "Maybe it easier to go the beach."

"Yes, in the greatest country in the world." Humphrey looked at the screen and shook his head. "It sure is. Equal, fair and honest, where everyone's welcome. If you wait in line."

"Why can't they just get visas?" a woman asked.

Humphrey turned to her. "Long process, meant to discourage them. It's hard to immigrate to Australia, refugee or not. And these unfortunate folks, well, they never seem to fit the profile."

"That was hundreds of years ago," Griff said. "It's not like that now."

Humphrey looked up at the TV screen. "Obviously. But, you've got a point. The White Australia Policy was enacted a hundred years ago. But do you know when it was abolished?"

Griff looked at Jane. The shrug of her shoulders was so slight to be almost imperceptible. But Humphrey didn't miss it.

"After the war," Griff said.

"Not quite. Whitlam ended it," Humphrey said, "in 1973. In practice. I think there are sections of Queensland and WA still hanging onto it. One Nation and Pauline Hansen, good God."

"Whitlam got the sack, didn't he?" Griff asked.

"Yes."

"Couldn't have done a very good job then."

Humphrey leaned on the bar, enjoying himself. "You're right there, Griff. He went a bit too far. The locals went quite ready for it all. But at least he brought the soldiers back from Vietnam."

"Australia fought in Vietnam?" asked the same woman from before.

"Yeah, and worse, they were conscripts, forced to fight."

"But why?"

Humphrey turned to the screen. "It's got something to do with this. Fear of the Asian peril. Our little outpost in south-east Asia thinks itself much more part of the western world, despite the geographic realities."

Griff stood up. "I'm outta here. I came in for a cold beer, not a bloody lecture. Come on, Jane. We don't have to sit around listening to this bullshit."

They walked between the empty tables, under the inflatable kangaroos that hung from the ceiling, past the boomerangs and didgeridoos stuck to the walls.

"Faced with the truth and they just run away," Humphrey said.

When they were gone, Darius looked at the screen again, at all those skinny people on the boat, and tried to make sense of it all.

"Hopefully," Humphrey said, "the whole world's watching this."

But the report ended abruptly and switched to the problems in the Middle East. Darius turned the television off and the restaurant's customers drifted back to their tables. The conversations started to pick up again and the room was pretty much as it was before.

"Hey, did you bring those flyers we printed?"

"You printed them, not me."

"I shoved them in your backpack before we left."

"That's why it was so heavy."

Darius reached for his backpack and lifted out the bundle of flyers. Humphrey snatched them and started moving around the room, handing them out as he went. The flyer had been Humphrey's idea; Darius thought it was way over the top, but sometimes there was no stopping Humphrey. Still, Darius thought, it might be a good way to gauge if the restaurant would have success; if people scoffed at the flyer, maybe they wouldn't come to the restaurant. Then, he could put a stop to it all before they got in too deep.

Darius picked up a flyer from the bar and looked at it. It had a newspaper cartoon in three boxes: the first had an Aborigine being shot by a white man in 1788; the second had the white man hitting the Aborigine with a bottle in 1888; the third had the Aborigine hanging dead from a prison bar in 1988 with the white man smiling and saying, "Look, no hands". On the rest of the flyer were song lyrics and quotes, and already Darius could hear people in the restaurant repeating them.

"'I believe we're in danger of being swamped by Asians,'" one person read. "'They have their own culture and religion, form ghettos and do not assimilate. Of course, I will be called racist but, if I can invite whom I want into my home, then I should have the right to have a say in who comes into my country.' From a speech by Pauline Hanson."

"If you want to learn more about the real Australia," Humphrey shouted, getting everyone's attention, "and eat real Australian food, then come to the True Blue Tucker restaurant. We're opening in September. Tell your colleagues, your family, your friends, even your

217

enemies. This is your chance to discover the truth about Australia."

"Tucker is Australian slang for food," one man said.

"And it'll be the real thing. No kangaroo steaks or crocodile burgers. There'll be the kind of things ordinary Australians eat."

"What's that then?"

"You'll have to come to the restaurant to find out."

He moved back behind the bar. "How lucky was that, eh? I mean, bad for the folks on the boat but great for us. The Aussie government just gave us a whole lot of free promotion."

"What d'you think'll happen?"

"We'll be full on opening day, that's for sure."

"If we open. I mean the refugees on the boat." And though he would never say so, Darius also thought they should be sent back to where they came from. Why did they think they could just jump on a ship, sail for Australia and expect to be welcomed? Who told them it would be paradise?

"The government won't let them in."

"You're sure of that?"

"There's an election coming up. Security's always a hot topic. Gotta defend our island continent. Keep it pure. Hah, you could say that insecurity's the biggest issue. The mates need to feel safe and protected. This could be exactly what Howard needs to get re-elected. Maybe it's all a set up. We say otherwise in public, shout about our multiculturalism and equality, but in our secluded shelters in the suburbs, when the lights are out and all the doors and windows are locked, there are plenty of Aussies who don't want these people invading our precious neighbourhoods and living in the house next door. We don't want our whole apartment building stinking of rice. You heard Griff. And he doesn't sound like he's stupid."

"Who'll you vote for then?"

"I don't vote," Humphrey said, moving back towards the kitchen. "I'm not on the electoral roll."

"Hypocrite," Darius said when he was alone at the bar.

Freddie entered the restaurant and came up to him.

"How's it going, Digger? Good night so far?"

"Yeah, bit quiet, but interesting."

Freddie looked around the restaurant. Most of the tables were full. He waved to a few of the customers he recognised. "It's good to have you back, Digger. The place wasn't the same without you."

"Thanks, mate." Darius reached out to grab the flyer that was on the bar, but the owner saw it first.

"What's this? True Blue Tucker?" He looked at Darius. "Your name is Tucker. You know anything about this?"

"It's my band."

"No."

"It's just an idea, Freddie. I was gonna tell ya."

Freddie marched towards the kitchen. As the owner argued with Humphrey, the whole restaurant quietened to listen. Humphrey strode out of the kitchen, Freddie following close behind. Humphrey took off his apron and dropped it delicately, from his thumb and index finger, to the floor.

"Well, now you know, Friedrich," Humphrey said. "Darius and I quit, effective immediately."

Freddie turned to Darius, his cheeks flushed. "You can't do that. We have an agreement."

"Sorry, mate. We don't."

"Then get out of here," Freddie shouted, pointing to the door. "And don't expect any money."

"We're going," Darius said, already with his backpack on his shoulder. He had heard a few nasty rumours that Freddie could get violent when pushed, especially when it came to money. "I'm sorry, Freddie. I wanted to tell ya.

"Too late."

"Forget the money. No harm intended. Come on, Hobo."

"See you all in a couple of weeks," Humphrey shouted from the doorway. A bottle flew through the air and he ducked just in time. It smashed against the door and a few people screamed. Darius went through the door and Humphrey followed, but he popped his head inside one more time.

"You throw like a girl, Freddie," he said, and he just got the door closed as another bottle smashed into it.

***

Freed from the Hole, they could turn their attentions to the restaurant. After the flyer handouts, and other posters they put up, a lot of people had contacted Humphrey, asking about the restaurant and when it would open. Humphrey was sure it would be a success.

The painting was done. It had cost more than Darius had expected, as everything was costing more, but they split all the costs 50-50. Humphrey mentioned something about tax refunds for business expenses and Darius hoped this was the case.

They bought a couple of televisions and had these tuned to an English news channel while they set about decorating the tables. They stuck documents and photographs to the tops of tables and then covered them with clear contact so people could eat and read at the same time.

"Mate, no one's gonna wanna look at this stuff while they're eating," Darius said, pushing the contact smooth with a ruler so there would be no bubbles.

"It'll be the easiest place in the world to make conversation."

Alice had sent over a few boxes of material. Humphrey called it evidence. This amounted to most of what was being put on the tables. Taken altogether, Darius thought it offered an extremely negative view of Australia, especially as Humphrey cast aside anything remotely positive. Darius was quietly ashamed and worried they would have to do a lot of explaining. Worse, he thought no one would come in, and if they did, they wouldn't come back.

The freighter was still stranded off the coast of Christmas Island, but news coverage was limited. The news reported that the Norwegian captain had tried to sail towards Christmas Island, but Australian SAS commandos had been sent out to prevent the ship from moving closer.

On the television, there now was a short report. The pictures on the screen made Darius stop and stare: the giant, motionless freighter, the people huddling under the blue tarp, the commandos circling like the ship was Australia's mortal enemy.

"I read some of the Aussie papers online this morning," Humphrey said when the report was over. "You won't believe what they're writing. Utter rubbish. One journalist claimed that the captain himself might be a people smuggler. And this is the guy that rescued those poor folks, probably costing his company millions."

"Nothing's happened yet. They're still there."

"I read that the government tried to pass something called the Emergency Border Act."

"What's that?"

"It would basically give us the right to destroy any ship sailing into our waters. Like we're being invaded. And they could turn refugee ships back no matter what condition the boat, or the people in it, is in. Not exactly a fair go, is it?"

Darius shook his head. It wasn't, but he couldn't help agreeing with the Prime Minister. There had to be a limit. "We've got the right to protect our border."

"To a degree, sure. But we could be a little more humane about it. Fair go. What a joke that is. The mates scream for it when they're hard up, but hate it when others get it, especially the ones they consider undeserving. Anyway, a fair go is never about equality and honesty. It's about money. And there won't be many Aussies who think a fair go applies to boat people."

"Probly not." Darius picked up the flags Humphrey had bought online. "Where should we put these?"

"Near the door. People will see them and will want to know what they represent. You know, that reminds me, we're gonna need to hire some staff pretty soon. We can't do all this ourselves."

"What happened to you in the kitchen and me behind the bar?"

"Yeah, well, I've been thinking about that and I think it's better if I work out front. People are gonna read this stuff and they're gonna ask questions."

"So, you'd be a waiter then?"

"A waiter. Yeah."

"Hobo, how are we..."

"Wolfie said he'd help out. He told me yesterday he's got some guys for us. Hopefully they'll all be gay. That'd be fitting. It'll give our place an edge, a connection to our convict roots, pun intended. All that blokey, matey masculinity is just extreme homophobia asserting itself. That's probably why all those beach boys and surfers get their chests waxed and walk around with no shirts on."

"It's not like that," he said, recalling his youth, all those hairy-chested shearers. He remembered how, for a bet, his father had sheared Curly, back and front, when the man had passed out drunk.

"Not all of it. But you can't deny the history, the mathematics. Australia was settled almost entirely by men. Wild colonial boys. Currency lads. Call them what you will. We can only guess what

221

might've gone on in a men-only colony. Maybe those early bush ballads can be interpreted as love stories. Between man and man, or man and horse."

"What an awful thought." Darius pressed down and sealed a large piece of contact, finishing the last table.

Humphrey stood next to him. "It's looking better than I ever imagined. Remember those awful drawings I made in London?"

"You called them blueprints."

"Only because the serviettes were blue. Man, this place is gonna make history."

"Or make us broke."

"What?"

"Nothin."

They both turned when there was a knock on the door.

"Well, will you look at that," Humphrey said. "Shame her boyfriend's not with her. That guy's fun. A stereotype on two short legs."

"Griff's all right. I ran into him the other day. We had a coffee."

"And there you've got the start of your own bush ballad. Are you writing any poetry, Darius?"

"Not about Griff, that's for sure, or Miss Jane. Sounds like they split. Griff wouldn't say much."

"You need to find yourself a meaty topic. Something you can really sink your teeth into."

"Yeah."

"You gonna let her in?"

Darius moved towards the door. "I guess I should."

"Do it. Her opinion will be the clincher. If she hates it, gets all stroppy and calls us un-Australian and negative, then we'll know we've got it right."

Darius unlocked the front door. Jane edged inside. She looked around the room.

"How's it going? I thought I'd have a look before I left."

"You're leaving? What about Griff?"

"He's coming too."

"He is?"

"They cancelled his contract. They're cutting down. He's pretty disappointed and won't even let me read the letter, but hey, we're going home."

222

"Back to Melbun?" He looked behind him and was surprised to see Humphrey was gone.

"Yep, I'm gonna miss Munich."

When all you ever did was complain, he thought.

"We won't be here for the opening." She edged further into the restaurant, still looking around. "I guess those flyers and posters were just a joke. Shock advertising, you know?"

"Yeah, sure." He moved aside and let her pass. He watched her go from table to table.

"Oh, you didn't. I thought you'd be above this, Digger. Bozo's an idiot, but I thought you were smarter than this."

"It's just an angle. A way to be different from the competition."

"Where'd you get all this? And that quote from Hanson on the flyer, and that horrible cartoon?"

"The cartoon was in the *Sydney Morning Herald*," Humphrey said, coming out of the kitchen. "It was published at a time when healthy Aborigines were mysteriously killing themselves and dying of heart failure in prisons."

"The cartoon's a misrepresentation. A one-off incident doesn't account for the whole. If you studied history, you'd know. Instead, you take small little things and make them huge. Every country has problems."

"Maybe, but I think that's better than ignoring them entirely."

"I'd watch out if I were you. The boys at the footy club are talking about you. About both of you. I told them it was just a bad joke, that you wouldn't have the guts to go through with it. They don't like the idea of this place at all."

Humphrey shook his head exasperatedly. "Miss Jane, when you get home, jump in your little hatchback and drive north. Go up to Queensland, to the small country towns where Hanson's supporters live. Visit Palm Island. Go to Darwin, spend some time in the settlements in the Territory and in the north of WA. Get to know the locals. Talk with them. There's a lot more happening in our country than just real estate prices and interest rates in Sydney and Melbourne. Go and see it all for yourself. You're a history student. That's part of your research."

"I know my own history," Jane said.

"Yeah, yeah, crafty bushrangers and sacrificial Anzacs, every

223

convict a victim and every farmer a frontier hero. Eureka revolution. The sad part is that you actually know a lot more than the average Dazza and Shazza."

"You think you're so fucking clever."

"I also think that you're clever. Taking a drive to see the real Australia, now that would be clever."

"I'm not that clever," Darius said, trying to ease the tension.

"Yeah you are. And you've seen a lot more of the real Australia than she has."

"It's tough out there. A lot of times I looked the other way."

"Don't worry, Darius," Humphrey said. "I did the same. I felt so bloody guilty."

Jane sat down. "I know what you're talking about. I read *My Place* when I was at school. I'm really sad that it happened, but I don't feel guilty. It wasn't me, and it wasn't my parents."

"A lot of Aussies think that. And that's not wrong, but it also doesn't change things."

"And you think this restaurant will change things?"

Humphrey shrugged. "If it gets some discussion going, what harm can it do?"

"Then why you don't have some positive stuff too? For balance."

"She's right, Hobo. I'm with that."

Humphrey shook his head. "Freddie's got the stereotype covered."

"Yeah, and the Waterhole is always full. I can't see you guys having the same success."

"Well, we'll see. At least we know that if we don't get any customers, we can just change the decor from reality to stereotype and then everyone will come in."

"I'm sorry to say it, but I hope you fail," Jane said.

"And I hope you drive north and explore your own country."

"Maybe I will."

"Better take Griff. Some places up north aren't the best for a girl on her own. A white girl. A city girl."

Jane stood up. "I'm gonna tell the footy team what you've done."

"Go for it. If they don't like it, they don't have to come here. But they shouldn't deny others the chance to learn." He smiled broadly at Jane. "I guess what I'm asking for, Miss Jane, is a fair go. Why aren't you and the footy team willing to give us that?"

"Not for this." She turned and walked for the door.

"There's no such thing anyway," Humphrey said. His mobile phone rang. He went into the kitchen to answer it. Darius could hear his excited voice and exuberant laughter.

"You can do a lot better than this, Digger," Jane said at the door. "I thought you were a proud Australian."

"I am."

She shook her head slowly. Her earrings clanged together, but not in a musical way; the sound was annoying and made him want to yank out each earring one by one and throw them to the floor.

"You can't be if your name's on this restaurant." And she walked through the door, closing it gently behind her.

Darius watched her cross the street, her bleached hair bouncing in that peculiar, stiff way, like it was long dried grass. Her white legs shone from under her black dress. He felt a pang in his stomach. It could have been love, but it was probably just lust; the desire to fuck the girl he had always got so close to fucking but never did. He wanted to know what she looked like naked, to see if she might be a different person with all the layers removed. He was about to run through the door when Humphrey stopped him.

"Hey, Darius. That was Wolfie. A couple of guys are coming over for us to interview. He says they're experienced and reliable and that if anything goes wrong, he'll take responsibility for them. I reckon they might be part of Wolfie's little love nest."

"Great."

"Miss Jane gone?"

"Yeah."

Humphrey slapped him on the back and gave his shoulder a rather intimate squeeze. "Let it go, Digger. You have no idea how much better off you are. If anything, you should feel sorry for her, and you should feel really sorry for Griff. He might have to spend the rest of his life with her. Imagine that?"

"He told me they split."

"Maybe he just wants that."

"Yeah, right. You think she'll go up north?"

"When it freezes over."

"That'll never happen. Bloody hot up there."

Humphrey laughed. "Let's get back to work. Heads or tails?"

"Heads."

Humphrey threw a coin in the air. "Heads it is. You want the boys or the girls?"

"Toilet cleaning? Again?"

"We gotta pass the health inspection."

"All right. Girls this time. The men's lav was filthy."

"It still is. That's why we're doing a second cleaning. Come on, before our future employees get here."

They set to work. Sure, he was glad he wasn't Griff, but the rejection still hurt. She had chosen Griff instead of him. But then, he was the one who had left earlier in the year and had been glad it was over.

"Thanks, dad," he said into the grimy toilet. "You saved me from her."

Lewis: Speaking of history, what about the restaurant you opened in Munich?

Poet: Ha. That was really misguided. I was young. It was a mistake.

Lewis: How did it go at the start?

Poet: Not too well. The German people are pretty interested in Australia, and they were surprised to learn that it's not all beaches, lifestyle and multiculturalism.

Lewis: Australia's famous for that.

Poet: But it's not the whole story. Like you said, history casts a long shadow, and you can learn a lot from it. But we went way over the top. We thought we could change the world.

Lewis: Was that the thinking behind the restaurant? To educate people?

Poet: At first, yeah. But really we thought we had a gimmick people might be interested in.

Lewis: And were they?

Poet: Well, opening day was a huge success, but that wasn't our fault. That was luck. Bad luck for some and good luck for us.

~~~

Truth Soup

"Did you follow the story?" Alice asked.

"Yeah. Shocking. What happened to them in the end?"

"They're going to New Zealand, and to Nauru."

"Where's that?"

"In the Pacific."

Darius considered this as he poured another beer. It was great to have them here, for the opening day, sitting at the bar and watching him work. The place was about half full. Wolfgang invited a lot of people for lunch, but the crowd had thinned out since. Still, there were people inside, and Darius thought that wasn't too bad for a Tuesday afternoon. He noted not many of them took notice of the decor, and if they did, then they didn't seem too fussed about it. It actually looked like a lot of them were ignoring it.

"So, the government won. They didn't get in."

Alice nodded and sipped her Riesling. "If you want my opinion, I think they'll be left to rot on Nauru, but you won't read about that in the paper. In fact, you'll probably never hear anything about them again."

"Why don't they just stay home?"

"They think the western world is paradise. They only have to get there and everything will be better."

"Worse is that the western world presents itself as paradise," Harry said. "From what's seen on television and in films, from everything they can see on the internet, of course they think life would be better there."

"They're jealous then."

"That's simplifying it," Alice said. "They want a better life. And why shouldn't they?"

"Oh my God!" someone shouted.

Everyone turned to look at the television screen, at the thick grey smoke billowing out of a skyscraper.

***

"Terrible day," Humphrey said, locking the door. "But brilliant for us."

They stood on the street. Munich still bustled and moved with traffic and people, even in the early hours of the morning.

"Awful."

"But we did it, Darius. We opened a restaurant in Munich. Everyone loved it."

"They just came in to watch TV."

"So? Good for us."

Darius was still processing all the images he had seen that day: the skyline of Manhattan enshrouded in a grey cloud, the dust-covered survivors staggering through the streets, the dented Pentagon, the scattered debris of the plane that went down in Pennsylvania, and Harry cowering at the bar when the first claims of terrorism were put forward by newsreaders and military experts. "America Under Attack," one news channel had claimed, like World War III had begun.

"Yeah."

"We'll have to double all of our orders if this keeps up." Humphrey looked down the street, spinning the ring of keys around his finger.

"What ya waitin for?"

"I called a taxi. I can't be fucked walking."

Darius wanted to walk, to let the warm night clear his head, to think about what had happened. He also wanted to take the time to savour his moment of success. Yes, a shearer from WA with no education had opened a restaurant in Munich. This was the greatest moment in his life so far. He was the battler making good, and in a foreign country no less. Sure, it was his dad's money that had got the restaurant started, and the whole thing had been Humphrey's idea, but the restaurant had his name on it and he was the owner; well, co-owner.

The taxi floated down the street. It was a long, gleaming Mercedes. Darius was tempted, wanted very much to collapse into the leather seat and be chauffeured back to Viktuelienmarkt.

"The Germans know how to live," Humphrey said as he opened the door. "This thing's a limo. And rightly so."

"I think I'm gonna walk."

It was Humphrey who had done everything, Darius thought. Now, Humphrey wanted to ride in taxis.

"Come on," Humphrey groaned, already in the car. "Forget about the money. We made a killing today."

Darius looked at the car again, wanting to sit in it, wanting to feel like he deserved it. Then he looked at his friend, wanting to feel like he deserved him too. He saw that Humphrey was writing a message on his mobile phone.

"You go," he said at last, backing away from the car. "I need to clear me head."

"Yeah," Humphrey said, still texting, "a lot to think about. Last chance."

"See ya later."

"By the time you get home, I'll be fast asleep." Humphrey closed the door and the taxi took off down the street with a belch of diesel.

He started walking towards the apartment, but soon found himself cutting back towards the centre. There were still plenty of people around. Lots of bars and restaurants were open, spilling out onto the streets. Televisions were on in every place and the planes crashed into the buildings over and over. He found a lively looking bar near Marienplatz and went inside, wanting company, to have people around him and to let their conversations drown out the voices in his head.

At the bar, he ordered a *Weissbier* and turned to watch the television. The buildings imploded again, and again, in real time and in slow motion. It was painful to watch, to imagine each person trapped in the buildings, the life they'd had. What was going through their heads right before they died? he wondered. But few people in this bar were watching, or wondering. They were drinking, enjoying themselves. One large, boisterous group sat with their backs to the screen. They were laughing loudly, their table covered with empty glasses. He tried to ignore them, tried to tell himself he didn't need to be part of a group. He could survive in here on his own and the television gave him something to look at. It was still incredible to see the footage, and he still held his breath as the buildings drifted almost weightlessly to the ground.

A tall girl from the loud group came up to the bar and ordered a round of drinks. He gave her a quick look, but when she turned in his direction, aware he was looking, he avoided her eyes and watched the television. Strangely, she continued to stare and he felt increasingly uncomfortable under her gaze.

She tapped him rather hard on the shoulder. "*Entschuldigung.*"

He turned to look at her. She had striking blonde hair and her face was the colour of creamed honey. He wanted to lick her cheek, and then found himself wondering where that urge had come from, and so suddenly. She looked familiar; probably from the Hole, he decided. A lot of girls had come in there and he couldn't possibly be expected to remember them all, even if they all expected to be remembered. She was a very nice looking girl, but her bright, sparkling blue eyes and the confident pout of her lips gave her something more than prettiness. She looked like she knew something about the world and about herself, some great secret that lent her power. She was rather large, even with her body hidden by the shadows of the bar and the dark pants she wore, but it looked like she carried it in the right places. Buxom, he thought, liking what he saw. She was young, but her eyes were experienced. It looked a little like arrogance, but she was sweet enough to seem innocent.

"What?"

"Oh, you're English."

"Australian actually."

"Look, I know this might sound like a line, but do we know each other?"

"I used to work at the Waterhole. Ever go there?"

"Don't know it." She smiled sweetly. It could have been the alcohol, because she seemed pretty drunk, but he decided to see what he wanted to see, being rather drunk himself. "I just moved here," she added.

"Me too."

Her drinks landed on the bar. She took the handles of three glasses in each hand. Darius saw she had strong forearms covered in faint slithers of blonde. Glasses in hand, she turned and faced him. Through the sleeves of her shirt, he could just see her biceps flexing.

"I guess that makes us strangers then."

As she passed him, she nudged him playfully with an elbow. She carried the beers back to her group, arching her back with the weight. When she sat down, she said something that made them all look in his direction and laugh.

Darius focused on the television again. And although he was embarrassed enough to want to leave the bar, he stayed, because even mocking attention was attention. When she wasn't looking, he tried to sneak glances at her. If she had been alone, he would have gone up to her, but she was secure behind the sociable wall of her group, laughing and shouting, so he just admired her from the bar. She was big, but he was attracted to her, felt the rather intense desire to unbutton her shirt, un-clip her bra and press his hands against her naked chest. From the looks of her, his hands weren't large enough. When she looked towards him, he turned to the screen.

He drank slowly, hoping she might come to the bar again, but she didn't; she even moved chairs so she had her back to him. With the foam drained from his glass, he took one last look at her, and at all the other girls left in the bar, though there was only a handful and none of them looked interesting.

Outside, Munich's long pedestrian mall was almost deserted. The church towers and the façades of buildings were shadowy outlines but the streets were well-lit, making him think it was early evening and not creeping towards the quiet hours before dawn.

He didn't want to go home, but also didn't know where to go next. It was terrible to realise that he knew no one in this town. He didn't want to become another aimless lonely drunk staggering from one bar to the next, trying to pick up girls who got prettier, younger and thinner with every drink.

"Digger?"

That sounded like Jane, he thought, turning expectantly. But the girl from the bar was walking towards him. Her dark corduroys made a loud spliff-spliff as she walked. She had long legs, he saw, rather thick, even with the black pants, but she was tall enough to make everything look like it was in proportion, just. She walked with power and strength, like an athlete, like someone who easily burst from a walk into a run. He wanted to see those legs, to admire her muscular thighs; he envisioned her round calves as hazelnut ice cream he could bite into.

"So, you were at the Hole."

She shook her head. Her hair bounced. "It is you. Amazing. The world's an amazing place."

"Yeah, it is."

He looked at her and nodded, trying to place her, trying not to look quizzical or confused. It was a strain to wade through the alcohol and through all those experiences in his life when he just hadn't paid attention. He knew that if he could place her, his chances of seeing her naked, or even of getting a date, would be that much higher.

"Amazin," he added. It sounded so pathetic, he wanted to run. A man rode past on a bicycle and he was tempted to push him off it and ride away as fast as he could.

She licked her lips once, making them shiny and pink. "You don't remember." She laughed. "I bet you remember Sabrina."

"Sabrina," he repeated.

And it came flooding back: the two girls on the highway, their dusty backpacks, their horsey, unwashed smell, his rocking hangover, his ridiculous hope of a threesome in Exmouth. That's right, Exmouth. She was the big girl hiding under the hat. He looked at her now, amazed that she was so different, so much thinner. Or was she? She had polluted his thoughts the whole way home, had gotten bigger and bigger in his mind until she became too large to fit in his head. Now, he couldn't even remember her name. He sniffed at the air, thinking he might get that same whiff of horse, hoping it might trigger more concrete memories, but instead he got a flowery fragrance that made him woozy.

"You were hitchin," he said, looking her up and down, wanting to pound all that tasty flesh. "In a pretty dangerous area too."

"That was my idea." She folded her arms. The blonde hairs on her bare forearms caught the light and glittered. "Sabrina was so scared. I wanted some adventure, you know, away from all those other backpackers in their cars and on the buses. I wanted to do it differently and see the real Australia."

"Humphrey says everyone should do that."

"Who's Humphrey?"

"Uh, a friend of mine. We live together, I mean, we're not together together. We're just friends." He cleared his throat as she laughed at him. "So, what're ya doin in Munich?"

"I'm interning at the *Sueddeutsche Zeitung*."

"You're makin all those long words."

"What?"

"Uh, nothin." He was losing her, was terrible with the kind of pick up small talk at which Humphrey excelled. "It's just a joke. When did you get back?"

"Last year." And it was clear to him, in her voice and in the way her whole body seemed to sigh, that it was a relief to be back. "I flew home from Perth. Sabrina got a job and stayed. She gave up university and everything. She's still there."

"I guess she likes it."

"I don't get it. I found Perth pretty dull. There's the beach, and that's beautiful."

"So are you," he said lamely.

"But there's not much else." She took a step closer to him, cocked her head sideways and lifted her gold eyebrows. "What on earth are you doing here, Digger? You're the last person I expected to see on the other side of the world. I thought you were one of those Aussies who never left."

Her closeness, and the fact she hadn't run away despite all the stupid things he had already said, gave him confidence.

"I'm seeing the world. Spent the winter in Canada. Was in London for a bit. Munich's great."

"Beats the hell out of Perth, doesn't it?"

"Perth? I hate the place." He had worked hard on this analogy and now let it loose. "It's like a big office complex, you know. All the parks and beaches are there just to keep all the workers happy. A real nine-to-five place. After that, everything shuts down and it's like the whole place falls asleep."

She laughed. Darius watched her; she was very voluptuous when she laughed, even prettier when she threw her head back and he could see the moist pink interior of her mouth. He liked the way her mouth was permanently wet, her lips glistening. She seemed so confident, so oblivious to everyone judging her; she just didn't seem to care what they thought. He wondered if she would be just as free-spirited in bed, if he ever got her there.

"I never thought of it that way," she said. "But now that you say it, you're right. Perth Inc."

Darius tried to smile, tried not to look too desperate. "You wanna, uh, get a drink somewhere? If you're still with ya friends it's all right."

"They're not my friends."

"Who are they then?"

"Colleagues. Yes, I want a drink. But first you have to tell me why you're here." She leaned closer so that he swam in her scent and he could count the small dusting of freckles on her forehead. "Are you searching for the real Germany?"

"Kind of. But you could say I'm searchin for the real Australia."

He tried not to look surprised, tried to maintain his air of quiet dignity, tried to make it seem he always said such clever things, but he failed on all counts, he knew it. And from the thin smile of recognition on her wet lips, it looked like she knew he was impressed with himself.

"Now that's interesting. Let's go, Digger. I know where we can start looking."

She grabbed him by the hand and they set off down the pedestrian mall, in the opposite direction of his apartment.

She talked incessantly, about Australia and Germany, about what had happened that day and about what she saw on the street. Nothing she said was dull. Every single word and opinion travelled right into the centre of his brain and stayed there. She made him laugh too, something no woman had ever done. Most surprising was that he could match her, simply by being honest and saying exactly what he thought.

She took him to a run down *Kneipe* in what was clearly the wrong part of town; he didn't even know what the area was called. She ordered beers and shots – all the other men had the same combination in front of them – and the alcohol fuelled their conversation and primed his confidence. She continued to say things he didn't expect, reacted in ways he couldn't predict. She laughed when he was serious, was silent when he made a joke. It kept him sober and sharp, and even as they drank and drank, still all her words went to the centre of his brain. He just could not tune her out. She became louder and more energetic, more voluptuous and achingly sexual. At some point, she had undone the top buttons of her shirt and an enticing acre of cleavage was on display.

When they left the bar, the first light of dawn was slithering between the cracks of the clouds. Darius let her lead him through the city, down streets he had never seen before, past train stations that were only ever marks on the big transport map, blips on the way from one place to somewhere more important. To his surprise, she led him to her apartment, upstairs, and into her bedroom. There were still unpacked boxes and the feel of a room not quite lived in.

"You don't remember my name, do you?"

She threw her shirt carelessly onto a chair, left her cords crumpled on the floor, one leg pulled inside out, and then stood in front of him in her white, very practical underwear. There was a lot of her, and when she put her hands on her hips, he wanted to dive right in, from a running jump. He wondered if his answer would dictate what happened next. His groin pounded. She was tall, a few centimetres taller than he was, well-rounded in the right places, strong and sensuous. Her legs were long and shapely. He was drunk, and though he could have recited everything she had said that night word for word, he could not transport himself back to the Great Northern Highway and to that moment when she had said her name.

"No," he said, the blood pumping out of his groin. "I don't. I guess that's it then."

He turned and headed for the door, to leave before being rejected, but two hands landed on his shoulders and twisted him around. She lifted his shirt over his head, nearly ripped it to pieces.

"Good answer," she said, and the loud unzipping of his jeans was like an erotic call to arms. His member stood at attention, ready for battle. "And not very Australian."

She led him to the bed and pushed him down onto it, his jeans around his ankles. When she fell on top of him, the bed creaked. He was amazed how perfectly their bodies seemed to lock together. Her body jiggled and bounced and she wasn't self-conscious: didn't care that the bed slammed against the wall, seemed to like having the windows and curtains open, was oblivious to the whole world seeing and hearing. Her sense of liberation was intoxicating, and Darius was soon clawing, pushing and pulling as much as she was, matching her groan for groan, bite for bite. She liked it when he handled her roughly; it was strenuous work and he briefly wondered if it was time to join a gym.

On they went, until the morning light filled the room and Darius could hear the neighbour upstairs walking the wooden floor in heels, clicking from bedroom to bathroom and back again; he even noticed when she changed shoes.

The girl was in no mood to stop, wouldn't let him. Then the alarm clock rang. She frowned and tried to tuck her tousled blonde tresses behind her ears, but the strands kept falling forward, the tips landing on his face and tickling his nose. She unstuck her body from his and sighed happily.

"Lovely. That's about as much of the real Germany as any foreigner can take." She leapt from the bed with energy.

Darius was left spread-eagled, his sticky legs stuck to the sheets. He pulled a sheet up to cover himself. "It's a cultural experience I'd be happy to have again."

She pointed a long finger at him. "That's a date."

She pranced through the room saucy and satisfied, arse shaking, breasts bouncing. She even stopped and put her hands on her hips in front of the vanity mirror and admired herself, nodding once with satisfaction before heading for the bathroom. Her large feet slapped the floorboards and she sang while she peed loudly, straight into the water. He heard the toilet flush, the shower run and more muffled singing. He looked around the room. There were still plenty of unpacked boxes and the shelves were empty except for the rather bizarre collection of large rocks that lined the bottom shelf.

He closed his eyes and almost fell asleep.

Then she was back, her hair wrapped in a towel, but the rest of her naked and dripping wet. She moved through the room, going about her morning routine like he wasn't there. She hastily picked out clothes from her wardrobe and tossed them on the bed. A purple shirt landed on his leg. She turned on the television. There was the footage, all those people dying again and again. One of his socks dangled in front of the screen, obscuring the view.

"Unbelievable," she said, shaking her head. "It's going to be a crazy day."

She pulled on a pair of grey slacks and slipped the purple shirt over her broad shoulders. She looked good, like a filled out swimmer, even if the shirt was a little too tight. The clothes seem to put everything in the right place, distributed her a little more evenly, and when she came back from the bathroom with her face made up, slightly, he couldn't help feeling proud of this conquest, especially the way it had happened and how he had behaved. He sat up in bed, interested again, wanting more, boastful. She looked at her watch.

"Well, Digger, time for work. I got to get all this news into print. All those long words."

He started to edge out of the warm, moist bed, trying to hide his manhood under the sheets. His clothes were scattered all over the room, flung in every direction when she had torn them off. She stood over him now, arms folded, her shirt straining around her shoulders.

She could have picked up his clothes for him, but she just stood there, smiling, staring.

"Come on, Mr Tucker. I've seen it all. Don't be shy." Then she giggled and added, "We're mates now, after all."

He made a naked jump for his clothes and pulled his underwear on hastily, backwards. She laughed loudly as he took it off again and got it right. He tried to smile, to look relaxed, to show he was comfortable with his body and with her looking at him.

"You know my name," he said, pulling on his shirt. It stank of cigarette smoke.

She picked up a few items and put them in her handbag. "I needed it for my thesis."

"What?"

"My thesis. Post-colonial gender studies."

"You wrote about me?"

"I did of study of the Australian male. Fascinating topic. You were one of my examples."

"What? When?"

"At university."

"I wanna read it."

"Sure. It's in German. I could translate it for you, but right now, I really have to go."

She pushed him from the bedroom and shuffled him towards the door. Outside, with the door locked, she didn't wait for him to tie his shoelaces, and he had to run down the stairs to catch up with her on the street. She walked quickly, with long, jumpy strides, gaining speed with each step.

"I hope you wrote something good," he said, running up to her. He grabbed her arm just before she went down the stairs to the underground station. Her forearm was firm; he couldn't get his whole hand around it. She turned to him, her wet mouth formed in a growl, and then gave him an unexpected and very sensuous kiss.

"I wrote the truth," she said. "As I saw it and based on my research."

When he let her go, she bounded down the stairs, taking them two at a time and weaving between slower commuters.

"Wait." He followed her, down the stairs and onto the crowded platform. "Can I see you again?" he asked loudly, and everyone turned to look.

"Sure."

A train rumbled and squeaked up to the platform. Everyone moved forward and she stood in the front line. The wind blew back her hair and through the gaps between all the heads, he could see her round cheekbones, that perfectly straight nose, those eyebrows that were like thin slivers of gold.

"But I don't have a mobile phone," she said over the crowd and the noise of the train. "And the land line isn't connected yet."

The train doors opened and a flood of people poured out. The crowd waiting parted, slightly, and as people passed him, he was bumped by briefcases, backpacks and shoulders. He struggled to get his hand into his back pocket, fought to keep his footing, but managed to snatch a business card from his wallet. He tapped the person in front of him on the back.

"Can you give this to her?"

Annoyed, the man did so.

She looked at the card and laughed. "True Blue Tucker? I should've used that for my thesis."

"It's my restaurant. In Maxvorstadt."

She was the first onto the train and the crowd followed her, but then she stood by the door, looking at him.

"Maybe I'll come by some time," she said as the doors slammed shut.

Then the train was gone, rumbling to another station that was just a blip on the map. Already, the platform was filling up again, everyone on the way to work and not so happy to be doing so, and every newspaper with smoking buildings on the front page. He fought against the crowd and climbed the stairs.

On the street, the morning was exceptionally bright and hopeful. Everything seemed to go in slow motion. Even his walking felt easy and unhurried, like he had all the time in the world and nothing he could do today would match the importance of what had happened last night. Her smell was still on him and the thought of her, every centimetre, filled his head. All her words still echoed, still resonated, and as he walked, oblivious of his direction, their conversation continued in his head.

"I'll get her to translate it," he said out loud, certain that she only could have written something positive. After all, he had picked the

239

girls up, listened to their criticisms, waited with them in the darkness and had helped them get the final ride to Exmouth, with his dad's connection.

"You'd like her, dad."

Eventually, he found his way back to the centre, to the pedestrian mall and close to the bar where they had met. No, we hadn't simply met, he thought; we connected. And then he remembered how she had looked out the window of the truck, and all those other times in the car when she had looked at him. If he had been open to it, more experienced, they would have connected then.

He found the hotel and went inside.

"Mornin," he said to the receptionist. "I'm looking for Alice Pickering."

She gave him a less than pleasant look and picked up the phone. "She must be in the breakfast room," she said when there was no answer. "First floor."

They were both hidden behind broadsheets running only one story today. There they sat, the Arab and the Aborigine, breakfasting in a room full of white people.

"Good mornin," he said, flopping into an empty chair.

"Darius. This's a pleasant surprise."

Harry folded the paper just enough to look at him. "Rough night?"

"I ran into an old friend." He was desperate to brag, to tell the world a beautiful girl had picked him up and screwed him senseless. "Literally."

"That Australian girl you talked about in London?" Alice asked.

"Nah, nah. A girl I met last year up near Karratha. A, uh, German girl."

"Watch out. They're a tough bunch. If they think they know something better, they have no problem telling you so."

"Nothing wrong with strong women," Harry said. "The problem is, most men can't handle them."

"Is that how it is where you're from, Harry?" Darius asked.

"It's a bit different than that."

"That's putting it lightly," Alice said. "Those women aren't allowed to do anything except cook, clean and breed."

"It will change."

"Not after what happened yesterday. They're already trying to pin this on bin Laden and his troop of suicidal boy scouts."

"Now you're being an extremist."

A few people nearby turned towards their table.

"The thing is," Darius said, "I can't even remember her name."

"When will you see her again?"

"Dunno. We made no plans." He took one of the empty cups and poured himself some coffee. "She doesn't have a phone." He tore three packets of sugar and dropped the contents into the cup. "I gave her the address of the restaurant. She said she'll come by."

"Sounds serious," Harry said.

"Yeah?"

"We'll be there for dinner," Alice said. "We're going to be tourists today. You're a local now. What do you suggest?"

"The art gallery's good."

"I'm in the mood for some German art. This country has a history of barbarism but they've given the world some fine art work."

"And music," Harry added.

"And cars," Darius said, keen for inclusion.

"Yes," Harry said, "you'd like to think it might all balance out nicely."

"At least they faced it," Alice said, making a few businessmen look up from their laptops and printouts. She turned to Darius and her voice became louder. "Good on you for opening your restaurant. And save a table for the next cover up, because if America tries to get revenge for what happened yesterday then you can be sure Australia will fight right alongside them."

"Alice, please," Harry said.

She lifted the newspaper and continued reading. "The Yanks won't just let this slide, Harry. Someone somewhere will have to pay. So, whatever you do, don't grow a beard. Maybe we can pass you off as an Italian or a Greek."

"I'm British," Harry said. "And proud of it."

***

She came for lunch, three long days later, with two other girls. They sat down at the Alan Bond table and she didn't even look at him. He watched from behind the bar. In the preceding days, he had all but given up and had struggled to move on; he'd considered standing in

241

front of the SZ building, but here she was in front of him. He had to do something, despite what anyone would think.

Their laughter rose above the sound of the lunchtime news broadcasts, which now included interviews with witnesses and speeches from earnest politicians. The world was still in a state of collective shock, but well-manicured fingers were already pointing towards the Middle East, to some network of terror led by a man Darius had never heard of. Again, there was an outcry for vengeance, for war. But against who? he had wondered the last few days.

But forget all that. Who cared if there would be war? There she was, her face hidden behind the menu. She was explaining things to her friends, pointing at the menu, and all those German words she spoke somehow travelled through the maze of noise and went straight into his ear. He didn't understand any of it, but heard every word.

"They look like a fun bunch," Humphrey said, looking towards the girls. "You think they're laughing because their getting the point or because they're missing it entirely?"

"Maybe they're ignoring it like everyone else does."

"Comfortable on that fence, Digger?"

"Looks like the one who's laughing's getting it."

"Yeah, Bondy's story is pretty funny. We need to get a copy of that ad he made. You remember." And he sang, "'They said you'd never make it.' That was a classic."

"Right," Darius said, wondering what Humphrey was on about.

"I reckon some explaining is in order. They've probably never heard of him." Humphrey smoothed the sleeves of his suit jacket and moved around the bar. "The refugee table needs another bottle of red."

Darius frowned as he opened the bottle, hating how already their roles were clear. Humphrey, in his slick suit, acted like it was his restaurant while Darius stood behind the bar like an ordinary employee. Humphrey wasn't really waiting tables as they had agreed; he had already hired two waiters to take care of that. He just went from table to table explaining things, to the few people who came in. Now, Humphrey was doing that right in front of her. Darius picked up the bottle of wine and edge around the bar, to get close enough to hear.

"It's a great Australian story," Humphrey said. "A rags to riches tale. He started out as a sign writer, made millions in the eighties when anyone with half a brain and all the right connections could have. But

242

then, and this is when it gets funny, he went to court for fraud but said he couldn't remember anything. Really. He sat there like a vegetable and just said, 'I don't remember.' Ha. Can you believe that?"

"I thought all you Aussies were honest?" she said.

"We like to think so, but whatever gives us an advantage, we'll use it."

"What about the fair go?" she asked, leaning back so that Darius saw the outline of her face and the impressive curve of her cleavage.

Humphrey cocked his head sideways, as he did when he found someone interesting. "Good question. Someone left it out in the desert, I think. Out near Lake Disappointment. Now, what would you like?"

Darius tuned out and focused on his work. He took the wine to the refugee table, walked straight past her, but didn't look at her, didn't flinch when he heard her laugh. He picked up a few empty glasses, circled around the other side of the restaurant and joined Humphrey back at the bar.

"That girl knows her Aussie."

"Yeah?"

"A real lively one, she is. A whole lotta Rosie. I might try to get her phone number."

"Don't interrupt their lunch, Hobo. Let her be."

"Can't hurt to invite her back. We need customers."

"Yeah. It's been pretty bare since Tuesday."

"Give it time, Digger. We're new on the block. Word will spread."

He hoped so. The restaurant was bleeding money. Every day there was some big bill to pay. Humphrey had already talked about going to the bank to apply for a line of credit.

The time ran. They ate their lunch quickly. Darius tried to keep himself busy, but there wasn't much work to do. He chatted with Micha; the barman seemed bored. At one point, Darius looked towards the Bond table and was stunned to see that she was gone.

"They certainly enjoyed themselves," Humphrey said, catching Darius looking.

"That right?"

Humphrey leaned against the bar. He looked even more angular and gangly in the suit; when he leaned forward, the bones of his spine stuck out. He held up a note and waved it like a tiny flag.

"She asked me to give you this."

Darius pretended not to be interested and just kept himself from snatching the note from his friend's hand. "Who?"

"Our little Aussie expert. Well, not so little. You know her?"

"She looked familiar, from the Hole maybe."

"Maybe."

"Are you gonna give me the note or what?"

"Woah, or what? Or you'll take me outside? Hah. He looks like your usual, everyday mild-mannered barman, but beneath that servile exterior is an angry, violent rebel desperate for a cause."

Darius tried to smile, to show he was enjoying the joke. "Give it here, Hobo."

Humphrey reached it out but pulled it back again when Darius tried to grab it. "You must not fraternise. Oh, screw that. Fraternise all you want. But you might need a fraternity to deal with her."

Darius snatched the note. Humphrey leaned over the bar as he unfolded it.

"What does it say? Phone number? Address? One hour hotel?"

Darius laughed loudly, louder than he ever had in his life; he nearly pulled a stomach muscle. His throat hurt from manufacturing this entirely new sound, a laugh that seemed to come from his testicles. He dropped the note on the bar. Humphrey picked it up.

"'I like your restaurant, Mr Tucker, but your waiter's a bit of an arse, and a badly dressed one at that. But the food's good and the tables unusual. I'll be back for dinner.'"

And the expression of shock and offence on Humphrey's face made Darius laugh even harder.

"Of course, you know," Humphrey said in his pompous British accent, "this means war."

"Fuck me, she's funny."

"I'd say I'm looking forward to dinner as much as you are, Mr Tucker. Hopefully by then, the world will have sorted itself and the universe will be back in order."

"Including you not being an arse?"

"That was never in doubt. It's the badly dressed comment that rankles. This suit cost 200 marks."

"Maybe she's a fashion expert."

"No way. What's her name anyway? She didn't sign the note."

"Dunno."

"What? She knows you."

"So?"

"Ve have vays of making you talk."

"There's not a lot to say."

"Well, how does she know your name?"

Darius couldn't look his friend in the eye. It was a good story, and it was getting better each day, but it still mattered to him what Humphrey thought.

"Come on, out with it."

"All right. We met up north, when I was driving back from the mines. She and a friend were hitching near Karratha. I took them to the turn-off to Exmouth."

"That's it?"

"Yep."

"And she remembers you? What kind of impression did you make?"

"Well, I waited at the turn-off until they got a ride."

"There's more to it than that."

"We, uh, kind of ran into each other on Tuesday night."

Humphrey nodded, putting it all together, but Darius knew not even Humphrey had the imagination to conjure how it had really been.

"Aaah. Did you break anything? You better go to the hospital and check if you've got a fractured pelvis."

"Hobo, that's enough. She's great."

"Yeah, come on, Digger. Give me another 'or what'. Take me out to the parking lot."

"I like her."

"You know, I was wondering what happened to you on Tuesday. It also explains why you've been moping around the last few days. Alcohol makes us do things we regret, doesn't it?"

"I don't regret it."

"She didn't even look at you when she was here. Were you limp that night?"

"Fuck you. She's like that. Unpredictable, you know?"

"Darius, I'm impressed. She's definitely smart. But come on, you can tell me her name."

245

"I don't know it, really."

"You mean you ran into a girl in Munich who you once gave a ride to in Australia and she remembered you and then took you back to her cave for a rollicking night on the Bavarian mattress and you still don't know her name?"

"Yeah. Amazin, isn't it?"

"I love this country. Aussie women, you know, a lot of them talk and talk about independence, but it's rubbish. If you've got something, you don't need to keep telling people you have it. They talk a good game, want a career and blah-blah-blah, but the minute a guy comes into their life, bang, it all becomes about him."

"She's not like that. She wears pants. Does what she wants."

"Too right. That's why German women are so much better than the Aussie versions. Dinner's a long way off. Let's hope she brings more of her friends with her. Having girls in here brings in the men and they're the ones who spend. Freddie used to pay girls to come to the Hole, you know."

Darius nodded, pretending that he did. He hoped she would bring some friends and that the men would come in, because they certainly needed more customers.

Lewis: You speak fondly of Munich, even if things didn't go well.

Poet: I made a lot of mistakes, but Munich gave me time to think.

Lewis: About your father?

Poet: Yeah, but more about Australia in general. The restaurant was a disaster at the start, but it was interesting to learn what other people think about us.

Lewis: And what's that?

Poet: Well, a lot of people expect us to be like Steve Irwin or Paul Hogan. You know, like we're all larrikins firing up the barbie and getting drunk.

Lewis: That's the influence of media.

Poet: Sure. The same way people expect Germans to be leather pants wearing beer drinkers and sausage eaters.

Lewis: A stereotype always has some basis, even if it gets stretched.

Poet: Do you wrestle crocodiles and drink like a fish?

~~~

Convict Casserole

"It's ordinary goulash," she said.

"No, it isn't," Humphrey replied.

"Your chef's Polish, I bet. Or Czech. I've eaten this before."

"Good guess. He's Polish, but he cooked this from a genuine convict recipe."

"Prove it."

"Can't. If I gave you this recipe, which is a historical document locked in my personal safe, you might sell it to our competitors and then my restaurant would be empty."

"Your restaurant?" She pointed at Darius. "It's got his name on it."

"Our restaurant," Darius said. "And it's empty."

"Anyway, it wouldn't matter if I had this recipe or not because everyone already has it." She lifted the empty bowl. "I could make this, with a packet of goulash powder from the supermarket."

"It wouldn't be the same," Humphrey said. "It would be missing a vital ingredient."

"What?"

"Suffering. Genuine convict suffering. You can taste it, can't you? That can't be copied."

Alice and the girl laughed at this, laughed together. Humphrey laughed too.

"That's just psychological," the girl said. "You could call it Soviet Goulash and everyone will think it tastes of communist suffering. You could call it Gulag Goulash. Your Polish chef's probably got his own name for it."

"Good point," Harry said. "I think she's got you there."

Humphrey turned to Alice. "Help me, professor, please. Set this lovely young lady straight."

As she looked from Humphrey to the girl and back again, Darius thought she was trying to decide who to support. Go with the girl, he hoped.

"Well," she began, "most convicts couldn't write so even if they had recipes, they couldn't write them down. The settlers and upper classes of colonial Australia ate pretty much an English diet. I'd say cuisine but England doesn't really have one. I doubt the convicts were allowed to cook for themselves, and they probably never ate as well as we just did. So, I guess it's highly unlikely such a recipe would be genuine."

"Thank you," the girl said.

"Sounds reasonable," Darius said.

"So," the girl said, "there you have it. You're lying to us. Admit it. There's no recipe."

Humphrey shook his head. "I'm not talking about convicts still in chains. What about the emancipists? Many of the convicts served their terms and were set free. Those men cooked for themselves and got married and their wives cooked. History may not have recorded it, but there had to be a convict cuisine. Alice, help me out."

"It's possible. But it's more likely they ate like the settlers, just not with the same quality or quantity."

"Hah. And when you don't show us the document, you basically admit you're wrong. Come on. There's just us. Show us this recipe."

"I would, but I'm not sure if you can be trusted. We don't even know your name."

"No, you don't. But if a name's all you need to trust somebody, then you're far too trusting for me. I know your name, but I don't trust you."

Harry and Darius laughed.

"A name is very important," Humphrey said over the laughter.

"A name means nothing," Harry said. "I've used lots of different names in my life. She's right. What's important is trust."

"He writes under different names for security," Alice explained.

"It was my publisher's idea," Harry said, sounding like he hadn't agreed with it himself.

"Not exactly brave," Humphrey said.

"If you want to know about courage, then you should read some of his work. If the wrong people find out who he is, they might try to kill him."

"I'd like to read it," the girl said. "Where can I find it?"

"Don't trust her, Harry," Humphrey said. "She'll sell you to your enemies."

Harry reached for his leather bag and pulled out a book. He handed it to the girl. "I was going to give this to Darius, but maybe you can share it."

"*The Shortcut to Paradise*," she read. "*Suicide Bombers and Martyrs*. Thank you, Harry."

"H. Abdur Raqeeb?" Humphrey said, leaning across the table to read the cover. "That was the best your publisher could do?"

"Actually, I came up with that one. It means servant of the watchful."

"I want to read it too," Darius said.

"So you should," Harry said. "Your name means he who informs himself."

"Really?"

Harry nodded. "It's from the Bible."

Darius turned to Alice. "Did you know that?"

"'Then King Darius wrote to all the peoples, nations, and languages, who dwell in all the earth: Peace be multiplied to you.' I learned that at school. In Scripture."

"Wow."

"Humphrey's a German name." the girl said.

"I know, I know," Humphrey said. "Peacemaker. What's your name mean?"

The girl smiled thinly. "Nice try."

"Anyway," Humphrey said, turning away from her, "names don't mean anything."

"It's not often someone contradicts themselves so quickly," the girl said, "or did you do it just to get a laugh?"

"You know, it's getting late. We've got another big day tomorrow."

"We do?" Darius asked. "Barely anyone came in today."

"Will we see you tomorrow for breakfast, Darius?" Harry asked.

"Uh, dunno. Let's see, eh?"

Everyone stood up.

"It was very nice meeting you," Alice said to the girl. They shook hands and the girl shook Harry's hand as well.

"Thanks for the book."

Darius walked them to the door and went out onto the street to hail a taxi.

"Don't bother," Alice said. "We'll walk. It's not far."

"Okay. What time's your flight tomorrow?"

"At four, but you don't have to come to the airport."

"I'm definitely comin. And I'll make it for breakfast too."

She leaned forward and kissed him on the cheek. "That girl. They don't build them like that back home, do they?"

"She's great."

"And don't worry about the restaurant. It'll pick up."

"Hope so."

She walked down the street and wasn't bothered when Harry didn't follow.

"I know what you're thinking," Harry said, moving close.

Darius looked down at the pavement. He would normally have felt uncomfortable having a man stand so close, but he liked having Harry there, felt a little more secure and included.

"My mother once told me that the most beautiful person is the one who brings out the best in you, the one who makes you better in ways you never could have imagined."

"I like that."

"You two look good together. You know, Darius, this is your life. It only matters what you think." He gave Darius's shoulder a comforting squeeze before walking away. "See you tomorrow for breakfast. I want you grinning like you were the other morning." He caught up to Alice and they walked hand in hand around the first corner.

Back in the restaurant, Humphrey and the girl were arguing, their foreheads inches apart.

"I think it's time to go home," Darius said loudly, interrupting Humphrey mid-sentence.

"What?"

"I'm leavin." Darius turned to the girl. "And I'm takin you with me."

"Yes, you are. This guy's getting my anger up," she said, jumping out of her chair. She swept Harry's book into her handbag and tried to tuck her hair behind her ears. Then her hands went back into her bag and she pulled out a camera. "But first, a photo, of both of you standing in front of the bar. And holding that Aboriginal flag."

"What for?" Humphrey asked. But he was already taking the flag down from the wall.

"For me." She took the photo and also snapped a few table tops. Then just as swiftly, she put the camera away, shouldered her bag and headed for the door. "Coming, Mr Tucker?"

"Yep."

251

"I won't wait up," Humphrey said, the flag hanging limp from his hands.

"You shouldn't," the girl said from the doorway. "Maybe you could sing a few convict songs to yourself to help you fall asleep."

"I won't be here for lunch tomorrow," Darius said. "I'm taking Alice and Harry to the airport."

"We're running a business here, Darius. Where's your commitment?"

"At least when I'm here I actually work."

"You tell him, Digger," the girl said, grabbing his arm.

***

The train rattled and screeched towards the city centre. The afternoon was warm but the yellows and reds on the trees signalled that summer was over. On the train, there were more suitcases than people, and the luggage made the wagon feel more crowded and cramped than it should have been.

He looked out the window, ignoring the flutter of maps, the nervous conversations of people new to Munich, the tired silences of the jet-lagged.

A strange sensation: sadness, yes, a familiar kind of emptiness, of being left behind and forgotten, abandoned as the car drives into the night. But it wasn't nearly as bad as when he had left London. There was no aching desire to run back to her now. She was part of his life and had brought an added dimension; a paternal figure who was encouraging, trustful and worthy of respect. If asked honestly, he would have said it was Harry he missed now. He had lived most of his life without his mum and, though he didn't want to, could quite easily factor her out again. But he wouldn't do that. He had parents again, and they would always be there, so they had promised, to support him and to help. So there was no reason to be sad, to still mourn the loss. He had a mum again, and a new father, honest and true, the servant of the watchful.

That all sounded good, but it was bullshit.

It was Waldtraut. Trudi. She filled all the gaps. She took away the emptiness, removed that feeling of abandonment: liked him, admired him, inspired him, wanted him, believed in him.

He grinned, recalling the clever way he had found out her name. After a long, drawn out physical attack on each other, another pleasurable cultural wrestle, they had laid on the bed in the sultry candlelight, in the hazy post-coital fug, and she had translated parts of her thesis. But she had cut the top off the cover page, removing her name. When she went to the bathroom, he rummaged through the garbage and found that slither of paper. The only problem was that he couldn't tell her that he knew.

That thesis of hers, so complicated. There had been a little bit written about his dad, initialled as JT, part of the section sub-titled Fathers First. As she translated, Darius realised Trudi must have done a lot of asking around, dropping his dad's name into every conversation, because she certainly knew a lot about him. Maybe she had even gone to his home town, to his house.

"In many other places in the world," she had said, "fathers want more for their sons and are proud when they succeed at things they themselves failed. But in certain parts of Australian society, there is a trend of fathers wanting to stay superior until they die, and are only proud if the son follows in their footsteps."

"That's pretty much it," he had said, amazed that she had perfectly summarised his own relationship with his dad.

"They openly support their sons, want them to succeed, but deep down, they're only satisfied when the son remains below their level."

"That's a bit hard, isn't it?"

"It's not like that in every case, but there's definitely a difference to other countries. Australia's a real man's country. That's what I discovered when I was there." She tossed the thesis aside, so the loose papers slid and scattered across the wooden floor. "Maybe if the women were a bit more empowered and had more influence, it would be different. I don't mean in the cities. I did a lot of my research in the small country towns. Out there, Australia is built by men for men."

"And Germany isn't?"

"It's a man's world. Here, the men hold positions of power, but not because women can't do the job. Life is meant to be enjoyed, and not to spend eighty hours a week working."

"I bet you'd like to be in a position of power."

"I already am. I do what I want, I live how I live, and I don't need some managerial position to make me feel better about myself. Power is all about insecurity. That's why men always need it. I'm in full control of my life, and more importantly, I'm in control in here."

The train rumbled into the main station. As he got off and walked to the exit, his legs felt like rubber, still weak from all that sex. She had wrung every drop out of him, until his skin was raw and he felt he was pumping semen all the way from his toes. It was Trudi, getting everything out of him, even making him uninhibited in bed, so every move, sound and sentence seemed completely natural.

Trudi.

She was tall, feisty and funny. She collected volcanic rocks. She lived in Munich, like he did. Here, he could do whatever he wanted, and if he was in love with a tall girl who maybe outweighed him, why the hell should he care? There were no Stevenson girls to pass judgement, no local bakeries for biddies to gossip in, no pubs where shearers and farmers congregated. There was only Humphrey and he seemed to like her too.

"Gotta apologise," he said as he negotiated the streets of Maxvorstadt.

He was glad to find the restaurant full. There was football on the television and the air was thick with tension and cigarette smoke. All the men, and there were only men, were watching the screens, sipping their beers but not moving their eyes from the action.

"Digger!" Humphrey shouted from the bar. Wolfgang and a few of his friends echoed the name. Darius smiled at the group and moved towards the bar.

"Good crowd," he said to Humphrey. "G'day, Micha."

"Hi, boss."

"It was Wolfie's idea, to put the soccer on. We'll do it every weekend."

"All these guys Wolfgang's friends?" Darius poured himself a *Weissbier*, giving it a nice long head.

Humphrey nodded. "He knows everyone. I'll take one of those, too."

Darius poured the second beer. "Hey, look, mate, I'm sorry for what I said last night."

"What did you say?"

"You know. About you not working. You do a lot around here."

Humphrey took the glass. "Bullshit. I do nothing but talk. But that's the whole point. We can hire another bartender if you want, but I know you like tending bar."

"Let's see how it goes in the next few weeks, eh? If we keep getting crowds like this."

"Then you and your lass can walk away together. I'd say run, but you know, she may not be up for that."

"Careful."

Humphrey laughed.

The crowd erupted as Munich scored. Everyone jumped up and down and hugged each other. Darius winced as a few cheeks, and lips, were kissed.

"She's beautiful," Humphrey said. "All of her. Did you find out her name? Or does being anonymous light her candle?"

"I know her name."

Humphrey raised his eyebrows, wrinkling his forehead. "Well?"

"It's Waldtraut. Waldtraut Winkel."

"Bless you. Whew, what a great name. I bet there's not another Waldtraut Winkel in the whole world. Sounds like a disease. You're suffering from a terrible case of Waldtraut Winkel. Ha-ha. And there's no known cure. What you need is bed rest. Take that disease to bed. Did you?"

"She called herself Trudi in Australia."

"I'm sure she did. The mates, with all those marbles in their noses and mouths, they'd struggle with Waldtraut. Trudi Winkel." He chewed the name and it looked like it tasted good. "That sounds better. She coming tonight?"

Darius shook his head. "She took the train to Boeblingen this morning, to see her parents."

"Booooooblingen," Humphrey repeated. "That fits her. What a fantastic rack. You could hang half your wardrobe on it."

"*Wie oberflaechlich*," Micha said.

"What?"

"You are so superficial. Women are not objects."

"Tell that to Hugh Hefner and the rest of the male population, present company excepted. And tell it to all the women who walk down the street with their tits hanging out. And tell it to everyone who ever set foot in Hooters. The whole damn world is superficial. Look at Adam and Eve and that studly hunk Jesus. Come on. Have you ever seen an ugly depiction of Jesus? Even God is superficial."

Micha turned to Darius, who was laughing. "Are you together with that blonde girl who sat with your parents last night?" Darius nodded. Micha turned back to Humphrey. "Then he's not part of your superficial world."

"Thanks, Micha."

"Yeah, Darius the tolerant," Humphrey said. "Forever informing himself. So, she's not coming. Good. That means you and I can do something together."

"Sounds good. Let's have breakfast tomorrow, but not too early. I need some sleep."

"You do. You look like hell. Does Trudi keep you from sheep counting?"

"Yeah, something like that."

"Well, there's worse things you could do during the night."

"Like singing convict songs?"

"Like singing lonely convict ballads to a pillow. But I tell ya, I made that pillow weep."

"Maybe, uh, maybe Trudi has a friend."

"Not interested. No business partner of mine is going to do any matchmaking for me. It won't be long before a parade of Munich's finest young lasses will be beating a path to our restaurant door. I'll be fending them off with a stick soon."

Darius looked around the all male restaurant. "Good luck."

"Don't need it. Anyway, there's no such thing. Look how far I've got without it. I'm the kind of person that makes things happen. I don't need luck."

The away team narrowly missed a goal and all the men "oooohhhed" with relief.

"That was lucky," Micha said to Darius. "Just missed."

"See? Lucky."

"Sports are different. In sport, luck is everything. How a ball bounces is completely random. And in this ridiculous excuse for a sport, a bit of good luck makes some uneducated teen a millionaire and a bit of bad luck gets the coach fired."

"And a bad decision from the referee makes the fans burn down the stadium," Micha said.

"There's no luck in that," Humphrey said. "That's just our violent human nature colliding with intense boredom."

256

Darius drank his beer.

"Anyway, when are you seeing her again?"

"She's back on Sunday night. She said she'd come here if she leaves early enough. She has to work on Monday."

"Where does she work? Or is she trying to keep that a secret as well?"

"She's doing an internship at your favourite paper."

"The SZ? Ah, a journalist in the making. That might explain why she's so opinionated and aggressive. Watch what you say, Digger, or you might end up in print."

"She's already done that."

Humphrey's eyes widened. "You mean we were in the SZ? Why didn't you say something? Wait. She took photos of us last night. What fantastic publicity."

"She didn't say anything about that."

"Then what did she write?"

Darius cleared his throat. "Her thesis."

"She wrote her thesis about you? A shearer from WA?"

"About Australian men. I was in the part about fathers and sons."

"I wanna read it. D'you have a copy with you? Give it to me."

"It's in German."

"How did you read it? You can't even buy a loaf of bread."

"She translated it."

"Yeah, on the pillow, right?"

"And then some."

"Then she can do the same for me. I reckon Trudi and I have a lot to talk about."

Darius tried to smile, to look like he wanted to hear that discussion, but quietly hoped his eyes weren't giving away his anxiety and jealousy.

A goal was scored and the men cheered and kissed each other.

***

She came straight from the station, pulling her suitcase on wheels, which looked pretty small in comparison, into the restaurant and collapsing into a chair at the Stolen Generations table. He quickly poured her a *Weissbier* and got to the table before Humphrey spotted her.

"Hi. Nice to see ya."

"You sound surprised. You thought I wouldn't come?"

"No, but, I, uh, just didn't want there to be any pressure."

She leaned back in the chair, turning towards him. "What then?"

"I think things are going great."

"Trudi. I've been waiting for you, Trudi." Humphrey pushed past Darius and fell into a chair.

She gave Darius a short, searching look. "At least someone was expecting me."

"I was. I'm really happy to see ya."

"What's this I hear about your thesis on the Australian male," Humphrey said, unable to get the words out quickly enough. "I've got some very strong opinions on this subject, but I wanna hear yours first. And they better be good because a foreigner can never expect to know a country better than a local." He turned to Darius. "Bring me a beer, will you?"

Darius grimaced, hesitating, lingering too long. Trudi raised her eyebrows at him. Her large forearms were folded, resting on the heads and bodies of a group of Aboriginal children, photographed in front of a church mission. He wondered if his reaction would influence much of what would follow, because it felt like he was losing her, and he feared that Humphrey might sweep down and steal her.

"In a minute."

He sat down, squeezing in next to Trudi.

"I think you should stay at the bar," Humphrey said. "You know how slow Micha is."

"There's no one to serve. And I wanna hear your opinion as well."

"You've heard it. Weren't you listening?"

"Yeah, but maybe it's changed." He turned to Trudi. "He has the habit of changing his opinions."

"I know. He did it on Friday."

"Right."

"And Hareem said as much as well."

"What did Harry say about me?" Humphrey asked. He waved it off. "Forget it. You shouldn't trust an Arab anyway. They ram planes into buildings just to get all those virgins in their heavenly paradise. There's nothing political or religious about it. If anything, it's pornographic."

"You need to do a bit more reading, Humphrey," she said. "There's a lot more to it than that."

"Yes, okay, yes, I'm a little behind on my Middle East studies. I'm catching up."

"And I don't think all the Muslim people will be happy that you lump them together with extremists. I thought you might be more intelligent than that. The actions of a few fanatics don't make every Arab guilty."

"Well, you would say that. Spread the guilt so far and so thin that it disappears altogether."

"What does that mean?"

"Nothing. Forget it."

"No, no," she said. "Go on. Call me a Nazi. Go for it."

"I didn't say that. I'm not gonna say that."

"Tell me to open a Nazi–Holocaust bar in downtown Melbourne. Should I do that?"

"Calm down."

"I'm calm, but stop trying to pass the guilt onto me."

"We're talking millions of people, incinerated."

She looked down at the table. "And we're talking thousands of children, stolen."

Humphrey held up his hands. "Don't put me in that boat. The Boragarts are clean. And you can't exactly compare it."

"No. You can't. Inhumane is inhumane, no matter what the statistics."

"Okay, okay. I agree with you there. Sorry."

"You don't look it."

"Apologise, Hobo."

"I just did."

"With feeling."

"I'm sorry, Trudi."

She looked at Darius. "So you found it out. Bravo. You could've just asked me." She turned back to Humphrey. "My name's not Trudi."

"Waldtraut then."

She slapped the table with her hands. "You know what. I'm off. I've had a pretty crappy weekend. I shouldn't have come here." She gave Darius a push. "Let me out."

"Hang on," Darius said. "We're all taking this too seriously. Let's just have a drink and relax."

"No, I've had enough. This restaurant's a joke. An empty joke."

"We're facing our history," Humphrey said. "We want the world to know the real Australia."

She turned to Darius. "Do you?"

"Well, it's an interesting take, isn't it? It can't all be about inflatable crocodiles."

"You mean you want to profit from this?" she asked, pointing at the table.

"That'd be better than losing everything. Hobo, we better go to the bank tomorrow and try to get that credit."

Humphrey nodded. "Let's give it a few more weeks, all right?"

"So that's what this is all about. You think you've got an angle, a different way of selling Australia. Shock value. Get people talking, make a pile of cash."

"We already put a pile into this place," Darius said.

She pushed him and he had to stand up.

"Trudi, wait a minute," he said.

"Hang on," Humphrey said. "You blame us for profiteering, but you did the same with Darius. He was your project. You used him. You wrote about him in your thesis and you're probably writing something else about him now."

Darius turned to her. "Are you?"

She looked at the floor. "I'm not going to lie. I wrote an article about this restaurant. I did it yesterday and I wish now I hadn't sent it. I'd like to rewrite the whole thing."

"For the SZ?"

"No."

"What then?"

"For a newspaper in Australia."

Darius felt his body stiffen. "Did you use our names?"

"Of course. I thought you were proud of what you're doing. I thought you were taking a stand. But now I know you're just in it for the money."

"We're running a business," Darius said. "Not a museum."

"Then tell your mate to get off his soapbox."

"Tell me yourself," Humphrey said. "I'm right here."

"Fine. You've got some nerve to put all this on display. You don't even have a direct link to it. You're not Aboriginal. So, don't talk history when you're only interested in money."

Humphrey stood up. "We're losing money because of this history. No one's interested in it."

"Good." She marched towards the door, pulling her suitcase behind her.

"She's getting away, Darius," Humphrey said.

Outside, she had already stopped a taxi and had the door open. Darius called out her name and she slowly turned to look. He ran up to the car.

"It's not what you think. We're just trying to survive."

"I'm disappointed. I thought you were really trying to do something different."

"We are."

"For a profit."

"And to educate."

"So Humphrey says, but I don't believe him. What about you? Is that what you want?"

"Well, uh, look. I know this. I wanna be with you."

"I don't want to be in a relationship right now. I was fine with just having fun."

"We can do that too. See what happens."

"Do you want to know what I really think?"

"Yeah."

"You choose your friends poorly, Mr Tucker. Our friends reflect who we are. But I learned that Australians don't really make friends. They make alliances. And I would have told you my name. You just had to ask."

"You've lost me. Why are you goin?"

"This isn't right. I don't agree with what you're doing. Turning suffering into branding? That's wrong, Darius. History isn't one-sided. I hope you guys fail miserably."

"Thanks."

"This isn't what I want."

"What do you want?"

She fell into the taxi. "Art. Passion. Humour."

"Poetry?"

"That too. But you're a long way from that."

She closed the door.

"Wait a minute," he said, but she stared straight ahead and the taxi was already at the end of the street before he started running after it. He walked back to the restaurant, keeping his head down when he entered.

"What happened?"

"I dunno. She's gone."

"Just like that?"

Darius sat down. He took a long sip of Trudi's abandoned beer. "I guess she saw a side of me she didn't like."

"Women, eh? Can't live with them, let's have another beer."

Lewis: There's more to Australia than that.

Poet: There is.

Lewis: You captured that well in *The Informer*. Every verse is told from the point of view of a different character.

Poet: Yeah, right. They're all different people.

Lewis: And yet they're also similar. It's the Australian psyche divided into characters, each verse representing a certain part.

Poet: Like you said, there are a lot of different elements that make up our identity. The stereotype is part of that too.

Lewis: Indeed. After the success of *Dad's Bush Burial*...

Poet: I wouldn't call the local rag a publishing success. And the circumstances I wrote the poem for were not the best.

Lewis: No, but did you write any poetry while in Munich?

Poet: A bit. It was awful. Love poems.

~~~

The Culture Club

He poured the beers while watching the group. Their separate bills were lined up just behind the bar. He calculated them in his head, with difficulty, and got a satisfying result. They needed more nights like this. The members who knew him from the Hole came up to the bar and called him Digger. He wondered what Freddie would do when he found out the Aust-Schland Club were having their monthly meeting here.

They were all Germans, fascinated by everything Australian; a few had even been there. They did boast two Australian members. Darius knew Mitch and Bevan, had heard their stories at the Hole: came for love, got entrenched and secure, were forever homesick but too afraid to leave. They usually came to the meetings late and left early. They were both drifting aimlessly towards middle age, yet living in Europe made them different from all the Gregs and Darrens they had grown up with. At least, that was Humphrey's take on it.

Darius hoped they wouldn't come tonight. If they did, there might be trouble. They lived in Germany but they were still patriotic and proud, capable of anything if pushed hard enough. They might quickly turn from mates to enemies and fight for the country they no longer lived in.

But again, those were Humphrey's opinions. Darius hoped they wouldn't come because he didn't want to have a confrontation, didn't want to have to explain himself. He was sick of doing that. Why couldn't everyone just let him be?

"Great place, Digger," one group member said at the bar. "We know a lot about Australia but we always want to learn more, good and bad."

"Thanks."

He would have liked to have said "Thanks, Juergen," or "Thanks, Hans," but he didn't know the man's name. He didn't know any of their names.

"How'd you find out about us?" he asked.

"It's a funny story. My daughter, she studies in Melbourne now. She saw an article in the *Sonntagsblatt*. That's the German paper in Australia."

"I know it," Darius lied.

"She read it and sent it to me. She couldn't believe there was a restaurant like this."

"D'you have a copy with you?"

"Sure. There was a picture too, of you and Humphrey. I'll get it."

He moved back to the group.

Darius wondered what she had written. His loneliness ached as he thought about her again. He could still put all those sentences she had said in perfect order and replay every conversation in his head, including their last one. She resonated. He could hear her talking and laughing, could see the round curves of her naked body all flattened and pressed against her mattress.

Where was she?

He had rung her bell until his finger hurt, until a neighbour came down and told him to go away, threatened to call the police. When he'd sat in front of her building all day, she hadn't come home. He stuffed notes in her mailbox, wrote long letters and love poems, but she never replied.

"Let her go," Humphrey had said. "If she wants to love you, she needs to love all of you, the bad stuff too. Come on, Digger, hasn't it been great hanging out again?"

That was true. They had patched things up, and this had made it easier for Darius to convince himself that he was better off, that she was too big and that he could do better. But the few girls he met in Munich knew little of the world; many of them expected him to be either Crocodile Dundee or a surfer boy. Or both. He hoped these girls would drive away his loneliness, that's why he chased after them and worked so hard, but it only made him yearn for Waldtraut more. The girls were nice, but the one girl he managed to take home was uptight in bed, full of expectations and learned moves. She made him feel inhibited and self-concious, like she was rating his performance for a *Cosmopolitan* survey. But Waldtraut, that beautiful beast, had set him free.

The Aust-Schland Club had a couple of women who had already eyed him; Humphrey had called shotgun on the redhead.

The man came back to the bar and held up the article. Darius took it. There was Humphrey, dashing in his suit, but the Aboriginal flag looked inappropriate and out of place, as if he might just as quickly burn it as hold it aloft proudly. He saw himself in a rumpled shirt, slouching, looking tired but happy and relaxed. He missed that Darius. In a touch perhaps reserved just for him, she had published the article under the name Trudi Winkel.

"It's very well written," the man said. "And there's much about you in there. You had a very interesting life."

Darius scanned the article, finding his name many times and Humphrey's only twice.

"A shearer with his own restaurant in Munich. Your parents must be very proud."

"They are." He still hadn't told them he had lost her, and it was weeks ago now. "Can I keep this?"

"Yes. I made copies for everyone."

"Thanks, and thanks for comin too, for bringing the whole group."

"We were tired of the Waterhole." The man looked towards the door. "I hope Bevan and Mitch get here soon. They will love this. They always complained about how kitsch the Waterhole is."

On cue, Bevan and Mitch entered the restaurant. Darius was surprised to see Griff trailing behind them. The group cheered their entry, but then started bombarding them with questions. They pointed at photographs, read quotes from documents and repeated, word for word, things Humphrey had already said. Bevan and Mitch were stunned, though Darius was sure they were pretending. Griff must have said something, Jane too; they all knew each other. Darius watched Humphrey linger around the edge of the group.

"G'day, Digger," Griff said at the bar. He propped himself on a barstool, making himself a few inches taller. "Congrats on the restaurant."

"Thanks."

"Can I get three beers?"

"I got it," Micha said.

Griff looked around. "Nice place. When did ya open?"

"Nine-eleven," Darius said, using the catchphrase Humphrey hated.

"No way. Can you believe that shit? I'm fucking glad we're gonna join in and get those Al Qaeda pricks."

"The Coalition of the Willing," Darius said. Humphrey turned in his direction and mimed a laugh, his hands clutching his belly. He tilted his head towards Bevan and Mitch and did it again. "Australia never misses a war," Darius added, repeating what Humphrey had said about the coming attack on Afghanistan.

"They deserve it," Griff said.

"Who?"

"You know, the terrorists."

Humphrey came up to the bar. He grabbed two of the beers. "My little friend, I hope you can point them all out. That'll make things easier. Ha-ha. Maybe you can smoke em out, like Bushie wants."

"G'day, Bozo."

But Humphrey was already heading back to deliver the beers to Bevan and Mitch, who were both moving around the restaurant, going from table to table.

"So," Darius said, keeping an eye on them, "you're still here."

"Yep." Griff paid Micha for the beers, not tipping.

"I thought ya lost ya job."

"Bevan found me one where he works. Me and Jane, you know, it didn't work out. She went home."

"Shame. Nice girl."

"Yeah, woulda been great to be back home."

"So go. I bet there's a plane leavin tonight."

"Nah, good money, Digger. A coupla years of this and I'll have enough for a deposit on a place in Cronulla. And Mitch said you can work here five years and get all ya pension money back."

Darius shrugged. "Worth the winter?"

"Bevo's gonna take me skiing. He says ya gotta ski to make it through."

"Can you?"

"Fucking eh, mate. Hate the cold, but I'll give it a go."

Mitch's shouting made them both turn. "What the hell's goin on in here? You can't put all this on show?"

"Why not?" Humphrey asked.

"You a fucking Kraut or something? No Aussie would ever do somethin like this."

"I'm as Aussie as you are, whatever that means. All of us came from somewhere else. How many generations does it take to make an Aussie anyway?"

"My great-granddad fought at Gallipoli," Mitch said.

"Of course he did. And even if he didn't, he did. Mine too."

"He was a true Anzac. I'm the great-grandson of an Anzac and that makes me a real Australian."

"That's great. You should be so proud. Make sure you check out the Gallipoli table in the corner. You great-granddad was part of the greatest blunder in military history." He turned to the group. "In the First World War, Australia had to attack Turkey."

"Well, we fight wars, but we never start wars," Mitch said.

To everyone's surprise, Mitch, in his conservative grey banker's suit moved towards Humphrey. But despite his aggressive airs, he clearly wasn't a fighter.

"Fair go, Mitch," Humphrey said. "We're allowed to have an opinion, even if it's not the same as yours."

"This's a bar, mate. People come in here to have a drink and hang out."

"And they can have some intelligent discussion as well."

"Yeah, but not about this. It's a thousand miles from the Australia I know."

"Then you need to see a bit more of our homeland. Read a few more books."

Mitch went to one table and tried to lift the contact with his fingernails.

"Hey," Humphrey said. "What do you think you're doing?"

Darius moved around the bar. He managed to pull Mitch back from the table.

"Digger? What're you doing here?"

"Working."

"You were better off at the Hole. And so are we. Let's go, Bevo. Griff."

"No," Humphrey said. "Stick around. You might learn something."

Though he had said nothing, Bevan seemed a whole lot angrier than Mitch. "You're fucked, mate," he said now. "We know people in this town. We'll have this place closed in a week."

"We also know people, namely the local police and a few good lawyers. If anything happens to us or our restaurant, we'll know exactly who it was." Humphrey smiled at the group of Germans. "And we've got witnesses too."

"You think ya so fucking clever," Bevan said.

"You seem pretty clever too. I guess you know all of this already. See them out, will you, Darius?"

"Come on, guys. Griff? You too. We don't want any trouble."

Darius herded them towards the door. Outside, he said, "Fellas, relax. It's just a gimmick."

"It's a fucking joke," Bevan said. "Jane told us about it, but I never thought it would be that bad."

"Then why did you act so surprised? Look, we're just working, like you guys are. But between us, I wanna change the place. Redecorate it, you know? Make it right."

"You should," Mitch said.

"You have to," Bevan added.

"I'm on it. We thought people might be into this, but they're not."

"Why would they?" Mitch asked. "That's not the real Australia. Come on. Let's get a beer."

"Have a good night, fellas. Sorry, eh."

Back inside, the group were huddled around Humphrey.

"I can't believe their behaviour," one member said. "They're normally so nice and funny."

"I think we're going to need some new Australians," another said.

"Would you like to join our club?" asked the man who had copied the article. "We could hold our meetings here and tell all our friends about the place."

Humphrey looked at Darius. "Where do we sign up?"

The man clapped his hands together. "Great. I never expected Mitch and Bevan to be ashamed of their country. They always spoke about it so positively."

"They're probably just angry," Humphrey said, "like I am, deep down. They know all about this, but maybe they just don't know what to do about it. A lot of Aussies ignore it for that same reason. They don't have a solution."

"This stuff about the Stolen Generations and Aboriginal deaths in custody," one man said, "it's nearly as bad as Apartheid."

"I think it's worse. The world knew about Apartheid. Ironically, people in Australia protested against it. But when it comes to what happened to the Aborigines, a lot of Aussies just look the other way, thinking that it's not their problem. It's always been like that."

"I'm shocked."

"You should be."

The evening went on like that. The group asked questions and Humphrey answered them. But, Darius observed, Humphrey stayed off his soapbox and was fair, trying to give both sides of the story; he was even apologetic about Mitch and Bevan, and promised to contact them and bring them back into the club. That was good of Humphrey, but Darius knew it was a decision more based on economics than mateship or Aussie loyalty. They needed more customers. Otherwise, he didn't think they would survive until Christmas.

As the group chatted and laughed, circling around Humphrey, Darius sat at the bar, mentally picturing the redecorating he wanted to do. He thought about his pub back home, where he had spent so many nights watching his dad drink, and then drinking with him when he was old enough. He wanted this bar to look exactly like that one.

We'll talk about it tomorrow, he decided.

***

"I can smell croissants," Humphrey said from the kitchen. "And one stinky Digger."

Darius entered, still sweating. He was surprised to find Humphrey alone, the SZ spread out in front of him. He had seen the redhead earlier, wrapped in a bed sheet; she had skipped past him on the way to the bathroom while he tied his running shoes.

"Where is she?"

"She hightailed it."

"And?"

"And what? She came, she saw, she conquered. Then she came again."

Darius dropped the croissants and rolls on the table, the paper bag damp with grease and his sweat. "She go to work or somethin?"

"I guess."

"I'm gonna take a shower."

"Yes, do that."

"Then we need to talk."

"What about?"

"Making some changes."

Humphrey's phone rang and he grabbed at it. "Wolfie. What's

270

shakin?" Humphrey grinned. "You're joking? Yeah, we'll be there soon. Can you do me a favour? Call the press. Maybe we'll get on tomorrow's front page. Ciao."

"What happened?"

Humphrey snatched a croissant from the bag and bit into it. "We're under attack," he said with a mouthful of it. "A few windows broken, nothing major by the sounds of things."

"What're we waiting for? Let's go."

Humphrey picked up the paper again. "Take a shower. We want you looking your best for the camera."

Still, Darius showered quickly. Back in the kitchen, dressed and dripping, Humphrey was still seated.

"There's coffee," Humphrey said, gesturing with his mug.

Darius poured himself a cup, loaded it with sugar and drank it fast. "I think we should start."

"Yeah," Humphrey said, buttering a roll, "we should. You ready?"

Darius nodded. He made himself a roll to take with him. Humphrey went and got dressed, taking his half a roll with him. When he came back out of his room, Darius was standing by the door.

"Shall we walk?" Humphrey said.

"Aren't we in a hurry?"

"Not really. All right. We'll take a taxi."

"What d'you mean we're under attack?"

"Sounds like vandals. Maybe Mitch and Bevan had a few too many beers last night."

They got into the taxi. Darius ate his roll as they rode to Maxvorstadt. Humphrey spent most of the short journey texting.

"Good thing Wolfie made us take out that big insurance policy," Humphrey said.

"You said it was just a couple of windows."

"Yeah, but who knows what might follow?"

There was one police car and a large green van. A handful of police officers stood in front of the restaurant, lacklustrely trying to stop a photographer from getting close ups of the shattered front windows and the "Al Qiada rules" spray-painted on the door.

Darius grimaced at the scene, but Humphrey was chuckling quietly.

"What's so funny?"

"They spelt it wrong."

"Yeah?"

"Idiots."

Humphrey was shaking his head when a policewoman came up to them, an open notepad in her hands and a clipboard under her left arm. She was tightly packed into her uniform, almost jammed into it. The green pants hugged her hips and arse, giving her a very visible panty line, back and front.

"G'day," Darius said. "English please."

"You speak no German?"

"We're working on it," Humphrey said, "but we don't have the required terrorism vocabulary."

"You are the owners, yes?" She had a deep voice that seemed to struggle with the English words.

They both nodded.

"Not terrorism. Broke windows. No bomb. You're happy."

"Happy? You mean lucky."

"Yes, you're lucky."

"It was a terrorist attack," Humphrey said. "And it's probably because Australia's sending soldiers to Afghanistan. This is clearly an attack on Australia because we're helping to fight the war on terror."

The policewoman smiled while she made some notes. She was pretty, Darius thought, more handsome though because she had a man-shaped face. He could understand some people falling for her, but she wasn't his type. She didn't have the soft features of Waldtraut, nor that beautifully formed mouth that was always twisting and turning, morphing from laughter to mockery to anger to pleasure. He felt a dull ache in his stomach.

"Any problems before? Telephone calls, letters?"

"Nope. All of our customers are just people interested in experiencing a little bit of Australia in this great German city. But what it does show, as the World Trade Center showed, is that terrorists can strike anywhere and that no one is safe."

"Ah," she said, bored. She handed Humphrey the clipboard. "You must fill out these forms. For the insurance. Can I have your passports?"

They handed them over. Darius was nervous. Their visas were in order, but he still thought something might go wrong.

"Is that your real name?" the policewoman asked.

"Darius Tucker is pretty special, isn't it?" Humphrey said. "The restaurant's named after him."

"No, I mean Humphrey Boragart." She looked at Humphrey and smiled, her lips thinning and her teeth showing. Her whole face softened. "*Casablanca* is my favourite film ever."

Humphrey seemed to like the look of her. "'Play it, Sam,'" he said. "'You played it for her, you can play it for me.'"

She laughed, throwing back her head and making her ponytail swish from side to side. "You should be on television."

"Yes, I should. And while we're on the subject, I have to ask, why is everything in this country dubbed? You'd all learn English a lot faster if it wasn't."

She shrugged thoughtfully, agreeing, maybe disagreeing, it was hard for Darius to tell. But her posture changed as she relaxed slightly. She shifted her weight onto her right leg, bending the knee a little, stretching her pants so the outline of her panties made a perfect V.

"Good question," she said. "I ask my sister. She works in television."

"I'd like to know her answer. Maybe you should come by and tell me in person." He reached for his wallet. "Here's my card. That's my mobile number. Call that whenever you want."

"Are you finished?"

Humphrey handed her the clipboard, placing his card on top. "All done."

"Thank you." Then she walked away, her panty line shimmering from side to side.

"Why did you say that?" Darius asked.

Humphrey was still watching the elastic hugging her arse. "What?"

"Why did you say it was terrorists?"

"Aussies fighting Aussies is hardly newsworthy. But a terrorist attack on Australians abroad, that might get us on the news and in the papers. Those dickheads have given us the best publicity possible. Maybe we should send them a thank you note."

Darius ran a hand through his still wet hair.

"How about that cop, eh? I'd like to see what she hides under that uniform."

"Maybe you'll get lucky."

273

"From the look in her eyes, I won't be needing it. Did you see those hips shake as she walked away? Of course you did."

"What about the redhead from last night?"

"Good point. We need to keep the Aust-Schland Club coming back."

"And to get others to come in. That's what I wanted to talk to you about."

"Promotion? We just got a whole lot of it, for free."

"I mean changing the decor."

"What? So you can win Trudi back?"

"So we don't go bust."

"We can't do that now. I don't want Mitch and Bevan thinking that they've won. Anyway, this's gonna turn it around for us."

"You hope."

A horn sounded. They both looked down the street to see a television van coming towards the restaurant.

"Let me do the talking," Humphrey said.

Darius took a step backwards, not wanting to be involved.

***

The place was empty, except for Wes, the owner of the Munich Star Hostel, and a few of his American friends. All other potential customers stayed away. With nothing to do, Humphrey sent the staff home. The phone rang a few times. Darius had a long chat with Alice, assuring her everything was all right. He told her it was all a hoax; just local vandals.

Freddie called. His voice was jittery and he feared his restaurant would be next. Worse, Freddie said, his place was empty.

The policewoman from earlier in the day rang and said she would come by later that evening, when her shift finished. Darius hoped she would bring the whole Munich police force with her.

"Lord," Humphrey said, looking at the ceiling, "please detain that lovely redhead, wherever she might be."

"No worries there," Darius said. "No one's comin in. You should've said it was Aussies."

"Where's your sense of honour, Digger? We can't dob in our fellow countrymen."

274

A few members of the Aust-Schland Club called to offer their support, but none of them stopped by in person.

Waldtraut didn't call. Each time the phone rang, Darius rushed to it hoping it would be her. She must know, he thought. Doesn't she care about my safety?

A television van came again in the afternoon and the empty restaurant made for a good follow up story. "Al Qiada rules" was still painted on the door, the front windows still cracked.

"This is the best kind of defence against terrorism," Humphrey said to the reporter. "To keep going like before. We all have to show that we're not afraid, that these extremists will not stop us from continuing our lives. If we start changing the way we live, then we will let them win."

Wes and his friends clapped and cheered. They chanted together, "U-S-A, U-S-A."

"Thanks," said the production assistant, "that was great. We'll make the evening news. Maybe my sister will get here to watch it with you."

Humphrey playfully punched her on the shoulder. "Hey, you're the one dubbing everything."

"There's eighty million people in this country. I think that's a reason."

"Fair enough. But you'd still learn English quicker. Look at the Scandinavians."

"Maybe. You're good on camera. Did you ever do any acting?"

"Just at school. Regional theatre, for fun."

She motioned for the cameraman and crew to leave. "Let us know if there's another attack."

"Will do," Humphrey said, saluting rather stupidly. He closed the door on the crew and came to the bar. "We'll be on the news at eight."

"Great."

The door opened. Griff entered.

"Well, look what the foul easterly wind blew in," Humphrey said.

"G'day, fellas. You guys all right?"

"Sure."

"If those two mates of yours show," Darius said. "I'll knock their fuckin heads off."

"Oi, steady on. It wasn't them."

"Bullshit."

"Look, mate," Griff said, taking a seat at the bar, "we kicked on to another bar last night but then split up at the main station. They said they were heading home. We all had to work today, you know."

"Look at the door," Darius said, pointing. "Those idiots spelt it wrong."

"Yeah, I thought that was amiss. Good thing ya didn't tell the cops. They could get deported or something."

"We just tried to do the right thing, mate."

"On ya, Digger. No harm done."

"Not yet."

"Where is everyone?"

Humphrey sat down next to Griff. "I guess they're all a little scared of being blown up."

"Sorry, mate. They only told me that they did it. I wasn't part of it. I don't agree with what they did. But, you know, don't hold it against them. They're good fellas."

"You wanna beer?" Darius asked.

"Yeah."

"Divvy one up for me too," Humphrey said. "Someone's gotta drink it before it goes flat."

Darius started pouring the beers.

"Can I do that?" Griff asked.

"You know how?"

"I worked in a bar when I was at uni."

Darius took another look at Griff. He had a plain, innocent dog look, his mouth hanging slightly open, his blue eyes soft and watery. The perfectly trimmed goatee didn't make him look as tough as intended, while the weighty gold hoop in his left ear lobe looked a little gay.

"Go for it," he said.

They swapped positions. Darius took Griff's seat at the bar.

"So, Griffith," Humphrey said. "Looks like you've changed teams. When your mates said they knew people in this town, they weren't kidding. Who'd have thought they'd be members of Al Qaeda?"

"What? They're not fucking terrorists."

"He's joking, Griff," Darius said.

Griff smiled as he slid the beers across the bar. He poured himself one as well and they raised these together.

"Cheers."

They all drank. Darius looked around. Wes and his buddies had left.

"How's it been today?" Griff asked. "Like this?"

"The phone rang a lot," Darius said.

Humphrey looked into his glass. "Who's been callin?"

"Mostly people we know. Aust-Schlanders. Coupla crank calls. Some guy named Arnold or Alan from the embassy in Berlin called too."

"What'd he say? Is the Aussie government gonna protect us?"

"He's comin to Munich. To talk to us."

"That'll be interesting. Maybe some extra promotion."

"We need it."

Humphrey took a long drink. "I gotta confession to make, Darius. I thought we'd clean up with this place. You know, open True Blue Tuckers all over Europe. Start a chain, become millionaires."

"Way off," Darius said. "A few more months of this and we'll be done. We need to redecorate."

"That's not what we set out to do."

"Look, Hobo, we gave it go and it hasn't worked. Let's fix it before it breaks us."

"I still say it needs more time."

"Why not just cover it up," Griff said.

"What do you mean?"

"Put some tablecloths down, then people won't see what's on the tables. For a while, see what happens. If the people want to know, they can lift it up and have a look."

"That's a good idea. Hobo?"

Humphrey was nodding. He sipped his beer and nodded some more. "Yes. Yes. That's exactly what we should do. That's what Australia did and we'll do the same. Thanks, Griff. A fitting contribution."

"I reckon the problem in here is not the decor, it's the atmosphere," Griff said. "Maybe the decor's causing the bad atmosphere."

Darius slapped the bar. "That's what I've been tryin to say. No one wants to look at this stuff. It puts them off. It's fucking depressing."

"You're right, you're right. We'll put tablecloths down. Yeah. Cover it all up. Brilliant." Humphrey went into the kitchen and came back with a pile of white tablecloths. "The former tenants left these. They'll do for starters. Maybe we can get some special Aussie tablecloths. Don't look at me like that, Darius. Simple, inoffensive stuff, I promise."

The three of them spread out the tablecloths. With all the tables covered, Darius thought the place felt a little more inviting.

"Big difference," he said. "Feels cleaner too."

The door opened. The policewoman walked in with two friends.

"Hey," Humphrey said. "You made it. Just in time for the news. Darius, get the TV on."

The policewoman came forward and shook Humphrey's hand. "I'm Annette. This is Sarah and Julia."

"Thanks for coming by. Thirsty?"

The three girls sat down at a table. Annette smoothed the creases in the tablecloth.

"Three beers," she said.

Behind the bar, Griff got to work. "Coming up."

The news started and everyone watched. The report on the restaurant was short, and what Humphrey had said was translated into German.

"God, they even dub me," Humphrey said. "I don't sound anything like that guy."

With the news finished, Darius turned the TV off. All of them sat together at one table. It was very pleasant, sitting and chatting with the girls. But they only stayed for one beer. When Annette left, her two friends went with her. Humphrey went too, giving a rather ridiculous thumbs-up as he went out the door.

"You reckon he'll get all three?" Griff asked.

"He'll be lucky to get one," Darius said, locking the door. "But then he'll say it had nothing to do with luck."

Griff laughed. "He's a real character."

"He'll strike out. Annette didn't exactly ask him to come along. He just left with them."

Griff laughed again.

"You can go too, if you like. I'm just gonna clean up and then scarper as well."

"I'll stick around and help."

"You don't have to."

"I got nowhere to be. Where's you regular barman anyway?"

"Micha? Sent him home, when it was clear no one was coming in."

"How'd ya end up hirin someone like him?"

"What d'you mean?"

Griff moved behind the bar and poured a beer. "You know."

"Our real estate guy sorted it all out." Darius took the beer Griff offered him and sat down at the bar. "He organised all our staff. Cheers."

They clinked glasses, but Griff didn't look him in the eye. On their first night out together, Waldtraut had taught him always to look a person in the eyes when toasting.

"They make it good here, don't they?"

"They do a lot of things good," Griff said, "and did a lot of things bad."

"So did we."

"Yeah, but nothing like that. You been to Dachau?"

"Sure."

"Miss Jane take you?"

Darius laughed. "Mr Squildo. That's still funny. Hobo took me, just after I arrived. He said it was necessary."

"Bloody shocking, isn't it? I'm glad we don't have that kind of guilt on us."

"Take a look under the tablecloths. We've got that kind of guilt."

Griff shook his head. "You can't compare. Anyway, the Aborigines pretty much have themselves to blame. They need to get up and change things, not sit around waiting for government handouts."

"Careful. Me mum's a quarter caste. Now she's a professor in London."

"But that proves my point. They can make it, if they want to. She'd be a good example for all the others back home. Why doesn't she teach there?"

"Doesn't like it. She said she had better chances overseas. And it's too racist."

"Yeah, but you're from the country. It's different in the cities. Sydney's the most multicultural city in the world."

"Yeah? How many Aboriginal friends do you have in Sydney? How many Asians? How many Muslims?"

"You've obviously never been to Sydney. But you travelled a lot, eh? Jane said you were in Canada."

"Spent the last winter there."

"You ski?"

"Of course."

"Maybe we can go skiing this winter. Hit the Alps."

"What about Bevan and Mitch?"

Griff finished his beer and poured himself another. "They went too far. I don't agree with everything in here, but what they did was un-Australian in my book."

The loud knock on the door made Darius jump. Slowly, he went to the front and peered through the window, half expecting to see the angry, revenge-seeking faces of Bevan and Mitch, and perhaps the rest of the footy team. But there was just a man in a blue suit. Darius opened the door.

"We're closed."

"I'm Arnold Jamison, from the embassy. I called this afternoon."

Darius let the man come in and then locked the door behind him. "I'm Darius Tucker, one of the owners. Humphrey, the other owner, went home."

"Was he on the news?" Jamison asked.

"Briefly," Darius said, leading the man to the bar. "You were quick, Mr Jamison. We only spoke a couple of hours ago."

"I flew down as soon as I could. The Ambassador considered it urgent."

"Just a coupla broken windows. No big deal."

Jamison stood up straight, trying to impose himself and show his government-aided substance. He was middle height, broad-shouldered, though that could have been the extra padding in the suit jacket, and running to fat so the buttons on the lower part of his suit jacket strained a little. He looked barely over thirty, but wasn't fresh-faced or innocent. He looked like he had seen the world and dealt with difficult problems, maybe even crushed of few immigration dreams or had people deported. His face was pale and would have been boring if not for the exceedingly ambitious arch of his eyebrows. Without them, Darius thought, he would have looked like an ordinary clerk who pushed visa applications from one tray to another. But with them, he looked like an up and coming diplomat, one who might be willing to step on the backs of friends for added leverage.

"This was a terrorist attack on Australian subjects abroad," he said. "The report I write will go to the foreign minister himself."

"That could be a downer," Griff said.

Jamison turned to the small barman. "And who are you?"

"Griff Swindon."

Jamison popped the button of his jacket so his belly showed even more. "You work here?"

"He's a mate of mine," Darius said. He slapped Jamison on the back, trying to welcome him into the fold. The embassy man was edgy and made it worse by trying to act like some outback fella of resource and humour. Darius wondered if Jamison was used to intimidating people simply because of his position and the influence he exerted. But Darius wasn't intimidated.

"What about a beer, Mr Jamison?" he asked.

"I'd love one, and call me Arnie. Are you Digger?"

"That's me, Arnie."

Behind the bar, Griff went to work pouring three more beers. Darius was a little surprised to see Griff had already finished his second.

"Are you in the Army Reserve?"

"Nah, mate. I'm a shearer, not a fighter."

"From WA, right?" Arnie took the beer. "Thanks."

"Yep, down south. Near Wagin. How do you know that?"

"I called around. Friedrich told me a lot about you. Some good, some bad."

"We kinda shafted him a few months back. I thought he'd forgiven us by now. We sent him an inflatable kangaroo as a peace offering. What about you? Where are you from?"

"Bunbury, but I moved to Perth to go to uni."

All three drank.

"You know," Arnie said, speaking with a thicker accent than before, "my uncle has a big farm over Wagin way. Murray Stevenson. You ever heard of him?"

Darius smiled thinly, reminded of what a small world it was back home. He had always felt out of place there and had told Humphrey he hated always running into people he knew, especially those who knew his dad, but now he missed it; those simple connections that made socialising that much easier. Arnie's mother was a Stevenson girl. In a flash he saw the shimmer of their dresses at his dad's funeral, the rhythmic swaying of their narrow hips and the fresh openness of their mouths.

"You just made me very homesick," he said.

"You know him?"

"Me and me dad used to shear all his skinny sheep."

"Jack Tucker," Arnie exclaimed. He seemed to pounce on the connection like a starving animal. "You're his son? He's a legend down there. What do they call him?"

A sob got caught in Darius's throat. He just managed to get the words out. "The Ripper."

"That's right. Jack the Ripper. Uncle Murray was always telling stories about him. He must be pretty proud of you."

"He was. He died last Easter in a car accident."

"No. I'm sorry, really."

"It's all right. I guess news doesn't travel as fast in Germany as it does in WA, except when there's a terrorist attack."

Arnie nodded sombrely. "What happened?"

"A roo jumped in front of his car."

"No, I mean last night."

"Not much to tell. We got a call this mornin. The police were here when we got here. They talked to us and we organised some workers to come and fix the glass. They haven't come yet."

"And Al Qaeda's still on the door."

"Humphrey wanted it left there."

"What on earth for?"

"He reckons it'll keep them away for a while. You know, that they've made their point. Still, I'm happy with a few broken windows as long as they don't blow the place up."

"I'll drink to that," Griff said, drinking to that.

"We can't guarantee your safety," Arnie said. "This war's putting Australians everywhere in danger. We know we're going to be targeted."

"What war?" Darius asked.

"The war on terror," Arnie said, making it sound like he was at the front line.

"Don't worry," Griff said. "There won't be another nine-eleven."

"That's why we're involved in the war."

"Good luck," Darius said, thinking that Arnie sounded

unconvincing, was selling secondhand rubbish. He took a big gulp of beer. He was tired, but he didn't want to go home; there was the possibility of having to listen to Humphrey screwing Annette. It was actually quite nice to sit at the bar, his bar, drink a cold beer and talk with two of his countrymen. Arnie and Griff both seemed to have their heads on straight.

"Reckon we might need it," Arnie said.

"Just kill em all and let God sort em out." Griff drained his beer and then quizzically looked at the bottom of the glass, wondering where the contents had gone. He poured himself another, missing the tap with his first attempt.

"Brilliant idea," Arnie said. "Let's hope the Muslims aren't thinking the same thing."

"Terrorism is political," Griff said, "not religious."

"It's religious, believe me, and it's also about power and making voices heard."

"I think you're both wrong," Darius said, remembering what Harry had once said. "It's about money."

"Oil? You might be right," Arnie conceded, making Darius like him a little more, "but you didn't hear that from me. So, are there any other Aussie places in Munich?"

"There's the Waterhole, but you know that place. It's run by a German and the last thing truly Australian in that place was me."

Griff and Arnie laughed.

"I think we should talk tomorrow," Darius said, "when Humphrey's here. He's got a copy of the police report."

"When are you open?"

"Eleven."

Arnie drained his glass and stood up. "Then, I'll see you tomorrow."

"About time you went home too, Griff," Darius said.

Griff gulped down his almost full glass and then followed Arnie to the door, staggering slightly. Darius unlocked the door and shook Arnie's hand.

"You're taking this well. I expected you fellas to be jumping with fear. But you're the Ripper's son and that explains a lot."

"You little ripper!" Griff shouted. When Darius tried to close the door on him, he said, "Whas up, Digger? Ya not comin? Let's kick on to another pub."

"I got some work to do." He turned to Arnie. "See you in the mornin. Try to remember a story about me old man. I miss hearin em."

"Will do, Digger. G'night."

Darius pushed Griff out and locked the door. Back at the bar, he poured another drink and switched on the television. The restaurant wasn't on the news. It was a new day in most parts of the world and more newsworthy events had already taken place. There were reports from Afghanistan, more trouble in Israel, people starving in Africa, speeches from politicians promising to rid the world of terrorists. It was all very depressing, but he kept watching, his only company a dolled up newsreader and all those empty beer glasses he lined up on the bar.

Lewis: Were any of them published?

Poet: I think they all got burned. Or thrown in the trash. That's probably what they deserved. It was a pretty difficult time, for me. The restaurant was attacked. I broke up with my girlfriend. It looked like we were gonna go broke.

Lewis: Did you think about closing down and leaving?

Poet: No. Then you let them win.

Lewis: Still, there must have been some anxious moments when someone of Middle Eastern appearance came in?

Poet: Why?

Lewis: Well, uh, they might have been a suicide bomber.

Poet: I never even considered that. And fair go, mate. Not every Arab is a terrorist.

Lewis: No, of course not. But you stayed in Munich.

Poet: Yeah. I had a good bunch of mates there. And the restaurant started to do well.

~~~

Sleeper Agent

"We goin anywhere in particular?"

Harry stared straight ahead. "I thought we'd just ride the bus for a while."

The red double-decker ploughed through damp, grey London, adding putrid exhaust to the city's gaseous cocktail of haze and threatening to clip the pedals of every cyclist it passed. The city looked moist, overused and uninviting. Darius missed Munich's buffed streets and cleansing alpine rain. Next to him, Harry seemed to look out the window and see the same version of London, and perhaps also missed another cleaner, more welcoming place. Harry had shaved off his moustache, and his top lip was slightly paler than the rest of his face.

"What's with the backpack?"

Harry glanced at it, nestled between his knees. "Research. I've been doing this since we got back from Munich. Every day I ride a different bus, on a different route."

"Don't you have anything better to do?"

"I like to sit on the top deck, at the front like this. You can see a lot from up here, and the people don't know you're watching them."

Darius followed Harry's gaze. He saw miserable Londoners struggling under black umbrellas, pushing and shoving on the footpath, there faces lit by the Christmas lights that hung from every shop window and awning.

"This's a great city," Harry said. "I loved London from the moment I got here. And you can't ignore the history. This city shaped the world. Crusades, empire, Shakespeare, Darwin, Industrial Revolution, Africa. You could almost say that everything that ever went right and wrong with the modern world started from here."

"A lot to answer for."

"Yes, but I don't think any of these folks have time for history. They've got to find a present for that uncle they never visit, finish that important end of year report for their boss, organise that package holiday to Spain. They probably don't know half of what this city has done."

"Australia's the same. What happened a hundred years ago is not nearly as important as what the average Darren faces every day."

Harry looked at him. "Sounds like something Humphrey would say."

"Yeah. But ya got to live in the present, you know?"

"What about your educational eatery?"

"We changed it a bit. Not so confrontational anymore."

"And? How's that working out?"

"It's made a massive difference. Things have really picked up in the last month. We had to hire more staff. We've got this Aussie guy, Griff. He works behind the bar now. He's a real laugh."

"I'm happy to hear that. Alice and I were worried you might go bankrupt."

"It's all good."

"How's Humphrey?"

"Yeah, busy. He got cast in some TV show. Lucky bastard. He was gone for a couple of weeks while they filmed it."

"Reality TV?"

"Some crime show. Tat...something. He's been pretty cagey about it. Hasn't said much since he came back. I think they made him sign some kind of agreement."

"Non-disclosure."

"That's it. The show's gonna be on in February."

"Good for him." Harry rubbed at the fogged up window. "No other attacks?"

"The first one was a hoax. I told you that."

"Still, some people might've tried to copy it."

"Nah. People forgot about it. Now they're comin in droves."

"Yes, more people living in the present. Where I'm from, it's a little different."

"How?"

"The past is always called up, especially when it's useful, and religion plays a part in everything. People there are already calling the invasion of Afghanistan a crusade."

"So?" Darius wondered what the Crusades were actually about. The best he could think of was that Indiana Jones film: knights, eternal life, the Holy Grail, Germans as the bad guys, good beating evil.

"That word has a powerful meaning in that part of the world.

Crusade. One side's successful conquering is another side's bitter invasion. There's all this talk now about fighting for God. When Bush talks about his God and fighting for beliefs, he's no different from bin Laden. They're both extremists, they're both dangerous and there's a good chance they're both wrong."

Harry stopped talking when a man sat down in the seat across from him. The man opened a tabloid and began reading. On the front page was the photograph of a soccer player, involved in some sex scandal.

"But this invasion of Afghanistan is a crusade," Harry said, his voice lowered, "a battle of gods. Bush is turning this into a religious war, making everything worse. His jihad has been rebranded regime change. And it justifies the extremists, on both sides, to fight dirty and show no mercy, because they think they're doing it for the greater good."

"Australia's involved too. We never miss a war."

"No, you don't. That's a mistake. Don't be surprised if something happens to Australia."

"An attack?"

"And more than a couple of broken windows. Your countrymen should just stay home and fix their own problems."

"Yeah, they should."

The man across from Harry lowered his paper. "Australia doesn't have any problems."

"It has a lot more than you think," Harry said.

"They're sending soldiers to Afghanistan because they don't want to be left out."

"There's more to it than that."

The man shrugged and went back to his paper.

"It'll be over pretty quick, won't it?" Darius asked.

Harry rubbed the smooth, pale skin where his moustache had been. "Don't be so sure. The Americans have all the firepower, but they won't be able to fight on their terms. It's an amazing place, Afghanistan. But there wouldn't be many westerners who would think it hospitable." He sighed and shook his head. "The Taliban are a nasty lot, but there are worse groups in power around the world. The Americans will have their work cut out for them in the mountains. People will die, and whatever happens, it won't be over quickly."

Darius sat back and looked out the window as all those words and ideas bobbled around in his head. The sentences echoed, but then the gaps between the words seemed to disappear, so what Harry had said became a pile of jumbled letters. But he had to say something, and even though he liked Harry and wanted to be interested in his world, he couldn't really care less about what happened in the Middle East. He silently wished they would all just fight in their own countries and blow each other clear off the planet. Then maybe they woudn't get into boats and try to sail for Australia; they wouldn't bring their own problems to his country. He still didn't really understand why the hijackers had flown those planes into the World Trade Center. What had the people working on those buildings done to deserve that? What point had the terrorists been trying to make?

"Well, they can't just do nothing after nine-eleven," he said.

Harry played with the straps of his backpack. "The media talks of terrorism like it's a new thing. The new enemy. It's the oldest form of violence. Terrorism is about spying and sabotage, weakening your enemy and planting seeds of fear. And the most successful and dangerous terrorist organisation in the world is the CIA, not Al Qaeda."

Darius looked down at his hands. It had been three days but still they smelt of beer. He hoped Griff and Micha were coping all right, and that the restaurant was full. I'm earning even while I'm here, he thought.

The man got up, leaving his paper on the seat, and went down the stairs.

"Hey, Harry?"

"Yes?"

"I lost, uh, I'm not together with Waldtraut anymore."

"The girl from the bar? What happened?"

"I dunno. She got really pissed off about something, the restaurant, I think, and then she was gone."

"I'm sorry. I liked her."

"Me too."

"Did Humphrey put his foot in his mouth?"

"Yeah. No. It was something to do with me. I think. I tried to contact her but I think she left Munich."

"Shame."

"Yeah. You got anything to eat your backpack, Harry. I'm starving."

"Did our morning gallop make you hungry?"

"It did. I've been running in Munich, but not that often."

"Sorry. No food."

"What's in there then? It looks pretty full."

A young couple, with several shopping bags clutched in their hands, sat down in the seat across from Harry. The man picked up the abandoned paper while the woman looked at Harry and then at his backpack. Darius watched her tug the sleeve of her boyfriend's jacket and then lean close to whisper to him. The man smiled and shook his head.

"You know something, Darius," Harry said. "I've lived in this country for nearly thirty years. I played tennis at university. I taught theology at Oxford. I cried when Diana died. Every year, I stand in line at five in the morning for tickets to Wimbledon. I'm a British citizen. I'm married to an Indigenous Australian. I've spoken out against extremists and religious oppression."

"I didn't read your book, Harry. Waldtraut's got it."

"I'll give you another copy when we're home."

"How's it selling?"

"Very well. Since around the middle of September."

"Brilliant."

"Yes. It's good that people are interested in the background. There are lots of people who want to know why these things happen. Understanding is important."

Darius saw the couple whispering together again. The man laughed.

"Oh, all right," the man said to her. "We'll change seats."

She looked out the window. "No. There's Marks and Sparks. Let's get off. I still need a present for Aunt Lindsay."

They stood up. The man smiled briefly at Harry as he passed.

"We're leaving," Harry said to Darius.

"The bus?"

"England."

"What? Back to Scotland?"

"Alice got an offer from the University of Auckland. We're going after New Year. She hasn't been able to tell you because she likes having you close by, but who knows, maybe you'll move back to Australia."

"I'll come visit. I'll take some weeks off in January. I'd like to see New Zealand."

"That'd be great. Alice feels bad about leaving, but it's a great opportunity for her."

"I'm happy for her. For both of you."

An elderly man sat down. "Morning."

"Good morning," Harry said.

"Doing your Christmas shopping? It's mad out there on the streets."

"Awful weather for it."

"Everyone's buying presents. Good for the economy, I guess." He looked at Harry's backpack. "Looks like you finished your shopping. Or do you have a bomb in there?"

"Do you think that's funny?"

The old man laughed. "Not if you have got a bomb in there." Then he muttered, "Maybe's it's enough when you outpopulate us."

"Excuse me? I'm British. Would you like to see my passport? My driver's license?"

"Harry, settle down," Darius said. "He's allowed to have an opinion."

Harry nodded. "You're right." He turned to the elderly man. "I'm sorry."

"You should be. You made the world this way and now we have to live with it."

Harry turned and when he spoke, his voice was steady, his tone conversational. "Well, now we've got ourselves an interesting paradox. I think it's more that you made it this way and now everyone has to live with it. I love my fellow Brits, but English history is tainted with mistakes, and I mean world-changing errors that still have an impact today, centuries later. It was the English who tried to force Christianity on the Muslims, with all those Crusades, with all that pillaging and murder. And it was the English who invaded half the world and left ancient civilisations in tatters. It was the English who wrecked Africa. And it was the English who proved to the world we were once monkeys, refuting the same religion they had killed and invaded for."

"You blame us for everything then," the elderly man said. "And terrorise us as a result."

"Not me. Like I said, I'm British. And terrorists are an incredibly small minority."

"But they cause a lot of damage."

"Yes, they do, and that's very bad, but people are more interested in the who and the how, when they should be interested in the why."

"They should just leave innocent people alone."

Harry stood up and rang the bell. He bent over and lifted his backpack. The bag looked heavy, was bulging in certain places. The elderly man watched him.

"Are you getting off?"

"Yes," Harry said.

"So am I."

Harry let the elderly man go down the stairs first, then followed him. The bus started to slow down. All three stood in the doorway. Darius was glad to see the rain had stopped.

When the doors opened, the elderly man was first out. He looked around for a little bit and then walked towards the police car parked in front of a shoe shop.

"Where to now, Harry?" Darius asked.

Harry was watching the exchange. The elderly man looked in Harry's direction. A policeman got out of the car.

"Just a minute, Darius. Let's see what happens with this. It could be good."

"He's from a different generation. You know, probably thinks all Arabs are terrorists, and all Germans are Nazis."

"I'd like to think the people here are more enlightened than that. More tolerant at least."

The policeman came towards them. "Morning."

"Good morning. Everything all right?" Harry asked.

"Well, the gentleman over there, was he on the bus with you?"

"Yes."

"He's a little worried you might have something in that backpack of yours."

"Is he?"

"Can I have a look?"

Harry gestured towards the street, at the few people who had stopped to watch. "Are you going to check everyone's backpack?"

"If you're going to take that tone, we'll check it in the bag of the wagon. You too."

Darius didn't move. "I didn't do anything."

"Come along."

Harry nodded at Darius. They followed the policeman. He opened the back door of the wagon and all three got inside. Harry and Darius sat on the narrow bench on one side, the policeman on the other.

"What've you got, Heath?" asked a voice from the cab. Darius could see his face through the mesh divider.

"Probably nothing." Heath turned to Harry. "Give me your pack, please. Just a routine check."

"Do you do this with everyone?"

"There's a lot of people on the street at this time of year. Security has been upped since nine-eleven."

Harry handed over his backpack. There was loud zip as Heath opened it.

"What's he got in there?" asked the voice through the mesh.

Heath pulled out the statue of a fat, smiling man with a bald head.

"That's Buddha," Harry said.

"What's he doing with a Buddha in his bag? Is it ticking?"

Harry laughed.

"Quiet," Heath said. He kept pulling items out of the bag.

"What else is in there?

"There's some weird kind of elephant, a crucifix, a chain of beads, one of those hats Jews wear."

"A kippah," Harry said. "A yarmulke."

"Right, and there's a bunch of old books."

Then the bag was empty.

"Is this what you wanted to show me?" Darius whispered to Harry.

Harry smiled and spoke to the policeman. "Are we under arrest?"

"I've never been arrested before," Darius said.

"No. No." He started packing the bag together again, jamming the contents inside. "You're free to go."

"Thank you." Harry shouldered his backpack.

The policeman opened the door. "Sorry about that. Can't be too careful. I hope you understand."

"No problem."

Outside, it had started to rain again.

"Let's have a cup of tea," Harry said. "I know a place around the corner. They have shishas too."

"Is that a kind of cake?"

"It's a waterpipe."

Harry took a left down a narrow street and Darius followed.

"What was that all about?"

"The backpack? Research. Mostly, people just stare at me. That was the first time the police were involved. But he was pretty friendly about it. Still, this is going to make a great introduction."

"You're writing another book? What about?"

"It's about how the attack on the World Trade Center has changed the world. And if you don't mind, I'd like to include that you were put in the police wagon with me."

"Yeah, sure."

"Don't worry. I'll change your name."

"Okay."

Harry stopped in front of a small cafe. "I hope someone has the courage to publish it."

Lewis: What turned things around with your restaurant? Did the Australian Embassy help you out, provide any support and protection?

Poet: Not really.

Lewis: You sound disappointed. Did you expect more?

Poet: I didn't expect anything. No one was hurt in the first attack and we really didn't think it would happen again.

Lewis: And no one thought Bali would be targeted either.

Poet: The world's full of surprises.

Lewis: Like shearers becoming poets. Why were the love poems so bad?

Poet: I was trying to impress a girl. I wasn't writing from the heart. They were terrible, and she said so too. Love wasn't really my specialty. I guess I relate more to pain and loss and disappointment.

Lewis: All negative things.

Poet: That depends on how you look at it. I don't think of myself as a negative person. And I think all the poems about my dad are really uplifting. I want to be like him.

Lewis: A true blue Australian.

Poet: Right. And others should want to be like him too.

~~~

Ol' Boragie

He moved through the steel and glass of the terminals, weaving between all the lazy idiots just standing on the walkways. Hate airports, he thought, and flying too. Who designs the seats anyway? Anyone over six feet gets wedged in like a sardine. And then every bastard tilts their seat back taking away even more space, and they run their hands over their balding heads, flicking hair into the plastic food and leaving dandruff floating in drinks.

"I'm really jetlagged," he said to himself.

He just wanted to go home, have a hot shower and sleep. Still, being back in Munich, back at the airport, another country under his belt, he felt different. He was progressing. He knew a few words of a foreign language and could convincingly reel off travel yarns, even if not all of them were his own. He could even boast he had been to Hong Kong, but leave out that it was just a two hour stopover on the way back.

New Zealand. All the images were still stark: the flat green plains, the misty hills, the way the rain fell in sheets, the rock faces dripping with moisture, and the moss so lush and soft he had wanted to grab a handful and eat it. The bare, sheep-scattered highways, the bustling small towns, the pockets of beauty nestled so closely together, and everything so green, natural and healthy.

He had hated it.

Because there was no one to enjoy it with, no one to turn to, smile, and say something like, "Did ever see something so beautiful?" He had no hiking partner, no dining partner and no bed partner. It was just him, moving from town to town, without even any hitch-hikers to pick up. So he hit on scrawny middle-aged waitresses, struck up pathetic conversations with over-ripe bakery assistants, and stayed in crowded, smelly hostels when he could have afforded, and would have preferred, hotels. He loitered at universities, flirted with supermarket cashiers, and followed girls into perfume and clothing shops. He reeked of desperation, he knew, was trying way too hard. The girls smelt it, felt it and, quite rightly, ran away from him.

And the whole time, even when he was with Alice and Harry in Auckland and the late January days were bright and hot, he wanted to be back in Munich. There, he was somebody, a successful restaurateur. He decided he would go back looking the part. In Auckland, he set about making some changes, to cultivate a new Darius. Looking back now, he thought he had gone a little overboard, but he liked what he saw in the mirror and liked the way other people looked at him.

It was that Darius who moved through the string of terminals at Franz Josef Strauss Airport. His silk shirt was tight in the shoulders and loose in the arms, as the tailor had recommended. He had forked out a good wedge of cash for the chunky slab of metal and silver that dangled from his wrist; it also told the time and could do a few other things he didn't fully understand yet. But it looked good, felt right, as did the designer sunglasses. They dulled the nasty fluorescent lights of the terminal and when he glanced in the mirror, it was vindicating to see he looked more than a bit like a rock star on holiday. The hair was helping; it still held that styled messiness he'd let the hairdresser punish him with. He'd learned how to keep that style too, even if took a good fifteen minutes. He carried his big backpack casually, one strap slung half over his right shoulder. He tried to carry it like he didn't need it, didn't think it a status symbol, and could easily just drop it and walk away. His walk was important. He'd thought about it on the plane, had practised a little up and down the aisle. It required a kind of bored, self-important ease, to be loose-limbed and confident, but his alligator-skin shoes, squeaking loudly and attracting attention, were so uncomfortable, he could barely walk at all.

Griff was standing at the ticket machine.

"G'day, mate. You look like hell."

"Griff? What the fuck?"

"Didn't you get my SMS?"

Darius pulled his mobile phone from his back pocket, flipped it open and turned it on. It beeped loudly and buzzed several times. He read through the messages.

"Hobo's on tonight. I forgot all about it."

"No worries. We've got everything organised." Griff stepped forward and relieved Darius of his backpack. "We've even rented a big screen and a projector. That was my idea."

Darius was still going through his messages. "Yeah? Sounds great."

"Fuck, what've you got in here?"

"A few souvenirs."

As they walked towards the exit, he wondered how much he had missed, had been missed. He shoved his phone back into his pocket and took off his sunglasses to rub his eyes.

"What time is it?" he asked, looking curiously at his enormous watch, at all the hands flicking and turning, completing tasks he couldn't quite comprehend.

"Ten past. Come on. We're gonna be late."

Griff looked even smaller carrying the backpack. He walked with short, jumpy steps, trying to show he wasn't struggling under the weight.

They got in the back seat of a taxi, the big backpack between them. Griff made small talk, filling the air with inane comments and questions. Darius kept his head turned away from Griff, listening with one ear. He looked out the window, watching the fields become suburbs and the suburbs become city. It was still winter in this part of the world and now he missed the southern hemisphere summer. He sighed loudly a few times when Griff was in mid-sentence.

"Hobo still talkin about openin a place in Stuttgart?"

Humphrey hadn't written much in his emails and Darius wanted to get up to date as quickly as possible. While away, the idea of a True Blue Tucker in every major European city had become increasingly appealing to Darius.

"He was there last week. He had an audition for another cop show and looked at a couple of potential locations."

"And?"

"He got the part, but he reckons Stuttgart's a nothing town with nothing goin on. We're lookin at Berlin and Hamburg instead."

He turned to Griff and smiled. "Good on him. Hobo's gonna be a star, and on German TV."

"It'll mean great things for our restaurant."

It was Sunday evening and the city was quiet. When the taxi pulled up, there were a few people gathered out the front of the restaurant, including a big guy in a black suit standing at the door. Griff paid the driver and waited for a receipt. He took all of the change and Darius saw the driver sneer.

"Give him a tip," Darius said.

"I rounded it up. That's enough."

Darius pushed his sunglasses into his hair and lifted his backpack out of the taxi. At the door, he was stopped by the man in the black suit. Darius tried to push the big hand off his shoulder but it stayed there, holding him to the spot.

"Hey, mate!"

"You on the list?" he demanded, his voice squeaky and high, his accent American. His muscles bulged unnaturally under his tight suit and his eyes were far too close together, perhaps the result of spending a decade or two staring down at his own pectorals. He had terrible skin; a rash of pimples on his cheeks and forehead stood out pink and proud from under a layer of moisturiser.

"List? Get outta my way. I'm Darius Tucker."

The bouncer looked at his clipboard. "Your name's not on the list."

"It's above the fuckin door."

"It's all right, Alfonso," Griff said, pushing past Darius. "He's with me."

"Of course, Misser Swindon." The man moved aside.

Darius tried to laugh, to shake his head coolly. Griff lead the way into the crowded restaurant. Humphrey saw Darius and pushed his way towards him.

"Digger!" Humphrey shouted, putting his arm around Darius's shoulders. "We thought the Kiwis might've kidnapped you, to keep you from seeing my debut performance."

"Wouldn't've missed it for the world."

"Welcome back."

"Good to see ya, mate."

Darius wanted to relax under Humphrey's arm, to feel part of this. But he felt self-conscious with his alligator shoes, clunky watch, silk shirt, messy mullet, and all the other parts that made up his contrived whole.

Humphrey whispered in his ear, "Nice makeover."

The crowd parted, slightly, as Humphrey led Darius towards the bar. A few people shook his hand, members of the Aust-Schland Club, whose names he could never seem to remember. He once again wished they'd wear name tags. More than a few people stared at him like they'd never seen him before, surely wondering what role he played in Humphrey's life. He kissed Annette on both cheeks and shook Wolfgang's hand. He dumped his backpack behind the bar. Micha smiled at him and put a cold beer in his hands.

"You look fabulous," Micha said. "Welcome home. Next time, take me with you."

"Cheers, Micha." He turned and faced the crowd. Glass in hand, he climbed up onto the bar. "Excuse me, everyone." The crowd quietened down. "I want to thank you all for comin'." He raised his glass in Humphrey's direction. "And I want you all to toast my best mate Humphrey Boragart. You're the most incredible bloke I ever met. I know you'll be a huge success tonight." He lifted his glass. "To Humphrey!"

The crowd echoed him and drank. It had been a while since he had done so, but still he forced himself to drink the whole beer at once. A few people cheered him on and clapped loudly when he got to the bottom. He didn't tip the empty glass on his head like he should have, and when he jumped down from the bar, it was an effort to stay on his feet. But he pulled it off, got a loud round of applause and held up his hands in triumph. He then took a seat at the bar and tried to steady himself. He gritted his teeth and managed to keep all that airline food from spilling onto the floor. Thankfully, the screens lit up, the lights went dark and the show began. Everyone went quiet. In the opening scene, a girl was killed, but you could only see the lower part of the killer's body and his hands.

"That's me," Humphrey whispered to Darius. "Can you believe it?"

"Nuh."

"You understand any of it, Digger?" a voice whispered in his other ear.

"Arnie," Darius said loudly, making people turn to him and shush. He lowered his voice. "What're you doin here?"

"Humphrey invited me." He wore another blue suit, tie-less to mark the relative informality of the occasion. The top buttons of his white shirt were open and a heavy tuft of dark hair poked out the top. "It's not often Aussies get on TV in this country."

"Good to see ya."

"You know this show?"

"Nuh."

"It's called *Tatort*. It's been on for years. Different detectives in different cities. Every Sunday, it's set in a different location."

"Interesting."

Arnie turned to the woman next to him. She wore a grey business suit, was broad in stature and rather tall. She loomed over Arnie, but Darius thought that she had something over the embassy man beyond height. Was she the Ambassador? he wondered.

"This is Sally Roach."

She held out a large, tanned hand and Darius took it, liking her strong handshake and cool palm. He only knew one other girl who had shaken his hand like that, and hated all those others who shook his hand like they were not even there, giving nothing to grip but a slimy dead fish.

"Nice to finally meet you," she said in a low voice which broke sweetly on a few words. "Arnold told me a lot about you."

"It's all lies."

Sally raised an eyebrow. She had long eyebrows that suited her large face, and they were darker than her short brown hair. She was pretty, with a face that exuded health and vitality. Her red lips seemed to curl upwards and would beat anyone to a smile. She had a long, straight nose, but it got lost among her other over-sized features, so it looked all right, except when Darius saw her from side on. That seemed to be how she faced people, looking through the side of her brown eyes, a delightful smirk on her face. There was a glint in those eyes, at least Darius thought he saw one; eyes that seemed to already have guessed his intentions and were pleased and intrigued by them.

"I hope not." She twisted her head back and upwards a little so her nose looked like a diving board. Darius imagined a tiny man springing off the tip of her nose and swan-diving into her mouth. It made him want to bite the end of her nose, to see if it was as soft and springy as it looked.

"Sally's from TA," Arnie said. Darius looked at him, wanting him to go away. "Tourism Australia. She's taken over the Germany desk and is on a bit of a tour, getting to know the place."

"Welcome to Munich," Darius said. "If you need a tour guide, I'm your man."

Sally edged past Arnie to take the bar stool next to Darius that had just been vacated by a man rushing outside to answer his mobile phone. But before she sat down, she took off her suit jacket and rolled up the sleeves of her blouse to her elbows; a farm girl looking for work. Darius saw she had strong forearms with small brown hairs that were flattened and straight, like they had been combed.

"I might take you up on that," she said. "I'd like to get an Aussie's take on Munich."

"I knew you two would like each other," Arnie said. "She's from the country too."

Darius turned to Sally. "Whereabouts?"

"Blackheath. In the Blue Mountains."

"Beautiful area," Darius said, wondering where the hell it was.

"Have you been there?"

"Sure."

"Come on, Sally," Arnie said. "Everyone's been to the Blue Mountains, even blokes from small WA country towns."

"And so they should. Like Digger said, it's a beautiful place."

The crowd cheered as Humphrey's face was shown on screen for the first time. He had a scraggly moustache, badly trimmed.

"He looks all right," Darius said.

"He looks like a giant porn star," Sally said. "Is he standing on a box or something?"

"It's because the other actors are so short," Arnie said. "All actors are."

Darius wondered why Arnie was still standing there, was still trying to be part of his conversation with Sally. Couldn't he take a hint?

On screen, Humphrey delivered his first line, spoken in a thick Australian accent. He sounded like he was copying Crocodile Dundee.

"They made me speak in English," Humphrey said loudly. "I'm working on the German."

"And so you should," a voice in the crowd replied.

Sally leaned close to Darius. He could smell her, could just get a look down her shirt at the shadowy crevice between her breasts which was wide enough to hold a cigarette packet.

"Is he gonna become a regular on this show?" she asked.

"Dunno." He tried to keep it together. He nearly slipped of his stool but managed to steady himself by putting an elbow on the bar. He wanted to throw this big country girl over his shoulder and haul her out of the restaurant. "He's got another part in Stuttgart, but I don't know much about it. I just got back today."

"From where?"

"New Zealand," he said, rubbing his eyes. "I stopped over in Melbourne too."

Sally turned to face him. "What's it like?"

"You've never been to New Zealand?" Arnie asked.

"Hey, fair go, Arnie," Darius said. "She's promoting Australia, not our little brother."

"True," Sally said, "but I don't think they like being called that." She laughed and Darius copied her. They shared a moment.

"Sorry," Arnie said, though he sounded far from it. He gestured at the screen with his full glass. "Humphrey's a good actor. Very natural on camera."

Darius leaned towards Sally. They're shoulders touched. "He's just playin himself. But that's probly more than enough."

Sally chewed her lip thoughtfully as she watched Humphrey on the screen. "You know, he might be good in one of our ads."

Then she was on her feet and moving in Humphrey's direction. Darius watched, was a little shocked to see what a big arse she had; the seams of her skirt looked like they strained and stretched with every step. She had long legs, but they were thick and lumpy, far too unathletic to be shown so brazenly with such a short skirt and lifted with such high heels. He wouldn't be put off though, because she had strong, square shoulders and her back had an attractive curve. He liked her animation and energy, the way she kept moving, throwing her head back, laughing, smiling, really expressing herself. Like she was now, speaking with Humphrey. Darius was glad that both of them seemed to undertake the conversation with professional intentions. He saw Annette watching too. Humphrey and Sally shook hands, striking a deal. Sally tried to make her way back to the bar.

"Reckon you're in there," Arnie said. He winked once and then moved slightly away when Sally returned. Her bar stool had already been taken so Arnie made space for her to stand between them. She needed quite a lot of space and took all of it, wiggling her arse into it like she was parallel parking. Darius offered his stool but she waved him off. Arnie drained his beer and headed towards the bathroom.

"He likes the idea," she said. "He invited me over for breakfast tomorrow, at your apartment. Is that okay with you, Digger?"

"Sure. We live together."

"Yes, he said that."

"Not together together. If you like, I could take you round Munich afterwards."

He wanted to add something dirty, some witty sexual innuendo that would convince her that the quickest route to the breakfast table would be from his bedroom. But he couldn't think of anything clever, and even if he had a killer line, he knew he would never be able to deliver it with the required panache.

"Sounds great," she said.

"I miss anything?" Arnie asked, taking his place at the bar again.

On screen, Humphrey's character was arrested and put into the back of a police car. Darius smiled, recalling how he and Harry had sat in the police car last Christmas. He'd read Harry's first chapter while in Auckland and was eager to tell Humphrey about it. No. What he wanted was tell to Waldtraut about it.

Eventually, the credits rolled and the crowd cheered and clapped. Darius recognised a few of the minor co-stars who chatted with Humphrey and shook his hand; they were all pretty short. But they didn't stay long, scampering for the door, en route perhaps to another more important party. He saw Arnie follow a group of women outside. In fact, so many people left at once that Sally seemed to feel obliged to leave as well.

"I should be going."

"You don't have to," he said, but she was already pulling on her jacket, straightening the sleeves and sucking in her chest to fasten the one button that disappeared under her cleavage when she exhaled. That button might only reappear if it broke its thread and flew into someone's eye, he thought.

"It's late." She tugged at her skirt, trying to get it below her knees but meeting too much resistance at her hips.

Darius looked at his chunky watch. He could only guess the time. "No, it isn't."

"It was nice to meet you, Digger," she said, holding out her hand. Darius shook it, thinking he might get a rush of electricity, some chemical reaction of skin on skin that would result in more body contact without having to go through all the necessary rituals, to jump through all the hoops. He felt nothing.

"Same here."

She let go of his hand and withdrew, taking a few steps backwards and trying to keep eye contact, but Darius made a point of looking away.

"See you tomorrow," he said, now looking past her and watching Humphrey press the flesh at the door.

As each person left, Humphrey made them laugh, including Sally on her way out.

"Attack of the fifty foot woman," Griff said. "Who was that giant, Digger?"

"She's from the tourism department, or something like that. I dunno."

"That was her?"

"Yeah, and I've seen you take home much worse."

Griff shrugged. "Hobo said someone from TA was coming. Why didn't you introduce me?"

"You looked busy."

Humphrey came up and took a seat at the bar. "I'm thirsty."

"You were great, mate," Griff said. "Wanna beer to celebrate?"

"I think a bottle of bubbly would be more appropriate."

Darius looked at Micha, who had already proven he had a feeling for such occasions. Sure enough, he sent the cork flying across the room.

"Onya, Micha," Darius said.

"Shit, it's good to see you." Humphrey slapped Darius on the back. "You have no idea how boring it was around here without you."

"From what I hear, it's all been happenin'."

"It's been Boretown, population," he counted, "four. And everyone's been asking about you."

"Yeah?" Darius reached out to grab his glass of champagne, but Annette grabbed it before him.

"I hate the way they show the police on TV," she said. She took a long drink, tilting the glass high because of her bulbous nose.

"Tell that to your sister," Humphrey said, turning his back slightly to her and facing Darius. "So, good trip? How's that brother of mine?"

"Yeah, good, good." Darius had a glass of champagne now and he sipped it, though he hated the stuff. "They've got a pretty nice little place, in St Kilda. It looks like Peer's gonna be a monster."

"Les says he eats like a Boragart. And the Idol Bomber?"

305

Darius laughed. That nickname was still funny. Even Harry had liked it. "Still idle, but he's writing."

"A book? You in it?"

"First chapter. It's pretty funny, the way he's written it. It's like slapstick, you know?"

"The world's getting paranoid," Humphrey said.

"When I flew to Ibiza for Christmas last year," Micha said, "there were two Middle Eastern men in the departure lounge. Half of the people changed their flight."

"Did you?" Humphrey asked.

"No. Why should I?"

"Better safe than sorry, I reckon," Griff said.

"That's a terrible attitude," Micha said. "The worse kind of prejudice."

"Hey," Griff said defensively, but with that humorous tone he always employed when cornered or threatened, "I come from a multicultural country so you can't call me prejudiced. We had a Leb in our school cricket team. He was a top bloke."

"Was he any good?" Humphrey asked.

"Opening bat."

"I wonder if he would've been a top bloke if he'd sucked?"

Griff hesitated a little too long. "Yeah, course."

"That sounded convincing," Micha said.

"As always, Griffith," Humphrey said, "your honesty is admirable. Still, I wouldn't want to be an Arab. Like our enlightened little barman here, people talk about equality and freedom but none of them will want to sit next to an Arab on a plane, or have a Muslim family move in next door, or have a Mosque in their suburb."

"Harry says we should just live like we always did," Darius said.

"He would say that," Humphrey said. "He might be sleeper agent after all."

"Bullshit. Terrorism is about fear. If everyone's afraid, they don't even need to blow anything up."

"Sounds like you and the Idol Bomber talked about this a lot."

"He's got some strong opinions. He's against the war. He said the Yanks just can't invade any country they want."

"They do it when it suits them. And it's also another good example of how our country, the littlest, yappiest mutt, always sides with the biggest dog."

"Australia's not a little dog," Griff said. "My bro's in the navy. We could fight off anyone. Our navy's one of the best in the world."

"Yeah," Humphrey said, "they're brilliant at pushing refugee boats back out to sea."

"The boat people get blown way out of proportion."

"Maybe they should get blown out of the water," Darius said.

Humphrey laughed. "That's good. Howard's probably got his finger on the button. Still, I don't think they'll be using them in any tourist campaigns."

"Hey," Darius said, "did Sally ask you to be in an ad?"

"Who is Sally?" Annette asked.

"The big girl I spoke to earlier," Humphrey said, not turning to look at his girlfriend. "She's from the ATC."

"*Eine wichtige Elefantin*," Annette said under her breath.

"Hey," Darius said. "Fair go, Annette."

"You understood that?" she asked.

"The elephant part, yeah. I never thought you'd be so superficial."

"Darius likes the big ones," Humphrey said to Annette.

"No, I don't."

"Nice shoes, by the way," she said, sipping her champagne. "Nothing superficial about them."

"I love em," Humphrey said, "even if somewhere an alligator's freezing to death. Did Sally tell you she's coming over for breakfast tomorrow?"

"Better hide the butter," Annette said.

Humphrey ignored her. "What fantastic irony. Me doing ads for Australia. Maybe they'll paint my face, put me in some bark underwear and stick a boomerang in my hand. Hah."

"A lovely image," Griff said. "Your star's on the rise, Hobo."

"I'll drink to that." Darius raised his glass of champagne. They all toasted Humphrey's burgeoning success.

"I don't need to be famous," Humphrey said.

"Good," Annette said. "As a police officer, I think foreigners should keep a low profile."

Humphrey turned to her, his face blank. "Sounds like us foreigners aren't very welcome."

"You're from Australia. That doesn't count."

"Why not?"

"Probly because we look like them," Darius said.

"*Genau.*"

"What about him?" Humphrey asked, pointing at Darius. "He's part Aboriginal."

Annette looked disbelievingly at Darius. "He probably just says that to get the girls."

"That would get him nowhere back home."

Small droplets of sweat ran down Darius's back and got caught in the silk folds of his shirt. He tried to feign indifference and laugh it off. Why did Humphrey have to say that? Even Griff was looking at him differently, and he knew already.

"Well, I can't see it," Annette said.

"Maybe Sally'll want you for the ad instead of me," Humphrey said to Darius. "You know, as the token Aborigine. There's always one." Humphrey reached out and stroked the sleeves of Darius's shirt. "Looks like you'll need silk underwear instead of the basic loincloth."

Everyone laughed, with Griff laughing the loudest.

"Don't give me a boomerang," Darius said, "because those things just become sticks in my hands."

More laughter.

"Good. Then you're no competition." Humphrey stood up and went to the front door.

"We're closin?" Griff asked, as Humphrey locked the door.

"Everyone's already left," Darius said, wanting to leave as well, even if it was nice to hang in his restaurant with his mates.

"I reckon we should celebrate in private," Humphrey said walking back to the bar. "Not my screen triumph but the return of prodigal." He slapped Darius on the back again. "I graced the small German screen tonight, but that doesn't compare to having my best friend back."

"Thanks, Hobo. It's great to be back."

"Now get behind that bar and pour me a *Weissbier*," Humphrey ordered.

"Yessir." He didn't like the order, but was happy to have something useful to do, a task that might allow him to tune out sometimes and get his thoughts in order, to think about what he might say and how to say it.

Micha made room for him behind the bar while Griff ducked between the two of them and climbed onto the vacated stool next to Humphrey. Darius started pouring beers, Griff made jokes, every sentence Humphrey spoke was clever and they all laughed into the night. Annette, bored and being ignored by Humphrey, left early, pouting and remonstrating at the door when Humphrey wouldn't go with her. Micha followed shortly after, donning his motorcycle jacket and tucking his helmet under his right arm.

"He and Wolfie are a couple now," Humphrey said as Micha closed the door. "They're trying to get married."

"Yeah?"

"Don't look so shocked, Digger."

"I'm not."

"Well, I was. I thought he'd swing forever. And Wolfie's got about twenty years on him too."

"I'm happy for them," Griff said, raising his glass. He drank long and pleasurably, eyes closed, like he was in a beer commercial.

"Don't be picking out your monkey suit just yet, Griffith. I don't think you'll be invited to the wedding."

"Why not?" Darius asked. He smiled as Griff shrunk defensively, hunching his small shoulders forward and putting his head over his near empty beer glass like he wanted to dive into it.

"You missed some excitement. Micha's convinced that Griff's homophobic."

"I'm not. He's full of it."

"And I dared him to prove it. So, a coupla weeks ago, he kissed Griff, right on the mouth, spun him around when he wasn't ready. And you know what happened? Griff decked him."

"Yeah?"

"He took me by surprise," Griff said. He rubbed his mouth with the back of his hand, as if the kiss still lingered. "I never woulda done it otherwise."

"As always, love your honesty." Humphrey turned to Darius. "It gets better. You see, he didn't punch him. He slapped him, like a girl, open hand, right on the cheek. I think he even let out a girlish shriek of protest."

"It was a reflex action," Griff said. "You woulda done the same. Digger, help me out."

Darius, laughing, held up his hands. "I've seen worse than that."

"Care to elaborate?" Humphrey asked.

"You and Hannah in Woodlow."

"I bet she slapped me harder than Griff slapped Micha."

Darius laughed again.

"I don't wanna to go to some fairy wedding anyway," Griff said, draining his beer.

"I'm stunned," Humphrey said. "You actually said something honest."

"Look, fellas," Darius said, "it's great to see ya, but I'm wrecked. I'm gonna head home."

"Yeah," Humphrey said, "I need my beauty sleep to look my best for long tall Sally tomorrow."

Griff was reluctant, making them all drink a shot of Tequila before leaving, but soon they were out on the street. Griff headed for the train station and Darius got into a taxi with Humphrey, his big backpack between them. The taxi rumbled and weaved through the city, the slow rocking movements nearly putting Darius to sleep.

"You look awful, if your hair's anything to go by."

"Long trip."

"You miss Alice?"

"Bit," he said, though he missed Harry more. He just couldn't seem to connect with Alice. She was so different, and this time she had been too busy with her new position in Auckland. "Hard to think she's on the other side of the world."

"At least she's there."

"They're gonna come over and visit, when things have quietened down. Harry hates flying at the moment."

"He should stop carrying a backpack."

"Hey, what's up with you and Annette?"

"Don't ask. That girl is such a handful. Why are the skinny ones always such drama queens?"

"Maybe she doesn't eat enough."

"Maybe she does but doesn't keep it down."

"Anyway, I thought that was the point, that she's a challenge."

"Some girls are a challenge, and others just require maximum maintenance. I can't stand it any more. I'm starting to second-guess everything I say. I don't want to set her off."

"So end it."

"Her sister keeps getting me auditions."

"Aah."

"It's not like that," Humphrey said. "Actually, it's exactly like that. She's my casting couch. You saw me. I'm pretty good, aren't I?"

"I always said you were a good actor."

"And I'll get better. Like anything, the more you do it, the better you get."

"Maybe you should take some lessons or something?" It was a good idea but Darius knew Humphrey was a proudly self-taught man.

"Don't need it. I'm learning it by doing it. I just need to keep acting."

"Then you'll have to keep seeing Annette."

"I guess all art requires suffering. If I do this ad, maybe I won't need her any more."

"It's just an ad."

"Did Sally say anything? It looked like you two were getting on all right, that you weren't far from getting it on."

"She's leaving in a coupla days."

"Even better. Then you wouldn't get stuck in the dire situation I'm in. But she's Australian, and they tend to be clingy and possessive. Ah, screw it. Come on, Digger. Get her into bed and secure that contract for me."

"Maybe she's more your type."

"I'd love a crack at her, but I'm scared Annette's got the apartment watched or bugged or something."

"Maybe Sally's her spy. And this is a test."

"She's not that smart."

"Who? Annette?"

"Both of them. Sally's Australian, so that's her excuse. Annette's just a little cop."

"She's not that small. She once told me they have a size limit for the police and she reached it easily. She just looks small standing next to you."

"I do tower, don't I?"

The taxi pulled in front of their building. Darius opened the door.

"Arnie reckons you're too tall for TV."

"That idiot doesn't know the first thing about acting," Humphrey said, getting out, "even if he does work for an exceedingly successful theatre company." He looked at Darius's backpack. "Bring back a coupla sheep or something?"

"Just a few presents," Darius said, enjoying the pack's weight as he shouldered it.

"All for me I hope."

"And a few things for breakfast."

"Anything but Vegemite."

"Come on, I love the stuff."

"I backpack full of 'mite, am I right? You lousy expat. You can buy it here, you know. You don't have to smuggle it across the world."

"It's not the same."

"You've said that before."

"I'll get Sally to prove it tomorrow."

"Get her to lick it off your fingers."

"Anything for your precious contract, Hobo."

They walked up the stairs in silence, but once inside the apartment, Humphrey's tone was soft and genuine. "It's good to have you back, Darius."

"Thanks, mate."

"You wanna cup of tea?"

"Nah. I'm gonna crash."

In his bedroom, Darius unpacked, taking his time to hang up the numerous silk shirts and tailored pants, to stack the jars of Vegemite neatly on his desk; he even built them into a small pyramid. He put the large volcanic rock on the desk as well and spent a few minutes admiring it, remembering how he had hiked through Tongariro National Park near Taupo and had stolen it. He put the bottles of whiskey on the desk too, still in their duty-free boxes, and then climbed into bed. He thought about setting his alarm and played with his watch trying to figure out how to, but gave up and was asleep before he had time to conjure all the clever things he could say to Sally tomorrow.

***

He slept long and deep, sexually dreaming of a girl who started out vague and out of focus but then morphed from Sally to Waldtraut and back again, and became, at one point, an elephant. The elephant started laughing, and it was that laughter that woke him.

He opened his eyes. He heard the laughter again, coming from the kitchen. He pulled on his jeans and an old shirt. In the bathroom, he splashed water on his face and checked himself in the mirror; his hair looked exactly like it should and he hoped his dishevelled, jet-lagged look might be seen as ruggedly handsome.

"You're mad," he heard Sally say as he walked down the hallway. "We could never do that."

"It's brilliant. It'll be front page everywhere. It could be the worst ad ever but think of the publicity, the controversy. Think of how many groups will protest against it."

Darius stood in the kitchen doorway watching them, timing his entry. On the table in front of them were the plates, knives, jars and crumbs of a half-consumed breakfast. Darius noticed that Sally, wearing another skirt, had her legs hidden under table.

"They'd never go for it," she said.

"Who? The public?"

"My bosses, and the old boys in Canberra."

"You're probably right," Humphrey said. He turned and saw Darius leaning against the doorway. "Ah, shearing beauty has finally surfaced."

"Mornin." Darius rubbed his eyes and stumbled into the kitchen. His mouth had the taste and texture of the underside of an economy class seat-tray.

"Hungover or jet-lagged?"

"Looks like a healthy mix of both," Sally said.

"If you want some coffee," Humphrey said, holding up the empty jug and shaking it, "you better make some." He turned to Sally. "I really missed him. He makes a great brew."

She smiled at Darius, her red lipstick glistening. "I'll have another cup, Digger."

He moved slowly around the kitchen, finding things where they should be and thankful their weekly maid always put everything back in the right places. As he made the coffee, he felt that they were waiting for him to speak. Sally was still smiling at him, and his brain slowly formed something half-clever. He heard the lame sentence in his head. It'll have to do, he decided.

"Your laughter makes a good alarm clock," he said, and it sounded even more pathetic when spoken. "What's so funny?"

"Humphrey had the ridiculous idea to use a swear word in one of our ads."

"Not a really bad word. Something relatively innocent that

would get people's attention and cause a stir. Show how liberal and laid back we are. Sally, we're talking about selling a lifestyle, letting people know everything's a bit more relaxed and easy-going down under. This would show how blasé we are about such things, and how uptight and prudish the rest of the world is."

"My favourite is, 'It's about time you bloody well went.'"

Darius chuckled, but his brain was working too slowly. He willed the coffee through the decanter, hoping that a steaming cup of his supposedly exceptional brew would clear his head.

"Too demanding," Humphrey said, shaking his head. "It's too much like an order."

"You're good at givin those," Darius muttered.

"A question would be better," Humphrey went on. He sat back and looked at the ceiling. "Something like, 'You bloody coming or what?' I can see the ad now. You take stereotypical mates from the cities and the outback, you know, young larrikin types with toothy grins and wrinkly foreheads, and you put them in situations people would expect. On the beach, in Kakadu, Sydney Harbour, Ayers Rock, Barrier Reef, some country bar. Typical stuff. Then, cut from them one by one and have each of them turn to the camera, smile in that laconic way we're all so good at, and say, 'You bloody coming or what?'" He clapped his hands together. "Why aren't you taking notes, Sally? This stuff's gold. I really should work in advertising."

Sally laughed again.

"See how seriously she takes me?"

"Can you say bloody on TV?" Darius asked. He poured the coffee, filling Sally's cup first. The fragrant steam blew away the fog of the continents and time zones he had crossed. "People might get the wrong idea."

"Finally," Sally said, helping herself to milk and sugar, "a voice of reason. If we use a word like that, the whole world will think we're nothing but a bunch of uneducated, uncouth antipodes."

Humphrey held up his hands. "Aren't we?"

"Well, I'm not. And none of my friends are. Maybe you sandgropers are like that but that doesn't mean the rest of us are."

"I think I've just been insulted. Darius, a little help, please. I'm just an ignorant country boy and none too smart. Did she just insult us?"

Darius took a seat at the table. "Reckon she did. Let's take her round the back of the shearin shed and give her a good floggin."

"Yeah, that always sorts out these uppity city intellectuals."

"Rubbish," Sally said. "I'm from the country and nobody behaves like that."

"Like you said, we sandgropers are different. They say it's the inbreeding, or the water, or the lack of it, but," he pointed at Sally, "you're to blame."

"Me?" Sally was shocked at being fingered. She tried to smile through it, but it looked like her jaw was tightening.

"Yes, you. You and all your mates at TA and in Canberra. You made us. Shrimps on the barbie? Come on. You spent millions of dollars promoting us and we've all tried to become what the world expects of us. As a result, you've unleashed a generation of global swagmen who all think they're the love child of Steve Irwin and Kylie Minogue."

"Save that performance for the camera," Sally said. "You exaggerate far too much."

"He often exaggerates," Darius said. "You get used to it."

"If it gets my point across, then yes I do. Sometimes you have to be extreme just to be heard."

"You'd make a good terrorist then," Sally said.

They lapsed into silence. Darius watched Sally as he sipped his coffee, peeking over the rim of his cup, trying to decide if she was worth the trouble, the effort. She was disappointing him, with her words and movements. He thought he could almost predict everything she would do and say. Strangely, now that he wasn't interested, she seemed to smile even more in his direction.

"Forget it. I can't undo all that brainwashing." Humphrey turned to Darius. "You got any more Vegemite? We finished the old stuff."

"Yep." He went to his room and took a jar from the top of the pyramid. He saw the rock again and put his hand on it, feeling comforted by it. The kitchen was silent when he came back. "It's different, isn't it, Sally?"

"What?"

"Darius thinks the Vegemite you get here tastes different."

"Tastes the same to me," Sally said. Darius offered her the fresh jar and she sampled it. "Yes, it's the same."

"I told ya," Humphrey said. "It's all in your mind, Digger. And

315

while the world fights for consumer gods and consumer goods, we sit here debating the purity of Aussie breakfast products. Now, Sally, about this ad campaign."

"There'll be no dirty words.

"Of course. I was just pulling your leg."

"I spoke with my boss this morning," she said, her voice becoming pertinent and business-like. She sat up in her chair and made professional gestures with her hands that looked practised. "He really likes it. I only had the idea last night while watching your film."

"What idea?" Darius asked through a mouthful of Vegemite and toast. It definitely tastes different, he thought.

"To use a local personality in the campaigns for important countries. Someone with a public profile in that country. A lot of Germans travel to Australia and we want to make an ad just for them. I think you're perfect."

"Me too," Humphrey said. "But I have one condition."

"What's that?"

"I'm not doing any ad that includes images of Indigenous Australians. You can show the parks and all the famous sites, but not those people."

Sally looked at Humphrey and seemed to be processing a thousand thoughts at once, none of them positive. "Why not?"

"I don't agree with how you've always used Indigenous Australians to promote tourism. Or left them out altogether. It's an insult. And don't get me started about Uluru." He gestured at Darius. "Ask him. His mother's quarter-caste and a history professor. I bet she'd be none too happy about it."

Sally looked quickly at Darius and then back at Humphrey. "But statistics show that potential visitors are interested in our Indigenous culture. They want to experience that when they visit."

"Yeah, what's left of it, or what's been packaged and prepared just for tourists. But the government doesn't have any right to use it as a selling point, not after all the dirty things they did, not when they can't even muster a simple sorry. Tell her, Darius, your mum was taken, wasn't she?"

"Okay, okay," Sally said. "I'm sure we can come up with a, uh, with a concept that doesn't involve Indigenous culture."

"And no background didgeridoo music either."

"You're making a lot of demands for someone who hasn't even been offered a contract yet."

"I've got my principles. And I think you might have trouble finding an Aussie in Germany with my kind of public profile and abilities. I've got more work lined up too. In a year, I'll be getting mobbed in the streets."

"He's exaggerating again, Sally," Darius said. "Aren't ya, Hobo? And I reckon he's pulling your leg again."

"Are you?

Humphrey looked at Darius, then at Sally. "Yeah. Yeah. Hah. I'll do whatever you want."

Sally let out a sigh. "You scared me a little there. Whatever happens, the concept will come from the top. What they come up with, we'll have to do, with you or with someone else."

"No problem." Humphrey put his hands behind his head and leaned back in his chair. "I'm flexible."

Sally drained her coffee and stood up. She checked her watch. "You might want to be ready at short notice. When I took over this position, one of the first orders of business was a new marketing campaign."

"I'll be ready when you need me. Will I have to go to Australia for the ad?"

"We'll fly you in. It'll only take a week or so, I'm sure." She reached out a hand for Humphrey to shake and seal the deal. "I'll be in contact when I'm back at the office, when I've got more to tell you."

Darius stood up to shake her hand too but she turned to pick up her handbag and didn't see him standing there with his arm extended. He lowered it, and then she started backing out of the kitchen.

"Thanks for breakfast," she said. "I better get going. I'm flying to Frankfurt later today to visit the consulate there."

"No tour of Munich?" Darius asked.

"Next time. I'll be in touch."

Darius heard her heavy footsteps in the hallway, the door opening and closing, and then her footfalls on the stairs. He sat back down.

"That was close. You just saved me from putting one foot in my mouth and the other up my arse."

"Fuck, Hobo. You nearly lost it."

"I know, I know. Thanks."

"No worries. Do the ad, mate. It'll mean great things for our restaurant."

Humphrey chuckled. "You believe that shit?"

"What?"

"She thought I was mad because I didn't want Aborigines in the ad, but then she ran for the door the minute I mentioned your mum."

"No, she didn't. She's gotta go to Frankfurt."

"Yeah, she does."

"What she said about WA, that's what pissed me off. She's probly never even been there."

"I guess she didn't take a look under our tablecloths last night."

"You wouldn't get the ad then."

"Maybe not. It's all rather fitting, isn't it?"

Darius stared down at the messy remains of breakfast, at his own half-eaten piece of toast, at the smudge of red lipstick on the rim of Sally's coffee cup.

"You really think she left because of me mum?"

"Who knows? But she certainly left in a hurry. And I'm pretty sure she's spent her entire life with white skinned-people in Blackheath and Canberra."

"I guess."

Humphrey looked at him. "You must've kept that secret well growing up."

"What secret?"

"Having an Aboriginal mum."

"She's quarter-caste. I don't remember it being a big deal when I was a young kid. Me dad told me, just before he died, that everyone liked her, that she fit right in." Darius took a sip of his coffee. "But when I was older, people were always talking bad about the Aborigines. Not to their faces."

"That's how it is. I've been to townships up north and spoke to people. Every Australian needs to do that."

"They won't be putting those places in your ad."

"Nope. And why would they?"

"Make the ad," Darius said. "Even if they use Aborigines. Be the larrikin, play the stereotype, and then everyone will come into our restaurant."

"I like the way you think, Digger. Maybe we can invite Sally and that clueless embassy idiot to our opening in Berlin."

"You wanna open a place there?"

"Yep. If the ad goes well, we should really think about expanding. We've made a killing the last couple of months."

"It's going great. I stopped sweatin in my sleep."

"Griff's volunteered to run the place."

"You're jokin, aren't ya?"

"We might have trouble finding the right Aussies," Humphrey said.

"That depends on what kind of restaurant we open."

"We're not doing the stereotypical thing. True Blue Tucker is not gonna become some branded joke like the Walkabout bars, or like Freddie's Hole."

"Why not? Our place is only doing well because we covered it all up."

"That's true. We could just make the other places the same. A big cover up."

Darius took a bite of his Vegemite toast. "I reckon Griff drinks a bit too much to run a restaurant on his own. What about Les?"

"He's entrenched in suburbia. But Griff's all right. Miss Jane had her pierced tentacles wrapped around him when we first met him. He's changed a bit since then, you know."

"Yeah, he's all right. But we need someone we can trust."

"You don't trust him?"

"The alcohol. That's what worries me."

"Well, he's priming himself for Berlin and is telling everyone what to do. You better come in and cut him even further down to size."

"I'll be there in the afternoon. I got a coupla things to catch up on." Darius stood up, keen to start the day. "I'll see ya later."

Humphrey picked up the jar of Vegemite and threw it at Darius who caught it. "It's all yours now. You don't have to share it with me. Use that black power. I'll bring you back a box of it when I go to Australia."

"You really think it's gonna happen?"

"Without question. It's meant to be."

Lewis: From the way you describe him, Jack Tucker is certainly a person to emulate.

Poet: Yeah, and even when things are hard, there are lessons you can learn. Good things that can come from bad, ya know? I got that from him.

Lewis: That comes through in your poem *Birth Death*. There's not much that's uplifting about a mother dying while giving birth, but Jack Tucker finds the positives.

Poet: Right. Maybe if the mother had lived, the father and son would never have been as close as they were.

Lewis: Like you were with your father.

Poet: Yep.

Lewis: And the fact that it takes place in a ruined barn in the middle of a cyclone makes it even more powerful. Almost like the birth of Jesus.

Poet: Something like that.

Lewis: Is that how you were born?

Poet: I'm no Jesus. But that poem is inspired by a story my dad used to tell.

Lewis: "He was spat out in a storm, pink and raw, a protesting kid. The wind blew the roof off, took her soul, a parting gift. His dad raised the baby, let out a roar, from promising lips."

Poet: Great yarn, isn't it?

~~~

Myth Selling

The familiar hum was comforting. The voices rose and competed, bouncing off the walls and getting into every corner of the restaurant, his restaurant. Even the lulls were nice, when everyone collectively started to lower their voices, reacting to the level of everyone else until most people were whispering, but then the volume would slowly rise again until the room echoed with shouts.

It was great to be back, working with Micha and Griff behind the bar, pulling beers and joking with the regulars. He made a point of learning people's names and greeting them when they came in. Everyone knew him as Digger.

Things were going just great. The three of them, Darius, Humphrey and Griff, got together not long after Darius returned from New Zealand to come up with further ideas for the restaurant. Wednesday became quiz night, Thursday was Australian cinema night, when they would show an Australian film, Saturday was given over to soccer, and on Sunday, in keeping with the precedent set by Humphrey's debut performance, they put the *Tatort* on. As a result, True Blue Tucker was the local of choice for a lot of people who lived in Maxvorstadt, and was also popular with students. The Technische Universitaet was just around the corner, the University of Munich too.

They printed flyers and put up posters. There was an article about the restaurant in *Spotlight Magazine* and even a short blurb in the SZ.

But she did not come.

Disappointing, yes, and no matter how much he tried to gloss it over by focusing on the restaurant, his success and popularity – that he wasn't just another ordinary Aussie expat and certainly no dumb outback shearer – the rock hadn't got her attention and that hurt. He'd lugged the bloody thing halfway around the world convinced it would be exactly the kind of intimate and meaningful gift that would garner a response, an immediate one at that. He had even written one last love poem, composed, decomposed and recomposed over several rain-soaked days on the Coromandel Peninsula. He found his attempt to capture in verse that first night they had met and spent together appalling, but surely such artistic and sensitive outpourings were what girls wanted, even if she had already ignored the poems he wrote last year.

The poem and the rock went into a package he placed underneath her postbox. He had even gone there a second time to see if the box had been moved. It had, and that was even more disappointing. He had written his mobile number at the bottom of the poem and every time his phone rang he dropped whatever he was doing and snatched at it.

But she didn't even call to say thank you.

"You choose your friends poorly, Mr Tucker," she had said.

He scanned every edition of the SZ hoping to find her by-line.

A week passed, two, three. The first few quiz nights were a riot. Humphrey was a brilliant quizmaster and wrote all the questions himself. Bevan and Mitch came to the third quiz night, bringing members of Munich's AFL team with them and presenting Darius and Humphrey with a signed jersey which they hung on the wall. Mitch was vaguely apologetic but Darius waved him off and gave him a pitcher on the house. All mates now.

They showed *Strictly Ballroom*, *Dead Heart* and *The Castle*, and there wasn't an empty chair in the place. The *Tatort* screenings attracted a full house as well. Griff said that the restaurant had become the living room for many of the people who lived in Maxvorstadt.

"They live in such small apartments," he said, "so they hang out here."

That was fine for Darius, because they all spent money.

They played only Australian music. Humphrey went online and bought band posters: Midnight Oil, Australian Crawl, Cold Chisel, The Cruel Sea, The Church, The Triffids, Hunters & Collectors, The Hoodoo Gurus, Yothu Yindi, Goanna, all the bands he could think of. They stuck the posters on the walls and even on the ceiling.

They bought new tablecloths. Each one had a big map of Australia on it, and this made a great talking point because people could point at the map and talk about places they'd been to and places they wanted to see. Of course, nobody ever looked underneath the tablecloths and Darius was glad about that.

A rep from Foster's came by and offered them a great deal on beer; they just had to use Foster's beer mats and hang the blue Foster's Australia map logo out the front. Done.

Humphrey got the call from Sally and flew to Australia, business class. Griff took over quiz night duties, but Darius thought Griff wasn't nearly as good as Humphrey. It was still fun, though.

The best part of Humphrey being away, Darius thought, was having the apartment all to himself. He decided it was time to find his own place. He called Wolfgang and asked him to look into it.

All these positive developments, all in a short time, but there was no word from her. Not even a sign.

He gave up. There were plenty of girls coming into the restaurant, many of them interested. It was fun to take some of them home, and he was thankful they didn't ask for much more than a good time. That was all he wanted too: satifsaction, relief and distraction. They didn't get rid of his loneliness entirely, but they helped, and with Humphrey still in Australia, there was no one to judge him. He sometimes struggled to get it up, struggled even to get it out. A few times, he woke up and wondered what to do with this strange person who had found her way into his bed. I fucked that? he would wonder. Why? One girl rolled over, sleep-wrinkled and looking nothing like she had in the dim-lit restaurant the night before, and demanded commitment before asking for coffee. Others left the pillows bruised with make-up and were quite happy to be cast aside, even happier to cast him aside.

And so the weeks passed. Darius held sway at the restaurant and then Humphrey was back, brandishing a tan and an unmarked DVD. Another event was organised and invitations sent out. Darius called Arnie at the embassy, but he couldn't make it. He also sent an invitation to Waldtraut, but even while licking the stamp and printing out her address, he knew she wouldn't come. Why would she want to celebrate Humphrey's success? Why the fuck didn't she at least say thank you for the rock?

On the night of the screening, the restaurant was so full, they had to turn people away. The Aust-Schland Club, which had nearly tripled its membership in the passing months, was there, and there were plenty of guys from the footy team as well. Griff made a speech, as did Humphrey, but Darius remained behind the bar, deciding to let Humphrey have the moment, glad his friend hadn't screwed it all up. It was Darius who dimmed the lights, on Humphrey's order.

The ad started with an aerial shot of the Great Barrier Reef.

The camera zoomed in on a lone yacht surrounded by turquoise water. The camera got right up close to the yacht and then dropped underwater. Humphrey's angular frame floated across the screen. His head popped out of the water, as did the camera.

"G'day," he said, lifting the mask and snorkel from his face and smiling broadly, "*Wilkommen in Australien.*"

Then the didgeridoo music started, upbeat and catchy. On the screen, Humphrey went from the Barrier Reef to drinking a beer at a trendy bar with the Sydney Opera House in the background. Then he was feeding kangaroos in what Darius guessed was the Blue Mountains. Then he was driving along some desolate gravel highway like the ones leading to the mining town up north. Then he was hiking through what looked like the Territory, Kakadu maybe. All quick shots, a second or two. Climbing Ayers Rock, walking along the cliffs at Port Campbell, falling off a surfboard, bungee jumping from the Sydney Harbour Bridge, standing under a waterfall, cuddling a koala, kayaking with crocodiles nearby. He finished back on the yacht, standing over a barbecue and slowly flipping large fillets of fish. He wore an apron that said "Kiss the Cook". A pair of bikini-clad waifs lounged on the deck, champagne glasses in hand, and seemingly ready to remove their bikinis and do Humphrey there and then, perhaps blow him while he cooked dinner. He turned to the camera and smiled.

"Australia," he declared, "*eine bessere Lebensart.*"

Then the camera pulled away, ending like the ad had started, with the picture of the lone yacht in the green waters of the Barrier Reef.

The crowd cheered and clapped. Darius watched Humphrey absorb the praise like it meant nothing, like it was undeserved. Griff brought the cake out of the kitchen, struggling under its weight, almost dropping it. It had been Darius's idea to have it in the shape of Australia, with orange land ringed by blue icing.

"Brilliant, eh?" Griff said. "My idea. You deserve it. That was fantastic. You were fantastic."

Humphrey slapped Griff on the back. "Where's Tasmania?"

Behind the bar, Darius laughed.

Griff put the cake on a table. "I guess, uh, the delivery boy ate Tassie on the way here."

"Well, it's not the first time Tassie's been left off. Who wants a slice?

But you have to name the place before getting that piece. Whoever can pinpoint Canberra gets two pieces."

People crowded around the cake, yelling out the common places everyone knew, working from the coast inland until all that remained was a large chunk of central and northwest Australia nobody present could name. So Griff just cut the cake into pieces and gave it to whoever was next in line. Darius chose the Northwest Cape. At the bottom of that massive tongue of land, he had dropped off Waldtraut, and she had stared at him from the window of the truck, and had kept staring until the big vehicle was around the first bend.

"What'd you think?" Humphrey asked.

"About what?"

"The ad. Shit, weren't you even watching?"

"Not an Aborigine in sight."

"But you heard the music. Anyway, I like it. It adds to the irony." Humphrey looked around and then whispered, "Before you ask, no, I didn't do either of those girls on the boat. It would've been like screwing a skeleton."

"Was Sally there?"

"Only for the part in the Blue Mountains. I had dinner with her at her parent's house in Blackheath. Her dad was a real mean old bastard, a paid up member of One Nation, I'm sure."

"But not Sally. She's all right."

"Yeah, but I met a few other people while I was there. We need to talk. I've got a cracking idea."

"Hey, Hobo," Griff shouted. "Let's show the ad again."

"Darius, breakfast tomorrow. Griff, you too. I've got plans."

Humphrey moved towards the projector. Griff followed close behind. Darius took his cake back behind the bar and offered the rest to Micha.

The ad started again. Darius watched, homesick.

***

Humphrey slept late, still jet-lagged. Griff and Darius breakfasted together.

"Great night, last night," Griff said.

"Yeah."

"The ad's so fucking good."

"Humphrey said they're gonna show it here in cinemas and on TV. There'll be billboards too."

"Good for us. We should get Berlin open before the campaign starts, milk that publicity."

"We don't even have a location yet."

"We'll find one."

Darius sipped his coffee. "I did a bit of research. Berlin has half a dozen Aussie bars."

"Ours is better."

"I think Hobo's got something else planned."

They both turned as the toilet flushed. Humphrey came into the kitchen, eyes half-closed and yawning.

"Never again," he said.

"I thought in business it was all right," Darius said.

"No matter what seat you're in, it's still twenty-four hours in a plane."

"You want some coffee?"

"The biggest mug we've got."

Darius poured the coffee. Humphrey sat down. He took the full mug and drank it, without milk or sugar.

"Ah, that helps. But I am not hungry. That airline food is still in transit in my small intestine."

"We were just talking about Berlin," Griff said. "Getting a place open up there before your ad campaign starts."

Humphrey shook his head. "Not enough time. The ad's already approved. The old boys in Canberra love it. It'll be on in a couple of weeks. I think the website's already up and running. Speaking of running. You look pretty fit, Digger. Like you lost some weight. You been out hitting the footpaths?"

"Every morning. The spring's inspired me."

"The summer down under was awesome. I miss that."

"I never thought I'd hear you say that, Hobo."

"I'm a beach boy at heart. I grew up surfing, remember that."

"You fell off the board in the ad."

"The director told me to."

"Did you really go to all those places?" Griff asked.

Humphrey nodded. "In three weeks. It was a whirlwind. Those

shots, they last like two seconds, but we travelled for hours to get out there. A whole day in a bus for a split second shot. Bloody nice country, though."

"Stop it," Griff said. "You're making me homesick."

"Have some more Vegemite." Humphrey took a long sip of his coffee. "I know I badmouth Australia sometimes, but the place is fucking beautiful. There's no denying it. They didn't have to pay me to say those lines. I would've said them for free."

"I was gonna tell ya that," Darius said. "You spoke with conviction. You weren't acting."

"Well observed. I wasn't. What we need to do is to set ourselves up so well here that we can spend the summers down under. You know, spring and summer here, then summer there. Perfect."

"Ideal," Griff said. "Let's open some more places."

"Steady on, Griffith. Don't forget that me and Darius are the ones who own this whole thing. If you're willing to invest, then you can open a place too." He turned to Darius. "That all right with you?"

"Ah, yeah. Well, I dunno."

"Come on, fellas," Griff said. "You know I don't have the funds for that."

"Berlin's already got a bunch of Aussie restaurants," Dairus said.

Humphrey stopped mid sip. "How'd you find that out?"

"Internet."

"You're really becoming computer proficient."

"Griff gave me some lessons while you were away. I'm gonna buy myself a lapbook."

"A laptop," Griff said. "Or a notebook."

"What's the diff?"

"Same thing, different word."

"Ah."

Humphrey laughed.

"I'll take you shopping today," Griff said between laughs.

"Hey, Hobo, you mentioned last night you had a big idea."

"I do, Digger."

"Come on. Out with it."

Humphrey sipped his coffee, draining the mug. "More, please." Darius topped up the mug. "You make a good brew, my friend."

"Thanks. Now talk."

"Right. You know I got to visit Les and Loo. In Melbourne. I only had a couple of hours before I had to go down to Port Campbell."

"How are they?"

"Good. Les is really happy there. Loo as well. They made a good choice. Les and I, we had this long talk. I told him I'd had a bit of an awakening, at Uluru of all places. We spent the night there, at one of the resorts, can't remember the name. It was so bloody hot, I couldn't sleep. It was like three in the morning and I went for a walk. Pretty stupid, when I think about now, because there must've been all sorts of snakes out then."

"My dad found one in the radiator of his ute once," Darius said. "It was entwined inside the whole thing."

"How'd it get in there?" Humphrey asked.

"Good question. Maybe it was an elaborate way to have an anecdote to tell."

"He put it in there."

"Maybe."

"Can I finish my story?"

"Sorry, Hobo. Go on."

"So there I was, out in the desert, in the middle of the night. It was fucking hot. I just had a pair of shorts on. There was no moon, but there was like thousands of stars."

"I know that kind of sky," Darius said. "I saw it up north. Did you pick up handfuls of dirt?"

"Why the fuck would I do that?"

"Just asking."

"Anyway, I stood there, looking at all these stars, and I thought, I've got it way wrong. I've been fighting this country, when all the time I should just accept it and embrace it, good and bad. There's no changing the mates, Darius. We can't do it. But we can look up at the desert sky. We can go down to beach in the morning. We can do all these great things in an incredible country. But we don't have to turn miners into culture buffs, or shearers into historians. That's not our job. I said this to Les. And you know what? He just looked me and said, 'It's about bloody time you realised that.' Dairus, your girl got me thinking about it too, what she said about me being on a soapbox and her comment about inherited guilt. Fuck all that. It's not our job to educate everyone. You can't re-educate adults anyway. It has to start in the schools. We should be enjoying what we have. Like here, in Munich. We've got this great restaurant. The quiz nights, the films, it's a blast. We could get some people in to play live music as well."

"I like that idea," Griff said.

"Me too," Darius said, "but what's your big idea? A realisation out in the desert isn't an idea."

"No, Digger, it's not. Who's a clever boy then? But, the realisation brought me to it. And Les helped too. We need to focus on what people want. And I don't mean the stereotypical stuff of Australia, the stuffed crocs and the boomerangs. Oi, that's not a knife. No. I mean the things we really have, the things that are really us. Like what we've been doing. With the films and the music, and showing the cricket and the footy. The places we open should focus on that."

"So, no more decorated tables?"

Humphrey nodded. "That's a big part of us, but we shouldn't put it in people's faces. We could show films instead, and play the music. *Beds are Burning, Solid Rock, Treaty*, all that stuff. We are facing our history, even if a lot of Aussies look away. And like your girl said, you can't open a German restaurant with a Holocaust theme."

"That's you big idea?" Darius asked. "We open more True Blue Tuckers just like this one? We already had that idea."

"No, no. I mean, yes, we can do that too, but what's really missing is the food. When I was in Oz, we had a catering service that went with us all over the country. The main cook, this guy Luke, he made the most amazing food, and he did it with stuff he found locally. I was really impressed. He took so much pride in what he was doing, real Aussie cuisine. He's coming over."

"To do what?" Griff asked.

"To revamp our kitchen. That's the idea. True Blue Tucker. Real Aussie cuisine. You see? You see? We can do both. We make it a fantastic restaurant and a place for people to hang out, where everyone feels comfortable and at home. They can have emu egg omelettes and have fun at the quiz nights. They can eat occie-seaweed salad and watch *Muriel's Wedding*. You see? The Maxvorstadt living room, like Griff said, but the Maxvorstadt kitchen as well. And Luke's the bomb. He's practically writing the book on Aussie cuisine. But he's too experimental for your basic restaurants back home. No one wants to take him on. That's why he does catering jobs. When I told him about our place, he jumped at it. With him on board, True Blue Tucker will be unique, without competitors."

Darius sat back. "He went to Australia and came back an entirely new man."

"Hey, Mr Alligator Shoes, you went to New Zealand and did the same."

"Yeah, I did."

"So, what do you think?"

"It's brilliant," Griff said.

"I didn't ask you. Darius?"

"If Luke's as good as you say he is, then I'm in. But I wanna meet him first."

"He'll be here in a week."

"What if I'd said no?"

"I knew you wouldn't. The way it all happened, getting the TV role, the ad from Sally, meeting Luke on set, the night in the desert, it was like I was being pushed in this direction. This could be big, Darius, and I'm talking locations all over the world and bestselling cookbooks. All that can start from the True Blue Tucker in Munich. Real Aussie cuisine."

"Sounds good, but let's not get too far ahead of ourselves. Let's start with our place and see how it goes."

"Yeah, sure. It's gonna work. Aussie cuisine. There really is such a thing. Luke proved it. We've got positives to give the world, Darius. We can do it all and the people will love it. We'll put Freddie out of business."

"Let's just hope he doesn't steal the idea. He started showing films as well."

"He won't be able to match us, not when we've got Luke. You remember. Freddie had a kitchen full of Africans."

"They cooked ostrich and said it was emu."

"We're gonna do the real thing. No more stereotypes." Humphrey turned to Griff. "Can you do me a favour?"

"Sure."

"Go to Saturn and get a copy of *Priscilla*. I wanna show that movie this week."

Griff stood up. "You got it."

When Griff was gone, Humphrey said, "I had to get rid of him so we could talk. You don't want him involved, do you?"

"Not as a manager. I'm happy with him working the bar, but I just don't think he can do it. Something tells me he'll do the dirty on us, if he can."

"And he drinks too much."

"Actually, he's cut down, a bit. He met an English girl. She told him what a dick he was when he was drunk. He changed it, started to drink less, especially on the nights she comes in."

Humphrey laughed. "I guess she sucks a mean cock."

"Well, that's lovely."

"Maybe he'll come even further around and earn your trust."

"Let's start with Luke and go from there. There's no point opening new places until we know that the concept's popular."

"But we should start planning, so we get in before others copy us."

"Yeah, we should."

Humphrey yawned. "I think I'll go back to bed."

"It's good to have you back, mate. How d'you feel?"

"Upside down and inside out."

"The ad's great."

"It is. Annette thinks so too."

"She come home with you last night? I didn't see her this morning."

"No. Early shift."

"Did you miss her?"

Humphrey shook his head. "There was too much going on. But it was good to see her. She wrote me this long email while I was away, in English. Must've taken her ages to write. She wants to get married, you know. The whole nuclear package. Kids, dog, house, everything."

"Yeah? You'd be a good dad."

"You're joking. I dunno. Maybe. But not now. My career's just starting, acting-wise I mean. If I keep going at this rate, I might be able to make an assault on Hollywood. Imagine that."

"I can't."

"Yeah, I hate LA anyway."

"Maybe you should just focus on the restaurant. This big idea of yours will take some work."

"It will. But if it flies, then we can sit back and roll in the dough."

"Then live for summer, right? Summer here, summer there."

"I'd love to have the summer in Oz again. I even miss Esperance. I'm a bit pissed that Les moved. You just don't get that kind of raw

331

natural beauty anywhere else in the world. It makes you feel so small and insignificant. The people are ordinary, and they'll be the first to tell you that. I'm an ordinary Australian. That's what they all want to be. But the land, Darius, the beach, the smell of the wind, the pull of a big wave dragging you out. The way you can look in every direction and it seems like the land never ends. You're all alone. You can't tell me you don't miss it."

"I do."

"And there's lots of other places I wanna go to. I don't wanna end up here in Munich married and living in the suburbs. There's Europe and the States. You have no idea how much I wanna drive a Cadillac across America, diagonally, like Seattle to Miami or Boston to San Diego. And it's gotta be a Caddy with big steer horns on the front and bright pink upholstery."

"I'm in. We could go to Vegas."

"What d'you dream about doin? Come on. I've seen you at the bar staring into the dishwater like you're trying to see your future."

"Motorbike trip. Dunno where. Just get on a bike and go."

"I'd come, but I don't know how to ride. I'd have to sit on the back. No, better, a side-car, with fly goggles and skull caps."

"Sounds good," Darius said, but his vision didn't include Humphrey. The motorbike trip with no real destination had Waldtraut on the back.

"You know what, I'm gonna apologise to Waldtraut. Can you give me her address?"

"I was gonna write to her too. Really let her have it."

"Why?"

"Because it wasn't fair the way she left. And things have changed now."

Humphrey laughed. "What a letter that will be. An apology from me and a rant from you. Let's do it."

Humphrey got up and left the kitchen. He came back a few minutes later and handed a piece of paper to Darius.

"Here. My sorry speech. Ha. It's really not that hard to say sorry. You'd think Mr Howard might be able to do it."

"I'll write the letter and send it today."

"Do that. You've got nothing to lose. Let her have it. Now, I'm going back to bed."

Darius found some lined paper in his room. He put this on the kitchen table and spread some Vegemite on a roll. He made a cup of tea, thinking about the last six months. He remembered their couple of nights together, with him being honest and saying what he felt.

"No holding back," he said to himself. He picked up the pen.

He started slowly, trying not to be mean, but then something snapped inside him and the words flew across the page. He outlined and explained all the ways she had hurt him: how she had ruined his life, treated him unfairly, played with him, poisoned him, and would not make one single response to all of his letters, poems and gifts. He listed the girls he had slept with, described the lonely trip to New Zealand, talked about the changes they had made to the restaurant.

How easy it was to write. The pages piled up.

And what a relief it was to have it all out. He felt free, unburdened, like the spell was broken, all those voodoo needles pulled out of his heart one by one, sliding out with a sweet ache of pleasure. He didn't read through the letter to correct his mistakes, all the misspellings and the words left out in haste, and he didn't even waste a stamp on her. He took it to her apartment and shoved it in her mailbox. He laughed at himself for those pathetic poems he had written, scorned himself for stealing the rock; for trying so hard and suffering for so long. It was over now, and she would know exactly what he thought of her.

***

The next morning, he came bounding down the stairs in his running gear feeling great about the world. He ran along the Isar and did a loop of the Englischer Garten.

It felt good to be fit, to be running in Munich.

It was spring. There were buds on the trees. He and Humphrey had decided that when Luke was there and working in the kitchen, they would revamp the restaurant: get rid of the old tables and invest in better furniture. They would keep the pub feel, but try to have a comfortable dining area as well. An Aussie bar and grill. Darius was excited. He was looking forward to meeting Luke. He ran with energy. There were lots of possibilities and potential, and the run helped him put them in order.

When he got back to Viktualienmarkt, she was standing in front of the door to his building.

"Waldtraut?"

He stepped back to look at her, to be sure that it was really her. She hadn't changed except that her hair was shorter and she didn't look as big as he remembered, though he conceded that could just have been his mind trying to make the transition easier.

She stepped towards him and slapped him hard across the face.

"Why did it take you so long to show some spirit?"

"Huh?"

"Was it that brainless, ignorant friend of yours who told you to write poetry? This letter," she said, holding it up and flapping the pages, "this is what I was waiting for."

His eyes moved from the letter to her face and back again. She looked good, angry and pretty. She seemed to be waiting for him to respond, to defend himself, but he was struck dumb.

"Well? Are you going to take me upstairs or not?"

He knew it was a bad idea, knew he should have left her on the street, but he just couldn't refuse her. By the time they were in his bedroom, it seemed like there had been no gap between their last physical tryst, no period of banishment and disillusion.

"Let me take a shower."

"No. You stink, but I don't care."

She said nothing more, didn't even look around his room to admire the big flat-screen television, the pile of CDs, the brand new notebook. She simply strode into the room and removed all her clothing. Her behaviour was contrived, he thought, but he wasn't complaining, because even when she did something even the slightest bit contrived, it was still more real than anyone else could muster. And she was in his room, naked, spread out on his bed, all curvy and rounded and shimmering, and more sexual and carnal than his imagination had been able to conjure during his lonely nights. And he knew, with that first squelchy, tingly thrust, that this was love. It was chemical, it was electric. The tiny hairs on his ears stood on end and fluttered, and the buzzing behind his eyes had the colour of exploding stars, like his brain was shooting fireworks at his retinas, celebrating and rejoicing. When he closed his eyes and filled her, he saw all those fireworks explode in a crash of bright colour that made him want to scream.

334

But more than anything, it was easy. So easy. He really could just be himself: no movement was stupid, no sentence lame, no expression offensive or derisive. He could let go, forget all the lies and myths his life had been built on.

The bed shook, threatening to collapse despite the expense, and each corner banged against the floor. They both moaned loudly, sometimes together, sometimes soundlessly, sometimes just with a smile; her smile made him feel that everything was just right. There were satisfying smacks of slippery flesh, two awkwardly shaped bodies that seemed horribly mismatched happily gyrating in unison as if that was the sole purpose of their making; at once fighting, reacting and protesting, but working towards a common goal.

"You really made me suffer," she said after the first round.

"You made me suffer," he said, rolling her over to start round two. He couldn't help thinking it was like flipping a tender, succulent steak.

"You deserved it."

And then they were at it again, all electricity and chemistry and ferocity, pounding flesh until noises in the hallway made them stop, mid-thrust, to listen. Darius heard the familiar clomp of Annette's police boots on the wooden floor getting slightly fainter until the door slammed and he heard her going doing the stairs.

"He lives here, right?" she said.

"Yeah."

"It was good of him to apologise. Tell him I appreciate that. But I think he's in love with you, Mr Tucker."

"What?" He lowered his voice. "No way. He's got a girlfriend."

"Sounds like she just left." She pushed the remaining sheets and blankets from the bed and propped herself up on one elbow, a glorious nymph. Every other woman Darius had known would have covered herself with a sheet but she just lay there, gleaming.

"She's difficult," he said, smiling at all of her curves, tracing them with his fingers. "I don't feel comfortable around her. We've got nothin to say."

"I guess your friend doesn't feel comfortable around her either, being gay. It can't be easy to keep that going."

"Humphrey's not gay."

"I love it when you get angry. That letter was pure pornography. I didn't think you had it in you."

"Yeah, well, callin my best friend gay makes me angry. You probly think he called you a Nazi cause he was jealous or something."

She looked him square in the eyes. "You know, you're really not as stupid as you pretend to be. Don't worry. I know why. But if you want to keep me, that has to change."

"What d'you mean?"

"For starters, stop asking questions like that. Questions you already know the answer to. And stop acting like a simple country boy. You can be so much more if you tried. You're an Australian and you can be proud of that, but that doesn't mean you have to wear your country's insecurity and mindlessness like some badge of honour. That poetry you wrote. I hate poetry. But some of it was good and if you just wrote about something real, it might become great."

He looked at her, admiring her broad shoulders, her large pale breasts, the thin tan lines. He would have liked to have written another poem about her, but promised himself he would try to write one with more depth and meaning.

"I've got something to show you." He got up and retrieved the newspaper from the drawer. "Here. I wrote this for my dad's funeral."

She took it and read it. When she was finished, she said, "Good. It's good. Maybe you should write about him."

"Yeah?"

"I mean it."

"We'll see. Where'd you get the tan?"

"I spent part of the winter in Australia. I pretty much gave up on you and had to get away. I worked for the *Sonntagsblatt* in Melbourne."

"You wrote about us in that paper."

"You saw that? I'm amazed that didn't ruin you. They liked your story but they edited out a lot of the stuff I wrote about Humphrey."

"Quiet. He might hear you."

"I don't care. He's as much a hypocrite as all the Aussies he thinks he's nothing like."

"I think you might find he's changed a bit."

"Hey, thanks for the rock, by the way. I would've preferred your friend's head in a box, but we can't have everything we want. So, you weren't ruined?"

"Nearly. The place was empty for weeks. A few Aussies vandalised the place but that had nothin to do with your article."

"I thought that was a terrorist attack. I saw Humphrey on the news. He looks ridiculous on camera. Like some dolled up Frankenstein."

"It was spelt wrong, Al Qaeda. Humphrey talked terrorism because he thought it might be good publicity."

"Like doing an ad promoting a country you only ever talk bad about."

"He's changed, really. Did you see him on *Tatort*?"

"Again, Frankenstein, but without the bolts. I wasn't surprised. I think he's been practising his whole life. He's got himself a nice little niche here. And it makes no difference how bad he is."

"His girlfriend's sister works for ARD."

"Well, that explains everything. He's definitely gay then."

Darius tickled her angrily and she squealed with delight, but they both stopped when there was a loud knock on the door. Darius pulled the bed sheet over them both just as the door opened, though Waldtraut hardly seemed to care if Humphrey saw her naked. Humphrey's head appeared in the gap.

"Trudi. I thought I recognised that voice. Nice to see you. Darius, I'm going to the restaurant. See you later, maybe."

He closed the door and Darius managed to hold in his laugh until he heard the front door close.

"See?" she said. "He's clearly jealous."

He let the laugh out. "Yeah, of me."

"It doesn't matter anyway." She climbed back on top of him, making him wince with as much pleasure as pain. "Come on, Mr Tucker. I waited a long time for this."

"Me too. I thought I'd never see you again."

"And I thought your restaurant wouldn't last."

"We changed it. Put tablecloths down."

"Yeah? That work?"

"It did."

"A cover up. I knew you were never into it. Profit from suffering. It was all Humphrey."

"I shoulda told you earlier."

"And I thought the minute it was over you would leave Munich."

"I'm not leavin unless you go with me."

"I'm not going anywhere with you."

337

"Yes, you are."

"That's the spirit."

***

He walked all the way to the restaurant, his groin aching and still sweating, his stomach rumbling. He felt faint, and had to stop a few times to buy coffee; he even bought a bottle of multivitamins in the hope a couple would get his strength back up for a late evening tussle. Barely half an hour had passed and he wanted to be inside her again. More, he wanted to hear her speak, to talk with her, to have her make him laugh. She gave him confidence and power, the motivation he needed to become the person she wanted him to be.

"Good thing you own half this place," Humphrey said as he walked in. He was standing at the door and Darius guessed he had been waiting. "Or you'd be the world's worst employee."

"We're not even open yet."

Behind the bar, Darius tied an apron around his waist to protect his old jeans. Waldtraut had laughed at his designer jeans, and had gone into hysterics at the sight of his alligator shoes. She liked his watch, though, and had showed him a few of the things it could do.

"Micha and Griff can handle things without me," he said, alluding to the time – soon, he hoped – when he wouldn't be there at all. He poured himself a big glass of orange juice. "And I'm happy to hear I'm still one of the owners."

Griff squirmed on his stool, like he was stubbing out a cigarette with his arse. "Berlin's still a goer, I say."

Humphrey banged an open hand on the bar counter. "I want details. Come on, Digger, you brought home better looking girls than her. Girls with more manners too. Girls who wouldn't clean out our fridge."

Darius tried to remain aloof but those comments rankled. No, he told himself. The old, superficial, lying Darius would get angry. This Darius doesn't care what people think.

"Well, Hobo, you can think whatever ya want. I like her, so don't chase her off again."

"She ran."

"Who's the girl?" Griff asked.

338

"His heart's been captured by a Kraut," Humphrey said. "She's got him pinned down, literally."

"Watch it, Hobo."

"Oooo, what'll ya do? Take me outside?"

"Steady on, fellas," Griff said.

"If you keep insultin my girlfriend, then I might have to."

"You've been insulting mine for ages."

Darius scanned the restaurant.

"She's not here. Say whatever you want."

"You only..." Darius began, but he couldn't finish. He looked down at his running shoes.

"Only what?"

"Nuthin. You wanna beer?"

"I do," Griff said, raising his hand. He was wearing that pinky ring with a skull on it that Darius hated so much. But he didn't have time to imagine making Griff swallow it because there was a loud knock on the door. Humphrey went to open it.

"Luke! What the fuck?"

"I jumped on an earlier flight." Luke dropped his backpack. He and Humphrey hugged.

"You're here. Brilliant. Come on in. This is Darius, Griff and Micha."

Luke shook everyone's hand. He was much younger than Darius had expected; he'd pictured someone over forty, he didn't know why, a failure of sorts. But Luke was barely out of his teens and had a baby face. He was rather regular looking, normal height, normal weight. Ordinary and average, Darius thought, and he hoped Luke would be far more than that in the kitchen.

"Nice place," Luke said. "Can I see the kitchen?"

"Follow me," Humphrey said.

When they were gone, Darius said, "Hey, Griff, can you give me a hand?"

"With what?"

Darius stood up and went to one of the tables. "You too, Micha. Let's get all the contact off these tables. Clear all this crap away."

"Now you're talking," Griff said.

The three of them set to work. It wasn't hard. The contact came off easily and soon the tables were bare. They put it all in a couple of big garbage bags. Micha took the bags out back while Griff and Darius put the tablecloths back down. The place didn't look any different, but Darius thought it felt different.

When Luke and Humphrey came out of the kitchen, the three of them were back at the bar. Luke already had an apron on.

"He's starting today," Humphrey said.

"Just to get a feel for the place."

"We'll work on a new menu in the next few days. He's gonna crash on our couch. That all right, Darius?"

"Sure."

"I booked a hotel for the first coupla nights," Luke said. "Didn't know what I was getting into."

"You can stay with us when you're ready."

"Thanks, Humphrey." Luke picked up his backpack and took it into the kitchen.

"Maybe he can have your room while you get tortured in Trudi's little sex den."

"I was thinking of moving out anyway," Darius said.

"What?"

"Yeah. Sorry to say, but I liked it when you were away. It was nice having the space."

"Then Luke can move in with me."

"Into your little sex den."

Humphrey laughed. "Annette keeps forgetting her handcuffs."

Darius checked his watch. "Let's open up and put Luke to work."

Humphrey went to the door. "It all starts today. Real Aussie cuisine." There were people waiting outside. "Hi there. Yep, we're open. Welcome to a little slice of Australia in Munich."

***

It was early evening when Arnie charged through the door.

"Can I have everyone's attention," he shouted. "This restaurant's closed until further notice. Please leave. You don't have to pay your bills."

Humphrey went up to Arnie. "Have you lost your fucking mind?"

"This place is an absolute disgrace. Do you have an idea what you've done?"

"Nuh. Did you come all the way from Berlin to shut us down?"

"Bloody right."

Arnie's face turned a darker shade of red. He walked up to the bar and Darius could see a vein throbbing on the side of his face.

"All right, Arnie?"

"No. Far from it. I didn't get a good look at the tables the last time I was here. The place was too full. But if I had, I would've shut you down then."

"You shouldn't've spent all you time perving on the girls, and drinking yourself into a stupor," Humphrey said.

"I would really not want to be in your position. We're gonna take your ad off, too, and you'll have to go to court for violating your contract."

"I didn't violate anything."

"Come on," Arnie shouted. "Everybody out."

"Sit down," Humphrey ordered. "Darius, call the police."

Arnie held up his hands. "That's not necessary."

"You can't just walk in here and close us down. Your embassy's just a little office in this country. You don't have any real power. Anyway, we've done nothing wrong."

Darius stepped towards Arnie. "I think there's been a mistake. Someone's given you false info."

"We got a call this morning. She told us to check your tables. Slanderous material, damaging for the image of Australia."

"So, have a look." Darius went to a table that only had a few drinks on it. "If you don't mind, folks."

The people lifted their glasses and Darius pulled back the tablecloth.

"Darius, don't," Humphrey said.

"See? You've been led up the creek."

Arnie looked at the bare table.

"I'll confess, Arnie. We had some stuff on there for the first few days, but nobody liked. We didn't even like it. We took it all off. True Blue Tucker is all about the real Australia."

Humphrey stepped forward. "That's right. We've even got a new chef. An Aussie making real Aussie cuisine. You hungry?"

"Yeah, uh, sorry, fellas. Looks like I got a bad tip."

Darius put an arm around him. "Sit with us at the bar. Have a beer."

Arnie's phone rang. He answered it. "Sally? Yes, I'm at True Blue Tucker...No, it's not like that at all. Everything's fine...Sounds like someone was trying to put out bad words about the place. Maybe one of the competitors..."

"It was Freddie," Humphrey said. "Say hi to Sally for me."

"Humphrey says g'day...Yes, the response has been really positive to the ad...Okay...Sorry this kept you up...G'night."

Arnie pocketed the phone and took a seat at the bar. "I'm really sorry, fellas."

"Forget it," Darius said.

"I came all this way for nothing."

"I'm glad you came down. It's good to see ya, Arnie. Give him a beer, Griff."

"Already done."

Griff put the beer on the bar, placed on a Foster's beer mat. Arnie took a long drink.

"What happened?" Darius asked.

"Sally got a call as well, so it wasn't just me," Arnie said. "Sally said the person asked about tours. Is there a Stolen Generations tour? Can I visit a refugee camp? Can homosexuals visit Tasmania? Nasty stuff like that. She said she learned about it all from this restaurant. From your tables."

"Someone's out to ruin us," Darius said. "But we're clean. There's nothing slanderous about True Blue Tucker."

Humphrey came to the bar. "Are you gonna stick around, Arnie. Tonight's quiz night. You can be captain of one of the teams."

"Yeah. All right."

"Darius," Humphrey said, "a word."

Darius got up and followed Humphrey into the kitchen.

"What did you do?" Humphrey asked.

"We got rid of it all, earlier today."

"What made you do that?"

"I dunno. Instinct."

"That was lucky."

"Yeah. It was."

They watched Luke working.

"He's on it," Darius said. "Knows his stuff."

"Who do you reckoned called?"

"Miss Jane?"

"Why would she do that now?"

"Maybe she saw your ad. Or the website."

"Maybe."

"You got your questions ready?"

"I worked on them on the flight. Some really funny ones."

"Let's do it."

"Hey, guys," Luke said, holding up a plate. "What do think?"

"What's the yellow bread? Is that damper?" Darius asked.

"It is. Walnut and almond damper."

"Looks great, Luke," Humphrey said. "You're hired. And you've got a place to live."

"Sweet. That was easy."

Darius turned to Humphrey. "All right if I scarper?"

"Where're you going? Don't run away on me now. We need you here tonight."

"No, you don't. Besides, you're the one who does all the running, like when you abandoned me in Woodlow."

"You still haven't forgiven me for that."

"Les told me you've done it to him plenty of times."

"He exaggerates. He only married an Asian to prove he's not racist."

"I'll tell him you said that."

"He knows what I think. I know a lot more about Les than you do. He has his secrets too."

"Don't we all."

"Yeah, and I heard what Trudi said this morning."

Darius hesitated. His old self would have said nothing, like when his father threw him out, like when Humphrey drove Waldtraut away. But he was different now. Spirit, that was what she wanted from him.

"That's right. She thinks you're gay."

"I am," Luke said. "It's good I told ya now and got it out of the way."

"It doesn't matter," Humphrey said. "You can be anything you want. Half of our staff is gay." He turned to Darius. "And you're one to talk with your silk shirts and styled hair and flirting with Micha."

"You always do this. You turn things around and put everything on everyone else. You talk about people needing to know the truth

343

but you don't know any of it yourself."

"That's good coming from an uneducated shearer."

"Yeah, who saved our restaurant tonight, and stopped you from blowing the ad."

"Don't stop there. Go for the throat."

"And, and you're just a university drop-out who can't act except when he's playing the typical Aussie."

Humphrey opened his mouth to respond. It looked like he had a lot to say. Darius knew he had gone too far. He hadn't wanted to, but Humphrey had provoked him.

"You guys always this open with each other?" Luke asked. "It's really refreshing."

"When did you get so sharp, Digger? You always stand at the bar like you don't understand anything, but you get it all, don't you? I shouldn't be surprised. Your mum's clever. Who knows what you could've become if someone had nurtured that brain of yours. I can see now why it hurts so much that she left."

"I respect her for what she did and I don't blame her. We talked it out in London."

"But she did the wrong thing by leaving you."

"I got by all right. With a little help."

"This's normally when friends say sorry, but I'm not sorry for anything I said. It was worth it to see you get pissed off for real. All that fair-go-easy-mate bullshit always annoyed me."

"You learned the same script."

"Yeah, but I threw it away in high school. And it was around then that everything started going wrong. Or right. Depends on how you look at it, I guess."

"So? What we do now?"

Humphrey put his arm around Darius and led him back into the restaurant. "I think we should go back inside, have this quiz night, and then when everyone's gone, Griff included, we lock the door and do something quintessentially Australian."

"What's that?"

"Get drunk, mate."

***

344

"How is she?"

"Good, good," he said, his head throbbing. Even the static of the phone made his brain ache.

"We were hoping you'd find each other again."

"Yeah. We did."

"Is she there now? I'd like to say hello."

"She's gone to church."

"Church? She never struck me as the religious type."

"Me neither. I think she's writing an article."

"And how's Humphrey?"

"Good. He says g'day."

Humphrey passed on his way to the kitchen, wearing just his Australian flag boxer shorts. He mouthed "Coffee?" Darius nodded, his brain bouncing painfully against his skull.

"Did you see his ad?" he asked.

"Yes. I never thought he'd be chosen to do such a thing. Or that he'd do it, if asked."

"He's mellowed. How's Auckland?"

"Still a mess. We haven't unpacked half the boxes."

"Better get to work," he said, happy his own world was in great shape. Waldtraut, Humphrey, the restaurant. It had been great last night, getting drunk and recalling all the adventures they'd had together: the mining town, Woodlow, Munich, London. Waldtraut came to the restaurant, well after midnight, when he and Humphrey were very drunk. She went home with them, but Darius woke up to find her gone. She left a note on his desk, scrawled on a piece of torn newspaper: "Gone a praying, love W." He liked that, the giant W, with its sharp corners and perfectly straight lines. It seemed to reinforce that everything was right in his world, that all his angles were uniform and his lines symmetrical.

"All we do is work. Harry's busy writing and university just eats up my time. We need a holiday."

"You comin over?"

"We don't have enough weeks for that. Sorry, Darius. I hope you're not disappointed. We're going to explore our new hood, maybe go to South Island as well."

"Do it. It's great," Darius said, and he recalled his lonely rental car foray, going from one beautiful place to another with no one to share it with.

345

Humphrey walked past, put a cup of coffee next to the phone and then went back into his room. Darius sipped. It was instant and tasted like sludge, but at this point, any injection of caffeine would be useful.

"How's True Blue Tucker?"

"That's another story entirely. We've got a new chef. An Aussie. Things are gonna change. We're gonna open places all over the country."

"Without the history?"

"We've still got it. But we're doing it in different ways, like playing music and showing movies. Luke says we can do it with food, too."

"Is Luke the new chef?"

"Yep. Top bloke."

The doorbell rang. "Hang on. There's someone at the door."

"It's probably that girl of yours. I'll let you go. Harry says hello and say a big hello to Waldtraut from both of us."

"Will do. Thanks for callin, Alice."

"Take care."

He hung up the phone and opened the door.

"Annette? You lose your key?"

"Is Humphrey here?"

She was dressed in street clothes and, as always, looked exceedingly uncomfortable in them. She wore tight pants pulled up too high, and sure enough, there was that panty line. But it didn't offer the comfort of the familiar this morning. Instead, he felt there was something threatening about it, that the elastic was drawn so tight that it might snap off a finger if someone tried to tug at it. A challenge, that's what it was; a divider, a line in the sand.

Darius stepped out of the doorway and let her past. "He's in his room."

She knocked on Humphrey's door and went inside. Darius lingered in the hall, wanting to hear her first sentence, but there was only silence. So he went back into his own room, drained the rest of his coffee, got undressed and climbed into bed. It still smelt of sex, of her, and the bed sheet was sticky and dried in some places. But he gladly immersed himself in it again. She would be back soon and then they could add another layer of stickiness to the sheet.

"Gone a-praying," he said.

He closed his eyes and was almost asleep when a door slammed loudly. Then there came a knock on his door. It's her, he thought. He kicked off the sheet so she could jump straight onto his naked body.

"It's open."

"Woah," Humphrey said, looking away, shielding his eyes with his hands. "Didn't expect that."

Darius pulled the sheet up.

"Aren't I the one who's supposed to be gay?" Humphrey asked.

"I thought it was Waldtraut."

"Bad luck. Only me."

"Was that Annette leavin'?"

"Yeah." Humphrey stared at the floor. He sipped his coffee and lowered himself into the swivel chair in front of Darius's desk. The leather squeaked, as did the chair as he swivelled from side to side.

"What happened?"

Humphrey swallowed his coffee like it was lemon juice. "You won't believe it."

"What?"

"She proposed."

"You're kidding."

"I know. It's unreal, isn't it? I thought shit like this only happened in movies."

"This is life, Hobo. You can't act now."

"No."

"What'd you say?"

Humphrey blew the air from his cheeks. "I said I'd think about it."

"You don't sound too sure."

"She wants the whole shebang. If I say yes, in a couple of years, I'll be behind the wheel of some economical family van ferrying little brats to soccer practice."

"Is that what you want?" Darius was asking himself the same question.

"I'm twenty-four. Ugh, I feel like such an adult."

"How old's Annette?"

"Twenty-eight, I think."

"So what'll ya do?"

Humphrey shrugged his broad shoulders. He sat there in his Aussie flag boxers looking like an overgrown man-child. The boxers had ridden up a little and Darius could just see one hairy pink testicle hanging out the bottom. He looked away quickly, but even without looking at it, and not wanting to, he could still see it.

"I came in here thinking the new clever Darius might give me the answer."

"Honestly?"

"I wouldn't want anything less. Lies are a waste of everyone's time."

"Well," Darius began, trying hard not to look at that testicle, "to be honest, I dunno. Maybe you should. She's a nice girl. You could move to Australia."

"But that'll mean the end of summer here and summer there. And she wants to keep working. She likes being a cop."

"Then you live here and go on holiday to Australia. You could have a couple of kids and make them into something great. Give them everything you missed out on."

"Wasn't expecting that. Life's suddenly full of surprises. You been thinking about my situation or yours?"

"I don't think you ever really gave her a chance. Me neither. You only thought about what she could do for you."

"I'm not sure I like this new Darius. I think I prefer the old submissive, say-what-others-want-to-hear Darius, or the say-nothing Woodlow Darius."

"Everyone can change. You did."

Humphrey chuckled. "Not sure if I could live in Australia again. Annette's got a big family here and they're pretty close. Melbourne's nice, but I'm scared once I'm back living in Oz, the place will start giving me the shits again. All those contradictions eat at my sanity. And think of all the Rods and Janes I'd have to deal with day in, day out."

"Not all the guys are like Rod."

"Some are."

"Maybe it'll be different this time."

"No. The life's here, with or without Annette. And we've got some serious expanding to do. Beyond Germany. I want us to open places all over Europe. Put the Walkabouts and imposters like Freddie out of business."

"Let's get Munich to the top of the tree first."

"Now I've got conservative Darius." Humphrey sipped his coffee. "Where's Trudi? Wasn't she here last night? I can't remember much after we got in the taxi."

"She went to church."

"Yeah? She's a weird one, and a real screamer too. Or was that you doing all the squealing. I remember that much from last night. It was like she was screaming in my ear. Great sound, really carnal, not like that Texan girl in Woodlow, what's-her-name. She sounded like she was giving birth to a monster."

Darius looked at his chunky watch. Next to it was an ashtray. He was surprised to see the remnants of a joint in the bottom. He didn't remember smoking it but it did explain the throbbing hangover.

"I think we better get to the restaurant. You think Arnie's still in town?"

"I hope so," Humphrey said, standing up. "I could use a laugh. Can you believe him yesterday? Charging in to close us down. I kinda wish you hadn't cleaned up the tables. You know, just to see his response."

"I saved us."

"You did. Again. Now it's superhero Darius."

"Look, mate, you don't have to come in today. Luke's got it going in the kitchen, and Griff'll be there. Why don't you go and talk to Annette?"

Humphrey stretched a little. "You reckon Griff dobbed us in?"

"Why would he do that?"

"Good point. But I still wanna know who it was."

"Probly Jane. She never liked you. Maybe she wanted revenge on Griff too because he didn't go back with her. She saw the ad and was reminded of it all."

"You might be right. Boy, I better pay attention. This clever Darius has some good things to say."

"Tonight's Aussie cinema night, right?"

"We're showing *Priscilla*."

"How about we skip it. All four of us have dinner. You, me, Waldtraut and Annette. We'll buy a heap of food and cook it up in our kitchen."

"That's a fantastic idea. You call yours and I'll call mine. I'll do the shopping and the cooking. Dinner at seven."

"Deal."

Humphrey got up and started to leave the room. He picked up a shirt from the floor. "Is this my shirt?"

***

349

The restaurant was busy. It was only Luke's second day, but people were already commenting on the food. Before leaving for the dinner appointment, Darius went into the kitchen to chat with the new chef.

"All right?"

Luke was hard at work, enjoying himself. "I'm in my element. This is exactly the chance I've been waiting for. I can let loose my creativity."

"It's great to have you here. They love it out there."

"Of course they do."

"We'll do everything right by ya, get ya papers sorted."

"Is that difficult? Hey, Lars, not so much oil. Let it cook in its own juice."

"We've got someone who helps us out. Anyway, getting a visa here, for work, just means being able to do something none of the locals can do. And when it comes to Aussie cuisine, you've got that covered. It'll be easy."

"Sweet. Thanks, Darius."

"No worries. So, uh, where ya from?"

"Brisbane. I grew up there, but I was born in Perth."

"Another sandgroper. Me and Humphrey are both from WA."

"Yeah, he said that."

"If you give me your passport, I'll get the paperwork started."

"It's in my jacket. Hanging on the wall. Inside pocket."

Darius pulled out the passport and flipped it open.

"Don't laugh at the photo. A real mug shot."

"Lucas Stevenson."

"Yep."

"What's ya dad's name?"

"Roy."

Darius shook his head. "Small world. The Stevensons are a massive clan where I come from."

"I know. Down near Wagin."

"Right. We all wondered what happened to Roy."

"That's why he left. He hated all that small town bullshit. And he wanted more than just being a sheep farmer."

"What'd he do?"

"He renovates houses. Creative like. Does great work."

"I'd like to meet him."

350

"Maybe he'll come over and visit."

"Did he ever patch things up with his brothers and sisters?"

Luke smiled. "See? That's why he left. All those fucking rumours that circulate. He's always been in contact with them. We used to go there for Christmas. Dad was always happy to see them all, and always happy to leave."

"I know Murray Stevenson pretty well."

"Everyone does, down there, even people who don't. He never liked me much."

"Well, you're safe here, Luke. I'll bring your passport back tomorrow. All right?"

"Yep." Luke pulled out a piece of paper from his back pocket. "And I need these ingredients. I was up all night planning what we can do. I don't know where you do your shopping, but if we're gonna do Aussie cuisine, we're gonna have to import a lot of stuff. And it'll need to be fresh. Or as fresh as can be. Goanna, emu, wombat, crocodile, king prawns, squid, occie. All that. I know some guys in Australia we can order from. And we need to talk contract soon."

"I'll talk to Humphrey about it."

Luke came up close to Darius. "I'm gonna need better help in here too," he whispered. "These guys can't even make sandwiches."

"We're gonna revamp the whole place, take it up a notch, the staff too."

"Good." Luke nodded. "Good. This's gonna be big, if we do it right."

"We will."

Darius went out the back door. He took a taxi home. Upstairs, Humphrey was busy cooking, with Annette helping. They had music on. Annette was shaking her hips to the rhythm as she cut carrots.

"Get out, get out," Humphrey shouted when he saw Darius in the doorway. "We're not ready yet."

In his room, Darius sat at his desk and thought about Roy Stevenson, about the rumours that had been spread and the nasty things his dad had said. Roy wasn't gay. He had just wanted a different life.

"Like me," he said. "Dad just made it all up."

His dad had told a lot of stories, like the one that miner had told just before the fight with Humphrey. The city fella story. His dad had used that one a lot.

351

City fella, he thought.

He took a piece of paper and a pen. He wrote, "Blew in on a slither of dust."

The words came easily, rhyming as if by magic, like they were supposed to go together.

When he was finished, he read through it and liked it. He wondered where it had come from. The story, he knew that, but how had the words formed themselves like this on the page, so rhythmic and sounding so nice?

"What to do with it now?" he asked.

"Publish it."

He turned. "When did you get here?"

She was lying on the bed, on her stomach with her feet in the air, reading the book Harry had given her last year. There were small bits of paper sticking out of the top of the book, close to the spine.

"You didn't even notice me come in. I think you grunted. Once."

"I was so into it."

"I like it."

"I haven't shown it to you yet."

"I read over your shoulder, while you were writing."

"You did?"

"Are you stoned?"

"No. No. I guess, I just got lost in what I was doing. You really think I should publish it?"

"Give it to your local paper again. They'll run it."

"Yeah. That's a good idea." He got up and went into the hallway. He found the number in his address book and dialled.

There was a long delay before it started ringing. It was late in the evening in that part of the world, and he thought about hanging up and trying tomorrow. But the phone was picked up.

"Hello."

"Murray, g'day. This's Darius. Darius Tucker. Digger."

"Mate, good to hear from ya. How the hell are ya?"

"Good. Look, I'm sorry for calling so late."

"You can call in the wee hours, Digger, I'd answer. Where are ya?"

"Munich."

"That's good. Miranda's flying over. I was gonna call you to see if you can keep an eye on her. But I couldn't find your number."

"You got me now."

"Your number too. I can see it on me display."

"Is Mizzy comin to Munich?"

"Took her to the airport meself. Today."

"She studying?"

"Yep. Six month exchange."

"Look, if she needs a job, I could help her out. I've got a restaurant here. An Aussie place. Doing real well."

"Congrats."

"Thanks. We can always use an extra pair of hands. I know she's good in the kitchen."

"All the Stevenson women are. What's it called?"

"True Blue Tucker."

Murray laughed. "That's brilliant."

"And it's going great guns."

"When Mizzy touches base with me, I'll tell her about it. And I'll give her your number. True Blue Tucker. Old Jack would love that. Tucker's Run is a gold mine, by the way. We put wheat in last year. Bumper harvest. I was thinking of using the profits to start some kind of charity. You know, put some money into the community, using your dad's name."

"The Jack Tucker Foundation. Great idea."

"It's good to talk to ya, Digger. I was worried."

"Why?"

"You were in a dark place when ya left."

"I'm all right. It was good for me to leave, to get some distance, ya know."

"Yeah, I know. Ya comin back soon?"

"Dunno. Maybe. We'll see, eh?"

"Be good to see you again."

"Thanks, Murray."

There was a brief silence. The phone crackled.

"Ah, Murray?"

"Yeah?"

"You remember that poem I wrote about me dad?"

"It's framed and hanging on me wall."

"I've written another one. Can I send it to ya? Maybe the local rag'll run it."

"Sure. Stick it in the post."

"Thanks, mate. Say g'day to everyone for me."

"I will."

"And tell Mizzy to get in contact."

"Take care, Digger."

"Bye." He put the phone down.

"Who's Mizzy?" Humphrey asked.

"No one important. Maybe we can give her a job, at the restaurant. I owe her dad a favour."

"Was that him on the phone?"

"Yeah."

"What was that all about?"

"Incredibly, poetry."

"You've written another bush ballad. Can I read it?"

"If you want."

"After dinner. Waldtraut! Dinner's ready!"

Darius followed Humphrey into the kitchen. Waldtraut came in as well. All four sat down at the table.

"This looks awesome," Waldtraut said. "All that praying made me hungry."

The dishes and bowls were passed around and they all took what they wanted.

"*Guten Appetit*," Annette said.

"Yeah," Humphrey said. "Good eating."

"Thanks for cooking, Hobo." Darius took a forkful of pasta salad. "Oh, it's good."

"Where did you learn to cook like this?" Waldtraut asked.

"Lester the almighty. We never had a dad. Les took care of me most of the time while my mum worked. I'm the reason he's become such a good dad."

Darius and the two girls laughed.

"Les is a great guy," Darius said to Waldtraut.

"A real top bloke," Humphrey added.

"And what about you?" Waldtraut asked. "Will you be a good dad?"

"I'd like to have Hobo as my dad," Darius said.

"Darius has found himself a new and improved father," Humphrey said. "Smarter, faster, more revolutionary, and has got into bed with the enemy in the process." When Darius sneered at him, he added,

"Oh, don't look like that. You know I'm joking. Harry's a diamond."

"Still generalising, I see," Waldtraut said.

Humphrey held up his hands innocently. "Hey, I'm just going on facts. He and Darius were arrested last year in London for taking a bomb on a bus."

"We weren't arrested," Darius said. "And there was no bomb."

"What happened?" Waldtraut asked.

"Nothing. Harry was doing research for a book. We got on a bus and he had a backpack."

"The idol bomber," Humphrey said.

"The backpack was full of religious stuff. You know, idols and books. A few people on the bus stared but nothing more. This old fart totally flipped out and got the police. Harry went along with it to see what would happen."

"And?"

"They checked his bag and that was it. The cops were pretty friendly about it."

"It'll get worse." Humphrey said.

"We have to keep a look out for everyone," Annette said. "That's what they tell us."

"We're safe here. All the nine-eleven guys lived in Hamburg. They won't strike against their home turf." Humphrey turned to Waldtraut. "So? How was church?"

"I didn't go to church. I went to a mosque."

"Really?" Annette said. "Is that possible?"

"Sure. I wore a headscarf."

"What'd you do there?" Darius asked.

"I went in, met a few people, sat down, prayed."

"To Allah?" Humphrey asked.

"To whatever higher power there is. I don't know any gods personally, so I don't know their names. But when you think of all the religions in the world, that nearly every society believes in a force greater than themselves, there must be something going on."

"Or everyone on the planet is dillusional," Humphrey said.

"You need to talk to Harry," Darius said to Waldtraut. "He thinks the same."

"I only went to a mosque to see if I could get in, being white, blonde and female."

"And a Christian," Humphrey said.

"I'm not anything."

"So where the hell will you two get married?"

Darius looked at Waldtraut. "Vegas?"

"Slow down, Elvis, I'm not that easy."

"What happened at the mosque?" Annette asked.

"I was very welcome. I spoke with some of the women there. I've always had a lot of respect for Muslim women. They're very strong, especially when you consider what kinds of barriers they face everyday."

"Are you writin an article?" Darius asked.

Waldtraut shook her head. "Not everything has to go into print, Mr Tucker. When I was in Australia, I had the idea to travel the world disguised as a Muslim to see how they get treated at airports and in different cities. You should have seen the looks I got today when people saw me come out of the mosque, from regular German people."

"No one would publish a story like that," Humphrey said.

"Not in your country, but the media's different here. It's not all owned by two greedy old men. Freedom of the press is a real thing and not just some catchphrase that gets thrown around. A few magazines were interested."

They were quite a way through the meal now, but the table was still covered with food.

"I think I've had enough," Waldtraut said.

"Me too," Darius added. "How about you and me talk a walk around the block?"

"Yes. Let's walk it off and come back for dessert. Is there dessert?"

"There's ice cream and cake," Humphrey said. "And brandy and cigars will be served on the balcony."

"We'll be back for all that."

The two of them left the apartment and walked down the stairs. Outside, the early April night was crisp and clear. They walked in the direction of the Isar. Darius told Waldtraut that Annette had asked Humphrey to marry her.

"Let's hope he says no, for her sake."

"You still don't like him?"

"He's growing on me, like a nasty wart. Oh, I'm so full. I need a massive glass of schnapps."

"We've got some at home."

"How was the restaurant today?"

"Full. Like always. The new chef's already making a difference."

"Good to hear."

Darius stopped and sat on a bench. Waldtraut sat down too. They stared at the river.

"Lovely night," Waldtraut said.

Darius put his arm around her. "Why did you call the embassy? And Tourism Australia as well?"

She laughed.

Lewis: All the poems are great stories. And there's so much Aussie spirit in them.

Poet: There is.

Lewis: May I call you Digger?

Poet: Course.

Lewis: Did they take long to write?

Poet: The poems? Coupla months. Once I started, it all poured outta me. One poem kinda led to another. But it took a while to get them published. No publishers were interested.

Lewis: I can't believe that.

Poet: It's true. I sent poems off to stacks of publishers, but I just got these form rejection letters. I don't think they even read what I sent.

Lewis: I bet those publishers are regretting that now. Your book's a bestseller. You've already out-sold Paterson and Lawson.

Poet: It only became a book with the help of a mate back home. He thought the poems were pretty good and decided to invest in my work.

Lewis: So, he paid to have your book published?

Poet: He was like my editor. Whenever I wrote a poem, I sent it to him. He put them in the local paper. Everyone said they were so good, he put a book together.

Lewis: And it's become a huge success. There's already talk of a movie adaption, for the life of Jack Tucker.

Poet: I got lucky. It all happened really fast. Word of mouth, the bush telegraph in overdrive. Another mate knew some people in Canberra, high up in the government. He sent the book to them and it just kept snowballing from there. I'm still amazed by it all.

Lewis: And now you're on a reading tour of Australia.

Poet: Yep.

Lewis: Sounds like you're surrounded by good people.

Poet: I am. And I consider myself really lucky for that. You should choose your friends carefully. Because your mates reflect who you are.

Lewis: Digger, I have to say, yours is a great Australian story.

~~~

The Last Bush Poet

It was a glowing introduction. He took the stage and raised a modest hand to the standing ovation, the same hand that had once held the scruff of a sheep's neck and had poured thousands of beers. He shook hands with the Minister for the Arts, who had given the introduction. At the podium, he adjusted the microphone, scratching the front of it and sending a screech of feedback through the auditorium.

"G'day," he said. "I'm Digger. Thanks for having me here. It's my first time in Canbra. Before I read, I'd like to send my sympathies and best wishes to all the families and friends of the Bali bombing victims."

The crowd clapped sombrely.

"My dad was an amazing man. He was exactly the kind of bloke who would've run back into Paddy's Pub to save people. He was selfless, honest and true blue. He was my dad, and he was also my best mate, the best mate anyone could have. I know he's here with us in spirit, and I'm glad I can share his stories and yarns with all of you." He opened his book to the page marked. "This poem's called *City Fella*."

Blew in on a slither of dust
To pocket a hefty wage, he must
Smoggy smile, Cottesloe tan, pink hands
Broken history, ponderous lies, no man
Of course, the Ripper gave him a go

Heavy wrists eager for a break
Drainin the thermos, snatchin the last bit of cake
Suspicious snigger, third person tales, sweaty shears
The lowest total, rich excuses, never shoutin a beer
In due course, the Ripper let him know

Thin denials echoed through the shed
The circling men snorted, saw red
A necessary challenge, "Outside", a line in the dirt

"Let's have ya, city fella, off with ya shirt."
Of course, the Ripper was up for the show

Cocky and young, swung big at the air
Aged experience scented softness there
Let him hit, once, twice, confidence up
Winner's grin, natty strut, not nearly enough
A matter of course, the Ripper landed a blow

Fell soundlessly after a superfluous crack
The men closed ranks with pats on the back
Flat out, laughed at, humiliated in the dust
A kick for good measure, puke the colour of rust
Of course, the Ripper told him to go

He slowly closed the book. The crowd clapped.
"Thanks."

He shrugged, trying to smile modestly, to pretend it was really nothing and that they all shouldn't be so impressed.

But they were. The whole country was.

His poetry had graced the pages of magazines and newspapers and was being quoted by people from all walks of life. He had captured the Australian spirit, the reviewers proclaimed, and revamped an identity which had been floundering in the shadows of terrorism, technology and America. He had people reaching for the bush poems and ballads of a hundred years ago, grasping at the hands of Anzacs of yore. The conservatives gobbled it up, made reference to it, worked fruitlessly to get The Digger to speak at their meetings and endorse their party; to get him to join forces with such obviously kindred spirits.

The book of poems, simply yet touchingly illustrated, self-published by the Jack Tucker Foundation, danced off the shelves, making The Digger a household name. But it was the beer commercial that made him instantly recognisable, followed by the ad for WA Tourism. Another book was set to be published and there were calls for him to be Australian of the Year.

Humphrey joked that it was the greatest deception in over two hundreds years of deception. He loved the poems, thinking they summed up Australia past and present better than any of his diatribes ever could. And he was the first to admit the poems were captivating, that they spoke of a world you wanted desperately to have some kind of link to, some reference point that might let you compare yourself with that bloke to end all blokes, Jack the Ripper.

From the country to the cities, from the hip inner quarters to the rank and file of the suburbs, *Me Old Man Ripper* found its way under Christmas trees, onto book shelves and next to birthday cakes. In offices and sheds around the country, the bloke was making a stunning comeback. Chest waxers in Sydney and Melbourne went out of business while beer and ute sales soared.

Darius tried to be humble and laconic, as was expected. He acted like he didn't deserve the attention or the accolades; he was just a simple country boy who had the good fortune of being blessed with the power of lyricism. His was a great story and the media grabbed hold of it with both fists, one from Murdoch and the other from Packer: the battler made good, the shearing balladeer, the self-made man and modest achiever, the son of an Australian outback legend. He gave ordinary city folks more reason to be proud Australians. He warmed the hearts of city intellectuals who had believed for years that there was no culture in the bush, and not much in the cities either. He offered relief to the country people who had feared they had no more stories to tell, or at least, no one who could aptly tell them. They were proud to be farmers and shearers, happy to be interviewed by current affairs programs in search of more outback characters like The Digger. What other outstanding artistic talent was wasting away in a shearing shed somewhere, or shouting a round in some dusty bar miles from the nearest highway? There were thousands of gems out there in the desert waiting to be discovered.

As he toured Australia, reading his poetry and drinking with locals, he was everybody's best mate, the quintessential top bloke, and nobody talked about him badly. Complete strangers drove hundreds of miles and came up to him at book signings and events acting like they had sheared together in the old days; that their country bond made them more than just passing acquaintances. They slapped him on the back and pumped his hand up and down, rubbing their callouses against his, winking at him as if they shared some great secret.

Waldtraut went everywhere with him. She was the one who kept telling him to give the Australian people what they want.

"Nearly every country holds on to an ideal about themselves that's far from the truth," she told him. "If you've got the talent and the right delivery, you might as well profit from it."

"No profit from suffering," he said.

"This isn't suffering. And if your restaurant taught you anything, it's that myth pays better than truth."

"It does."

Lewis: So, Digger, what's next for you?

Poet: A few festivals. I'm reading at Parliament House on Anzac Day. I've written a poem for it. My great-granddad died at Gallipoli. The poem's about him.

Lewis: What an honour. Any other readings or speeches scheduled?

Poet: I'll be pretty much touring for the rest of the year. America, Canada, Europe. And we've got a True Blue Tucker opening in Sydney as well.

Lewis: Well, thanks for coming on the show and sharing your story with us. We wish you the best of luck.

Poet: My pleasure, Mike.

Lewis: And I'd like to personally thank you for bringing Australia back to its roots. The book is called *Me Old Man Ripper* and its available wherever good books are sold. From all of us at *Australia's Own Heroes*, it's good night.

The credits start to roll. The music is John Williamson's *True Blue*. Lewis and the poet appear to continue talking until the picture fades to black.

~~~

Appendix I

Excerpts from *Me Old Man Ripper*

Ballad of the Ripper

He was born inna slantin mud hut
Down south o'er Wagin way
Was shearin before he could walk
Our prodigal here to stay
Was a mighty six feet high and wide
Before his whiskers grew
Could hold hisself in drink'n'fight
His heart was hard and true

Followed in his father's steps
To sheds across the state
Was torn up by the old man's death
They was the besta mates
He buried him behind the house
And then he grit his teeth
Swore he'd be the best damn shearer
The world had ever seen

So he charged inta every shed
Ripped from our hands our shears
Carved those beasts in half the time
His eyes all wet with tears
And it's here that the legend grew
Of a man so stoic and slicker
He earned a place in all our hearts
Our very own Jack the Ripper

A-ha now don't you be mistook
By such a dev'lish name
For ne'er was there a topper bloke
Bred into the shearin game
His antics they is knew by all

Across the far and wide
Up north he saved a dozen lives
And took it in his stride

Our Ripper he has done it all
As miner drover shearer
But from dusty plain to sweaty shed
It's the shears that he holds dearer
He's set every single record straight
And never will they fall
But not for wont of tryin
Old Jack still kills them all

They come from far across the land
To knock him off his perch
And when he beats them to their knees
He don't leave them in a lurch
He grins a little and helps them up
Puts them back to work
Or shouts em a round at the pub
No rubbin in the dirt

And when people talk of mateship
Of loyalty and fair go
They don't what they're on about
Unless old Jack they know
He's agin now and gettin on
But still he shears them quicker
Let him rule us till the day he dies
Cause we love our Jack the Ripper

The Weedy Miner

Out back below the dusty plains
Where our shiny riches lie
And men of miscellaneous names
As one for corporate profits die
There rose a weedy, lanky bloke
Into a towering force of a man
Of who everyone soon quietly spoke
Specially those who knew him first hand

He came inta town well after eight
And parked in front of the pub
Then drank down two beers straight
While givin old Davo the rub
Davo grinned and gave him a slap
Thinkin he'd never be up for a blow
To his surprise the bloke threw down his hat
And out to the road they did go

That chemical wind was roarin an blowin
Swirlin the dust all round
This weedy bloke he looked like nothin
But dug his boots deep inta the ground
He lifted his fists dainty like a girl
Causin old Davo to laugh
But the blows came all in a whirl
And the victor trudged back to the bar

Saw him next day down in the pit
Shirtless and pounding the stone
Wondered how he packed such a hit
Inta arms that were nothin but bone
Work to do so no word he spake
He went down deeper for more
This young fella packed the strength of the state
In a weedy body gold to the core

And as every stinkin season passed
He showed us the worker's way
Shied away from the easiest of tasks
While drinkin his pay slip away
Thought nothin of riskin his own head
To save that of one of his mates
Taught us what was for him inbred
That we'd lost in our own selfish states

For a weedy bloke all bone and skin
Can the toughest of miners be
While poor us can only wish for such things
That for him came so naturally
Barely of age, Christ did he show
The true outback Aussie way
To dig ya boots in and give it go
And then quietly save the day

Birth Death

He was spat out in a storm
Pink and raw
A protesting kid
The wind blew the roof off
Took her soul
A parting gift
His dad raised the baby
Let out a roar
From promising lips

Buried her amongst the trees
In foreign dirt
A dissident task
Went back down south alone
That empty house
An indifferent mask
How was he gonna feed em both
Through the drought
A difficult ask

And still her memory lingers
In their dreams
Twenty years on
The baby has become a man
A promise kept
All fears gone
His dad's turned all dried and withered
A heroic shell
Now he's done

The Record

Here comes a yarn p'haps you've heard before
About a bloke who stunned us all
On a hot day in one of old Stevenson's sheds
When a mighty record did fall

Yeah, he was as cocky as he was good
His hands they moved like silk
But his strength and character we shoulda guessed
Simply cause of his ilk

We thought that record was etched in stone
Carved by his dad in his prime
A week after his death young Jack comes along
And starts shearin em two at a time

We all gave up, just marvelled an stared
As no beast got barely a scratch
And the totals ran up higher than the ringer could count
After lunch the record was matched

Now any other bloke woulda stopped right there
Cracked a beer to call it a day
But young Jack Tucker took it between his teeth
And sent us all on our way

"You lot take off," he roared, "I'll shear em meself."
And the blades were slick in his hands
No one was tough enough to match him that day
On a record that, yeah, still stands

The rest of us were shocked, left wonderin aloud
Why this fella had been holding back
But with the shears at a beast's neck he said
"I wanted me dad to go out the crack."

That had us bowin our heads with respect
That record coulda gone years before
Jack Tucker loved his dad and let him go out the best
And it's tragic his type are no more

Appendix II

Humphrey Boragart's *Short Guide to Australian History*

A few billion years ago, the continent now known as Australia was a clump of land attached to the bottom of what became Africa. When the oceans formed, Australia was separated and drifted east, coming to rest in a corner of the world no one cared about. And that's how it stayed, millennium after millennium, with the local people living in relative peace, unharmed by the outside world.

It couldn't stay that way. The world was open to discovery, to flag planting and land stealing, and Australia would be no exception. While the school-taught idea of 'Cook discovering Australia' is a fallacy, Cook's landing in 1770 does mark the beginning of myth-making in Australian history; the tradition of storytelling, truth-stretching and identity-construction that remains even today.[1] Long before Cook, the curious Europeans had their greedy eyes fixed on Australia, and in the 17th century, the hoarding, empire-building Euro trash were already charting the coastline and setting plaques and pewter plates on cliffs and beaches, to prove they were here first. The Dutch were prominent, mapping, landing and shipwrecking along the west coast (then New Holland) on the way to the Dutch East Indies (today Indonesia). Their curiosity was their own undoing as the reefs and rocks tore holes in their ships. If they landed to take a look or were forced ashore to survive, the land didn't hold much interest for them: flies, sand, no trees or water, weird looking animals, naked natives, more flies, a whole lot of nothing. Terra Nautilus, Terra Nullius, Terra Australis; an empty, nothing land belonging to no one.

That Australia was empty at the time of 'discovery' and 'settlement' is, of course, an utter lie, a fallacy of history, proven so by the landmark Mabo case in 1992.[2] So, when the British arrived in 1788 to make a settlement at what is now Sydney, the men and women who made up the First Fleet should be considered nothing less than pirates who invaded and stole the country from the local inhabitants.[3] The Australians (as the natives were collectively called by their invaders) were thought of as one small step higher than animals and were treated as such.

A number of theories have been put forward to explain why the British took an interest in settling Australia. The theories are normally lumped somewhere under gold, god or glory. Gold being the potential worth of Terra Nullius. God being the spreading of religion and passing on the supposed superiority of the European race. Glory being King and country, the British Empire, with Australia a strategic port/outpost as the European powers clambered to gobble up the remaining unclaimed lands.[4]

The most commonly held justification for settlement was the overcrowded prisons in England. With American independence, England no longer had a disposal location for its 'criminal class'. As the aristocrats continued to sweep the London streets clean of pickpockets and bread thieves, they had nowhere to put them other than in old ships (hulks) clogging up the Thames. The solution was simple: put some sails on those ships and with a collective tally-ho-good-show-sport shove, send those ships out to sea, heading south, down under, where they could be forgotten about forever.[5] Whether it was for gold, god, glory or to get rid of the criminals, the First Fleet under Captain Arthur Philip set sail in May 1787 with 1,487 people; half were convicts, the other half sent to guard them. They arrived in Botany Bay about eight months later.[6]

That the Australian nation had such clear criminal roots has been the topic of much spin-doctoring and historical revision. For about the first 150 years since the invasion in 1788, it was referred to as the 'convict stain': being a convict or having convict roots. It was something never mentioned and which nobody wanted, unless their story was woven and twisted as part of folk lore, like that of the bushrangers in the mid to late 19th century, notably Ned Kelly. Around the mid 20th century, there seems to have been a shift in the interpretation and level of acceptance of Australia's convict roots. Instead of a stain, it was now embraced. Those with convict roots (real or not) considered it a badge of honour, much like have an ancestor or relative who was an ANZAC.[7] Today, it is an extremely proud Aussie, normally the loudest in the room, who can claim direct ancestry with a convict.[8]

Australia, which today is considered to be one of the most liberal places on earth, began as a colony of invaders, with many who were already criminals. Colonial enactments and decisions were made to benefit the privileged few, as British society and class distinctions were imported and enforced. Along with the convict roots, this gave rise to a general distrust of authority and attainment[9], and a suspicion of education, intelligence and breeding that survives today in the myth of the larrikin.[10]

The colony survived, barely, and slowly managed to get further established, with more invasions of other areas of the continent. The colony delivered little to the British Empire until the discovery of gold in 1851 near Bathurst, Victoria. Not only would this spark the gold rushes that would draw quick-fortune seekers from across the globe, and extend to other parts of the continent, it would begin an industry on which the Australian economy would be built, which remains today the most integral part of Australian production and exports.[11] Suddenly with something to offer, and with more immigrants pouring into the country, the colony became relevant to the British Empire.

At around the same time, with such growths in population, matters of nationalism and racism came to the fore. Australia was on the way to becoming a nation, and already there were those who considered themselves more Australian than others, and there was growing division between those same Australians and the immigrants who arrived to seek their fortunes.[12] Despite being geographically part of Asia, Australia thought of itself as white and part of the western world[13] and the early racism of the colony was directed at Asia immigrants, especially the Chinese. There was also a growing concern about the Aboriginal problem.[14] At some point, the leaders of the colony were confronted with a growing number of half-caste Aboriginal children. Rather than stopping the problem at its source, they decided instead to implement a program of so-called Aboriginal protection whereby the children were put in missionary schools to be educated and trained for placement within society.[15] These children, forcefully taken from their parents and homelands, would later become known as the Stolen Generations. This practice of human theft and slave trade would run until the early 1970s.[16]

Australia formally became a nation in 1901. The first prime minister was Edmund Barton.[17] One of the first acts of the new federal government was to pass the Immigration Restriction Act, part of a broader policy called the White Australia Policy.[18] It meant that the immigration authorities could choose who to let into the country and who to deport. Part of this screening process was the dictation test, given at first in any European language and later in any language. The test was impossible to pass, if need be, or easy to pass, if the immigrant was desirable. After the Second World War, these restrictions were reduced, as Australia, fresh from a potential attack from the "Asian hordes of the north", felt it needed to "populate or perish".

There was a justification for such a fear, beyond expounded ideas of the yellow peril. The Japanese bombed Darwin[19] in 1942 and posed a stern threat in the Pacific during the war. Since becoming a nation in 1901, Australia has always felt isolated and under threat, and thus has attempted to stand with (or offer itself as cannon fodder to) the most powerful country on earth. Until the end of the Second World War, that was Britain, and this meant Australian soldiers fought in the Boer War, WWI[20] and WWII. But empires were finished by 1945. Britain's power had waned and a new power emerged. Naturally, Australia aligned itself with the U.S.A. and this meant soldiers were sent to fight in the Korean War, the Vietnam War[21], the Gulf War, and the incursions in Afghanistan and Iraq. The result is that Australia fought in every major conflict of the 20th century, and the first conflicts of the 21st century.[22]

Sending the young men of Australia off to fight the battles of other countries had the interesting effect of empowering women, if only for short periods. During World War I and World War II, women were encouraged to get out of the house and enter the workforce, to keep the industry and economy going while the men were off fighting, but only on the condition that they would go back to being breeders and housewives once the men returned. This reflects the traditional notions of family and household held by Australians, including the concept that the family lives in a house on its own block with a backyard, a garage and a shed. The house is a key component, along with the possession of several cars and other modes of transportation, of what would become the Australian dream.[23][24]

While fighting wars in other parts of the globe, Australia in the 20th century was also on the way to becoming an industrialised and economically fruitful democracy. Scholars, and Australians in general, would add here that it was also liberal, equal and free, but such words surely can't used when the said country has a government policy called White Australia, and is still stealing half-caste and quarter-caste Aboriginal children from their families, and is imposing restrictions on immigration based on race. Up until the 1970s, it can be said that Australia was, if anything, a highly backward country clinging to the racist ideologies and lifestyle practices of a century before. The country needed shaking up, needed drastic change to bring it into the modern era. That would happen with the election of Gough Whitlam as prime minister in 1972.

If asked to name a famous countryman or woman, the majority of Australians usually name a sports star, actor or Ned Kelly.[25] When asked about Gough Whitlam, the majority are able to say he was fired from his job but are not able to say why or have any clue what Whitlam did during his term as prime minister.[26] It is a simple fact of Australian culture and collective historical knowledge that Australians know much more about John F. Kennedy than they do about Whitlam.[27] Before being fired[28], Whitlam managed to enact a number of policies and measures which brought Australia out of its colonial cave and into the 20th century. Whitlam ended conscription for Vietnam and ended Australia's involvement in the war. He abolished the White Australia Policy, made university free, provided benefits for single parent families, abolished the death penalty, gave more equal opportunities for women, said Aborigines were equal and gave them back land, began a policy of multiculturalism, and entered into negotiations and trade discussions with China and other Asian countries. While his legacy is overshadowed by his dismissal, one can't ignore the visionary zeal he applied to modernising Australia.

Unfortunately, much of the good work done by Whitlam was later undone by John Howard, the conservative prime minister who presided over some of the worst crises of Australia's identity, government policies and conscience.[29]

The current situation in Australia is open to interpretation. Where some see social harmony and liberal equality, others see racial and religious intolerance, social discord and marked inequality. Fortunately, as the vast majority of Australians live in suburbs[30], they are not confronted with the moors of their own society. They can go home to their mortgaged abode, close the door, and not give credence to historical guilt or current problems. The lucky country, living with blinders on until the luck runs out.

Notes:
1. Some selected myths of Australia: the myth of settlement, the myth of the digger, the myth of the bushman, the myth of Simpson and his donkey, the myth of the underdog, the myth of the larrikin, the myth of Foster's beer, the myth of pavlova invention, etc, etc, etc.
2. A Boragart survey (conducted for a year 12 history project) of people in Esperance concerning the Mabo case had the following result: 82.4% of the approx. 500 people polled claimed they did not know what the Mabo case was about, or responded incorrectly when asked. The Mabo case was a landmark court decision in 1992 concerning Murray Island where the High Court of Australia decided that Australia was an occupied land at the time of settlement bringing rise to the concept of native title; but not, unfortunately, instigating a complete revision of history.
3. Which raises the question of whether the perpetrators of this crime shall be tried in absentia with reparations paid to the descendents of the victims. If someone can sue for a million dollars because their tongue is burned by hot coffee, surely the theft of a continent of almost 8 million km^2 warrants a damages claim of immeasurable magnitude.
4. Which would result in disastrous colonial forays (more pirates in ships planting flags on inhabited lands) during the scramble for Africa of the 19th century, the damage of which is still visible today.
5. The fascinating oversight here being that a farming colony was to be established by city criminals who had never even heard of green fields except in Irish song. They did not have a single clue about farming, and the colony only managed to survive from the generous number of supply ships coming from England. That is, the supply ships that did not sink. The colonials could have asked the Australians for help, as they had survived there for, oh, about 40,000 years, but they were animals, so what did they know.
6. It must have been a hellish journey for the convicts down below. Of course, once at Botany Bay, a whole different kind of hell awaited.

7.   Australia and New Zealand Army Corps. Name for the soldiers who fought in the First World War. Despite the acronym including New Zealand, the word Anzac, and everything it has come to stand for, has been appropriated by Australia. For example, an Australian sporting team in victory over New Zealand may claim to have taken motivation and drawn inspiration from the Anzac spirit, which, when thought about, is a really confusing thing to say. The same Boragart survey cited in note 1: 91.7% of respondents answered correctly as to what the acronym stood for, but when pressed as to why New Zealand was included, many respondents could not offer a clear answer. Some said that, at that time, New Zealand was part of Australia. It is also worth noting that 53.3% of respondents needed to have the word acronym explained to them, and 65.1% pronounced Corps with a hard P, which the surveyor found ironically amusing as many of the Anzacs were dead.

8.   It must be noted that the same proud Aussie will take great offense if it is pointed out to them that the said convict ancestor may well have been a buggerer, or a buggeree, or a rapist of Aboriginal women, or a beastialist, or all of the above. And no matter how many statistics are given regarding the unequal balance of men and women convicts (not to mention that they were kept separated), nor the telling numbers of half caste Aboriginal children that became such a problem that a government-enacted genocidal child-stealing solution had to be employed, nor the examples of Norfolk Island and Port Arthur, it must be noted that the proud Aussie and a bunch of his friends will beat the living shit out of you if you try to clarify and correct the history he himself has attempted to rewrite. Port Arthur was where the worst convicts were sent; mostly, those convicts who had committed further crimes and were considered a blight on the colony. Norfolk Island and Port Arthur were described as places were humanity and civility no longer existed.

9.   The best example being the Eureka Stockade in 1854, and also the various bushrangers of the 19th century. See Ned Kelly, Ben Hall, Mad Dog Morgan, Bold Jack Donohoe, et al. The Eureka Stockade was a short rebellion on the gold fields of Victoria crushed by colonial soldiers. It's sometimes noted by historians as

the revolutionary birth of the Australian nation. But comparing a handful of miners grumbling about licenses and taxes on their gold fields to something like the French Revolution is drawing a rather long bow.

10. A word used by Australians often to describe themselves and the other Australians around them. It is linked to ideas of self-deprecating humour, an aversion to authority, a love of sport, a give-it-a-go attitude, fairness, humility, hard work, and to a lesser extent bravery and sacrifice.

11. It should also be noted that this same industry resulted in the ravaging of many thousand square kilometres of sacred Aboriginal lands.

12. The Aborigines had no place in such arguments, with Darwin's *On the Origin of Species* (1859) having given scholarly and scientific credence to the long-held idea that the Aborigines were sub-human and should be treated as nothing more than animals.

13. And to a certain extent still does.

14. The concern being not for the Aborigines themselves but for how to stop the problem being a problem, or to make it someone else's problem.

15. Better known as slavery.

16. It must be noted that the record of treatment of the Aboriginal and Torres Strait Islander peoples of Australia is horrendous and rivals, if not exceeds, the practices of slavery in America and Apartheid in South Africa. Why every single Australian does not feel an enormous amount of guilt (or at least a smidgen of guilt) for this historical legacy is beyond the comprehension of this researcher.

17. A Boragart survey conducted for a year 11 politics assignment: 78.4% of respondents could not say who the first prime minister of Australia was or answered incorrectly. Interestingly, 56.9% answered correctly when asked who the first president of the USA was.

18. Which stayed in effect until it was abolished in 1973.

19. But not with the Pearl Harbor/Hollywood intensity that has been described in some history books.

20. Including the shockingly disastrous attack of Canakkale, which Australians remember as Gallipoli.

21. For which Australia controversially and confoundingly had conscription.

22. Resulting in more than 100,000 deaths in wars that, aside from the Japanese attack of Darwin, had absolutely nothing to do with Australia.

23. The average Australian today has the highest household debt in relation to disposable income in the world. It can be argued that the Australians' obsession with and addiction to ownership stems from the country's convict roots. That is, from people who had nothing and valued highly even the smallest thing that was their own. Another argument could be that deep in the Australian psyche is the fear that the land is not theirs, never was, and will one day be taken away.

24. Like so much of Australian culture, the Australian dream is a bastardised version of something already defined: the American dream. It is very much a suburban ideal. Donald Horne, writing in the 1960s, called Australia the first "suburban nation". He also called Australia "the lucky country". And not in the sense that Australians are lucky to live in Australia, but that the country lives on luck (discovery of gold, happenchance of fortunate events, etc) and that one day that luck will run out.

25. Famous bushranger who was proudly of Irish stock.

26. Conclusions drawn from the same Boragart survey for year 11 politics assignment (see note 16). It shall be noted that Esperance is a small country town in Western Australia and many of the opinions there may not necessarily reflect those of more diverse populations in centres like Sydney and Melbourne, but that surveys conducted in Esperance do result in some very interesting statistics.

27. Which pretty much says it all.

28. A task carried out by the Governor General John Kerr. As part of Australia's constitutional monarchy, the governor general is the go-between for the King or Queen of England and the prime minister of Australia. The powers of the GG were mostly ceremonial and it came as a shock to many Australians in 1975 to learn that the GG could in fact fire the PM. It has not happened since, despite the fact that John Howard should have got the axe more times than can here be noted or outlined (see note 29 for examples).

29. Including, among many other examples, Australia's participation in the incursions of Afghanistan and Iraq, Howard's response to the Tampa Crisis of 2001, the refugee situation, the sorry debate, etc, etc, etc. Interestingly, or shockingly, it was precisely his handling of these crises that got him re-elected. Refugees, illegal immigrants and boat people remain a hot topic in Australia. The new refugee camp on Christmas Island has been compared to, and declared worse than, Guantanamo Bay, and Australia's human rights record in regard to refugees has been highly criticised. When compared with other countries, one can only wonder why this topic is so hotly debated. For example, from 1997-2003, Australia received around 86,000 asylum seeker applications; in the same period, Canada received approx. 300,000, France approx. 350,000 and Germany approx. 950,000. Plus, Australia has one of the lowest population densities in the world. The continent could easily support a population up to ten times the current 22 million, yet there is major uproar when 4,000 try to get to Australia in one calendar year.

30. Australian population statistics: almost 90% of the approx. 22 million people in Australia live in urban areas. Aboriginals and Torres Strait Islanders make up 2.7% of the population and on average live about 10-12 years less than non-Indigenous Australians.

Travel Page (cont.)